CATCH
OF THE DAY

To Rick, You deserve credit
for part inspiration, but I
won't tell you which part.

Viv

Published in the UK in 2021 by DR Enterprises

Copyright © Douglas Roberts 2021

Douglas Roberts has asserted their right under
the Copyright, Designs and Patents Act, 1988,
to be identified as the author of this work.

Paperback ISBN 978-1-7399182-0-0
eBook   ISBN 978-1-7399182-1-7

Cover design and typeset by SpiffingCovers

Revenge doesn't die with you

CATCH
OF THE DAY

DOUGLAS ROBERTS

Chapter 1

The Simpleton

Carl Jenkinson, had he known it, was quite possibly from Icelandic decent. The Viking habit of adding 'son' at the end of the family name ensured the continuance of the male lineage that, to this day, can be traced back to the earliest settlers sometime between the Dark and Middle Ages. Around the same time that the Romans invaded Britain, it is believed that when Erik Jenkinsson was banished from Norway for the relatively minor crime of accidentally killing a fellow combatant during a 'friendly' tournament, he took his family and the rest of his remoter issue in search of a fabled island (possibly one of the Orkney Isles) but ended up in Iceland. They built their long houses close to the shoreline but, with nobody else to interact with, and the help of mead, they amused themselves at night by singing and procreating. Erik was quite a good bard by their standards, but he was a really terrible singer. Nevertheless, the rest of the clan had little option but to persevere with his endless lyrics as there were few among them who could write, let alone compose more than one line that rhymed with the next. Folklore depicts Erik as a vomiting poet and one of those who founded today's modern Iceland. Not bad for a humble poet from Norway.

Had Carl ever wondered or taken the time and trouble to investigate, he may well have been able to trace his forefathers back to Erik, for he too had a penchant for poetry, as well as an awful voice. This tenuous similarity on its own would certainly not impress a genealogist as it probably describes half of the human race including the likes of you and I. From a very early age, his father had drummed into him that it was his Icelandic great grandfather who had ended up in Scotland while on a wallowing Icelandic fishing smack near the Outer Hebrides shortly before the start of the First World War. Neither fortune nor the Germans had smiled on the family during the Second World War, as their tenement, along with several streets adjacent to the Clydebank docks, had been levelled by bombs in one particular air raid. The entire family had been killed during that raid, apart from Carl's grandfather who had been posted to one of the many minesweeping flotillas at the time.

His father, Jon Jenkinson, was the issue of a one-night stand, literally, in a back alley behind one of the seedier pubs in Clydebank. Normally he could be found with glass in hand, in the smoky and warmer interior of The Cobblers Arms, accompanying an ageless piano player singing about the demise of the Jacobites, two centuries earlier. Anyone wandering past the pub would have quickened their pace to escape the dreadful din, while trying to decide whether the singer or the piano was the more out of tune. It would have been virtually impossible to find a pub in that neighbourhood that was anything but disreputable, or where the landlady would not have charged for the temporary use of a flea-ridden room upstairs; hence the necessity of a dingy back alley where the rats scurried about their own affairs between decaying wooden beer barrels.

Carl really didn't care that his 25th birthday was approaching as he spent his last few coins on another 'pint of heavy', but it would be payday tomorrow and he would be able to eke out his meagre weekly wages until next week. He only just managed to grasp the reality of the worth of money by paying his landlady after work every Friday night as he returned to his rented flat, and then by visiting the local store for a week's worth of food. Thursday nights was barrel-changing time at The Cobblers and in exchange for a couple of pints, he would remove the empties and replace them with full ones. Normally a two-man operation from the street to the underground cellar, he would manage this all by himself with ease.

In many ways, he was very much like his father in that he was larger than those around him; very large in fact but not fat. He was tall and strong with a huge mop of thick fair hair covering his ears, and the size of his hands would have made any goalkeeper proud. If there was anything large and heavy that needed shifting down at the docks, his workmates would nod in his direction and not bother to look back to see if it had been done, as it was commonplace. Why use a forklift when you had a 'Carl' around? Had he the time, money or inclination, he would have visited the barbers more than once a year and it was only when he had had his hair cut that his face was revealed, at least for the first couple of months or so. A strong jawbone gave way to a widish mouth bracketed by slightly dimpled cheeks beneath his shaggy beard, giving the impression that he was constantly smiling. His straight nose perfectly dissected his even blue eyes which somehow highlighted his unfurrowed brow. All in all, he wasn't just handsome, but an Adonis in disguise, and this might well start to impress a genealogist.

Whereas his father was a depressed drunken old loud sod, Carl was quite the opposite and kept very much to himself in his own contented world. Working at the docks as one of the cargo handlers, he carried out every order issued by his foreman with ease; others may have physically struggled, but not Carl. He rarely spoke more than a few words, but enjoyed the company of the others, particularly during the tea and lunch breaks. He even managed to laugh on the few occasions when he could understand their jokes. They noticed that nothing ever enraged Carl, except on one occasion when a brave little man had questioned his sexual orientation. He had ended up with a broken collarbone and his black eye had lasted over a week, and that was from just one punch; a mere tap as far as Carl was concerned.

Despite being a little slow on the uptake, Carl had an aptitude for making things and he did so with extraordinary delicacy. Despite his strong oversized hands, his deft touch could artistically deliver the perfect amount of paint exactly where it was needed on his own models. Ships were his favourite, made from discarded bits of wood left lying around the streets and alleys. They were beautiful. From the smallest lifeboat to the exactly spaced rigging on the largest cutter, it was evident that he had crooned for hours over every last detail, even down to the little figurines on the decks. His favourite wood was walnut and, where possible, he would polish a certain knot to accentuate a particular feature, such as the figurehead. When it came to metalwork, if anything his talent surpassed his carpentry skills: not only that, but he would repair any item that was bought to him, as long as it wasn't electrical. In recompense, but without asking, payment would come in the form of cakes, quiches, pies and the occasional bottle of beer. His rented bedsit was beginning to become cramped with not just models, but weird-shaped sculptures, although he had never considered selling any of them to make more space. They were his friends that reminded him of his dreams: dreams of the open sea and battling the elements while trawling in a decent catch of herring, or exploring far-off lands where volcanos spewed and glowed on the distant skyline.

Carl was the epitome of contentedness, without appearing to have any interest in the opposite sex, and to the outside world he was just another worker with a hobby. No doubt this life would have continued along this serene path had it not been for Alistair Gowern, the Union's shop steward who, upon his retirement, had been presented with an ornamental gold watch and accompanying chain across his waistcoat, accentuating a portly stomach.

As usual, Carl stood with his back to the wall adjacent to the counter in The Cobblers Arms with a half-empty pint, and while admiring one of the few unbroken etched mirrors behind the bar that depicted a schooner under full sail, he realised he was being addressed by Alistair.

"Now that I've a bit more time on my hands, I've noticed you're in here quite a lot, especially on a Thursday. Mind you, the wife would like me to pay more attention to her, but it's still not the done thing to bring a wife to the pub unless it's a special occasion. And there don't seem to be so many of those anymore. Take Douggy's funeral the other week. We gave him a fair send-off in The Masons Arms and she dressed up to the nines for it."

He looked up to see if he was getting any reaction from Carl and, when he saw him turn his head, continued.

"O aye, she enjoyed herself right enough. Her and Douggy's missus must have knocked back a bottle of Glenfiddich all by themselves. God knows where they got it from, and I had to half-carry her all the way back to Hilldon Street. Ha! She even managed to break one of the heels on her stilettos, but the old cobbler's gone sick so I won't be able to get that mended until he's better. I suppose she'll want me to buy her a new pair now."

He paused again to see if what he said was getting through to Carl and took the opportunity to drain most of his pint.

"We're going to have to start watching our pennies now that I'm retired, but she's worth it. Aye, a fine lass is Gwen."

Carl looked down on the portly man who was obviously bored and had no one else to talk to. He recalled that it was Mr Gowern who had insisted that they strike for better pay and conditions on several occasions. With the help of a handheld loud hailer in front of the gathered workers he would bellow about the unfairness of society. He was someone to look up to as he stood on a pile of girders; someone who one had to listen to, and someone in authority and therefore had to be obeyed. But Carl didn't realise that he was no longer his shop steward and supposed that the other chap with the loudhailer was just standing in for him.

"I can fix that for you if you like."

Alistair looked up at the towering frame beside him and realised he had never heard this man's deep gentle voice before. He'd just been another head or hand in the crowd when it had come to the vote.

"Well, that'd be handy as the Social Club's got a do on in a couple of weeks and it'd save me a whole lot of bother trying to get another pair of flashy shoes for the wife. Do you really think you could fix it?"

"I don't see why not. After all, it's probably only a piece of wood that's come away."

Alistair smiled. "I'll tell you what. Why don't I bring it over here tomorrow night and you can have a look at it?" He saw little reaction from Carl. "And I'll buy you a pint."

Still no reaction from Carl, but he held his silence as he could see Carl thinking.

"Bring both of them so that I can make sure they match," Carl gently boomed.

"Aye. That's a good idea. Now why didn't I think of that?"

About a month later, Alistair walked back into The Cobblers and threaded his way between the sparsely populated tables towards Carl. "Here. Let me buy you that pint I owe you. Heavy, wasn't it?"

"Heavy will do nicely, thank you."

Alistair stretched into his deep trouser pocket for some change and addressed the overweight barmaid. "Two Heavies and put another one on tap for my friend here."

Carl raised his eyebrows just a fraction, which meant he was thinking. "Thank you again."

"My pleasure. She didn't manage to break either of the stilettos this time so that in itself deserves the second pint. And you can't even see the join. Cheers."

With one gulp, Carl finished his original pint and curled his hand round the freshly poured dark liquid. "It was easy."

The clack of dominoes falling onto a table in the background accentuated the silence between them, but eventually Alistair seemed to come to a decision. "Look, I've got a friend who I met the other day and I mentioned that you may be able to help him. Nay, not shoes this time, but he wants an unusual item made."

Although Carl was looking at him, there was no reaction and he was forced to continue. "Have you ever heard of a Rubik's cube?"

He studied Carl's face to see what he would make of the question and had to wait.

"Yes. But I've never held one."

"Well, this friend of mine wants one made, but it won't be an ordinary one. You see, he wants it made out of metal, not plastic like this one." He delved the brightly coloured cube out of his coat pocket and put it gently on the bar counter between them. "You see, they don't make metal ones and he really likes unusual one-offs."

Eventually Carl picked up the multicoloured cube, hefted it in his hand and turned it over to look at the six multi-coloured surfaces. "What does it do?"

Alistair was hoping he wouldn't have to explain in too much detail as he really had no hope at all of twisting the individual squares back to their original positions. He showed Carl by rotating one surface, a second, and then back to its original configuration before putting it back on the counter between them.

"They get jumbled up and I'm told that the youths of this world can put it back in less than ten seconds, but it's beyond me. That's about all I can manage, otherwise it gets all too mixed up and I can't put it back again."

Carl picked it up again and peered closely at it. "I'd have to take it home and see how it comes apart, but I don't see why not. Does your friend want the same colours or can they be a bit different?"

"Oh, I'm pretty sure he'll want similar, but I'll ask him when I see him next anyway." He paused, wondering if now was the right time to ask how long it might take, but decided against it. He also wondered if he ought to mention that there would be some money in it this time, but decided against that as well. He watched Carl as he inspected all sides close up and was surprised at the reaction, when it eventually came.

"I wonder why they make children's' toys more difficult

than grown-ups'?"

"Oh no, it wasn't designed for kids, but mathematicians. You see, it's supposed to be all about numbers and the like, but I hear that there's a simple version out there for those of us who can't do it and I suppose that includes kids." He automatically assumed that Carl would be among those who would be incapable of solving the perplexing puzzle, as he associated it with those whose hands were, well, smaller.

Carl finished the first pint in one easy gulp, pushed his glass to the back of the counter for the barmaid to refill and looked down on Alistair. "I've never made something that moves quite this much. It's a bit different from propellers and beams, but I suppose the principles are the same. It might be easier with aluminium rather than steel. Do you think your friend would mind?"

This was not a question he was expecting, nor one that he was qualified to answer, but he needed to give at least some guidance. "Oh, I don't think he's really worried about that, just so long as it's not plastic." He felt he needed to emphasise. "You see, he's a metal fanatic and particularly likes the smooth feel, so as long as it's got that kind of sheen and weight to it, he'll be happy."

Alistair felt that this next bit was likely to be a bit tricky and he nervously fiddled with his pint by rotating it on the counter. "He would also like to see how it's put together, so he can take it apart again." He paused trying to get the explanation out. "He's one of those sorts of people who wants to know how everything works, you see." He raised his eyes from pretending to concentrate on his now still glass and looked at Carl for his reaction and was a bit surprised to see him being stared at. He was determined not to show his nervousness by focusing on keeping his pint steady, but found himself bringing it up to his lips. This gave him a legitimate reason not to say anything further for at least a few seconds more, and he took his time drawing out the last dregs of foam from the bottom. When Carl's response came, he felt a surge of relief.

"I don't see why not. After all, there's no secret about it is there?"

"None. None at all." He looked at his watch in pretence. "I must go... an old Union colleague wants to talk to me about something, so see you sometime next week eh, and errr... enjoy your pint on behalf of my wife."

Alistair put his collar up against the squally weather as he left the pub, naturally looking first right, then left, before crossing the road, and headed for a side street nearly opposite that would provide him with a little shelter from the damp gusts. He took up position in a recessed doorway and watched the entrance to The Cobblers, as well as the sheets of rain that appeared out of nowhere. He found that if he crammed himself into the left-hand corner, the drip from the broken gutter three storeys up didn't splash so much on his trouser leg, but after five minutes, he got bored. "Bugger this," he muttered, then braced himself and continued down the narrowing street to his next destination. It was only a few minutes' walk, but before he knocked on the door of the tenement, he briefly looked over his shoulder into the rain to see if he was being observed. He wasn't.

A small wiry man with short dark hair and beady eyes opened the door in the narrow hallway, recognised him, turned without saying a word and returned to the room from whence he came; Alistair followed. He had hardly entered the small front living room, his eyes adjusting to the familiar sulphurous air that emanated from the smouldering coal fire, when the man spoke.

"That didn't take long."

"Long enough for a pint that cost me," he lied.

"Don't bother taking your coat off. I'm just leaving." He pre-empted Alistair's unbuttoning regime just as he started to do so. "What did he say?"

Alistair realised this was going to be a very short meeting, looked down for a moment to watch his raincoat drip over the worn carpet, then tried to look the man directly in his eyes. As before, he found that he could only do so for a fleeting moment, as in his own soul, he knew very well who this man was and what he represented. He chose a point towards the top of his head to focus on instead, aware that he was being scrutinised.

"He'll do it."

"Did he say how much?"

"He thought it might be about five hundred pounds," he lied again.

The small man studied him for a moment. "How long?"

"I... I didn't ask, but like I explained before, this chap can't be hurried." Betraying his nervousness, he started fiddling with one of his coat buttons.

"Next time ask him. We must know. I'll get you two-fifty for this time next week and the rest later. Yours is over there." He gestured with a nod to a small brown envelope on the sideboard next to him.

He reached out and tucked it in his coat pocket, looked up and saw the man just standing there looking at him. "Right then, until next week then." He half shuffled before exiting the room, turned up his collar in anticipation and left through the same front door and, without bothering to look around, headed for home.

The small man watched him through the net-curtained window until he was out of sight, noting that the street was otherwise deserted before retrieving his mobile phone from his trouser pocket. His text consisted of just two words: 'Game on.'

***

Nearly two hundred miles away across a very choppy sea, three men gathered round a kitchen table sheltering from the inclement conditions in a remote farmhouse. They stopped what they were doing when a mobile phone pinged.

"Well go on then, have a look and see what it says."

The man at the far end ceased his cleaning, put the pistol down on the table and picked up the phone. The other two watched as his lips parted in a smile. "Looks like Aiden's found someone." He looked up at the others. "Someone on the mainland."

"And...?"

"And nothing else. It just says 'Game on' which was our agreed code. Keeping text to a minimum as told 'cos otherwise we might give something away. And we'd like it to be a surprise, wouldn't we?"

They all laughed a little at the rhetorical innuendo.

"If he's moved that fast then it may be ready in time. If not, we'll just have to hope it is for Armistice Day."

"You know I've always favoured Armistice Day anyway. There's likely to be more live TV coverage."

"Just leave Aiden to it. He knows what he's doing."

***

Carl really wanted to finish off the last few strands of the forward rigging but his mind, as well as his eyes, kept occasionally wandering to the relatively brightly coloured cube he had placed on the shelf next to the door. He kept telling himself it could wait, but the more he tried to ignore it, the more it intrigued him, so he gave in. He'd casually looked at it once he'd returned from The Cobblers, but its mere presence now irritated him; he just had to do something about it.

He inserted a blade he had fashioned himself between two of the squares on one corner, twisted it and off popped one of the elements onto the floor. He retrieved it and continued with the others until he was able to see how it actually all went together. He could now see that the entire device relied upon the elastic properties of plastic, but Alistair had told him that he wanted it made out of metal. He very quickly worked out that only the outer surfaces needed to be metallic and then formulated a way of fashioning replacement surfaces. He decided it would need to be finished in aluminium and he looked over in the corner of his room to where he knew he had an old off-cut. It would be difficult folding and lining up the corners, but he now relished the challenge; and to replicate the colours he would use enamel paint, then lacquer after polishing.

Other than his duties at The Cobblers, every evening after work he would spend hours on either his latest clipper or moulding the thin metal on the cube, unless he decided to quench his thirst.

One such evening a couple of weeks later, Alistair found him in his usual place at the bar and as casually as possible, joined him. In his own mind, if he were to be seen with him too often, it might well be noted by others that the two of them were becoming friends, so had resisted the temptation the previous week.

"Bloody wet again." He started the conversation as nonchalantly as possible as he beckoned the barmaid over. "Another Heavy, Carl?"

His reaction was to curl his hand round the half-empty pint, down it and place it back on the counter. "Yes, please, and thank you."

Alistair didn't want to sound too eager, but wanted to broach the subject as soon as possible, just in case someone came in and started talking to him. He had noted the same trio of men playing dominoes in the corner by the front window, each nurturing and eking out their pints, as well as a solitary man sitting near the dying fire and staring into the middle distance.

"How are you getting on with that cube I gave you?"

Carl took a sip, emptying half the glass before looking at him. "Oh I've started and it's not going to be as difficult as I first thought, but I needed to mend Mrs Jason's fire irons, so I'm in the middle of that at the moment."

This wasn't what he wanted to hear and decided to prompt a little. "Is it the metal that's taking so long?"

When Carl didn't answer straight away, he thought he'd hit the nail on the head, but then realised he was thinking. He thought he could almost see the cogs turning in Carl's head, and waited with a lengthy swig of his pint for what was coming next.

"Aluminium's easy, but it's the folding that takes time."

That was it. And if he wanted to know more, he'd have to lead him by the nose. Getting Carl to talk freely was as difficult as getting blood out of a stone, so he persevered, especially as Aiden had been on to him about progress the day before yesterday.

"About halfway through?"

Again the delayed response. "About halfway."

Silence was interrupted by the resetting of the dominoes in the corner.

"Well, I suppose I ought to leave you to it then. You seem to know what you're doing." He hadn't meant to finish his pint so quickly, but felt he ought to just leave. "See you next week then."

"Bye."

***

Two of the three men across the water waited in a parked car behind St Stephen's Chapel, not far from the border. It was a little-used beauty spot overlooking a small tarn and well shielded from the road by a stand of fir trees. The older driver had placed the ordinary-looking saloon car behind the lonely building in such a manner that they would be able to see anyone approaching down the track, and make a quick getaway if necessary.

"Here he comes now."

They watched the car bounce down the potholed track between the trees towards them and as it neared, the younger one commented, "You're sure that's him?"

"Yes, that's him. If you've ever been to that chemists' shop, you'll recognise him."

The estate car drew up beside them and the man looked across the gap and saw one of the two men motion with his head. He got out, looked around and went to join them in the back seat of the saloon. He coughed at the stale stench of cigarettes.

"Well Eamon, have you done it?"

"Of course it's done, and it's ready in the back of the shop, but I want your assurance that it's not going to be used on anyone local."

"Eamon, you know us, we don't shit on our own doorstep."

"Fellas. This stuff is really lethal and if you don't treat it with the greatest of respect it'll kill you quicker than that rotten whiskey you drink."

The two in the front glanced at each other. "Since when did you care?" the older one asked, and continued after a pause. "We've all done what's been necessary, including you, so what's changed?"

"I have a wife, a child and a respectable business now, that's what's changed."

"That's exactly why we're doing what we're doing so that you can enjoy not only your change, but ours as well; but the bloody Brits haven't changed. Don't tell me you've changed that much?" He looked round. "You're not going soft, are you?"

"Of course I'm not, but I've got in-laws to think about as well now."

"Don't worry, it's not them we're targeting, and in any case, they'll never know where it came from." A thought came to him. "It's not traceable, is it?"

"Definitely not. Impossible in fact. How soon?"

"Not too long... maybe a couple of weeks or so. Depends upon Aiden."

The talking stopped while they watched a lone cyclist stop at the head of the track to adjust his helmet before continuing along the road.

"Two weeks back here then. Same time?"

"Same time. With any luck, there'll not even be a bicycle within five miles."

Eamon got out and left. "I never knew it was him," the younger one commented as the estate car meandered down the track.

"That's the beauty of our group. There's only half a dozen who know who we are."

"Plus our chap in London," added the other older one.

"Yes. Nobody but nobody ever mentions him... do we? So just make sure we keep it that way, laddie."

"He's the same bastard who refused to serve me a pack of Durex a few years ago."

"I'm not surprised. He could probably see the nappies poking out from under your jeans. And anyway, he's a proper Catholic that one."

"Bugger the Catholics."

"As long as you just bugger the Protestants first."

"Well, we're going to do that aren't we?"

"Oh yes... oh yes. Very much so. Come on, we've left him enough time. Let's go."

With the shortening of daylight came the inevitable complaints about the nasty weather, but to cheer everyone up, adverts of special Christmas offers abounded on the TV and radio. It didn't matter if you were Protestant or Catholic, the retailers still crowed about what a good deal there was to be had – at least in most places. Less than thirty shopping days left. With more people visiting his shop with cold and flu symptoms, Eamon had difficulty convincing his wife that now was a good time to leave her to run the shop while he attended a seminar in England. The clincher had come when he had had to mention that all costs were being met by donations, and she immediately understood that orders had come down from someone in the organisation. She well knew of her husband's nefarious past and indeed had strong sympathies with the same cause, but as respectable shopowners now, hoped that their direct involvement would stay in the past. In the back of her mind, she knew otherwise and reluctantly conceded that it would never end.

During the short easyJet flight from Belfast to Birmingham, Eamon had time to ponder on his relatively simple task ahead. To be seen as legitimately attending a lecture being given by a notable international proselytizer of new medicines, followed by a series of practical workshops the following day, was all important to maintain his appearance to the security forces. He didn't know if he was on their 'watch list' but better to take no chances. His itinerary was to check into his modest hotel nearby, present himself for accreditation to the receptionist at the respective hall at the University of Birmingham, make sure he was seen by the CCTV, attend the first lecture, and then feign being unwell before returning to his hotel. There he would change his smart clothing for casuals, as well as add a moustache, hat and gloves and then walk to the station and catch a train to Glasgow, where he would meet Aiden in a backstreet coffee shop. There he would be given the Rubik's cube and could return the same way and be back at the University the following day. Nobody would be any the wiser.

It had been decided that he should catch a plane back to Belfast with the innocent cube in his hand luggage as a trial run to see what the security thought of it as it went through the scanners. If it was picked up on the X-ray machine, as it was thought it would be, inspection by any officer would reveal that it was just a metallic Rubik's cube. Even if anyone turned it to see if it worked, he could always protest that it was a gift and could it please be put back to its original configuration.

Several years had passed since he had undertaken anything like this and certainly not with such a grand prize as the end result. Not only that, but he had never carried out any sort of operation on the mainland, having only dealt with local opposition mainly in the rural communities, but he inwardly cringed as he recalled how he had nearly been caught and taken by those ugly Ulstermen on one occasion when he had been to Belfast. That, the best part of twenty years ago, was also supposed to have been an easy job, but now his responsibilities and loyalties lay with his wife and child. The IRA's idealistic policies had all but disappeared along with its leaders, who were now far too diplomatic, and the more violent side left to those who had little care for their own future, or anyone else's. Respectable he may be right now, but his brother's brutal death at the hands of the three soldiers who had cornered them in the backstreets and literally kicked the shit out of him until his bile had dribbled onto the dirt, was so vivid that he had to open his eyes every time it came back to him. This single incident – and growing up without his teenage brother – was responsible for his outlook on life in Northern Ireland, and he soon became a young 'gopher' for the local cell, and later on, for those in the upper hierarchy of the movement. The foremost thought of revenge did not diminish with his maturity, and was never very far away, yet he realised that his aptitude lay in the medical profession and he excelled when it came to formulas. Working as an apprentice in his cousin's pharmacy not only taught him what it would take to run such a business, but also provided him with a superb method of connecting with the local population, and discovering who was up to what, and just as importantly, when. He enrolled in an Open University course, managing to obtain the necessary qualifications for him to stand-in whenever his cousin was unavailable. This unavailability consisted mainly of violent acts and it really came as no surprise to anyone that he met his demise while caught smuggling arms across the border. The recently qualified Eamon naturally inherited his cousin's pharmacy, and outwardly he continued to provide an excellent service to the local community – including his future wife. Inwardly, his anger at the security forces still bubbled away and whenever he was asked to produce something that would enhance a bomb, or the like, he would ensure that the paperwork that went with whatever the substance was would tally.

At the request of a senior IRA commander, he had obtained, and accounted for in his own manner, a quantity of cyanide. When mixed with a small amount of compressed hydrogen, he estimated that it would produce a gas that would kill anyone within breathing distance – in his own words, 'farting distance'. He was told that he would need to insert the deadly compound into a specially made Rubik's cube, so that when the recipient twisted the squares, it would release the fatal gas. He was not told who the target was 'for your own safety' – which meant it was really for the safety of others – only that it would take place in Westminster and shake it to the core.

"There is one single man whose removal would catapult the current peace initiative into the sea, and then we can get back to the proper business of unity once again. All this bloody talk around a table at Stormont is getting us nowhere, but once he's gone, they'll see our logic, and come round. Especially as we've other plans in the pipeline, so don't you worry, you'll get your revenge." The commander knew Eamon's family history well.

There was indeed one Englishman upon whom Eamon

wished all manner of ills. He had been a captain in the British army unit stationed in Northern Ireland at the time and all these years later, was now the government's Northern Ireland secretary. It had been he who had been responsible for the vicious actions of those under his command, and he who was responsible for his brother's death. Although the commander had not mentioned him by name, Eamon had felt a surge of hope, a chance of retribution at last, an opportunity to finally tell his brother in his grave that he had found and killed his murderer, and that he could now rest in peace. Revenge was a far more emotive factor than any political aim.

The commander continued. "Now don't say a word. I know you're about to mention a name and we're not going to do that, even here, though I'm sure you can guess who it is. The best part about it is that they'll never know who to look for afterwards, so you can rest assured that you, your wife and baby boy will be safe." After a short pause, he added, "We'll all be safe." He looked at Eamon for a moment, seeing a man whose sole thought was one of concentration on the task ahead. "Come on Eamon, you'll be our unsung hero and the lads will be raising more than a glass to you down the pub. It'll be your moment of glory we can all talk about for years to come."

Now he stood in line with others at Birmingham City Airport waiting nervously for the tray containing his hand luggage to go through the X-ray machine, and as suspected, it was singled out.

"Is this your tray, sir?" asked the uniformed man across the conveyor belt of mobile trays as they bumped their way towards the stacking end.

"Not mine," the chap next to him answered, and looked around innocently.

Eamon found that his palms were sweating, even though it was a perfectly innocent toy that had set off the detector.

"That's mine. Anything wrong?"

"Can you open this holdall please, sir?" Polite but firm.

"Surely." He took a pace forward and unzipped his overnight bag that held not only the Rubik's cube more or less in the middle, but other such necessities for a brief stopover. "What are you looking for?"

"Did you pack this bag yourself?"

"Of course. Why?"

"Please empty the contents into this tray." He slid an empty one across so that it was parked next to Eamon's.

He started to pick out the clothes from the right-hand side first and out of the corner of his eye, saw that a second uniform was looking on from a different angle. When he got to taking out the cube, he noticed a reaction from yet a third uniform who had moved up behind him.

"What's this, sir?"

"It's a Rubik's cube for my nephew." He looked from one to the other while hovering it over the half-empty tray. "What's wrong with it?"

After a short pause the second uniform plucked it out of his hand and looked him straight in the eyes. "It's metallic and set off the alarm. They're not usually made of metal, are they?" It was a statement as well as a question.

Eamon gave a worried look on purpose, hoping that it would portray his innocence. "I don't really know. It was in a shop and I just bought it."

"And why's it not still in its wrapping then?" The third uniform had come round on Eamon's right.

He hadn't thought of that one but quickly retorted, "I thought I'd have a go at it, but it's beyond me."

The second uniform turned one facet and was about to turn another when Eamon interrupted him. "Please don't do that. I had to get one of the waiters in the hotel to put it back for me and unless it's the right way round, I don't know anyone back home who can do it again."

He watched the man peering closely at it before returning it to its correct configuration, rotated it to inspect all sides and placed it back in Eamon's outstretched hand after a nod from number three. "Hope your nephew has more luck with it than you. OK, you can carry on."

Instantly the three of them turned away to other duties leaving Eamon to re-pack his bag. He made a strong mental note to make sure that, the next time, the cube would be in a sealed cardboard and plastic packet. He made his way down the aisle as nonchalantly as he could, aware that he may still be under CCTV scrutiny, and realising that he was more stressed than he ought to be. 'Relax,' he told himself. 'It's a harmless toy.' But at the back of his mind, he knew that the next time it would be a deadly weapon and he had better be prepared for a different story other than one about a fictitious nephew.

When it came to passing messages, it was all too easy. On an official-looking prescription-sized piece of paper would be written time, date and place, as well as the fictitious medicinal order. Handed over to Eamon – or even his wife on the rare occasion – he would simply go to the back of the shop, unlock a cabinet where he kept the small bottles of placebos, and hand one over to the messenger with the usual repartee of 'not to be taken with too much alcohol'. Had he responded with 'they'll be in next week', the messenger would pass on down the line that Eamon would not be available, and that another 'prescription' would be needed.

On this occasion, Eamon had handed over a bottle to the

spotty youth who nervously held out his hand across the tall counter. "Three times a day and no alcohol for you. Off you go."

He watched the youth adjust his hood to suit the angle of the rain as he left through the shop door and join another on a push bike. He looked up at the shop clock and pondered that whoever it was who was sending these messages through, they knew his opening times. Later that afternoon and almost to the minute, he would have enough time to close up, lock up, cash up, turn off the lights, leave via the back door and drive to the rendezvous. He suspected the source of this latest summons and didn't dwell on the matter, instead turning to serve a young mother, noticing that she too held a prescription in her hand; a normal prescription.

He bolted the door and pulled down the blind behind the last customer, threaded his way behind the counter to the locked cabinet and retrieved two cubes, one still in its packet. He put them side by side on the countertop and cast a critical eye over them both, before lifting the clear plastic cover and swopping the cubes over. They were virtually identical apart from their weight. Certainly the colours were off a bit, shadewise, and the edges looked shiny rather than black, but otherwise it was the same basic shape and only just a fraction larger. He admired his handiwork, trying to spot the slight scratch marks where he had had to prise off one of the corners to access the inside. He had finally decided to use mini bladders in one form or another; one to hold the cyanide crystals and the other to retain the pressured hydrogen, both fitting into the limited space under the individual cubed colours. He had practised gluing the two together using salt crystals and oxygen rather than the real thing, and finally settled on utilising capsule covers taken from packets of antibiotics. When the bladders were twisted apart, they ruptured where they had been glued, even after the third dummy run. Eamon tried a fourth time, this time using compressed hydrogen, and was pleasantly surprised as he felt the faintness of the atmosphere brush over his hair. He chuckled to himself, 'now that's what I call real farting distance.'

That had been over a week ago, and now he was being summoned, possibly for final instructions. As he looked at the pair of cubes in front of him, he knew that revenge was getting closer.

This time they met inside a disused mill; at least it was out of the wind and a little drier, except where the rain found its way through the missing tiles. He saw the same two had been joined by a third man who he did not recognise, and in fact from the way he was standing – half in and half out of the shadows with a wide-rimmed hat covering most of his face – there was little chance of him making out any distinguishing features other than that he was tall and wore a brown trench coat. As he neared, the third man retreated a couple of steps into a darker doorway, even though he had clearly been noticed. Eamon wasn't in the least bit surprised by this kind of behaviour but recognised that it was the man's way of saying 'I'm not really here'.

"Have you got it with you?" asked the elder as Eamon approached the upturned packing crate.

He was going to enjoy this and took his time taking the last couple of steps. He paused, looked between the elder and the younger before briefly glancing into the doorway where the tall man stood. "You're going to like this." He produced the finished product from his raincoat pocket and placed it on the flaky wooden surface. All four of them just stood in silence looking at it; three of them almost expecting it to do something.

"Is it safe?"

"It's safe, and yes you can touch it," Eamon chuckled. "And it won't bite if that's what you're thinking."

The younger reached out and picked it up with one hand and automatically bought his other hand to it as though to start the twisting movement.

"But don't go turning it."

The younger one suddenly stopped, looked towards Eamon to see that he was grinning; he replaced the cube.

It took several seconds before the silence of dripping gutters was interrupted by the tall man. "Will it work?" His voice was surprisingly nondescript compared to the others.

"Oh yes. It'll work alright."

"No doubts at all then?"

"None," retorted Eamon.

Silence returned for almost half a minute but it was the tall man who broke it once again. "In that case, let's do it. We can all have a nice Christmas present, can't we?" He looked over at the older man and nodded.

Eamon watched as though he was a spectator, and saw the older man pull a brown envelope out of his coat pocket and approach him.

"All your instructions are in here, how to get there, where to go, who to see and how to get back, plus there's a bit of cash for expenses that you'll be needing. Remember, if it's untraceable, they can't get to us, so make sure you don't leave any fingerprints anywhere. Make sure you burn this lot once you've memorised it, OK?"

They looked each other directly in the eye across the packing case, separated by the cube.

"Merry Christmas, then." Eamon spoke first, put the cube back in his pocket, took the envelope, turned and left.

Back at his shop half an hour later, he sat on his tall stool besides his locked cabinet and re-read the instructions. He realised he would need to read them several times in order to memorise them exactly and he started going over in his mind how it would all happen.

He would catch the same timed flight from Belfast to Birmingham and from there, under the gaze of city centre and railway CCTV appear at a pharmaceutical company in Milton Keynes where he would be inspecting medical dispensers – by appointment, of course. Then onto London to do some Christmas shopping including a visit to Hamleys toy store, where he would buy a Rubik's cube. After an overnight stay in a Holiday Inn next to Heathrow Airport he would catch a flight back to Belfast the following morning. It would be at the hotel that he was to be contacted, and all the instructions said was that he should be sitting at the bar at around 10 pm. It worried him only very slightly that The Contact would know what he looked like, while he would have no idea what they looked like; that's the way the organisation worked, by keeping as many people in the dark as possible. He briefly wondered if he had met them before, perhaps in one of the Belfast clubs or even out in the sticks somewhere, and if so, maybe they could share some pleasant memories over a whiskey or two.

It was all so simple and if he were stopped at any one time, he would be able to justify his actions from start to finish. The only incriminating thing would be the loaded cube in a sealed packet; and that he would be getting rid of at the hotel. Then it would be over to someone else to deliver it and he would eagerly watch the TV for news of the death of Maurice Angus bloody Hamilton MP.

Chapter 2

Unhappiness

Chloe really had no idea what she was doing, fell out of bed as a result of trying to get back to sleep, and on the way down caught her ear on an upturned stiletto heel.

"Ouarrrrgh!"

Then she remembered it was hers. Not that she usually wore high heels, and bloody uncomfortable they were too, but her friend was wearing them and so she had had to as well. And they were at least half a size too small; certainly on her left foot.

With her eyes still shut, she fiddled around with her right hand to try and find the offending item, found it, grabbed part of it and went to throw it across the room, but it slipped out of her grasp and ended up clattering against a glass mirror a few inches away. She returned to the foetal position on the floor until she realised that due to her nakedness, she was getting cold; she felt the goosebumps begin to rise. Her logic found a way of solving that one using the minimum of energy, by grabbing the duvet that part-dangled down from the bed, and pulling it on top of her. It had barely settled on her as she tugged it this way and that so she could comfortably snuggle back to sleep, when a voice from nowhere cried out.

"Where's the duvet gone?"

Despite her severe hangover from too many shots and

cocktails – she could even still taste the last one which had grenadine in – she opened her eyes in an instant and found herself staring at cobwebbed dust half covering a lost hairbrush under the bed. She also regretted opening her eyes that quickly as the half-drawn curtains let in far too much light, but the voice was not one that she recognised and worse still, it sounded like a female voice. Yes, a female voice and she waited a few seconds hoping upon hope that she had been dreaming. That hope began to grow with each part of a second, but was shattered when a face appeared above her. At least it helped cut out some of the nasty light, but it was definitely female.

"Are you going to hog that all to yourself or should I join you down there?"

She quickly closed her eyes and a wave of nausea swam around her head as she pictured upside-down jellyfish trying unsuccessfully to escape her eyelids. She decided to open them again, but slowly and one at a time, but then they were wide open as she saw a woman slide over the edge of the mattress above her, lift one side of the duvet and join her in the relative warmth that had managed to briefly build up. Her brain struggled to comprehend why she was now being snuggled up to and she felt strange flesh come into contact with her own body, an arm entwined her torso and a leg slid down hers until toes met with hers.

"I haven't slept on the floor since I was a child, and that was in a sleeping bag, but this is fun. Don't you think? Oooooh, you smell lovely."

The last thing on her mind was how she smelt as she felt a coldish nose nuzzle her neck. Her mind was whirling with far too many possibilities as to how she was where she was, apart from having fallen out of bed – that was the easy part. Wide-eyed now and with a sense of horror beginning to creep over her, she felt the warm breath of… of… just who the hell was it and what were they doing in bed together? Naked. She wasn't a lesbian… was she? And what of her bedfellow? Perhaps she was the lesbian and this had all been a big mistake? Even if the woman next to her wasn't a lesbian, then what was she doing cuddling up to her? Was it something she herself had done that had led to them sharing her bed, and if so, what?

Her mind cringed as the number of possibilities expanded and shrank with every thought, and she found herself trying not to breathe. She wanted to put her hand 'down there' but didn't want to disturb whoever it was and alert them to… to… 'aaaaaaargh'. She almost screamed out loud. She had to go to the bathroom just to be on her own and collect her thoughts.

And now she had a fight on her hands. The way she had wrapped the duvet round herself meant that she really had to struggle to get out from under it without climbing over a naked body, and it seemed that the more she wriggled, the less it wanted to let her go, and ooooooouch, her head really hurt. She finally managed to escape its clutches with one knee still stuck to the floor, and then finding the damn stiletto with her outstretched hand, meaning that she had to stabilise herself by bracing herself against the mirror. She could just about see the outline of the bathroom door a short distance away, but reaching it upright on two feet was too much of a task, especially right now as she felt something trying to regurgitate itself. Crawling the last few inches to the doorframe, she steadied her body with an outstretched hand against it and went to do likewise with her other hand, missed and landed flat on the floor with her cheek hard against the skirting board.

Must get to the toilet… must get to the toilet. She gave up

trying to stagger and somehow decided that progress on all fours would be a safer bet; after all, once she reached the toilet pan, she would want to be in that position anyway to get rid of whatever was now rising fast in her gullet. All thoughts of her female companion were forgotten as she made her way in the dark towards where she thought the pan might be, and she didn't even have time to curse when she found that the lid was down. Precious seconds wasted lifting it so that it stayed up as she spew liquid in the direction of the gaping porcelain, only to find that the lid had decided to shut itself with a thump on her head. Her hands fumbled on the slippery lid, but at last she had her head fully over the water... with the lid resting on her head, but she didn't care just so long as the contents of her stomach ended up in it, instead of on it. She didn't care that the end of her long hair probably had its own bath, nor that any splashback might stick to her face, just so long as she could get rid of whatever was making her sick. She retched again as she realised what might be happening and was surprised at how loud the sound of it was as it echoed around the enclosed space.

She braced her hands on the floor each side of the toilet for another heave which seemed to go on forever, and it was only when it abated that she shifted her weight enough to finally lift the pan lid. She didn't lift her head until she was sure that the clang of it against the cistern meant that it ought to stay put, and as she did so, she froze.

"Well, that's not a very ladylike position is it?"

It took her a few seconds to realise what her companion was talking about. Her head was in a toilet pan, her body horizontal with pendulous breasts dangling down, her bottom was stuck up in the air and legs well splayed apart. And what's more, the light had been turned on. It was almost enough to make her heave again, but instead, she spat out the last remaining dribble and instinctively bought her legs together. Who was this woman?

She lifted up her head and turned to see a naked brunette smiling down at her. "Turn off the light." That was all she could think of on the spur of the moment. She watched as the woman pulled down on the cord and was very grateful when it went dark.

"Not your finest pose, but you do have a lovely backside. See you back in bed." The woman gave her a playful double slap on her right buttock and left her to it.

'Oh my God, oh my God, oh my God, but what have I done?' She could think of little else other than the embarrassment that made her feel like a scolded schoolgirl again, as she eased herself into a more comfortable position leaning against the shower screen. It felt cold against her back but she had other things to worry about, like the dampness her hair was making across her torso. 'Clean up… must clean up and think.' It was so difficult to decide what to do first. Stand up, turn the light on and have a shower, or sit on the toilet first. She eventually decided to shut the door first, turn on the light and then look in the wall-mounted recessed mirror. Squinting in the bright light, it was quite a shock seeing herself peering back. She parted her hair for a clearer look and recognised the first signs of maturity each side of her eyes and, widening them, saw how bloodshot they were. What had this person in front of her been drinking last night and what else had happened? She closed her eyes and instantly regretted it as she had to steady herself against the tiled recess. First things first – she needed a shower. No, not a cold one as that would be too much of a shock; and while she waited for an ambient temperature, she explored the area between her legs. She ran her fingers over her familiar-shaped pubes and then further down; at least there seemed nothing out of kilter there, so she hadn't been date-raped then.

Once she got used to the waterfall of warm water over her head and shoulders and started to shampoo, she set her mind thinking about what she could remember about last night. There had been quite a crowd to celebrate her closest friend Abergail's twenty-fifth birthday that had started off at Fino's Wine Cellar in Mayfair, a short taxi ride away. Mumm's vintage Cordon Rouge champagne had been ordered in advance by Abergail and no one in the party cared how much it would cost her, as she had let everybody know that today she would come into her extremely large legacy. Her being sole daughter of an earl and heir to the family fortune meant that her circle of friends would bear witness to the fact that she was now one of the wealthiest debutantes in England. Even before the meal had started, one girl had consumed far too much and had been sent home in a taxi, but Chloe was well aware of what lay in store for the rest of the night and, along with most of the others, had paced herself accordingly. Frivolity and gaiety emanated from the happy throng of girls and their laughter echoed off the vault walls.

Shortly after midnight, a matching pair of champagne-loaded limousines had collected them, toured the West End and chauffeured them to Annabel's Night Club in the heart of Mayfair. Only the well-heeled, rich and famous could pass the scrutiny of the doormen, or, as in this instance, had been pre-arranged with the well-connected owner. Abergail and her party of mostly unmarried girls, showing off their opulent jewellery, definitely fell into the category of the upper echelons of society. On occasion, even high-ranking royals could be found socialising and dancing the night away until the small hours.

It was all too easy to forget the outside world in the heady atmosphere of wealth in the luxurious surroundings, and at some point Chloe found herself needing to soak up some of the alcohol with canapés in the caviar lounge.

"I think you will find that oysters will do the trick."

She turned to see that a strikingly beautiful brunette had joined her on the next high stool. She couldn't but help stare at the exquisite aquiline features of her friendly face and felt an instant familiarity. She didn't know if she knew this woman, but felt certain she had seen her somewhere before. Her pose, her smile half-revealing perfectly aligned brilliant white teeth, the pear-drop earrings and matching pendant, manicured fingernails with just the right amount of expensive-looking jewellery reminded her of someone she had seen on TV, and then there was her made-to-measure dress that shimmered in the changing light.

"I think you might be right."

It wasn't that she was averse to oysters, it was that they were rather awkward to consume and although her father had taught her how to open and prepare them, she much preferred if someone else did it for her.

The woman leaned across as though to whisper in her ear, and she naturally leaned closer to hear, catching a waft of Chanel No 5.

"And they're only an aphrodisiac if you take them with ice-cold vodka." She looked around. "There's an empty cubicle over there. Come on, I'll show you how it's done." She turned to the man behind the counter and ordered two iced platters of Portuguese No 2 oysters and a bottle of Reyka vodka in an ice bucket.

She took Chloe by the hand and led her to the polished

curved leather settee. "Now, tell me a bit about yourself. I can see you're with Abergail's party and I know her family, but I don't believe we've met before." The music at the far end of the building was not so loud that she needed to crane her neck to hear what was said, and she detected a well-educated slightly husky voice with perhaps a touch of Gaelic.

"Oh, I've known Abergail since kindergarten. We grew up together, drifted apart and now live quite close to each other. Her father's got one of those big apartments in Belgrave Square and soon after leaving school, I just moved in with her, but I've now moved out into my own place in West Ken." She could see a slight questioning look on her face. "Well, actually it's not mine, it's my mother's. She owns one side of one of the roads down there and she said I ought to move into one of the empty ones as it's in need of refurbishment. But you ought to see inside… it's enormous and sometimes my brother comes and stays… that's when he's not gallivanting off on one of his treks across the Andes or getting lost somewhere in Peru. Yes, I think he's in Peru at the moment, but we haven't heard from him for weeks now, but we're not worried as he often does this sort of thing."

"Sounds fascinating. Do tell me more."

"Well." She shifted herself a little closer, and then had a thought. "I don't even know your name."

A hand appeared and rested on hers. "I won't tell you my full name as you probably won't remember all of it, but for the moment you can call me Erica."

"Erica. That's a lovely name. Mine's Chloe and sometimes just Clo." She felt that it would be inappropriate to hold out her hand as already intimacy was beginning to take over. "There's not much more to tell about Gavin at the moment, but he's a wonderful brother and always up to something." She laughed. "Last time he came back from climbing Popocatepetl – you know it's the highest volcano in Mexico – he bought me back a wooden vuvuzela type thingy. He'd just landed at Heathrow in the early hours and woke me up with it all the way from downstairs. It woke up next door as well and they weren't very happy about it. Half past five on a Sunday morning, but of course he hadn't a key and wanted to get in, so it was his way of announcing himself." She shifted herself to a slightly more comfortable position. "And then there was the time when he bought back half the England rugby team after they won something or other and that was rather early as well." She put her hand to her mouth. "Vulgar language but so good-natured; and their singing... They started using a couple of melons as rugby balls in the kitchen but one split all over this chap's head and he charged another with it still on. My friend and I were naturally the centre of attraction, but they didn't try anything on. Those muscles. Have you seen the size of their thighs?" She held her hands out forming a rough circle several inches apart. "I couldn't get my hands round even halfway."

Two dapper waiters appeared, one pushing a small trolley, the other with a standalone ice bucket and shot glasses. A two-tiered silver platter took up most of the space on the table in front of them; napkins, cutlery, water bowls and other accoutrements took up most of the rest.

"Just let it sit there and chill for a few minutes and let the aroma do its job. That way it will taste all the better. Now do carry on. You were telling me about your brother, but what about you?

"Of course, silly me. I tend to get carried away. Like I said, after I left uni, I moved in with Abergail for a couple of years and we lived in each other's pockets. The press were still describing us as typical Sloane Rangers back then and although Abby insisted we try to keep a low profile, her face was too well known, and the antics we used to get up to... We used to play cowboys and Indians with the photographers, we being the Indians, and mostly we managed to give them the slip. Abby knew one chap who ran this trendy bistro somewhere at the back end of Covent Garden and the press were all over us as there were rumours flying around about who she was dating – an Italian prince... Alberto. Abby dragged me into it and another Italian made up the four. When we came to leave, Alberto and Innis went out the front while Abby and I were shown out the fire escape at the back." She put her head back and laughed again. "The trouble was that somehow we got lost and ended up climbing all over the roofs and it took us ages to find our way back down again. It really was exciting looking down on the crowds below. We could see them but they couldn't see us. That's when we decided we were the Indians."

Erica's hand dropped gently on Chloe's. "I know exactly what you mean." She briefly looked around. "The doormen here are rather good at their jobs, but there's always one rogue or other who takes a sneaky snap and sells it on, so let's be on our best behaviour. Come on, let's start. Do you take yours with vinegar or naked?"

"Oh naked... I think. If it's too strong, I find it masks the taste, but I've never had them with vodka."

"I have just a pinch of cayenne, but take my advice. Have a glass ready and down it straight after. That way it will react with the pepper and give you that boost. Here... I'll show you."

Chloe watched her go through the motions of scattering a minimal amount of cayenne over the first of a dozen oysters and use the small fork to scoop one up into her mouth. She noted her delicate motions and that she still maintained her pose at the same time. In the past, and mainly at home, she had usually managed to make a bit of a hash of it, but Erica seemed to have everything perfectly under control.

"Now you try."

"Please don't laugh if I get it wrong." She found it easy and savoured the warming effect of the vodka as it followed the oyster down. Indeed, there seemed to be some sort of reaction going on in her stomach, but it was entirely enjoyable.

"Another." She was eager to repeat the procedure, and they both almost raced the second.

"One more and then a break," Erica suggested.

Chloe copied Erica as she dabbed her napkin to her lips. "Wow. Now I know why you take vodka with it."

"Don't hurry to get carried away. Both the oysters and the vodka will keep cold for a while yet. You were telling me about your escapades with Abergail, and excuse me for asking but so far you have told me about your friends and not yourself. No boyfriends knocking on your door?"

"Oh, I've had boyfriends. Well... more like friends who were boys, but nothing serious... yet. You know what it's like. The longer you keep them waiting, the longer their tongues get, and I certainly don't want to be tied down too young. Not while there's a terrific group of us. Don't you think it's great to have them chasing you and knowing that you can pick and choose as and when?"

She could feel the effects of either the vodka or the oysters starting to course through her, and coupled with the affinity she felt towards Erica, was really enjoying her time with her. It made a change from her usual circle of friends.

"Uni was a hoot and I ended up house sharing with

three other girls not far from Oxford's central campus, but I managed to come away with a 2.1 Bachelor of Arts in between visiting the usual clubs at weekends. On one occasion we all got a bit naughty and stripped off to draw each other nude." She made a cringing face. "And the next morning you should have seen the look on our faces when we saw what we had drawn. They were ghastly and looked nothing like us, all except Petra who swore it was her greatest portrait. She made my nose the same size as my boobs. It's not that big... is it?" Her genuine laughter revealed that she was relaxed about the whole affair. "Thursday was always a good night to start the weekend, especially at Fuzzy's. Do you know it?"

"Oh I know it, but not as well as you. What happened after Oxford?"

She decided it was time to tuck into the oysters again and reached over for the vodka bottle, but Erica beat her to it and topped up her shot glass.

"It all happened so quickly really. I'd bumped into Jamie just the week before the end of the semester and before I knew it we were on a train travelling around Europe. All I had time to do was drop my things back home and two days later we were across the Channel. Carefree. Just the two of us. It was wonderful being away from the constraints of exams and pressure from my family. From both of our families. He was the son of an MP and apparently they had great expectations of him. Paris, Amsterdam, Berlin, Venice – you name it and we went there – but when we got to Istanbul, he told me he wanted to carry on through India all the way to Burma. I wasn't so keen on the idea, but eventually we did and had a tremendous time. Then two things happened on the same day. I received a message saying that my grandmother had passed away and that I was expected to attend the funeral, and he went down with some foreign disease which meant we both had to fly back home sharpish."

She scooped another oyster and shot some more vodka. "It was a great pity as it bought us back to reality which was the last thing either of us wanted to do. He recovered and I still don't know what his actual disease was." She patted her chest. "Now, *that* went down well."

"Sounds like you were the perfect match. What went wrong?"

"Oh we did the usual thing, asking each other to Sunday lunches at each other's parents' home etcetera etcetera... bit strange really as I couldn't gel with his mother, but I got on really well with his father... You may have heard of him... Maurice Hamilton... Anyway." She repeated the oyster and vodka routine in between parts of her story. "I'd been invited to their estate near Shrewsbury on a shooting weekend and it was there that Jamie popped the question. He'd obviously not told anyone, let alone his parents, of what he was intending to do and it all became a bit embarrassing... for both of us." She tilted her head back to get the last drop of vodka.

"I take it you turned him down."

She rubbed her finger across her lips rather than dab the napkin and stared at her knees. "I couldn't speak... didn't have the courage to actually say no... instead I just went back into the house, found a quiet corner in the library, sat down and wept." She looked up at Erica with slightly misty eyes. "I'd left him on bended knee in the middle of the field surrounded by his family. He was such a nice chap but looking back on it, it was a typical holiday romance."

Erica extended her hand onto Chloe's again. "Well, I think you did exactly the right thing. In my experience those holiday romances tend not to last too long, and it's probably best you left when you did. Made a clean break of it."

"Oh no, that's not the end of it. You see, I still see Jamie from time to time and oddly enough, Maurice took me on as one of his assistants in the House of Commons soon after. I still help him out now and again when he needs some researching done. Had lunch with him last month when his wife wasn't with him but from what he tells me, she still holds a grudge, so I don't visit their house much anymore. He always sends me a Christmas present, and just to annoy his wife, I send him one as well." She laughed briefly. "I know I shouldn't do it, but I like to see the look on his face when he tells me what her reaction was. Lovely place though; surrounded by rolling countryside with streams, ponds, horses, and loads of geese and ducks." She went to take another oyster and noticed there were now only two left. "Yours or mine?"

"Oh, you help yourself." Erica topped up her glass up for her. "I've had my fair share. So what's in store for you now?"

"I have an agent over in Soho and she gets me jobs drawing sketches and cartoons for magazines. I know it doesn't pay all the bills but what with Maurice's bits 'n' pieces and mother's occasional demands, it keeps me busy." She necked the last oyster, downed the vodka and held out her glass for another top-up. "Also leaves me time to enjoy myself. Cheers."

She didn't notice Erica looking pensive. "Talking of enjoying yourself, a good friend of mine introduced me to a fabulous new cocktail. Fancy giving it a go?" She saw Chloe glance at the nearly empty bottle of vodka. "Oh don't worry about the dregs, leave those for the waiters. Come on, I know the cocktail barman here."

Her dazzling smile convinced Chloe in an instant; that and the alcohol, but she was a little unsteady as she rose.

"OK, but I really ought to watch myself and then get back to my friends. Just one. OK?"

Erica took Chloe by the arm, and to any casual onlooker, they were just two good friends making their way over to the relatively brightly lit bar. The two of them perched on adjacent tall stools and while Erica made the order, Chloe once again admired the way she held herself; not hunched over the counter, not awkwardly balancing on the rotatable stools, but upright with her ankles neatly crossed and resting on the crossbar. It then began to cross her mind that she still didn't know this woman who was several years older, obviously well-educated, travelled and apparently wealthy. Her nails perfectly manicured, eyebrows trimmed to perfection and enhancing her visage, natural lashes that accentuated her clear eyes. Was that a Dior dress she was wearing?

Before she could get word in, Erica beat her to it. "This cocktail is brilliant and called a Handgrenade and you're going to love it. I've ordered one too. It's got green chartreuse, Cointreau, vodka, lemon barley water, but it has got to be Robinsons, all shaken and topped up with lots of fresh soda over crushed ice in a large bowl glass. And the best part is the wedge of pineapple resting across the top, hinged by a cocktail stick... that's the pin you pull out before drinking it through a big straw. It's a wonderful reviver, especially in hot climes."

They could hear the barman shaking the silver flask and naturally turned to watch briefly.

"Callum's good at these, here, mind yourself." Chloe's foot had slipped off the cross bar and she had to steady herself on the counter.

"Looks like you and high heels don't get on so well."

"Abby suggested we wear them tonight and I didn't get a

chance to break these in. It's not that we're short at all, quite the opposite, but she can be rather insistent sometimes. I was just wondering, you seem so at home here... relaxed. Do you come here often, and I'm afraid I don't even know where you come from. Where do you live?"

Erica moved close enough to whisper, "Only when I'm on my own." She moved back a little and gave a knowing wink. "I'm not always in the country, but when I am in London and need a little distraction, this is the place to meet interesting people. Just like you." She extended an avuncular hand onto Chloe's again. "Here, try this."

Two large balloon glasses appeared in front of them on the counter; the frothy top made the drinks look enticing even if the pale green of the liquid below did not. Chloe adjusted the straw and took a naturally tentative pull.

"That's lovely... with a taste of pepper. Is there any in it?"

"No pepper. That's the green chartreuse." She saw Chloe take a longer pull. "Told you you would like it." She delicately sipped her own through the straw. "Now, let me tell you a little about myself."

Although Chloe heard what she was saying, very little sunk in, as the extremely alcoholic cocktail on top of what she had already consumed, went straight to her head. In short order, she had finished it and asked for another. She didn't notice that Erica had hardly touched hers.

"Try this one with a brandy chaser. It'll work wonders."

It certainly did, but before she was halfway through the third, Erica had to accompany her to the well-appointed toilets, swaying all the way.

***

Washing the last of the shampoo out of her hair, Chloe realised she had very little memory of the last hour or more, other than walking towards the cocktail counter. She gummed her mouth and thought she could detect a residue of oysters somewhere and looked over to her toothpaste and brush on the shelf behind the basin a few feet away. She needed more time to think and, playing the very noisy hairdryer in various directions, she tried her best to concentrate on why Erica had shared her bed with her last night, but could come up with no reason. She would just have to ask and hope that the answer wouldn't make her cringe too much. She looked at herself again in the mirror, took a deep breath and with a towel covering her midriff, opened the en suite door into her bedroom, expecting to find Erica in her bed.

Large though the bedroom was, there was no sign of her, and she didn't think she'd be hiding in the wardrobe; then on the dressing table by the window, she saw a note.

Dear Chloe. Thanks for the loan of one half of your comfy bed last night and sorry if I startled you earlier. Must dash to get ready for tonight's engagement. Catch up with you soon. Erica. PS: My number's on the back.

She sat down on the edge of her bed trying to concentrate and automatically looked at her bedside alarm clock. It took her a moment to realise that it was past four o'clock in the afternoon. She groaned to herself; she was supposed to be meeting... she couldn't remember who she was supposed to be meeting, nor where, but that had been at three o'clock anyway; wasn't it? She slumped her head back onto the pillow and instantly regretted it; it felt more like a rock than a gentle cushion.

A clear-headed Erica made her way by tube back to her rented apartment opposite The Queens Arms on Kilburn

High Road, occasionally chuckling to herself. It had been an amusing exercise, but she had enjoyed it; and she still couldn't believe how gullible the English were. She doubted if Chloe remembered a single word of what she had said after the first Handgrenade, but it didn't matter if she did. None of it could be corroborated, but she felt that she had given the right impression of being a well-connected mysterious jet-setter. Certainly connected enough to be known to the Hamilton family. She went to the bathroom and removed the blue-tinted contact lenses revealing her own brown eyes, wiped her lipstick off, and placed the fake Rolex watch and matching paste jewellery in a plastic box next to the hair tint bottle. She unzipped her dress, and carefully hung it up on a hanger; after all, it really was a Dior dress and the only item of clothing that actually was expensive. Dressed only in her panties, she leaned closer to the mirror and studied her visage, smiling to reveal her perfect set of teeth. She cupped her breasts towards the mirror and jiggled them briefly. "Still in good shape then," she said out loud. She felt that she was running out of time, especially as it was her thirty-seventh birthday next, but in herself, she had recognised years ago that she had natural beauty, and had used it to good effect.

She was bought back to reality by the pinging of her mobile phone in the next room; it would be a message. 'Yes/No. Meet?'

She replied. 'The usual. 9 2nite.'

When they had last met, Aiden had impressed on her how important this job would be, and that they were going to the greatest of lengths to ensure that nobody would be caught this time. It concentrated her thoughts as to the reason why she was taking these risks and reminded her that it would be her who would be smiling when it was all over. She adored her father with all her heart and still carried a small photograph of him; even though he had been in his grave for nearly a quarter of a century. With little to do for the next few hours, she fished around in the pocket of her handbag for it, started to panic when she couldn't locate it immediately, but with an audible sigh of relief found it and placed it on the bed in front of her. She'd had it encapsulated as it had been getting scuffed and faded, but now it was safe. He was right here. Right in front of her. She was on his shoulders, long black hair blowing in the wind with head half-back in delight. He was holding her arms out above his head to make sure she didn't fall as he trotted between the dunes along the sandy shoreline of Mallaranny in Co. Mayo, and had the biggest smile on his face that she could remember. One of her favourite memories was being swung round and round at arm's length, but he never let go. He'd told her that he'd never let go, and so now, neither would she. It still stabbed at her heart to remember the fondest of times they had enjoyed together, but they were clouded by one of the last times. Even though she was only twelve years old at the time, her aunt and uncle had taken her along with them to collect him from the police station at Enniskillen where he had been held, ostensibly for questioning. She had watched from the car as they helped him gingerly place one foot in front of the other down the stone steps, but it was clear that his right foot was unable to hold his weight. The front of his shirt and torn jacket were covered with blood that still dripped from his face and as they hobbled towards the car, she could see that there was a nasty gash on his right hairline. They had put him on the back seat and told her to comfort him until they got home. Cradling him in her arms and mopping up the blood away from his eyes with her uncle's handkerchief, she tried her best to tell him how much she loved him in the hope it would make him better. As her tears flooded out, she saw how they helped to wash away the blood from his face and wished they would never stop until it was all gone, but his glazed eyes just stared up at the roof instead of into hers. She saw his lips move and put her ear to them to catch his faint whisper. "Never let go... Never let go."

She took his hand to her mouth, squeezed it and kissed it, but there was no reaction and she watched as his eyes slowly closed for the final time. She rested her cheek to his and wailed until she felt her uncle's hand pushing her gently but firmly away from him, her eyes flooded with grief-filled tears.

Why had they done this to him? Why... why... why? He'd been the perfect daddy, but now the bottom had fallen out of her world; a world in which love had been her inspiration and sustenance and was all she had really known, but now that was replaced with misery. All she wanted to do right now was cuddle him and she started to nudge him, gently at first.

"Daddy... Daddy, wake up! Please wake up!" Her racking sobs descended into an ululating wail as she hugged him tighter, until her uncle opened the back door and pulled her away from him. She beat her fists uselessly on him. "Let me go! I want him back!"

He clasped his arms around her. "There's nothing you can do for him now. He's gone."

"No, no, no! He can't be!" He squeezed her tighter as she struggled to escape.

"He is, child. He's dead." She renewed her struggling but gave up quite quickly and instead clung onto him. Despite his own grief, her uncle realised that it was his niece who needed the greatest comforting that very moment, and he ran his fingers through her hair.

"Why?" she asked again, not looking up. She was not

asking herself this time but her uncle.

"Because."

She stiffened and took half a pace backwards to look into his face. "Because what?"

It took him a moment to respond, looking into those tear-filled eyes. "Because he was doing what he believed in." He watched as her face began to crumple. "Now's not the time and certainly not the place to explain. Not here in front of the police station, but you know what he did and what he did for others." The look on her face changed in acknowledgment of what he had just said. "He told me once that if a man's not prepared to die for what he believes in, then he can't expect others to do the same for him."

It took her a few moments to realise what he was trying to tell her and he saw a quizzical look come over her face. "Look... they bought him in for questioning because he was trying to protect the identity of someone." This was going to be awkward and he could see that he would need to choose his next words carefully. "Someone we all know." He looked over her shoulder at the buildings down the street, trying to find some inspiration, aware that he was being scrutinised by his niece. "They applied... pressure... and it looks like they failed."

"Failed... failed! They've bloody killed him! That not failure, it's bloody murder!" she almost screamed. "It's not right!" There was a look of concentration on her face as her eyes bored up into his, and it sent shivers down his spine. He'd seen that look before on his brother's face, and knew he had to control her.

"Not here. Not now."

"Who did this to him?" She'd taken a further pace back from his so that he had had to release his hold on her. "Come on. You know. Who?"

He fumbled in his own mind, not sure if he ought to tell her right now in front of the police station, as he didn't know what her reaction might be. He would have preferred to tell her somewhere in seclusion, knowing that she would likely be as much of a renegade as her father, but if he didn't tell her straight away, he was worried that she might do something rash.

"If you don't tell me, I'm going in there." She pointed at the police station. "And I'm going to…"

"Alright, alright. Calm down just a minute. I'll tell you." He'd seen a movement at a first-floor window in the police station. "But if I do, promise me you'll not do anything here." He saw defiance in her. "Promise me." God, but the look in her eyes. "Promise me now," he said forcefully.

Still a delay from her, but eventually she conceded. "OK. It's a promise, providing you tell me everything later."

He reached out and turned her around so that her back rested against his stomach, his hands resting on her shoulders. "Look at the first-floor window on the corner up there. You see that man looking down at us? Well he's the man who's in charge of the Brits in this part of the world, and he's a bloody animal. He's the man who ordered the arrest and interrogation of your father… and you're old enough to draw your own conclusions from that."

The wind ruffled their hair while they both stared at the vague figure behind the half-drawn curtained window, but they could not make out any definite features from that distance; the criss-crossed tape across the glass prevented a clear view.

She half-turned and with a thoughtful look asked him, "Who is he?"

"That's Captain Maurice bloody Hamilton in the window. That's who it is."

She turned back to the window to try to make out more features, but it was impossible, and then turned back to her uncle. "I'm going to kill him one day." It was a very deliberate statement, almost unemotional, and he believed her. "For Daddy."

"Not this day you're not. There's a whole company of soldiers behind those walls." He tossed his head in the direction of the police station. "And anyway, I doubt he'll be around long enough for that."

"Why not?"

"Because there's a queue wanting to do away with him and by the time you're old enough, he'll be dead."

She thought about this for a moment. "Then I had better grow up fast... because I will kill him... and make sure he knows why." Tears began to flow down her cheeks again.

"Come on back to the car, child. I'll tell you more when we're away from here and back home."

***

Wearing a medium-length lightly tinted blue wig and a shortish skirt, Erica pushed open the door to The Queens Arms and walked over to the bar; all the time hunching herself to make herself look shorter than she actually was. It was difficult for her to disguise her beauty, but the oval thick-rimmed glasses helped; especially as she had bent the nose stays to make them sit crooked. Apart from her legs, she reckoned that she was rather unattractive. Ordering a vodka and tonic, she looked round casually and spotted Aiden funnelling money into the juke box. Good move, she thought to herself. If anyone was going to try to listen into their conversation, they'd have trouble picking it up... especially over Shakin' Stevens. She wondered if he'd be putting on Elvis next. He looked round and motioned with his head a few feet away, to an out-of-the-way table under a wall-mounted speaker. Without being noticed as she was fishing in her purse for the right money, and where possible using the mirrors behind the bar, she made a mental note of who might be taking any interest in either her or Aiden. Being a Sunday evening, it was fairly quiet. There were only a dozen or so patrons and nobody looking out of place. She recognised the man she had nicknamed 'the old git' sitting by himself under the disused darts board off to the left.

She joined Aiden, placing her frumpish looking handbag on the table between them.

"If it weren't for your lovely lips and long legs, I wouldn't have recognised you. Since when have you taken up wearing glasses and wigs?"

"Ever since Liam got shot." She ignored his flattery and took a swig from her glass.

"Yeah. Real shame about Liam. But if the silly bugger had kept his nerve instead of running, he'd have got away with it."

"And Garthy."

"Well, nobody's going to get shot this time. We've made sure of that, so don't you worry your pretty little head. And anyway, you're probably the safest out of the lot of us." Aiden tried to put an end to the blame game she was playing.

"Well, I'm just making sure it stays that way, oh... and talking of which, I'll be needing those new ID papers etc. next week."

"Why next week?"

She looked at him as though he was stupid. "Because I'll be moving flats."

"You don't need to move flats. There's no way they're going to be able to trace you. Not this time."

"Listen Aiden, don't you know what's going to happen when they find out he's been murdered...? Come on then... what do you think they're going to do, eh?" She watched him formulating an answer but didn't give him the chance. "They're going to move heaven and earth to find us. First they're going to question our new friend and it's not going to be long before they start looking for her new girlfriend. Me... Yes me Aiden, me. Not you. Then they'll be traipsing through any and all video footage which will no doubt include all the bars and restaurants she's visited recently. After that they're going to photofit my face and run it through their computers which, I suspect, won't take very long at all. As well as all the street cameras, there's the underground and bus cameras, and while there's none right outside here, if they even get a sniff of the general area, they'll eventually find this flat. No... let me put it another way. I'd expect within three days, they'll be breaking down my door." She let him mull for a moment. "So you just get me that new ID next week, because I'm not hanging around for them to show up."

He slowly put his half-empty pint back down on the cardboard coaster in front of him. He'd noticed that she had raised her voice a little, and he'd surreptitiously glanced round the pub to see if anyone had been taking any interest in them, but everyone seemed to be ignoring them. Shakin' Stevens was still serenading anyway. Her mention of CCTV made him automatically look at the pub's which was pointed down the length of the bar, but he had found out from one of the barmaids several weeks ago that it was a dummy. That was why he had chosen this pub instead of the café across the road for their occasional meets.

"Ok... OK, I'll make sure it's here in the next few days... alright?"

"Alright." The fire that had been building up in her eyes, diminished.

"Where will you go?"

"Don't know yet... probably south of the river this time."

They sat in silence waiting for Elvis to come on, and when he did, he continued, "Come on then, tell me about Chloe."

The way she recounted the relevant parts of their 'chance' meeting the previous night, Aiden thought he detected an element of enjoyment, but he didn't let it show. He was still on his guard and watched a couple of blokes wander in and approach the bar; his eyes shifted now and again, looking for signs of surveillance, but nothing else had changed.

"Right then, here's what you do. You remember Eamon...?" He waited for her nod and as it didn't come straight away, he continued. "Don't you? You might remember him from a few years back when he was working in his uncle's chemist shop."

"What... young Eamon?"

"He's not so young now and he's the chemist, and it'll be him who you're to meet at the Holiday Inn at Gatwick Airport. Probably next week sometime and I'll let you know in good time. He'll be sitting at the bar around ten o'clock in the evening with the package for you."

She desperately wanted to know what was in the package, but knew better than to ask straight away and instead enquired, "How big is it?"

"Oh it's not so big. Easily fit into that handbag." He motioned at her tatty looking bag on the table. "Now, whatever you do, you don't open it." He waited for any sort of reaction from her. "Understood? Don't even try to open it until you get the say-so from me."

"OK, OK. I get the idea."

"What you've then got to do is wrap it up in nice Christmas paper with a pretty bow on top and a sparkly card attached to it addressed to Darling Maurice, and while you're at it, mark it from Father Christmas." He chuckled. "Then get your new girlfriend to give it to him."

"Why's she going to give it to him?"

He waited until Bing Crosby started his rendition of 'White Christmas', taking the chance to have another swig from his pint. "You might think you're a smart girl, but you haven't yet twigged why we set you up to meet her last night and get close to her. Come on, think about it."

She thought about it for a moment and considered she could have hardly got any closer, but knew that that was not what he meant; besides which, she hadn't told him about that part. She was just formulating an idea when he continued.

"It really is nice and simple. You give her the package just before Christmas and before she disappears off to her own family, with some excuse about not being able to do it yourself... say you're off to the Seychelles or somewhere exotic at the last minute and haven't time before catching your flight... and you don't trust the post, and you ask her to deliver it herself."

He had just clarified a plan similar to the one she was thinking about herself, but the way he put it definitely helped.

"Now you can see we've been planning this for years. You've me to thank for keeping tabs on both Hamilton and your new girlfriend, and I know pretty much down to the hour what they are going to be doing this Christmas. You see, I've spent weeks tailing them and now know what they'll be doing."

She recognised a smugness on his face and it almost made

her want to smack him just because of that, but she admitted to herself that this last part really was going to be simple. If only she knew what was in the package. She asked him.

She watched Aiden spin his nearly empty pint round in his hand while it rested on the tabletop, clearly considering whether or not to tell her. He knew her family history well and that her loyalty was beyond question, but he was weighing up the risk to himself as well as the organisation. He ceased his prevarication as she would soon hear about it. "It's a sort of bomb, and before you ask, no it won't be detected before it goes off."

"What sort of bomb?"

"Can't tell you that... it might expose others."

She visibly fumed and watched him lower his eyes. "Oh come on Aiden. If anyone has a right to know, it's me... and if it's me who's going to be handling it, I need to know what's in it." She watched him trying to decide if he ought to tell more. "You bloody well tell me or else you can find another mule to carry out your dirty work and I'll find my own way of nailing the bastard." She leaned over the table closing the gap between them. To an outsider they were just another couple having a minor domestic. "I've waited too long for this and I don't want to fuck up just because you think I can't handle it, so just bloody tell me. Now." She sat back sharply and finished off her vodka and tonic.

"Alright, alright. I'm just thinking of the others if anything goes wrong."

"It might go wrong unless you tell me. I don't want it blowing up in my face, or come to that, the wrong face."

"Oh, it won't do that... Not if you don't touch it, it won't."

"You've just told me I've got to wrap it. So come on,

what's in it and how's it going to get past their detectors, eh?"

Aiden looked over at the bar, finished off his pint and rose. "I'll tell you after I've got us another. Still V&T?"

She nodded and watched him put the two glasses on the counter, order and wander over to the jukebox. She concluded that he was stalling for time in his reluctance to tell her, but then again, she would probably do the same if she was in his shoes. She thought that their small but effective team had so far not been detected by the Brits, due mainly to their principle of keeping contact to a minimum. They all had their reasons, but Aiden was their mastermind, at least for their own particular cell. She'd heard about another operating on the mainland but never come across them and wondered what they were up to. She'd heard a rumour – no, not even a rumour but an intimation by Aiden – that this Christmas was going to be a focal point for action, and they were just pursuing their own particular plan. As he sat down, she heard 'Sultans of Swing' come on.

"You're right." He took a small swig so that the pint wouldn't spill if the table got knocked. "So I'll tell you." He went on to explain about the Rubik's cube, how it would work and what was in it. "With any luck, it'll kill his entire family and anybody else who's in the room."

Her jaw had dropped, but she snapped it shut. "Brilliant... absolutely brilliant."

He watched her reaction with a smug reflection of himself. "So you can see why I've kept this to myself for so long. Most of our other plans have been thwarted by MI5 because there's been a weak link somewhere along the line, but not this time. It'll make a real difference to those back home."

"But how did you come up with that idea? I mean why hasn't anybody thought of it before?"

"Let's just hope Bloody Hamilton hasn't."

"Hang on a minute. You said you had it made as a one-off. Are you sure whoever made it isn't going to talk to the police. After all, that must take some skill and there can't be too many firms around who could make that sort of thing. It'll be all over the news and somebody's bound to come forward."

"Not a firm dearie... a man. A man all on his own with an extraordinary skill." He sipped from his glass. "Shame he won't be around to enjoy this Christmas, so no worries there." He gave her a knowing look.

She smiled, emptied half her glass and shifted her buttocks nearer the edge of her chair. "Come on then... tell me more and why a Rubik's cube?"

"Hamilton was on telly a few years ago before he was appointed to the cabinet, one of those Parkinson-type interviews, and showing off about how he was one of the few who could solve a Rubik's cube in double-quick time. I wasn't paying all that much attention, but he did it in a few seconds and I wondered why he bothered. Apparently you have to have a mathematician's mind and can do it while only half-concentrating. But what caught my interest was that they replayed his doing it at the end of the programme at half-speed and it reminded me of how they used to wind up detonators in the old westerns. You know... when Clint Eastwood's blowing up a bridge with the train going over and he winds the handle on the box and the whole thing goes bang big time."

"Wasn't that Burt Lancaster against the Germans?"

"Whoever." He swigged from his pint, half waving it in dismissal of her correction. "And I thought, wouldn't it be ironic if Hamilton was the one blowing himself up. I could just picture him turning the cube and it going boom."

She butted in. "But then you needed something that wasn't going to be detected by the bomb squad."

"Got that from the film *Dune*... the one with the giant worms and spaceships in it. When the doctor bites down on his tooth and gasses half the room. Remember that one?"

"Not sure I've seen it." She wondered if watching old films was his hobby while he was passing the time in whatever bedsit he was in.

"Anyway, I had a word with Eamon and it was he who suggested hydrogen cyanide. The tricky part was getting the Rubik's cube made by someone who wasn't going to stand out, so not any sort of engineering business. I won't tell you how, but this loner got recommended. You know the rest."

"Just as well I'm on the move then."

"Maurice bloody Hamilton's going to get a fine Christmas present this year and deservedly so. Probably be his last, so he may as well enjoy it."

"Merry Christmas." She raised her glass to him.

Chapter 3

1985
(thirty years earlier)

The Cartwright twins still did everything together, even though they were no longer youths; well, almost everything. One naturally expects looks to alter as childhood develops into adulthood, but not these two. Their mannerisms, motions and thoughts coincided with each other to such an extent that all who were close to them were constantly having to double check which one they were talking to. The only person who could instantly tell them apart was their mother, who, with her sense of humour when they were born, had nicknamed them Brian 1 and Brian 2, but had eventually had them christened Eric and Ernie. Morecambe and Wise were her favourite comedians and the family joked that it was just as well that she hadn't named them after characters in *Fawlty Towers*. "Basil Cartwright just doesn't roll off the tongue as easily," she used to say when asked.

Naturally, they'd had a lot of fun growing up together and were referred to affectionately as Tweedledum and Tweedledee by the nursery staff since their mother had insisted they wear checked peaked caps to keep their heads warm. Not that they were rotund – quite the reverse – but with their wide smiles and being never far from each other, it just seemed to suit them.

Their time at the primary school a short walk away in the town of Leominster was not a lot different. They'd sharpen their pencils to the same length at both ends, put their hands up simultaneously, receive the same marks to the same questions, eat the same food and cross the finishing line together on the sports field; there really was little between them mentally or physically. Their headmaster had been in a quandary as there was a strict dress code, but asked their mother to at least put them in different-coloured shirts at the beginning of the day, but it didn't make any difference. They simply swapped them. At secondary level, they'd stick up for each other and soon see off any hint of bullying. It wasn't that they lived in a rough area, but as in any society, there's always one or two who want to stamp their authority on those who are weaker. Eric and Ernie found that they were often called on to keep the peace by their contemporaries and it was probably these occasional acts of kindness that led them to thoughts about their future as they approached leaving age.

"You could follow your father into the army," suggested the visiting careers advisor when the two of them sat in front of him in one of the classrooms. They'd been told to go in one at a time, but had ignored the instruction. "You're both fit strapping lads and your aptitude test is pointing you in that direction anyway."

Their father had only been a lowly private in the Gloucestershire Regiment but had been killed during a live fire exercise while on secondment to a NATO force while stationed in West Germany. The twins had never had a decent chance to get to know him, but had been told that he was a brave man.

Probably due to peer pressure, they took their sabbatical over that summer and spent it hiking round the wilds of deepest, darkest Wales. Camping out at nights, they did the odd job here and there for local sheep farmers to earn a crust and it was while they were crossing the Epynt military ranges on a particularly hot day that they came across a company of trainees on exercise. Not wishing to interfere and knowing that they ought not to be where they were, they watched them from the cover of a nearby wood as they deployed.

"We could do that."

"Yeah. Better than them as well."

"What do you think about old Chubby Cheeks' suggestion that we ought to join up?" It was a rhetorical question as they had both been thinking about the question posed a few weeks earlier and knew the answer. One, slightly before the other, retrieved a sandwich from his rucksack and they sat there munching and observing.

"Let's get down to Brecon first and then onto the Gloucester recruitment centre. Here, look at that chap at the back, he looks like he's in a bit of trouble."

They watched the rest of the company move off into the distance, all except for one who had taken the time to sit on a tree stump. He suddenly keeled over and disappeared into the long grass.

"Looks like he's been shot."

"Bit sudden like."

"I didn't hear anything."

"Nope."

They waited several minutes until the line of men vanished over the ridge, finished munching, drank from their canteens, rose together, and walked the couple of hundred yards to where they last saw the soldier. His darker army-issue camouflage stood out against the arid tall grass as he lay on the ground, barely conscious.

The two of them stood over him for a few seconds seeing that he was sweating profusely and panting like a dog with his eyes wide open.

"Looks like he's in trouble."

"Bloody hot day to be carrying all that gear about. Here, let's get him sitting up."

They shifted him upright so that he rested against the tree stump after disentangling his rifle and moving some of his other equipment out of the way.

"You look just about all-in mate."

They could see that he was trying to speak by the way his lips moved but heard nothing despite one of them putting his ear close to his mouth.

"Give him some water. That'll help."

"His canteen's empty," Ernie said rattling it in thin air. "Hold him a sec while I give him some. How much have you got?"

"About half."

"Me too."

It took them nearly five minutes of trying to get some water into his mouth and dousing him with a wet handkerchief before the soldier's breathing started to return to normal.

"Let's get this pack off his back. That'll take some of the weight off his shoulders and help him breathe easier."

"Bit heavy isn't it."

"Must be all of seventy pounds."

"No wonder he's collapsed. How do you reckon the others are managing?"

"Maybe they've got more meat on their bones. This guy looks like he's been on a crash diet. He's a bit skinny."

They watched as the soldier closed his eyes and his head lolled to one side.

"Now what are we going to do? He's passed out."

"Check his pulse."

"It's a bit faint."

They stood up, looked around over the desolate landscape in the hope of seeing other soldiers, or anyone else, but nobody. The views were magnificent in every direction other than the lonely stand of trees behind them, and about a mile or so away, the start of a forest that stretched to the horizon.

"Left or right?"

"Left."

They hefted the soldier upright between them; Eric on the left, Ernie on the right. The choice of which direction the twins should go was obvious to them and leaving the military kit and rifle on the ground where it lay, set off in the opposite direction of the other soldiers, downhill. Their unspoken logic dictated that they would head back to the remote farm in the valley they had passed several hours earlier. The heady summer atmosphere became heavier the further they descended and became positively wearisome when they entered the dense conifer forest. If it wasn't for a gate interrupting a long dry stone wall, they would never have come across Wyn Jones.

For five generations, Wyn's family had owned the extensive Tyn Bryn Farm which abutted the edge of the military's Epynt ranges, and he was well used to seeing all sorts of comings and goings at odd hours. Now, as dusk was approaching and, having finished identifying which sheep had escaped their annual fleecing, he was driving his Land Rover back home. As he passed one of the gates, he spotted the trio making their way across one of his fields. He almost ignored them and carried on, but then reversed back and waited for them; clearly the one in the centre needed help. He stood waiting for them by the gate.

"Get him in the back here." He spoke English rather than his native Welsh, guessing correctly that the two chaps either side were more likely to understand him. He then did a double take seeing that they looked identical. They eased the soldier into the back of the vehicle as gently as they could.

"Bit of luck you being here," remarked one.

"Yeah, real luck," copied the other.

"Jump in the front, lads. Let's get him down to the farmhouse."

It was a surprisingly smooth track once they passed through another gate which Ernie opened and shut to help ease their passage, but it was nearly a further couple of miles before the stone-built farm and connecting byre came into view. Wyn hooted as they neared, and out came a youth from a side door.

Wyn's Welsh was incomprehensible to the twins, but resulted in the youth dashing back inside, while Eric and Ernie eased the soldier awkwardly through the narrow doorway. The kitchen table had been cleared and to the twins, was obviously the place to set the soldier down, but as they went to do so, a female voice interrupted.

"Not on there, you bloody heathens. That's where we eat our supper. Put him in that chair in the corner over there."

They had hardly let go of him before the lady half-shoved them out of the way and bent over the half-conscious body, placed her fingers on his neck and started to undo his shirt.

"Dai!" The youth came forward from the recesses of the open plan room. "Go and run a lukewarm bath. On the cold side mind. Quickly now," she fired at him in Welsh.

She stood up and looked at the twins in turn. "You ought to know better than to go hiking over the ranges in this heat. Time and time again you wretched halfwits end up down here, half-dead and expect us to bail you out. Get him out of those clothes and upstairs into the bath before he really does snuff it."

The twins weren't expecting any sort of verbal tirade and initially just stood there with gaping mouths.

"Well come on then, now." The woman of the house patently expected her commands to be carried out immediately.

They sprang into action and soon had the naked soldier in the bath that was still running. "Out of the way." She barged them to one side, felt the temperature of the water with her hand and turned on the cold tap more. They watched her lift his delirious head and force down some cloudy liquid from a beaker she had bought upstairs with her, then apply a wet flannel to his forehead and turn the tap off.

"Well, downstairs with the both of you. I'll let you know when he's recovered. What's his name?"

The twins looked blankly at each other. "Dunno."

"What do you mean you don't know? He's your friend, isn't he?"

"No. Only met him this afternoon," offered Eric.

"Never saw him before today," added Ernie.

They saw her lips compress. "Well, whatever, you can't do any more up here, so get downstairs. I'll call you if I need you."

Wyn and his son Dai, were waiting for them, as was a pair of glasses of water. "You're not dressed like the normal type of squaddie we get round here. I don't suppose you can tell us what's going on, can you?"

In between sips and refills, they told them.

"You know, you'll probably end up having to do that same hike if you're going to enlist and if that happened when it's this hot, someone's probably going to end up either down here or in the morgue. Summer over the ranges can be stifling hot as it is now, and in the blink of an eye, change to a torrential downpour. Winter's just as bad but at the other extreme and tends to catch you out when it can. Dangerous place are the ranges. It's not just where east and west meet, or north and south... it's got its own climate and on top of that, it's steeped in blood. Here, have a top-up."

He went to refill their glasses with tap water, changed his mind, went to the fridge and got out three Heineken bottles and returning to the table was glad to see that the twins were intrigued by his last comment. He passed round the opener and waited for the third 'phut' before continuing, wanting full attention; They didn't get too many visitors but when they did, he liked to talk to someone other than his wife.

"So the story goes, centuries ago around the time of the Dark Ages, King Offa and an army of Druids took on a Roman legion and beat them well and truly in this very valley. The survivors escaped onto the ranges, hid in the dykes and between the rocks, anywhere they could, but were found and sacrificed. Only this sacrifice carried a curse with it. Now, you might think to yourselves that curses are old wives' tales, but you ask anyone round here, and they'll tell you that this one is very much alive."

The twins wondered just how many people lived 'around here' as they couldn't recall passing many other dwellings for miles.

Wyn watched them for a reaction. "You see, because the Romans had been so brutally oppressive in their pursuit of Welsh gold, enslaving whatever populous they hadn't already killed, the Druids had made their sacrifice to none of their gods. Oh no. Instead, as their blood flowed, their souls went with it; cursed into the ground. You haven't been up there long enough to notice the shape of some of the boulders nor that they're not always in the same place, and even some of the trees somehow tend to get in the way. You can go up there one day, and the same path will be blocked the next. It's like they're trying to find somewhere to go and if they can't, then they'll try to take anyone who can show them the way out of Purgatory. It's just as well you weren't camping up there last night." He paused, waiting for the obvious question, but it never came, so continued. "The fog's more of an atmosphere that clings and disorientates; penetrates the mind like. You'd have woken up and not been able to find your way back down and been driven to such distraction that you'd have wandered around in circles and eventually just given up and joined them."

He paused to take a swig and motioned with his head upstairs. "I keep drumming it into Dai not to go out on his own until he can find his own way in the dark, but he's a headstrong lad and listens to me less and less, but I suppose when I was his age…"

They heard footsteps coming down the creaky stairs and all turned their heads as Wyn's wife appeared with a look of thunder on her face and before she even reached the bottom step, she jabbered away in incomprehensible Welsh. She ceased her tirade after a few words from Wyn, stared at the twins and wrung her hands.

"I'm sorry lads, I didn't know you weren't with him. I thought you were just being awkward not telling me his name, but I understand now. I'm still not sure of his name, but his tag says he's a Private J. Ford and before you ask, he's going to be alright. He's resting now and Dai's keeping an eye on him. Hey, talking of names, I see he's given you a beer but I'll bet he hasn't told you my name, has he? It's Dilys, but you can call me D."

"Give me a chance, I was just telling them how dangerous the ranges are."

"Oh, for crying out loud. Not that old chestnut again." She turned to the twins. "I suppose he's told you about the place being haunted. Well, don't believe a word of what he's said. It's poppycock."

"Oh come on D, you know full well they still haven't explained those mysterious deaths a couple of years ago. And what about those three soldiers who were supposed to have died from dehydration a few years back? They couldn't have because their canteens were full when they were found. Now if you ask me…"

D and Wyn reverted to their native Welsh, swapping what sounded like insults to the twins who looked left and right as if they were watching a tennis match. Nevertheless, they picked up on the fact that both of them seemed to be singing while they spoke. The musical inflections rose and fell with sentences but they were caught out by the sudden cessation. It was Dilys who spoke to them in English first.

"You must think we're a right pair carrying on like that, but think nothing of it. It's perfectly normal. You see, there's no one else around to have a good argument with and it helps pass the time when we're not too busy. You two lads had better tell me what happened in your own words later, but first you'd better put your gear in the shed next door because that'll be where you'll be sleeping tonight. Our spare room's still full of Dad's old tat, otherwise you could have gone in there. There's an outside hose that doubles-up as a shower just round the corner and once you've cleaned up, you can share in some of my homemade cawl."

She beamed with pride at the thought of strangers

appreciating her stew, but then changed to a scowl.

"More like goulash soup," Wyn goaded.

Convivially, half an hour later, gathered round the bare wooden table, they tucked into D's traditional Welsh dish.

"I've just checked on him again and he's out for the count. Just as well you found him when you did. Sheer luck you seeing him tumble, and if the army finds out you were up there, well, I really don't know what they'd do, so you'd better say you found him down by our stone wall. You know, where Wyn saw you. No point in going down to the village and phoning them this time of night so we'll give them a ring in the morning and they can come and get him. Our phone line's been dead for a week now because of that last storm but they tell us it's going to be fixed soon."

"How many do you get wandering down here?" asked Ernie.

"Oh, not too many and certainly not often, but at least once a year."

Young Dai joined in. "We had half an army once and Dad got them to fix the bridge. It was great fun."

"Your Dad didn't do anything of the sort. They were here to repair the road bridge and all your Dad did was to mention that the old footbridge was also shot to pieces, so they mended that as well."

Wyn laughed. "That's right. Luckily it was the Royal Engineers lot. You know, the Sappers. Set up a zip wire and Dai and his sister spent half the day whizzing down it. You were bloody lucky you didn't break a leg or worse when you fell into the river."

"Just a scratch, Dad."

"Well, at your age you just bounce. These chaps wouldn't have. Tell me, which regiment are you thinking of joining?"

The twins briefly looked at each other but it was Ernie who answered for them. "Not sure yet, but probably an infantry one. We don't think we're cut out for anything fancy. Any ideas?"

Wyn finished chewing. "This being Wales, most join the Welsh Fusiliers, but as you're from England, well, I really don't know. My grandfather ended up in a parachute brigade in the Second World War and by Christ, did he have some stories to tell. Went all over the place he did. Italy, Normandy, and you know that film *A Bridge Too Far* that came out last year? Well, he was one of those and all he did was lose two fingers. Couldn't flick a V-sign if he tried," he chuckled.

"Don't forget he was deaf in one ear as well," added D.

"Yes, and don't we all know it. Said it came in handy when his wife was shouting at him."

They all chuckled. "Pudding, anyone?" D announced rhetorically.

As she dished out, she observed, "Somehow we don't get to laugh as much as we used to… only when we get together with the other village folk in the hall. How about you lads?"

They looked at each other briefly. "We have trouble making each other laugh because we know what's coming next."

Everyone stopped whatever they were doing for a second before they all burst out laughing at Eric's comment.

"I don't suppose you chaps want to give me a hand first thing in the morning, do you?" Wyn wiped his stubble and waited pensively. "I've got this rusty old bowser that's jammed up against one of the byres and just need an extra pair of hands moving it. Dai's not strong enough yet and it oughtn't to take long."

After a synchronised nod from the twins, Wyn added.

"Five o'clock then. OK?"

***

"Thank God the bloody rain's stopped," commented Eric quietly as they stood at ease, more or less in the middle of the parade ground along with the other seventy-odd soldiers.

"I think I forgot to waterproof my beret, 'cos it ain't half heavy and it's dripping into my ear," replied the man next to him they'd nicknamed 'Earache', even though his real name was Penache.

"Might wash some of that rubbish out of your brains then."

"Nothing wrong with supporting Aston Villa."

"Someone's got to."

A ripple of laughter went round those in earshot.

"Watch it. Here he comes now.

Sergeant Major Rowe, complete with swagger stick tucked under his right arm, emerged from the regimental headquarters directly in front of them, and strode across the tarmac as if he owned it; which he virtually did. When he was a few paces away, another sergeant in front of them shouted the order.

"Atten... shun!"

The Company had spent the previous six months going through basic training during a particularly wet winter and weren't far off their graduation parade. Consequentially when called to 'Attention', the response was pretty smart and in unison. They watched as Sergeant Major Rowe spoke briefly to his sergeant, who motioned in their general direction with his head. He then marched slowly up and down the three ranks, inspecting them firstly in front, and then behind, before

71

returning next to his sergeant.

"4845178 Cartwright, 4845179 Cartwright and 4845221 Apps. One pace forward." His voice carried the way one would expect and the three men stepped smartly forward.

"The rest of you. These three men are now lance corporals and will lead your respective platoons for your next exercise. You will need to protect them because they will be very important to you." He watched to see if anyone was going to query why they would be important, and was glad to see that there was no reaction. He continued. "They will be important to you because they will be your only contact with the outside world. They will be your radio operators and lifeline, and you will carry out their orders as if they came from me." He waited a couple of seconds. "Is that clear?"

"Yes Sergeant Major." Seventy odd men shouted together with the requisite vigour that satisfied him, but he still watched them like a hawk.

"At 04.00 tomorrow, you will draw stores and equipment for a three-day exercise from the Supply Depot. At 06.00 you will embark into the transports and be taken to the ranges in Wales where you will be given further orders." He waited again. "This will be your final exercise before graduating and officially becoming soldiers in the Queen's Army."

This time a long pause. "Well, what are you waiting for? God save the Queen."

"God save the Queen," shouted the company.

***

"Swain's the man," piped up a bored Earache.

"Rubbish. Just look how long he's been there and how many goals he's scored. Must be related to you, 'cos he's always complaining as well."

"He's had the most shots at goal this season and…"

"All off the crossbar."

"OK, OK. I'll grant you that, but sooner or later they'll start going in and then you'll see."

"Can't even tie his own bootlaces properly. Even a boy scout could do that."

"Twice… only twice."

"Three times."

"Twice."

"What about last year then, eh?"

"I'm talking about this year."

"Will you lot shut up a sec. I thought I heard something on the blower." Eric had his own ear glued to the receiver. Expectantly, nearby eyes from the platoon that was lined up along the waterlogged ditch turned his way and waited. They'd been there for over half an hour and were beginning to wonder if any orders were ever going to come through. The driving rain had soaked them through to the skin and dripped off anything that threatened to prevent it embedding itself into their camouflages. They were pretty well hidden and blended into the tussocks; all except the bright yellow stays that protruded from the end of their rifles, signifying that live rounds were not loaded. They heard him sign off and watched him consult the plastic-coated map and compass before looking round.

"About three miles north that way," he shouted and indicated with an outstretched arm. "We keep going until we reach a road just short of a place called 'German Village', so when you get there wait at the tarmac. Try not to be seen as we get there as they'll be looking out for us. Rory, you take the First Section off to the left, Terry, you the Third on the right, and I'll bring up the Second in the middle and a little behind you both. We've got two hours to get there, so go."

He watched as the extremities of men shambled up and started to move forwards over the uneven ground. "And spread out."

Eric's brother, Ernie received those same orders over his radio set, but his platoon, over six miles away in the opposite direction on the other side of German Village, were the wrong side of a lively river. Whereas Eric was out on the open plain, Ernie was in a deep valley surrounded by a conifer forest, and they too were getting just as wet.

"How the bloody hell are we going to get across that?" asked Greenage who was standing next to him on the moss-covered rocky bank. "They didn't give us any rope and I don't think Ian can swim."

"I never learned to swim either," added another a few feet away. "Don't think I can hold my breath long enough in that lot."

Ernie looked around to see the rest of the platoon converging on him and once they were near enough, he repeated their orders. All eyes naturally turned to look at the watery barrier. "Any ideas anyone?"

After initial blank looks all round at each other, chatter broke out in small groups until someone piped up. "How about we cut down one of these trees?"

They all turned to look behind them. "Better still, there's one that's half-fallen over there. How about we use that one?"

"There's another over there, look."

Ernie looked at Greenage then nodded. Everyone there knew there were no bridges for miles around as the previous day they had trekked from the bottom of the valley to just beyond their current location. Going uphill until the river became a crossable stream would take too much time and they had less than two hours.

Five minutes later they had both trunks on the steep bank next to the river. "They'll never reach," observed someone.

"They don't have to," stated Ernie. "We just push the shorter one down this side, wedge one end into the bank and the other against that rock in the middle, then get the longer one over to the other side and use them as rails. We won't get wetter than we are now anyway." His cheery outlook on their dampness raised few smiles.

Almost to the minute two hours later, they reached the edge of a stand of trees overlooking German Village. It had been a struggle as one chap had twisted his ankle badly in the river and another had fallen and cut his head on a rock; both had to be helped over the uneven terrain, but they had made it.

"Funny looking place isn't it?" remarked Greenage. "I suppose that's why they call it German Village, because it certainly doesn't look English."

"Or Welsh," commented another.

"Doesn't matter what it looks like, it's the defending platoon we've got to worry about."

"What do we do now?" a breathless lad asked as he tried to sit down on a mouldy log which disintegrated under his weight.

"We wait for orders," confirmed Ernie.

"Eric's supposed to be out there somewhere but I can't see any of them. Can you?"

"Not one of them. Do you suppose they made it?"

They all looked through the sheeting rain beyond the desolate village. "My brother's supposed to attack from one angle and us from another at the same time, but I haven't a clue where he is."

Ernie's radio squawked and he put his ear to it. Watched by all, they saw him listen and then look at his watch. "Right, who's got the flag?" Terry fished it out of his backpack. "We've got three minutes before we go down there. Our objective is to raise our flag on that pole from the middle tower. See it?" All eyes and heads swivelled. "Eric's platoon will be trying to do the same but the third platoon's down there trying to stop us." Ernie looked at them. "Ted, as you're the biggest, take Terry with the flag and one other, the rest of us will try to hold off the others while they get up that tower." He looked at his watch again. "One minute."

Dressed in clean uniforms, the three temporary lance corporals stood rigidly to attention three feet away from a desk. Off to one side, complete with swagger stick stood Sergeant Major Rowe, a paragon of his station. The three of them stiffened a little more as they heard footfalls, the door behind them opening, then slamming shut, and while keeping their eyes straight ahead, they watched Captain Hamilton walk round and sit in his wing-backed chair. Concentrating on looking straight ahead, they felt him glaring at them; and he made them wait. They didn't need to look at him as they knew his features well from their months of training. Almost on a daily basis he had appeared, whether it was in a hall, out on an assault course, or in the middle of a field, even on exercise. He would inevitably take their instructing sergeant to one side out of earshot, look at them individually as some sort of report was made, sometimes lasting as long as five minutes, and then march off again. They knew his gait well, mostly from behind, but they knew his face well. His body seemed to pivot from his hips, his longer-than-normal arms accentuating a slightly lopsided stride suggesting that there was some sort of injury preventing him from taking even paces.

At some point in his life, he may have been handsome, but now a receding black hairline revealed an arrow-shaped dark brown birthmark high above his left eyebrow. His angular but straight nose was repeated in the shape of his jawline and accentuated his very even stare through dark brown eyes. An always-clean-shaven face gave way to a flat forehead that didn't seem to have a finishing point near his smallish ears and the inevitable martial-style haircut around them marked him out as a military man.

He rarely dwelt on his past, to such an extent that he shunned his still-living mother and her entire family, but he had listened to his father who had instilled his own Victorian and religious attitudes into him right up to the point when he had had a sudden heart attack and died straight after one of their traditional Sunday lunches. An only son, he and his father were very like-minded and despite his teenage years, he'd had taken to the handed-down principle of 'work hard – play hard', but somewhere along the line a few years later, the 'play hard' part got left behind. When his housemaster at Harrow had broken the news to him that evening, he remarked afterwards 'that it was the only time he had seen the lad shed a tear'. He'd loved his father and his passing only heightened his resolve to emulate him. The only trouble was that being just fifteen and a junior in his house, up to that point he had had to endure the unpleasantries of embuggerance from his seniors. One sixth former in particular called Ackman was ever ready to take advantage, and two days later as he was searching for some cricket equipment in the box room, found himself cornered by the bully. A rage built up inside him. Then and there, he decided he would not put up with being pushed around and certainly not treated as a relief for someone else's sexual urges. He waited until Ackman had his trousers round his ankles and despite being half his weight, timed his kick to Ackman's groin to perfection. He felt disgust as the oversized youth grovelled around on the floor clutching his nether regions and decided to take his revenge; he spotted an errant ruler on one of the shelves, grabbed it, knelt hard down on Ackman's body and shouted in his ear.

"See how you like this then."

It took both hands to shove it up his arse and when he managed it, a feeling of great satisfaction came over him. He pushed it in further as Ackman let out another howl of agony but not as loud as when he tried to twist it. He thrust it in and out several times before the blood started to flow; the small increment indentations of the ruler tearing fresh cuts.

Ackman and his friends left him alone after that, and indeed the other juniors as well. Ashamed of what they had been doing to the juniors, they closed ranks and kept quiet about the whole incident. Ackman's absence at lessons due to his inability to walk very far did not escape the notice of his tutors, but they never did find out the truth, possibly half turning a blind eye to such issues. Only matron queried why Ackman's underwear was covered with blood.

When Hamilton was asked what he had done by one of his close friends the next day, he'd replied that he wished that he'd shoved it up further. From then on, he was known as 'Bloody Hamilton'.

Privileges came with entry into the sixth form and as one of the house prefects, he found he could abuse his position to satisfy his growing lust for domination over not just the juniors, but also his contemporaries. He had not forgotten his painful experiences a few years earlier, nor the gratification he had felt on getting his revenge and although he didn't possess those same sexual urges, he took enormous pleasure in watching others mentally squirm. His main rival and favourite to become head boy of his house the following year was also his closest friend, but it took him a while to make his mind up that he wasn't going to play second fiddle to Charles Ingham-Smith. About this time in his life, he realised that his competitiveness was beginning to overwhelm him, both in and out of the classroom. Of an evening after prep, he Charlie and a few other sixth formers could often be found round the house snooker table, and although a better player that any of them, he still had to resist the urge to cheat. Snooker is a gentleman's game and it rankled that he was expected to own up when accidentally touching the wrong ball; but he still did so whenever he thought he could get away with it.

He started to formulate plans, but it would make him unpopular if those around him discovered that it was he who had been the instigator, and he suspected that it might also scupper his chances with his housemaster. He approached the problem by dissecting it into phases with each part being unconnected to the other, and concluded that it would be better to use the system so that no blame could be attributed to himself. He didn't realise it at the time, but this method of thinking was the start of his military and parliamentary careers.

En route from the art block back to his house across the grass one evening, through a window as he was passing the masters' common room, he noted that while it was dark outside, he could see them clearly, but they couldn't see him, as long as he stayed outside with lightwash from the window. Pupils were definitely not allowed in the masters' common room, which was accessed through an ageing oak door at the end of a tunnel-like corridor in the north wing, and for most of the time that area of the school was deserted. He watched as one of the masters removed a book from a nearby shelf and retrieved a set of keys from behind it, unlocked the metal grill that secured the bar area, and returned them back to the bookcase. The master removed his hat, disrobed and walked behind the small bar where he poured himself a glass of whiskey, emptying the last out of the bottle. He watched the master look up as others entered, get out two more glasses, and open a cupboard at the back of the bar revealing several other bottles of spirits.

Looking around to make sure he wasn't being observed, Hamilton repositioned himself to get a better view, all the while staying in the shadows, and watched his teachers unwind after another day's tutoring. He had a bit of a shock when one master stood up and approached the window that he was looking through, and he ducked back to meld into the shadows of a nearby box hedge.

"When's someone going to fix this damn window? It never closes properly. Rufus, that's your department, isn't it?"

Hamilton heard a mumbling in the background.

"Well, get your chap onto it will you. Winter's coming and we don't need yet another draught."

The sound of chatter decreased with the closing of the window, but it clearly wasn't secured properly. At that moment, Hamilton knew what he was going to do, but it was the timing that would be all important and just for self-satisfaction, he would make it ignominious.

He shared the lower sixth dormitory with three others including Charles, so the opportunity to talk to him alone was frequent, and over the next few days, innocently planted the seed of wonder into his mind as to what it would be like to get drunk. The chance to start the wheels rolling came one evening while they were alone in the washroom.

"Bet you I can," boasted Charles.

"Bet you can't."

"You'll lose. What'll you bet?"

Hamilton thought about this for a moment. "I'll cover your breakfast duties for a week."

"Two weeks."

"No way, besides which half-term's coming up and the roster will change when we get back."

"OK then, one week." They smiled at each other. "Gin or whiskey?" asked Charles.

"Let's go for gin. My mum's got a stash at home and she'll never notice it missing. I'll pick it up next exeat. Sssssh. Someone's coming. Don't tell a soul."

The sixth formers knew that the biology lesson the following day was to involve ethanol and how it preserved organic tissue. Their teacher, nicknamed 'Bop' due to his expletives that sounded the same, asked who knew what other benefits ethanol had, and Hamilton grabbed at the opportunity.

"Charlie Ingham does, sir," he shouted out.

Bop looked over his glasses in his direction and then at Ingham-Smith on the stool next to Hamilton. "Well, Ingham?"

After a very brief glower at Hamilton, Charlie sat up straight and addressed Bop. "I think it has something to do with alcohol, sir."

"Ummmmm. And how would you know that?"

Charlie Ingham-Smith thought very quickly. "Something my father mentioned."

Bop held Ingham's attention, as well as the class's, for a moment. "Umm. You're quite correct but it's not the answer I was looking for," Bop continued. "It's one of the major constituents of petrol and has a complicated formula. If you turn to page 24, you'll see that ..."

When the lesson was over, outside, Charlie caught up with Hamilton. "What did you volunteer me like that for?"

"Well, we both knew the answer, but I thought you would want the credit... you know... being head-boy designate for next year. Thought I was doing you a favour. Here, talking of favours, keep an eye out on Noycey in your dayroom for me, will you? I think he's a bit of a troublemaker. I'm sure it's him cutting through the rugby boot laces, but my dayroom's further away from the boot room than yours and I can't keep trotting back and forth."

"Noycey eh?"

"Yeah. Sneaky little so-and-so."

This was another plan that Hamilton had been pursuing and he inwardly smiled as not only had he diverted Charlie's attention, but he would get him to do his dirty work for him at the same time.

Grooming himself, his diligence in the classrooms was consciously noted by his tutors, but in his spare time he played out various scenarios in his mind; he also started to make life as awkward as possible for Charlie. Their housemaster or his assistant would check their dayrooms of an evening just prior to prep when the pupils completed the essays or tests set by their teachers during their lessons. Charlie was in charge of one of the dayrooms, while Hamilton oversaw one of the others; there were four in all. When everyone was at supper, he would leave early with some excuse or other, but mostly totally unnoticed, and tamper with Charlie's room. Graffiti on the walls was found on one occasion, a missing windowpane or a leaking heating pipe, and then a bin full of rubbish scattered over the floor – all unattributable to him.

The 'black marks' against Charlie Ingham-Smith began to mount up. He found some cleaning fluid that smelt of alcohol in one of the janitor's cupboards, and towards the end of his campaign, lifted a floorboard under Charlie's 'horsebox', and emptied the gallon bottle into the void below. The previous night in the small hours, he had crept out of bed so as not to wake anybody, visited the masters' common room through the faulty window, stolen all the whiskey bottles, and secreted them under cobwebbed newspaper in one of the many lofts. Nobody would ever find them there.

After this incident, Charlie was called into explain himself to his housemaster.

"... and this last instance... the place reeked of alcohol last night. Well, what have you got to say about that?"

"Nothing, sir. We all smelt it but we don't know where it's coming from."

"There's no 'we' about it. I put you in charge of the juniors' dayroom and it's for you to make sure this sort of thing doesn't happen."

"I try to keep a good eye on the juniors and they're mostly getting good marks from their prep."

"Yes I know, but I'm beginning to wonder if there's not a troublemaker about, so let me know if you see anything suspicious."

That afternoon, Charlie naturally confided in Hamilton. "You reckoned it might be Noycey, but I haven't caught him doing anything yet."

Hamilton decided to create another smokescreen. "It must be him. Have you noticed the way he hangs about with Wilson? He was a troublemaker from day one. Bop caught him smoking behind the bike shed last term and he's always skulking around one place or another. Have you tried looking in the art studio because I swear they're up to something?"

While Charlie was busy following the innocent culprits, it left Hamilton free to pursue his own agenda. He waited a couple more days before again sneaking out at night to the masters' common room and found that they had replaced the missing whiskey. He figured that if he stole the whole lot there and then, they would have the window fixed and move the keys, so this would be his last chance. This time he took the remaining four bottles of Gordon's gin. He also made sure that the window was jammed ajar just enough for someone to notice if they were looking closely. On the way back to the main building, he emptied one down a drain, refilled it with water from an outside tap, and scored the label so that he could easily identify it. He took two bottles, one being full of water, to the old laundry room before hiding the others in the loft next to the whiskey. He smiled as he realised his stash was beginning to become a little bulky, but he purposely left the neck of one bottle exposed so that it could easily be seen from the hatch, which this time he left askew. Nobody would notice it was out of place unless they were looking up at the ceiling.

Hamilton had ascertained that in the main, the masters didn't open their bar until the evenings, and he had chosen his timing very carefully. He had until the following evening before the theft would be discovered.

The following morning, he beckoned Charlie to one side and out of earshot of the others as they were changing out of their pyjamas and into their day clothes ready for lessons. Two weeks earlier, he had mentioned that he had two bottles of gin hidden away in preparation.

"Half-term next week so tonight's the night. I've checked out where. The old laundry room upstairs because it's right at the end and nobody's likely to come wandering down there. Not even the night watchman, Old Charlie. OK?"

"I thought we might try the gym as it's away from the house," commented Charlie.

"Naah. Too far, and remember if we do get drunk, we've got to find our way back to the dorm afterwards and the hinges on the back door make a noise. Besides which, I've already hidden them up there."

Ever since his grilling by his housemaster, Charlie had been absorbed in keeping his nose clean and was a little reticent. "Can we put it off till after half-term. You know, wait until nearer Christmas?"

"Not a chance. Someone might find it and I can't keep stealing my mother's gin. She's bound to notice if another two bottles go missing. Naah. It's got to be tonight. How about we meet there at ten?" He could see Charlie wavering a little. "Or would you like to concede now?"

The thought of having to get up extra early for breakfast duties for a whole week more clinched it. "OK then."

"Don't forget your toothmug."

"Toothmug?" queried Charlie.

Hamilton glanced over Charlie's shoulder at a couple of juniors walking in their direction and lowered his voice further. "To drink out of. Here, watch it." And turned away.

As he walked alone along the tarmac path towards the language block for his first lesson of the day, French, he ticked off his mental list and inwardly smiled. The toothmug would be a nice little touch as he would purposely forget his, knowing that Charlie's would then be the only missing one from the line of mugs above the basins in the tiled washrooms. Even if their housemaster didn't catch him drinking or smelling of alcohol, he would at least query why his toothmug would be missing; there would be an obvious conclusion he would come to, whatever story Charlie told afterwards. Just a couple of parts of the operation to go.

Attendance at evensong in the chapel was compulsory at 6 pm, unless one had a valid reason to be elsewhere. Although lasting less than half an hour, a fair proportion of the pupils found one reason or another to avoid the daily dreariness, including Hamilton whenever he could. On this occasion, he chose to attend early and, knowing the routine well from his junior days, helped with the preparations. Setting out the choir stalls, mounting the correct hymn numbers on the board next to the pulpit, lighting the numerous candles and making sure the chaplain's cushion was in place, were just some of the menial tasks.

As Hamilton expected, Charlie arrived and sat down next to him in the pew, just before the chaplain appeared from behind the vestry door. Although his sermon was brief, it still seemed too long, but in unison they knelt with the others when those hallowed words 'Let us pray' were uttered.

While the chaplain droned on, Hamilton whispered, "Can you do the lights-out job for me at the end? Don't look too hard, but I want to follow Noycey and see what he's up to."

They both briefly peered across the transept at Noyce who was suspiciously passing something from his pocket to his friend on his left.

"OK."

Hamilton's prayers were being answered.

Once it was all over he filed out a few paces behind Noyce and friend with other pupils and the few masters. He wasn't the least bit interested in what Noyce was up to; that would have to wait. Not only was his attendance and assistance noted by the chaplain, but his heart soared as he fingered the prizes in his pocket.

Prep would have dragged on until bedtime and lights-out, had it not been for his doodling. At least that's what it would look like to anyone else, but to him it was his secret codified operation which he had called 'Thunderstruck'. Even when he lay in bed waiting for ten o'clock, he pictured what would happen down to the finest detail. He chuckled to himself as by now the masters would be on the prowl for anyone venturing near their common room, and he imagined Old Charlie holding a night-long vigil, deep in the bushes outside their broken window.

Annoyingly, at a few minutes to ten, a junior in his dormitory woke by banging his head on the metal frame of the bed and he had to wait until just after before the lad settled down again. With no slippers and no dressing gown, as he would need to get back to his bed sharpish, he silently opened the door nearest, and padded down the virtually unlit corridor to the old laundry room.

"Where's your mug?"

"Oh rats. Forgotten it, what with one of the juniors waking up. Doesn't matter though. We can drink straight from the bottle, just like they do in the Westerns." Hamilton went past Charlie, shifted several old cardboard boxes and rags in one corner until he produced a pair of green Gordon's gin bottles, making certain he had the marked one containing water, before sitting down cross-legged opposite him. He could tell that Charlie was still uncertain, and to ease his mind, immediately unscrewed the top and took a couple of swigs. He practised falsifying a splutter and had little difficulty repeating it as he purposefully let a dribble of water into his lungs.

"Wow... Now your turn."

He watched with glee as Charlie took half-a-mouthful,

and then swallowed. He too spluttered and coughed as the spirit trickled down his gullet; but not for the same reason as Hamilton.

"Gosh. Difficult to breathe. Is it supposed to taste bitter?"

"Not really sure. Had a sip out of Mum's glass once when she wasn't looking and that was a bit bitter. By the way, why do they call beer bitter?"

"I don't suppose we'll find out until we're older. Never tried it."

"We could try that next time," Hamilton said provocatively. "But let's see what happens with this first, eh?" He took another gulp from the bottle and this time, swilled the water around in his mouth, noting that Charlie was watching him. "Try washing it around your mouth before swallowing. Rather refreshing."

"Right-ho." Charlie took a larger swig than before, tried swilling it, but there was too much in his mouth. He swallowed and spat some out simultaneously with a 'phut'. Hamilton suppressed a smile as he saw some of the liquid spill onto his dressing gown, knowing that its odour would soak in and linger for some time. "God. Who invented this stuff?"

Hamilton knew the answer as he had already looked it up the library encyclopaedia, but he wasn't going to let on to Charlie. "I only know it's based on a plant or a flower. Probably the Egyptians or Greeks as they seem to have invented just about everything else. You know how Reddles like to harp on about them in class, how wonderful they were and how we owe our existence to them. So here's to the Greeks!" He took another mouthful and saw from under his hooded eyelids that Charlie followed him straight away. He reckoned Charlie was beginning to enjoy the sensation, but wondered how long it would be until he was too drunk to stop. More importantly, how long before he became legless?

Hamilton carried on the pretence for another thirty minutes or so while they both devoured nearly half a bottle each, and from Charlie's brashness, it was clear that he wouldn't need much more, as he suddenly burst into song.

"I'mmmmm dreaming of a White Christmas, just like the ones we used to know... with the..."

Hamilton hadn't allowed for this and was worried that the sound might carry far enough to be noticed. Too early he thought. For a couple of seconds he berated himself for not predicting that Charlie might become voluble.

"Sssssssush. We don't want everybody to join in."

"Why not?" It'sh a great shong and we sing it at home every Christhmas and I think I'll ask for some of this for a present." He waved the bottle. "I'm dreaming..."

"Come-on. We're here to drink, not sing. Drink up." He took a fake long pull on his bottle in encouragement, and saw Charlie do the same, but this time he had taken so much in that he sneezed some out of his nose.

"Heeeeehaaaaa." Charlie slipped over onto his side and started giggling with gin dripping from his nose, but still clenched the bottle. He raised his other arm pointing in Hamilton's general direction. "Shtay shtill while I count you." His head lolled in a circular motion and he burped

"Tell you what, I'll stay still if you do."

"OK," Charlie mouthed but then descended into a cackling laugh as he rested his head on his gin arm. "Heeeeey. Whhat's that tree doing?"

Hamilton saw he was looking more or less behind him at a faded greenish old cricket bag that lay on the floor, imagined himself in Charlie's horizontal position and surmised that it may well have looked like a Christmas tree from down on the floor.

Perhaps now was the time. "I'll go and have a look." He stood up, walked back and forth a couple of times in the cramped room while studying Charlie's eyes which weren't following him, and thought that they may have been pointing in different directions. He looked down on his hapless friend for a few seconds, emptied the water out of his bottle, partially over Charlie's dressing gown, and placed it flat on the floor.

He knew there was no need to rush. He went back to the green bag, retrieved the items he had put there earlier after his visit to the chapel, and left the room. On the high ceiling just down the corridor between the old laundry room and his dormitory, was one of the many newly installed smoke detectors. He stood stock still under it, listening to hear if anyone was around, but all he could hear faintly in the distance was Charlie still trying to sing about white Christmases. He looked at the two-foot-long taper in one hand, which was usually used to light candles in chapel, bent down and scraped one of the three non-safety matches on the flagstone floor, and lit the end of the taper. He had previously measured the distance needed to put a flame directly below the detector, and now held it a few inches away from it. If this didn't set off the alarm he would need to revert to plan B, and he held his breath. He jerked his arm down in surprise at the sudden ear-piercing noise and was momentarily stunned. Recovering quickly, he snuffed out the taper, went through a doorway into the washrooms, wrapped it in some toilet roll and flushed it down the nearest toilet. He then ran back to his dormitory and slid into bed as quietly as possible, sensing in the dark that the juniors were beginning to stir at the disorienting noise. He waited a few seconds, letting his breath catch up before getting up and turning on the lights. As prefect in charge of the dormitory of thirty or so juniors, it was his responsibility to get them lined up ready to exit. He trotted down the two rows of beds, shaking those who were trying to sleep through the dreadful din that interrupted their slumber, shouting for everyone to wake up, and line up.

"Wait here," he told the boy at the head of the queue.

He went through two connecting doors to Charlie's dormitory and found that in Charlie's absence, someone had had the presence of mind to turn on the lights. He repeated the alarm duties there, and as he passed Charlie's empty bed, he dropped the two matches next to it before returning to his own dormitory. He led the file of boys from both dormitories along the prescribed route to the fire escape door at the end of the long corridor and out into the chilly night air.

If any of the pupils were half asleep, the damp misty atmosphere soon had them fully awake. Dressed only in their slippers and dressing gowns over their pyjamas, it soon had the effect of animating their previously somnolent demur. Hamilton could see crowds of other pupils gathering in the lessening gloom as more and more lights were being turned on. Everyone was asking questions and looking for signs of fire, mainly at the main building from where they had just emerged; but there was none.

It didn't take long before masters started to appear and as Hamilton's housemaster approached and spotted them, he zeroed in rather aggressively on Hamilton. "What's going on?" he demanded.

"Not sure, sir. I've done a roll call and everyone's here except Charlie Ingham-Smith."

"Have you seen signs of a fire?" He looked over the boys and was met with several replies of 'no sirs'.

Another master appeared in the gloom, drew their

housemaster to one side for a few moments before disappearing again.

"Right. I want you to line up in dormitory order and we'll make sure everyone's here. Hamilton, do you know why Ingham-Smith isn't here?"

"No sir. The last I saw of him was at evensong last night." He waited for this seemingly irrelevant piece of information to sink in. "Do you want me to go and find him?"

He temporarily ignored Hamilton and raised his voice over the throng. "Has anyone seen Ingham-Smith?"

Again, lots of 'no sirs'.

He turned to Hamilton. "Carry out another roll call while I go and report to the headmaster... and don't let anyone leave. Understood?"

"Yes sir."

Captain Hamilton wasn't daydreaming as he kept the three lance corporals waiting; rather, he was relishing the moment. He knew he wouldn't feel the same elation as from the fruits of his operation that had led to him being appointed head boy, but it was one of those rare occasions when he briefly remembered the satisfaction of seeing others squirm. He hadn't had a decent opportunity to do so recently and looked forward to the next session with delight.

"You're a bloody shambles... all three of you." He looked for any kind of reaction and was a little disappointed that there was none; the sergeants had trained them well enough to ignore such jibes. "What makes you think you are remotely capable of leading men when you can't even carry out simple tasks?" His edgy voice made them mentally wince.

Sergeant Major Rowe knew what was likely to come next but managed not to bat an eyelid.

"You." Hamilton looked directly at one of the Cartwrights.

"When you didn't fan your men out, the enemy could see this from their vantage point and were able to concentrate on your advance just when it mattered most. Even if you had fanned them out, you didn't delegate a second and third in command to respond to such a failure. Then you had a second chance, but…" He harangued them each in turn for their own failings, finishing up with Lance Corporal Apps who thought he had done rather well by retaining their own flag in the tower. "You don't just sit on your arse and wait for the enemy to come to you unless you have a decent killing ground. It didn't exist, not with an attack from different directions. The field manual states…" The verbal lashing continued and still they didn't move, but inwardly they were wilting.

"Between the three of you, you'd have managed to get at least half of your men wounded, captured or killed. God, but if flogging hadn't been abolished you'd each get five hundred lashes for your gross stupidity." He glared at them hoping that one of them would rise to the criticism, and if anything, their lack of reaction made him more determined to mete out dire punishments. He was about to pronounce what they would endure when he picked up the sound of boots quick-marching down the corridor, then a smart rap on the door.

He simmered. "Come."

Lieutenant Herbert entered and saluted at attention. He had a worried look in his face as he knew what Hamilton was doing and would not want to be interrupted.

"Sorry to trouble you, sir, but a messenger's arrived from HQ and the colonel's asked for all company commanders to attend on him in the officers' mess immediately."

Hamilton felt anger rise in being denied at what he considered the most succulent part of his tirade. "Immediately, you say?"

"Yes sir. Immediately. Excuse me sir but I must alert the other captains." Without waiting, he saluted, about-turned and exited the room before Hamilton could react.

Hamilton stood up and rested his clenched fists on his desk. "Don't ever think of this as some sort of let-off... because it isn't, so you wait right here until I get back. Sergeant, keep an eye on them."

Sergeant Major Rowe waited all of ten seconds after Hamilton's footfalls had receded to nothing before telling the three of them to 'stand easy'.

"What's he likely to do, Sarge?" asked the unhappy Apps, and all three of them followed Rowe's measured steps until he stood directly in front of them.

He eyed them back and forth. "I'm not sure you want to know what he did to the last bunch who failed as miserably as you. It's just as well that flogging's not on the list anymore, because he'd do just that if he could." He paused a moment. "But we're a modern army now with modern ideas and corporal punishment's frowned upon, so it won't be just a kicking for you... more of a psychological punishment, and he won't let you or the rest of the companies forget it. He always seems to find new ways of belittling you in front of the others and you'll be lucky if you have any friends left by the end of it. You'll be broken men hardly able to face yourselves in the mirror, because that's all you'll have left – a mirror. Nobody else will want to talk to you."

From the look on their faces, they were quailing at the possibilities and he let them chew on it. "The only way you'll be able to exonerate yourselves is by an outstanding act of bravery... Volunteer for a suicidal mission and earn yourselves a medal each... But as you'll probably be demoted back down to privates and we haven't got many wars on at the moment,

I don't see that opportunity coming up very soon."

They waited over an hour before Hamilton returned, Sergeant Major Rowe bringing them back to attention just before he re-entered. Instead of sitting back down in his chair he stood behind it gripping his hands on the high back and smiled at them. His entire demeanour had changed. "It's your lucky day you miserable bastards, because we're being posted off to Northern Ireland for a tour of duty, so your punishment's going to be short and sharp as we've more important things to attend to before we leave next Thursday. Sergeant Major Rowe here will supervise, but you're on double duties until further notice. In the meantime and starting at 22.00 hours tonight, you're to parade this company outside every two hours in your underwear until 06.00 for the next ... four nights."

He thought back to the non-existent fire at school and how disgruntled everybody had been while they waited several hours for the all-clear. All they had wanted to do was to go back to bed and the longer they waited, the more they cursed and blamed their masters.

"The sergeants will make sure every man knows that because of your incompetence, they're being denied their beauty sleep. And that's just for starters. Now get out of here your grotty little shitheads. Dismissed," he shouted at them.

Chapter 4

1985

(thirty years earlier)

Their tour of duty had been extended due to the increasing insurgence of the Irish Republican Army and the retaliations from various Protestant groups. In addition, another battalion had been sent over to Northern Ireland to bolster the large number of troops already there as they tried to maintain some sort of peace and order in the province. Quite naturally, being away from their families, the entire company yearned for female attention, but as they were based in the relatively remote town of Enniskillen, they had been warned to watch out for alluring women who would lead them into deadly traps. Torture and garrotting were among the terrorists's methods of trying to ram home the IRA's determination for separation from the yoke of English government.

The Cartwright twins had indeed lost their status as corporals and were mere privates for the entire fifteen months in Northern Ireland. Due to their punishment, initially they had been very unpopular, but their sympathetic nature shone through and it didn't take long before they were accepted back into the brotherhood and in most instances, looked up to. Despite Captain Hamilton's constant needling, they turned out to be rather good soldiers.

Returning to the regimental headquarters at Hightown

Barracks in Wrexham, not too far from where England met Wales, they were all given an almost immediate six weeks' leave. Back in their hometown of Leominster, the euphoria of their return began to wear off but it was while they out at the local bowling alley one evening with an old school friend that they were introduced to the twin sisters, Mandy and Melanie. It was as though predestination had taken over their lives, because there was instant affinity between them. It was impossible for outsiders to tell who from who and passers-by would do a double-take, but Eric paired up with Mandy, while Ernie was with Melanie. Certainly, each could tell one from the other as their subtle differences were apparent only to them, but the two pairs of twins certainly had friends and family abuzz with conjecture. Their parents, following their careers, had moved into the area earlier that year, and their daughters had naturally moved with them.

A couple of weeks later in the same bowling alley, Melanie's ex-boyfriend confronted Ernie while he was at the bar buying a round of drinks. His initial friendliness soon turned sour as he had had designs on Melanie and he was looking to goad Ernie into a fight.

"So, you're going out with M&M then. Tasty are they? Like sugar?"

Ernie wasn't in the mood for any sort of showdown and ignored the jibe, but the ex continued. "Do you reckon that they really are soft on the inside and does she melt in your mouth?"

"What are you suggesting pal?" Ernie was becoming agitated and trying to get the attention of the barman at the same time.

"Oh no, I'm not suggesting anything. It's just that since they moved here, they've built up a bit of a reputation... know what I mean?"

"And what exactly do you mean?" He half-turned but kept an elbow on the bar.

"Well, let me put it this way. Where they used to live they were known as 'The Dartboard Twins". The other three were sitting at a low table some distance away, but he had raised his voice so that they could hear. Others within earshot also looked their way.

Ernie couldn't work it out, but suspected it was something derogatory and prepared himself.

With a sneer on his face and in a louder voice he shouted, "It's because they've had more pricks in them than a dartboard." His smile lasted all of half a second before Ernie knocked him unconscious with a fist directly to his face.

The barman looked over his shoulder to see what the noise was about, but Ernie had decked him so efficiently that his prone body couldn't be seen from the other side of the bar. Eric walked over and between them, they picked up the ex, carried him outside and sat him down on one of the pub benches with his head resting on his arms as though asleep. They then returned as though nothing had happened, all without saying a word.

On a Sunday, two days before they were due to return to their barracks, M&M were celebrating their birthday. The family tradition had been for all to gather at their parents' modest house for lunch every year, and cramped though it was round the table with over a dozen of them, including nephews and nieces – and on this occasion, Eric and Ernie as well – as usual, it was a joyous occasion; like a second Christmas to them, minus the paper hats and silly trinkets that flicked across the table from pulled crackers. At the end of the feast and before the family broke up to clear away the debris, in usual unison, Eric and Ernie stood, called for silence, then on bended knees each side of M&M, offered their engagement rings.

"Yessssss!" It was M&M's mother who led the gleeful shouting and she was joined by everyone else. When the whooping and clapping died down, all eyes turned to the intended girls at the end of the table, because they hadn't had a chance to respond.

"Well go on then, you silly girls. Say YES."

They were still in their seats; Eric and Ernie kneeling with their extended arms holding out Siamese rings. The shocked M&M sisters hadn't moved, and in the complete silence they looked at each other, smiled and together said "yes." Euphoric cuddles went round the room, all except for the waist-high youngest niece who sat still with a grim look on her face.

"What's the matter?" asked her mother.

The room fell silent.

With a crestfallen look she replied, "I'm waiting for the rings."

"But the rings are for Melanie and Mandy, dearest."

"I know... but I still can't hear them."

***

The regiment had been included in the pageant, and their battalion, still at attention on the parade ground, caught the departure of the general's car out of the corner of their eyes as it left the spacious grounds of Blenheim Palace. Standing squarely in front of them with the twin towers of the entrance to the courtyard behind them, Sergeant Major Rowe was in the process of dismissing them to their transports.

"... Wait for it... 4845178 Cartwright and 4845179

Cartwright, stand at ease. The rest of you are dismissed."

They stood alone with only their sergeant to keep them company while the rest ambled off towards their transports. He took the few paces forward towards them. "Stand easy, then." Despite his reputation of his bark being as vicious as his bite, he grinned at them; one of the very few times they had seen him do so. "Congratulations, lads." He shook hands with each in turn. "I gather you're out on the town with a few of the lads tomorrow night and if you'll take my advice, you'll not tangle yourselves with the local yobs." He grinned at them knowing that they would be tempted to indulge, but also knew that the Cartwright twins were known for their sobriety, not drunkenness. "They like nothing better than to pit themselves against proper soldiers and I'd hate to see you up on a charge on your wedding day." He craned his head a little closer to make his point. "Black eyes don't look too good in the family album, so just make sure you're back by 23.30 hours. All right lads, off you go with the others and report to Lieutenant Pages who's got your leave passes. Dismissed."

"Come." The young-looking Lieutenant Pages responded to the knock on his door in his broom-cupboard of an office and the Cartwrights had trouble standing abreast of each other in front of his table.

"I don't know how to put this, chaps... although I've got your passes here, I've been ordered not to give them to you."

They briefly looked at each other and together. "Why sir?" They were wondering if this was some kind of joke being played at the last minute.

But Pages was clearly embarrassed, looked down at the several paper passes on his table which he fidgeted with. "They were signed by the colonel a couple of days before he went to London last week, and certified by the adjutant, but he was rushed to hospital yesterday with suspected appendicitis, leaving Captain Hamilton as acting C/O... It's he who has rescinded all passes."

Despite Lieutenant Pages' youthful looks, he was a competent officer, and someone who the troops felt they could converse with, almost on even terms. He went on to explain further. "We all know you're both getting married and even though I reminded the captain just this morning, he was adamant that no one was to be given any leave while the colonel was away. After recent events in the town, he's worried that someone's going to bring disgrace down on the battalion while he's in charge and he doesn't want any more bad press or black marks against him. I do not suggest you approach him directly yourselves, as you won't get a different result... neither of you have ever been in his good books."

"But, sir..." Ernie was about to plead.

Pages held up his hand. "I'm afraid it's no good appealing to me as the matter is out of my hands, but between you and me only, I rather sympathise with your predicament. I know it's virtually unheard of being refused permission to get married these days, but I too have to obey commands."

There was only the sound of shuffling paper as Pages placed the passes in between a sheaf of other papers. "If it's any consolation, he virtually locked down the barracks for the next few days, and that goes for us officers too."

Eric and Ernie initially marched across the deserted square towards their barracks, but stopped more or less in the middle and faced each other.

"What right has Captain bloody Hamilton got? He's given a bit of power and instantly abuses it and upsets everybody. Who does he think he is?"

"God."

"Not in our eyes he's not. At least God would let us get married."

"We could ask the chaplain. Do you think that would help?"

"Not if he's locked down the barracks, but let's give it a go."

They marched off in the direction of the chapel, all the while cursing Hamilton and reminding each other of the arrangements that had been made. Family, friends, the church, food, and of course ale, as well as all the other arrangements would all have to be put on hold unless they could persuade the chaplain to successfully intercede for them. They had planned a simple double wedding with a reception afterwards in the local village hall next door. Not too many bells and whistles to help keep costs down, and just two family bridesmaids, one for each bride. Their future in-laws had relatives travelling all the way from Canada just for the occasion, and they were already on their way.

Captain Tervin hadn't been the battalion's chaplain for very long and didn't know Hamilton that well, but upon hearing their dilemma, had told them to wait in the vestry while he went and had a word. He returned a few minutes later with news that his appeal hadn't worked, and tried his best to console them. "You can't even contact the colonel as I gather he's away in London for a few days."

Walking slowly back to their barracks, the Cartwright twins were heaping all sorts of curses on Hamilton. As soldiers, they were certainly used to officers giving pointless orders and had learned to accept the military method of blindly following those orders, but this had now become a more personal matter.

"Look at all the arrangements we've now got to cancel. That'll cost us a pretty penny."

"Not just us either. Don't forget the Canadians who are

probably in the air right now."

"He really knows how to screw up somebody's life, doesn't he."

"And then there's the vicar who had to move something or other, just to fit us in."

"It's not only us, it's the girls as well. I hope they'll still want to marry us when this is all over."

"It's the sort of thing we ought to be telling them face to face, but we can't even do that."

"Here, we'll need to pick another date when we can."

"But we don't know when that's going to be, because we're due back in Northern Ireland next month."

"We'll just have to ask Lieutenant Pages if we can at least phone them."

"If Hamilton's got the barracks locked down, he may have cut the outside communications as well."

"Oh God. What a screw-up."

They had to wait while Lieutenant Pages dealt with another private who was also due to go on leave; they could hear part of the heated conversation through the closed door. It suddenly swung open and Private Hall, who they both knew by sight only, stormed out.

"Don't fucking bother. He won't even let me attend my grandfather's funeral."

Once again, they stood side by side in front of Lieutenant Pages. "There must be something we can do, sir. Try to contact the colonel?"

"Now listen lads, and pass this round to the others. Captain Hamilton is not going to let anyone, repeat anyone, out, and no, I cannot contact the colonel... or even the major come to that." He watched them trying to think up some other plea and pre-empted it. "Much as I regret having to say this, I'm afraid you'll just have to re-arrange your wedding and that's final."

"We've got to let them know, sir," pleaded Ernie.

Lieutenant Pages took all of two seconds to think about that one. "Yes of course. I think he will allow that. In fact it's better if you use my phone here... just to be sure you can get through" He picked up the Bakelite handset and spoke to the battalion communications corporal and then handed the phone to Ernie so that he could provide the correct number. Both Eric and Pages heard an exasperated voice through the earpiece which Ernie held slightly away from his ear, catching an occasional expletive. Ernie hardly got a word in but eventually managed to explain their situation.

Once he had finished delivering the painful news, he handed the handset to Eric who echoed what had just been said. He gently put the handset back down on the receiver. "I can hardly believe it. All that wasted time and effort, not to mention the money."

"And just because Hamilton's got a poxy bee in his bonnet." They looked forlornly at each other, turned and walked quietly out of Lieutenant Pages' office without saluting or waiting to be dismissed.

They were back on the edge of the square walking slowly across to their barracks; resigned to missing their own weddings.

"We could go AWOL?" queried Eric, but he knew that his brother had already thought of that and instantly dismissed it.

"Nah. He'd only send the MPs after us and they'd probably arrive just as we'd be getting close to the altar."

"What a bastard. A real shite."

"I'll frigging well kill him."

"Not before I do."

Chapter 5

1985

(thirty years earlier)

"Can you smell it too?" No reply, so he tried another question to goad some sort of response. "It's either the peat in the bog or the bog in the peat, but personally I think it's the bog in the peat." Still no reply. "My dad had an outside toilet that smelt better than what's coming off that... that... swamp."

"Shut up you twat," Eric and Ernie whispered in unison at Earache. His real name was so like earache that just about everybody had forgotten how to pronounce it, but Earache responded to what he had been called ever since he had joined up with both Eric and Ernie.

None of them could see each other in the dark of the night as they crouched behind a dry stone wall that delineated a field from the marsh behind them, and they knew their comrades were supposed to be evenly spaced along its length. Their squad, totalling nine, had been told that the half-height wall at the bottom of a shallow hill flanked the northern edge of the pair of farm cottages, and that their orders were to stop anyone trying to escape in their direction. They had all cursed as they had trudged nearly a mile through the morass that had threatened to suck the boots off their feet and now that they had arrived, none of them could envisage anyone going anywhere in a hurry in that direction. But orders were orders and they had silently taken up their positions, each less than a hundred feet apart and out of sight of the cottages, in case someone made a run for it. Silently that was except for Earache who every few minutes found something to comment about.

"Oh God, I think I'm kneeling in sheep shit... it smells like sheep... it even tastes like sheep..."

"Shut up you poxy twat. If Hamilton finds out that we gave ourselves away because of your whinging, I swear I'll shove all the sheep shit I can find down your gullet," Eric whispered.

"So keep your bloody trap shut," added Eric.

Unless someone moved, it was impossible to pick individuals out from the almost non-existent shadows cast by the waist-high wall and the corporal had counted them off by tapping each of them on the shoulder as they reached their destination and dispersed. Other than Earache's occasional comment, the only other sound was the wind as it swept across the coarse grass of the marsh behind them. And just for once it wasn't raining, but the damp permeated anyway.

Five minutes later, Ernie thought he heard Earache bleating again, when out of nowhere the corporal appeared and briefly crouched down next to him. "Won't be long now so keep your eyes peeled."

"Do we know how many of them there'll be yet?"

"Might not be any at all, but if there are, don't let them get past you." He disappeared off to tell the next man, Eric. As far as Ernie knew, Eric was the last man in the squad so would be on the far right of their picket line. The corporal said nothing on his way back and only his muffled footfall indicated where he actually was.

The dark can play tricks with one's mind, but both

brothers weren't the type to be put out. Even so, when one's been ordered to keep a good look out, shadows start moving all by themselves and the mind starts imagining things. Under Captain Hamilton's command, the rest of their platoon ought to be approaching the cottages from the opposite direction and if, as suspected, the occupants were up to no good, then they were likely to flee towards the marsh.

He was right in that they didn't have long to wait because first one, then another light came on in the right-hand cottage, and they could now see that their stone wall was some two hundred yards from the target. The wind carried faint noises of people talking and shouting, indicating that Hamilton had managed to surprise whoever was inside, and they saw another light come on, this time in the left-hand cottage.

"Keep down and stay where you are. Watch for any runners," the corporal repeated his orders in a loud voice to his left and right.

It must have been all of three minutes before anything further happened. The clouds dispersed enough to reveal a three-quarters moon, and in the moments before it dived behind the next ragged set of clouds, it bathed the landscape in front of them in a sea of shimmering silver. No more than fifty feet in front of Eric and Ernie was a small low-slung building covered by a corrugated tin roof, and next to it what looked like a stone water trough. As if on cue and once true darkness returned, they all picked out a torch running towards them from the cottages. This was exactly why they were there, and they waited for whoever was holding it to come to them. They couldn't see the person, but the torch took on the movements of a baton in a relay race as its beam swept about wildly. One second pointing towards the ground before arcing up to the sky, and the next moment off to one side as it headed towards

Earache. It was about halfway down the hill when it went out.

They held their breath in anticipation of hearing someone dislodging stones as they clambered over the wall, but nothing.

"Right. Those of you with torches, turn 'em on, but stay put. Three 'E's, over the wall and have a good look around." The corporal referred to Eric, Ernie and Earache as the three 'E's. "We'll cover you."

They had a torch each and while Eric and Ernie swept their beams methodically, Earache's was all over the place. Nevertheless, his beam picked out the low building and as they zeroed in, and from the smell of it, it was clear that this was a small pigsty. What was unclear was where the owner of the torch had gone, and this was the only place they could have gone to ground. They heard a faint metallic sound.

Now there were half a dozen soldiers approaching from the cottages, spread out in a line across the field. They met adjacent to the sty with Hamilton shining his torch on the three Es.

"Where is he, then?"

"Where's who, sir?"

"The person who ran down here."

"We're just looking for him now, sir."

"Right, then get on with it. The rest of you back to the cottages and the transport and wait for me there. That includes the rest of Corporal Callund's squad."

Ernie got Eric to hold his torch and rifle for him as he needed two hands to shift the numerous sheets of half-rusted corrugated iron to one side. "Hold your torch steady, Earache." This as a sheet slid down and threatened to cut his hand open. This gave him access to a big dented barrel and as he rocked it to one side, saw that there was a rather frightened looking boy, about seven or eight years old, hiding behind it.

Hamilton's torch picked him out also. "Get him before he runs off again."

It was easy enough for Ernie to clamp his hand round the boy's forearm and pull him into the open and when he did, Hamilton smacked him hard round the head. He hit him so hard that the boy's knees initially gave way and had Ernie not been holding tight, he may well have collapsed.

"Steady on, sir. He's only a small lad," Ernie commented.

Hamilton immediately rounded on him, virtually shouting, "You shut your fucking mouth. I don't need any of your useless comments. He's a fucking terrorist just like his fucking parents who we've just captured, and he fucking knows where the guns are. Don't you?" He shone his torch closely at the boy's eyes. "Where are they hidden?" He jabbed his torch sharply into the boy's face and the lad involuntarily went to put both hands up to protect himself. Ernie released his grip so that he could do so.

"Don't let go of that little shit because he'll run off and we'll have the devil's own job finding him again in this dark. Grab him, man, grab him."

Ernie clamped his hand round the boy's wrist again and wrenched his hand from his face.

"You two." Hamilton shone his torch at Eric and Earache. "Have a look in there and see if there's any weapons." He shone his torch back in the boy's eyes and instinctively the arms went up to cover his face. Hamilton smacked one away.

"Where's the bloody guns then?"

The glum-looking boy, dressed in his pyjamas and only one slipper, looked up beyond the torch but couldn't see what sort of man was at the other end of it. Neither did he see the fist that impacted with his stomach and caused him to double-over onto the sodden grass. Ernie let go and the boy had just enough breath left in him to let out a small cough.

"Guns… guns… where are they?"

When the boy didn't reply, mainly because he couldn't, Hamilton turned his venom on Ernie. "I didn't say you could let go, did I?"

Ernie was shaken by Hamilton's tirade and couldn't find the words to answer.

"Pick him up by the leg and hold him upside down. That usually does the trick." Ernie hesitated. "Go on, then. Do as I say."

Ernie reluctantly, but easily, picked up the light boy and dangled him with his outstretched arm in front of Hamilton.

"Higher," ordered Hamilton, and only had to bend down a little so that he could peer straight into his face. "Where-are-the-guns-you-little-shit?"

The boy was still struggling to regain his breath, and being the wrong way up didn't help. Instead he coughed and as he tried to take in another breath, Hamilton hit him in the chest, but this time a little harder. And then, using his fist with the other hand, clobbered him on the side of the head. Unsurprisingly, he passed out and his arms flopped down towards the ground.

This was too much for Ernie who carefully laid the young boy on the turf and checked him for a heartbeat.

As he rose, he shone his torch at Hamilton, and was taken aback by the ferocious look on his face. "That's out of order, sir. You've half killed him."

It provoked an instantaneous response. "Well, get him up again and we'll wring it out of the little bugger instead." Hamilton went to bend down, but that was enough for Ernie who put his arm on Hamilton's shoulder and prevented him from picking up the prone figure. His sense of fairness and in-built aversion to bullying overrode his military training.

"No, sir." He could see that his brother and Earache had finished their cursory look around the pigsty and were now each side of Hamilton shining their torches on the boy. "If you hit him again, we'll all be up on a murder charge. The boy's hardly breathing now and needs a hospital."

Hamilton couldn't believe what he was hearing – a private soldier telling him what he could and couldn't do. And not just any private but one that he had previously bollock for... for... for... he couldn't remember exactly what right now, he was so enraged. He wasn't going to take no for an answer. The bloody cheek of the man, and he'd deal with him later. "Out of my way, private." He brushed Ernie's arm aside and went to retrieve the boy, but then Eric intervened by stepping over the boy with one leg.

"Not this time, you don't."

Hamilton couldn't believe what was going on. Right in front of him on the ground was the answer to where the illegal guns and ammunition were hidden, which represented weeks of work. These soldiers, his soldiers, were denying him the chance to blow his own trumpet and enhance his opportunities to advance himself. How dare they. "Get out of the bloody way and I'll deal with you later too."

"You'll deal with us both right now if you touch that boy again... sir." Eric was joined at the shoulder by Ernie; Earache stood still in terror.

Faced with the twins standing over the boy, Hamilton initially ignored what Eric had just said. "What the fuck are you two playing at? I gave you an order. Now stand back," he shouted. "And stop shining your torches in my face."

Neither Eric nor Ernie moved. Something must have clicked within Hamilton because he suddenly realised what he had been doing. Up to that point he had been so focused on getting the information, that he hadn't realised just how injured the little boy was. His blinkered attitude had driven him to the point of madness but as rationale began to return to normal, so did his blood pressure, and raising his arm to adjust his helmet, he took a couple of paces backwards.

"OK, lads. Take him up to the cottages."

Illuminated by a pair of wavering torches, he watched the trio make their way back up the hill towards the civilisation of electric light. He turned off his own torch, gritted his teeth, and in the silence of the night, reflected on his behaviour. Certainly the intervention of those two had prevented him needing to explain the death of a small boy, but he still felt confident that he could have explained that one away to his superiors. After all, weren't the bloody Fenians murdering people all the time? He had to admit that the Protestants also carried out their fair share, but when it came to soldiers, it would have been a bit more difficult trying to explain how so small a boy had sustained those kinds of injuries before death. He knew that the coroner wasn't overly sympathetic towards the Brits, but also knew that there was a rumour that in exchange for pound notes, he would phrase his statements a certain way.

And then there was the subordination of those two poxy privates to deal with. His blood pressure began to rise again as he started to devise various punishments to suit their crime of disobedience. He was about to start walking up the hill but stopped as a very simple idea entered his head. He began to chuckle as he formulated writing up his report to show that it was the three privates who were beating up the boy, and that it was he who had come to the rescue.

Hamilton laughed out loud. Those three would be his catch of the day.

Chapter 6

Wet heat

Detective Inspector Patricia Eyethorne was good at her job; very good. In fact, just a couple of years ago, shortly before her thirtieth birthday, she had been presented with an OBE by the Queen herself at Buckingham Palace. She was that good.

It wasn't just that she had been dedicated to her job straight from school, nor that her shapely attractiveness was very photogenic, which helped no end, but as far as the police public relations department was concerned, she said the right things to the right people – namely, the press. In their eyes, she had been responsible for the recruitment of more female police officers across the country than any of their expensive advertising campaigns, and this went a long way to meeting the demands from their masters in Westminster. She had been detailed to promote the police force in schools, starting with St Olive's, Maidenhead just west of London, where she had been educated. It was fortunate that her visit there was rather successful, and so followed a succession of schools further afield. She really didn't feel the pressure as she was posted to the Criminal Investigation Department at the same time, but instead, enjoyed showing the next generation of female officers what they could look forward to.

Time and experience promoted her but it could have been the high-profile capture of a particularly nasty rapist that caught the public's attention; especially as it was her who had drawn the culprit out into the open. Her superior officers had initially appointed her as lead detective with every expectation of her failing, and thus be able to pass the blame onto a woman before appointing a male officer to carry on her groundwork and take all the credit. Had the press caught wind of this, there might well have been a hue and cry. A sympathetic colleague with a good ear had passed the word to her, and surprise surprise, she was suddenly promoted from sergeant to inspector by a red-faced superintendent.

Not too long after, what caught the public's imagination was that on most of the front pages was a series of high-resolution colour photographs taken by a passing freelance photographer. They showed her rescuing a very pregnant woman's child from being thrown into the Thames off London Bridge. She had clung on onto a metal stanchion with one hand, and pulled the dangling child to safety with the other, while the father attempted to unwrap her fingers from round the metal rung and thus send them both to a watery grave. The adulation was such that the Police Federation joined the throng in calling for recognition of her courage; hence the Order of the British Empire medal.

It was somewhere around this time that due to her dedication to her job she realised that she had no one to share it with. Single, with no brothers, sisters or children, and with her parents having emigrated to Australia a few years earlier, it had left her somewhat isolated, but very independent. She had decided she would remain single for as long as she could foresee and usually shunned the opposite sex. She was married to her job, when out of the blue came Justin. He was a dark-haired, clean shaven, six-foot bachelor stationed also at Maidenhead and attached to the diplomatic corps. He too was an only child and up until his recent posting, had lived with his parents on the outskirts of Oxford. He enjoyed his sporting hobbies and particularly his unmarried freedom. Up to that point, their paths had barely crossed.

The night-time diagonal wind-driven rain was threatening to turn to snow as she trotted from the police station towards her car. Cowering under a flimsy file on top of her head, she cursed at having left both her umbrella and raincoat in the boot of her car. She swore as she realised that she hadn't retrieved her keys from her handbag and ferreting around in it, caught a glimpse of them dangling from the ignition switch. Her initial surge of relief turned to dismay when she couldn't open the driver's door; nor any of the others.

"Bollocks."

A hooded Justin appeared right next to her out of the night and made her jump. "A brolly's no good on a night like this anyway."

Had the night not been so black, it would have turned blue with what came out of her mouth.

"Well don't just stand there getting soaked. Get in." He fingered his pocketed key fob to unlock his own car parked next to hers.

She went to look up at him into the teeth of the wind, only to find that he had vanished round to the driver's side of his car and was getting in.

"Oh crap." She felt the first dribble of rain penetrate her right foot.

She slammed the door behind her a little too firmly and then realised that she had just saturated the seat she was now sitting on.

"Shit." She wiped her hair and rain from her face then looked to her right at the man who had just saved her from a total drenching. Almost with horror, she saw him grinning at her, before the interior light suddenly extinguished itself. Before she could let out another expletive, he beat her to it.

"I'll think you'll find that people only lock themselves out of their cars when it's freezing cold and pissing with rain at night, and Murphy's Law states that it is incumbent upon the maiden in distress to offer fair recompense to the knight in shining armour. So. Your place or mine?"

She could hardly believe what he had just said and reactively swore. "Fuck."

"Not what I had in mind, but if you insist."

"What?" Incredulous, she peered across the gloom at his silhouette from the streetlights.

"Great minds think alike, but not when they're dripping wet. Oh, and don't worry about the seat. It's leather and will dry out quicker than you."

The cheek of the man's quick retorts unbalanced her normal logical thoughts and she went to feel for the handle that would open the door.

"OK, OK. Sorry about the innuendo, but you must at least see the funny side of it. After all, you might have left your keys in the ignition on purpose."

This was just too much and she decided to stand her ground. "Listen..."

"No need to thank me, just sit back and enjoy the ride. I'll drive you home and you can call the AA from there. Put your belt on."

It was only when they started to move out of the car park that the incessant pinging become so annoying, that she clipped her safety belt on.

"Which way?" he asked as they waited in front of the T-junction at the open-gated entrance.

She was not used to this sort of unexpected help. Self-reliance had been her way of life, but she acknowledged to herself that she could hardly shun his assistance. "Turn left. Towards Bray."

Once they had joined the short dual carriageway, he broke the frosty but brief silence. "My name's Justin Crawford, merely a police sergeant, and I believe I'm in the presence of the infamous Inspector Eyethorne."

His comment was more of a statement rather than a question and she now considered she could go one of two ways. Either accept his ride home and politely say goodnight, or face up to the reality of the situation and graciously take the help of what was an outsider to her ordered life. Her initial instinct was to carry on and leave things as they had been. Pursue her career. Return home to her rented flat, dry clothes and a comfy sofa. She was just weighing up the two options, inclining towards the former, when with horror, she realised that her flat keys were attached to the keyring in her car. She had no choice now. Damn. But this was awkward. She closed her eyes for a moment, trying to ignore the headlamps of the oncoming cars, but it didn't help much. With conscious effort, she decided to play ball.

"I can hardly help being infamous by doing my job, and I can't help what others think of me. We all have our part to play." She was still being reticent; the way she had always been.

"Oh come, come. Famous for five minutes I can believe, but twice?"

"And I suppose you've done nothing that warrants notoriety?"

"Nothing in the same league as you and you've got to admit, lady luck has played her part well with you."

She had already admitted that had it not been for that photographer, her life would probably be less exciting, but she had frequently recalled how painful it had been hanging onto the rung while the foul-mouthed foreigner had tore at her hand with his nails. She still had a scar.

"Turn left here, it's quicker."

"I know."

"Why? Do you live in Bray as well?"

"I share a flat just a bit further on past the cricket club... or The Fat Duck if you can afford it. Ever been there?"

"Famous I might be, but wealthy I definitely am not, and let's get one thing straight." She wanted to assert a bit more authority on the situation. "I've never been to The Fat Duck or Heston's place down the road, I shop at Morrisons, eat in a lot and have a normal life, so stop talking as though I'm from a different planet."

"OK, OK. Just wondering. It's just that us chaps in the diplomatic corps come across those who spend their whole life wondering which five-star gaff to spend their over-inflated salaries at. The hours I've spent just sitting in lobbies, starving hungry and watching them gorge themselves... Sorry to harp on. Talking of which, have you eaten yet?"

"Not yet. And I've a confession to make." The relative silence while they stopped at a set of traffic lights was only interrupted by the wipers threatening to squeak. "I've left my flat keys in the car as well."

"Looks like it's my place then." If it had been daylight and he had been looking at her, he would have seen her lips compressed. "No key under the mat?"

"No. Probably best if I call the AA now." She stretched down for her handbag to retrieve her mobile.

"Why don't you wait until we reach my flat? It's only

another half a mile or so." The lights had turned green. "By the way, you said you live in Bray as well. Whereabouts?"

Not wanting to let anyone else into her life, there were few who knew where she lived, but she saw no harm in telling Justin. "I rent a small cottage in Ferry Road."

He half-laughed. "We're practically neighbours then." He turned into a narrowing street with sparse old-fashioned streetlighting. "Just up here on the right, now let's see how close we can park."

He turned off the ignition and the interior light came on automatically. She noted for the first time that they were in a BMW. "Here... I've a brolly on the back seat somewhere." He leant backwards between the front seats, brushing against her.

"I thought you said it was no night for a brolly?"

"I might have been wrong." He straightened up. "Here. It's for you. I've got my hood. Follow me."

Once inside his flat, which had once been a house and was now divided, she watched him go through his 'coming home' ritual of turning on lights, parking the umbrella in a stand in the corner, firing up the kettle, removing his fleece and hanging it up on one of the hooks in the hallway. She noticed that there was a parka jacket with a fur-lined hood hanging there.

"Tea or coffee?"

"Tea, one sugar." She wandered into the small living room which was surprisingly neat. "Live alone?"

Somehow he had managed to stand right beside her without her noticing. "Yes and no." He said in a quiet voice. "Here, take your coat off and wrap this round you. It'll warm you up." He produced what looked like a tartan-patterned picnic blanket and draped it over her shoulders before returning to the kitchen.

Unconsciously, her detecting instincts surveyed the room in greater detail, skipping over what she would normally expect to find on average, but picking up on anything out of the norm. Magnolia-coloured walls, white ceiling, speckled carpet, a neutral smell, sofa, table, TV, hi-fi, and mainly nondescript wall-hung photographs. She stopped and looked at one of the smaller ones with a tatty frame depicting two chaps, arms round each other's shoulders and obviously posing for the camera. She recognised Justin, but couldn't quite place the other; he looked familiar. Moving on round the room, in one corner she spotted what initially looked like a square plinth, chest high with a mounted model of a red Ferrari on top, but what caught her interest was that this one had a pair of escutcheon plates; painted so that they blended in. She tapped it lightly with her fingernail, then went to shift it slightly, aware that she might have to catch the Ferrari if it moved. It didn't. She didn't expect it to. It could only be one thing.

"I see you've found my gun cupboard then."

She spun round to see him holding two mugs, one being held out in her direction. For the third time she realised he had appeared without her hearing him.

"Thanks. It's well disguised. What's in it?"

"Thin air. Here, come and sit down." He chose one end of the sofa and she joined him at the other end. It was a small leather three-seat model and had there been three of them, it would have been a snug fit.

"So. You have a gun cupboard with no gun?"

"Yeah, bit of a joke really. Soon after I joined the diplomatic corps a few years ago, I was detailed to look after an American bigwig general who was in charge of tactical operations in the UK. Namely the nuclear stuff. He was based at Upper Heyford but went all round the country. We got on rather well, but really I was little more than his chauffeur; mostly liaison. One day, some mad woman attacks him with a kitchen knife and I ended up having to wrestle her away from him. I've still got the scar on my arm to prove it. Anyway, this general didn't like the thought of himself being unprotected, and through official channels I was issued with a pistol and told to carry it whenever I was with him. I'd only just moved in here and without warning, these blokes turn up and fitted that cabinet. It didn't blend in with the rest of the room, so I just painted it. When the general returned to the States, I had to hand back the gun, but nobody bothered with the cabinet."

"Who are you protecting now?"

"Well, up until recently I was a floater for the foreign office. You know, visiting diplomats, dignitaries, minor heads of state. I filled in when people went sick or on holiday, but it wasn't as satisfying as being dedicated to one person, so I requested a transfer." He paused to sip from his mug. "Right now I'm one of six looking after Maurice Hamilton MP."

"What, Hamilton as in Northern Ireland Hamilton?"

"Yup, the very same."

"What's he really like? There's all sorts of rumours and reports in the papers, mostly negative."

"You're right there and yes he tends to upset almost everybody he comes into contact with, but somehow he does seem to get results. You know I said there were six of us... well... that's because he receives more death threats than the rest of the cabinet put together."

"Because of the Northern Ireland issue?"

"Not just because he's effectively in charge of Northern Ireland, but from what I've gathered so far, and remember I haven't been with him very long, he's made quite a few enemies along the way. There's even one of my fellow officers who wouldn't mind if he disappeared."

"What? People other than the IRA who really want him dead?"

"Yes, and ironically I'd be better off having a gun now more than before, but the PM won't allow it. Not in London or the Home Counties anyway. Bad publicity etcetera to have one's chauffeur seen carrying a gun all the time, but there's always an armed officer outside his London residence. Now that's the sort of thing the public do want to see. Reassures them that their leaders are being kept safe, and ergo they are too. You ever fired a gun?"

"Umhum." She sipped at her tea. "Was told to go on a day-course at Bisley shortly after I was promoted. Fired a .22 pistol and a .38. They give quite a kick, don't they?"

"Not too bad if you know which way they kick. How did you get on?"

"Well I hit the target a few times, but it was more about safety and recognition. You know. In case we're confronted with a gunman in public. I suppose you're very familiar with firearms?"

"Not overly, but we're required to attend a range every now and again. Some bring their own pistols along but I'm really not into it that much. Even if I did have a gun, I'm not sure where I left the keys to the cabinet." He glanced over to the corner. "Here, talking of keys, what are we going to do about yours?"

"I've been thinking about that." She looked at her watch. "One advantage of being local is that one gets to know who and where the criminals on the manor hang out and there's a lad called Eddy who drinks in the Royal Oak. He's an ex-con with a history of car theft and I reckon that's where we'll find him right now."

She saw a quizzical look on Justin's face, but only for a moment. "And you reckon he could do you a favour?"

"Breaking and entering's his form, especially high-value cars, so it ought to be easy for him to break into my old banger. Besides which, he owes me anyway, so if you don't mind running me around. Anyway, it'll give me a chance to quiz him on another matter." She finished her lukewarm tea, shrugged off the blanket and got up.

"I'd consider it a privilege."

"By the way." She turned just before she reached the door. "I recognise him but can't put a name to the face. Who's that chap posing with you in the photograph up there?"

Justin knew exactly who it was and didn't bother turning round as he wanted to see the look on her face. "Oh, only my mate Eddie."

"Eddie who?"

"Redmayne." He loved to see the inevitable reactions. "But it's a long story and we can save that for another time." He went past her leaving her open mouthed.

Their paths didn't cross again for nearly two weeks when the station superintendent gathered as many officers as were on duty, in the canteen. He was briefing them about the upsurge in mobile phone thefts by gangs on scooters and the new directive on how to deal with them. Patricia had seen all the relevant bumf, knew exactly how to enact the new strategy, but had had to wait until the super had advised everybody in his station verbally; particularly for those constables who had not bothered to read the several pages that had been issued.

"Fancy a curry tonight?" She recognised Justin's soft voice immediately behind her, but didn't turn her head. "A proper

CATCH OF THE DAY

curry in Slough."

She waited another minute for the super to finish before turning and replying. "Thai or Indian?"

"Oh, Goan. At least that's where they told me they came from."

"Sounds like your regular?"

"Not really. It's just that it's on the way back from London. Pick you up at eight?"

"Better ring me first. I may have to oversee a little job we've got planned for later." The crowd was breaking up and she spotted one of her sergeants heading in her direction; she knew exactly what he was going to ask her. "By the way, what are you doing here? I thought you'd be off minding."

"Three days off. But I need to catch up on paperwork. See you later." He gave way to the sergeant.

***

From the outside, The Spice of India looked like any other curry restaurant, and indeed the inside was no different; one soon got used to the Asian surroundings, polite waiters and background music.

"Mild or hot?" Justin asked.

"How hot is hot here?"

"Oh... about normal, but their lamb is really succulent. Poppadums?"

They went through the ordering procedures; she opted for medium-hot.

"Anything exciting happened in the smoke recently?" She asked, trying to start off a normal conversation.

"Nope. Rather dull really, but then again that's how it ought to be. Had to accompany Hamilton to Stormont the

124

other day. Flew out of Northolt rather than Heathrow. I was told to stay close while he met with Northern Irish leaders. Funny thing though… a chap from MI5 came along as well, and he was telling me how quiet it's been recently. They're rather concerned that the dissidents are cooking up something big."

"Aren't all dissidents always cooking up something big?"

"Bound to be, but spotting it is what the problem is."

"Tell me more," she enquired. "Or is it asking too much of the Official Secrets Act?"

"Not at all. Besides which, anything I tell you now will probably have changed by tomorrow."

"That fast, eh?"

They made way for the arrival of poppadums and chutneys, and once the waiters had disappeared to the background, he continued. "The problem's not so much on the ground but what's going on in cyberspace. All the usual texts, emails, Facebook, etcetera, they're all avoided now by most of the major players, but occasionally something comes out of the ether. When I'm not on minding duty, I'm slaving over a computer sifting through what the men in white coats send through. Mind you, there's hardly a white coat around these days. Some of them have ponytails and nose studs but you'd never guess their occupation if you met them in the high street."

"I know the sort. Difficult to sort the wheat from the chaff just by looking at someone. I suppose the biggest threat to Hamilton must come from the Irish contingent?"

"That's what most people think, but this MI5 chap wasn't there to act as minder as he vanished the minute we arrived and didn't reappear again until we were about to leave. He told me that he had to meet someone, and I didn't presume to ask whom. So one must conclude that they're keeping tabs on certain people. That's the worrying factor in all of this. Just because there's no smoke doesn't mean there's no fire."

"So you're the fireman then."

"I prefer to think of myself as a knight in shining armour." He smiled the same smile as when they had first met on that miserable night. "Enough about me and my job. I've two days left of my leave this month and I intend to enjoy them. With any luck and if the weather clears, I might even manage a round of golf with a friend of mine tomorrow. Do you play, and if not what do you do on your time off?"

It wasn't that Patricia was a shy person, but she had rarely been asked that question; the last time had been during her interview for promotion to inspector, and that had been purely business. Now the questions were being posed socially and she wasn't entirely comfortable revealing her personality to a relative stranger. She took a sip from her wine glass, not to steady her nerves but to pause for thought. Perhaps he wasn't such a stranger. After all, they shared the same office and he seemed a decent enough chap.

"Crazy golf's the nearest I've come to a real course. Many years ago at Thorpe Park with some school friends, so thanks for the offer but no thanks. As to what I do in my spare time… and that's a joke because I hardly have any, but when I do, I like to knit."

"What, knit as in jumpers, sweaters, gloves and the like?"

"Oh yes. It's very relaxing curling up on the sofa with a pair of number four needles and a few balls of wool. Once you get used to it, you can do it automatically while watching TV and I like to do crosswords at the same time. It helps clear the mind so I can concentrate on solving the mysteries of the local criminals."

"You call that relaxing?"

"Very. Would you like me to teach you, because the forecast's really not that great for the next few days?"

"Touché. But I've got this pair of favourite socks..."

"Oh no. Not in a million years..."

That smile was back on his face again, and she knew she'd been drawn. This time she laughed and realised she enjoyed his company.

"Let's put it another way." He didn't want to sound like he was fishing and tried his best to not let it come across that way. "What was it you used to enjoy but haven't done for a while?"

"Oh crikey, that's a tricky one." She twirled her wine glass on the tablecloth trying to recall. "Oh yes, I know. Mum used to take another friend and I ice skating whenever she could, usually at weekends. Probably just to get us out of the house, but she was very good and when the rink thinned out a bit, people would stop and watch her twizzles."

"Twizzles?"

"When you pirouette on one foot."

"I thought twizzles was a chocolate bar."

"No, It's a... Oh you wretched man, you're goading me again. And anyway, they're called Frazzles and they're a bacon snack."

He looked over her shoulder. "Talking of bacon, here comes our food." While it was being set out in front of them, he took the opportunity for a closer look at her features. Shapely indeed and dressed appropriately so that it showed off her curves without needing additional accentuation. Other than a locket on the end of a delicate gold chain that rested midway down her blouse and a pair of golden ear studs, he could see no other jewellery. Ostentation was obviously not her forte. Her shoulder-length light brown hair was neatly trimmed and set in a way that would have been easy to brush straight, and, if anything, highlighted her very even facial features. It was her infectious smile from her slightly wider-than-normal mouth that really bought her face to life. All in all, she was naturally beautiful.

They finished scooping spoonfuls of rice, vegetables and other bits 'n' pieces from out of the stainless steel dishes on the burners onto their plates, and Justin smoothly resumed.

"Talking of unusual activities, a good friend of mine took up horse riding and even went to India to train on Marawani or Malani ponies. Now, he's a leading stuntman and appears in all sorts of films. Gets to go round the world quite a lot, and as Pinewood Studios is just round the corner, we occasionally meet up. It was he who told me about this place. What do you think of it?"

"This is wonderful, and as you said, the lamb is just perfect."

"Yes. Quite a bit better than the curry they serve up in the canteen, eh?"

"You know our chef, don't you?"

"I know of him," remarked Justin in between chewing.

"Well, believe it or not, he's entered himself into a cooking competition." She waited for his expected reaction before joining him in laughter, as the dubious quality of the food served was the usual standing joke.

"In my job, I get to eat quite a wide variety of food. Day on day it'll be sandwiches or burgers from the high street, but then out of the blue, it'll be a sumptuous meal. Sometimes I and another colleague are required to sit on an adjacent table to Hamilton, incognito, acting as though we're like any other businessmen, and it would look daft if we just sat there with nothing in front of us. You see, he carries a tiny microphone in his top pocket at these meetings and I'm his Bluetooth link to the digital recorder in my jacket. It's disguised as a fag packet just in case. He doesn't want to be found having anything like that on him. Occasionally, diplomats can occasionally let slip with something if they think it's not going on record. Rather useful if someone's trying to deny something already said."

"So he's a sneaky so-and-so?"

"Oh yes, and to be honest, we're all a bit edgy being around him. I've only just heard that he had one of our chaps sacked on the spot yesterday. Not sure why yet and I expect we'll all find out sooner or later. Quite a shame really as I was just beginning to get on with him. Decent fellow."

"I didn't think one could be sacked on the spot these days."

"Oh don't underestimate Hamilton. He's a law unto himself. Anyway, the minute one signs the Official Secrets Act, you give up all those sorts of rights."

"Do you come into that category?"

"Unfortunately yes, but I still enjoy my job and what goes with it."

"Hang on a minute... I thought you told me you were a sergeant, which means you'd be employed by the county police, and therefore under their jurisdiction."

"You're quite correct and I am, but under secondment to the Home Office and have been for quite a while now."

"So what happens if you incur Hamilton's wrath. Will they sack you too or can they just take you out the back and shoot you?"

He laughed at the suggestion. "Of course not, but funny you should mention that. You know the death penalty's been abolished for ages now. Well, a friend of a friend claims that there's still a clause on the statute books dating back to

Henry VIII's time that's still in force. Apparently it states that anyone found guilty of high treason must be hung, drawn and quartered in the grounds of the Tower of London in front of five-hundred souls. The emphasis here being hung, drawn AND quartered... I'm not sure the public would put up with that these days and even if they did, the TV channels would probably make sure that more like five-hundred million had tuned in."

She finished her mouthful. "I'm not sure I would want to see somebody quartered, presumably by four horses, one on each limb?"

"Presumably. Most medieval. But then again there are those out there who would want to see justice actually being done. Only for the most serious of crimes like treason, of course."

She couldn't tell if he was being serious or not. On balance probably not, but she decided to play along and pretend. "Three cheers for Henry VIII."

"And just to prove that his methods were rather draconian, remember he had two of his wives beheaded."

"Just beheaded? Not that serious then, otherwise they'd have been drawn and quartered as well." She was trying her best to tease him.

"Obviously not."

"I wonder what he'd make of today's society with all these terrorists trying their level best to disrupt government including trying to knock off the likes of your chap Hamilton?"

"Oh, they were around in his day too, but they were mostly Catholics then. Nowadays it's anyone with a grudge who we've got to look out for."

"Especially the Irish."

He looked her straight in the eyes across the table. "Yes.

Especially the Irish."

From the earnest look on his face, she felt that she may have come a little close to a nerve. She didn't want to upset what was turning out to be a pleasant evening and, averting her eyes, she decided to change the subject in as subtle a way as possible. "One of the newcomers to my team is Irish. Now, if you want to take it out on anybody, be my guest to try it on Detective Constable Jerry Flanders. He's got a terrible sense of humour. Lives down Edgware way and seems to know everyone."

"Is he that tall young gingernut? If so, I heard the desk sergeant telling him to bugger off the other day. In the kindest sort of way if you know what I mean."

"That's him. With his warped sense of humour I suppose he'll end up running the station in another twenty years or so. Haa. He'll be welcome to it."

"You've got no aspirations in that direction then?"

"Who me? Why on earth would I want to become a superintendent running an entire station when I'm perfectly happy catching criminals. I enjoy detecting and I enjoy working with others who get out there, and I get to see how the criminal mind works. You see, it's a bit like an Agatha Christie novel but in real life where you need to consider every aspect, particularly the seemingly insignificant details. It's no good picking up a file that's been written by somebody else and expect to be able to solve it just by looking through it. They'll have missed something not obvious at the time, so it's important to follow the thinnest of threads from the outset. However well planned, every criminal will leave a clue somewhere along the line, and I derive great satisfaction from picking up that thread and following it through to its conclusion."

"It's been said that the mind of a detective is the same as that of a criminal, but the mind of a great detective prefers a great curry. I see you've enjoyed yours." Justin nodded at her plate that was fast emptying.

She laughed off his comment. "Now you're just trying to flatter me, and somehow you don't come across as the flattering type... oh I see, you were just trying to see if I'd rise to the bait. Well, you'll have to try harder than that."

"At least we now know where we stand with each other."

She was about to say that she preferred to stand on her own two feet, but stopped herself. Her recent thoughts about her isolated way of life was in contrast to spending this evening with somebody else and it bought it home to her. She had certainly received advances from the opposite sex, one of them not so long ago, but there was something charming about Justin and she felt that she really ought to give him a chance. After all, she could always say no at a later date, couldn't she? "Well, it's a great curry and thank you for bringing me here. Not sure about the wine though, and by the way, why are you drinking just water?"

"I've been told that there's some excellent Indian wines, but as far as I've found so far, they haven't yet filtered down to these kinds of establishments. As to the water, I rarely drink alcohol. It's not one of my vices."

"What are your vices then?" She instantly regretted asking such a personal question, but then again, perhaps that was exactly what normal people did. She asked herself if it was the sole glass of wine going to her head that was making her just a little foolhardy. On second thoughts, it couldn't be just that.

He looked at her for a moment, fork in hand, wondering how far he ought to go. "There can be quite a fine line between a hobby and a vice but it rather depends upon your definition.

Suffice to say I don't believe I have any vices. Not nasty ones anyway. Hobbies, I like to think I'm the sporty type, but I rarely have the time to pursue them. Not in my current job anyway, so I try to keep abreast with the latest, mainly over the internet, but there's only so much cricket one can watch in one go, and I end up fast-forwarding the highlights. Here, do you fancy the last of the passanda, there's a little left?" He had spotted that her plate was almost clean and motioned with his fork at one of the bowls on the burner between them.

"No thanks. I'm just about full. You have it." She put her knife and fork together on her plate and watched him scoop the last out of the bowl. "So, it looks like you're going to get the chance to catch up tomorrow."

"Maybe there'll be a break in the weather, about lunchtime would be good and anyway, if all else fails, including the English cricket team, again, there's bound to be a bulletin update on the threat board that'll need my attention. Oh, sorry. I've bought up that nasty subject of work again, haven't I?"

"Don't apologise. It's me who's usually accused of that."

"Looks like we're in the same boat there, doesn't it?" He wiped his mouth with the linen napkin and sat back as far as the chair would allow.

To her mind he was easy company, and while she had felt relaxed up to that point, she was beginning to wonder if he was going to make a pass at her before the end of the meal. She stopped fiddling with her clean spoon when the waiter came to remove their plates and other paraphernalia; another brushed away the few crumbs on the tablecloth. "Sweets?" he asked.

He beat her to it. "Not for me, thanks."

"No thanks."

"Coffee?"

Their eyes briefly met and almost in unison they replied "No." Justin added, "Just the bill please."

She wondered, and had she had time to think about it, half hoped that he would ask her back to his flat for coffee. She wasn't too familiar with the etiquettes that went with a first date, but from the little she had gathered from TV sitcoms, she waited for him to make the first move. She needn't have worried.

"You're a bit like me then. I find coffee tends to keep me awake at night, but you could always have decaf."

"I prefer tea anyway, but not too late."

"Somehow I see you as a cocoa person. Snuggled up with your balls of wool and crosswords with a cat on your lap."

"You see very well, other than the cocoa bit, and yes I do have a cat."

"What model?"

"Model? Oh I see. Just a British standard moggy that adopted me some years ago. I call her Sparkles because of her bright eyes."

"Lucky Sparkles, and very discerning too."

"My fault really. You feed them once out of pity and they keep coming back for more. The poor wet thing was waiting for me on my doorstep one night and before I knew it, she was in. Wouldn't leave until I'd given her some leftover chicken." She laughed at the memory. "And the next day she came back for more."

"How old is she?"

"I've no idea, but the vet seems to think she's probably the right side of ten."

Once the waiter had left after leaving the folded bill in a stainless steel tray, Justin announced that it was twenty-four pounds each; they went Dutch. It was still raining when they pulled up a few yards from Patricia's flat and Justin kept the engine running, keeping them warm and the screen clear of mist.

"I promise not to tell the papers where you live," Justin commented mischievously as he peered out of his side window through the raindrops. He turned to her at the same time as turning on the overhead courtesy light. "That was a very pleasant evening and thank you for sharing it with me. Much better than eating on one's own, don't you think?"

"Certainly was, but now I've got some catching up to do."

"Oh dear. Well, perhaps another time when there's less on our plates? Sorry about the pun."

She unbuckled her seat belt and reached for the handle; then paused. She really had found the evening enjoyable and thought she ought to thank him for forcing her hand, but didn't want to sound over eager. She wanted to get her own thoughts together before committing herself, but couldn't help what came out next. "Yes. That would be nice. Well... goodnight then."

She didn't know whether to shake his hand or just get out. In the end and with horror, she found herself giving him a quick peck on his cheek with her lips. She couldn't get out of the car quick enough.

She almost slammed her front door but caught it at the last moment, threw her raincoat onto the first chair she came across and nearly tripped over Sparkles before she could turn on her living room light. She was not thinking clearly and realised it. She continued through to the kitchen, opened a high-level cupboard door for a tumbler, then the next one when she remembered she had rearranged them only last week. She found a half-empty bottle of whiskey and poured out a small amount. She rarely touched the spirit, but on occasion found that it helped her think more logically. She took a sip and turned round only to see Sparkles' green eyes peering up at her as if to ask what was going on.

"Oh what a lovely cat you are… and what a lucky person I am. Maybe he's the one this time." She was bending down to address Sparkles.

Another sip before putting out some cat food and then she glided back to the living room and her favourite chair. Just before she sat down, she suddenly stopped. With shock, she realised she had been humming to herself and admitted that she didn't think she had done that since her school days.

With her head resting on the back of her armchair and after another swig, she closed her eyes and started to analyse the evening. It wasn't that he was all those things a woman would want to see in a man, but he was rather handsome to go with it. Politeness, humour, modesty; well, certainly not conceited. And he hadn't tried to make a pass at her. Sporty, dedicated to his job… her list went on in her besotted state. She nearly fell asleep in her chair thinking about him.

Twenty minutes later she rested her head on her pillow and looked forward to dreaming. One question raised itself as she drifted off… could she really take up golf?

Entertaining ladies as he had done so in the past, Justin was a little more pragmatic about the evening, but nonetheless quite content. Parking more or less outside his flat, he sat there for a few minutes, initially wondering if the rain would ease before tomorrow and mulling over DI Patricia Eyethorne OBE. It wasn't that he was in a hurry to settle down, nor that he'd had enough of his bachelor lifestyle, but with his twenty-fifth birthday on the horizon and quite a few of his friends now married, he was beginning to wonder if he ought not to consider more of a family way of life. For some reason Sophie came to mind. She was the daughter of an earl and had been great fun, expensive but just fun, and he still kept in touch with her. Then there was Riva who claimed to be descended from a Polish aristocrat, but she turned out to be one of those social climbers who used her sexuality to the utmost. At the other end of the scale was Dawn who, on occasion, liked to embarrass him, especially in public. He had to drag himself away from picturing his old flames. His natural instinct was to carry on until Mrs Right came along, but then again might not Patricia be the one?

A friend of his once told him that when it came to women there were always three options, even when there appeared to be only two. Obviously yes and no were two of them, but the third was maybe. Was she frigid or a 'goer' and there was only one way to find that out. Would he earn himself a proper slap in the face, or would she demurely accede? Tapping his key fob on the steering wheel, he applied that thinking. 'Yes' would lead him into a relationship and into the unknown, but it was the unknown part that always excited him; whatever the circumstances. 'No' would put an end to it and was rather definitive, so he dismissed that; they would end up occasionally passing each other in some corridor or other, politely nodding at each other, and this could well descend into awkward situations. 'Maybe' was a bit of a wishy-washy cop-out, but another evening out might well reveal which way he should go and would leave his options open. He ceased tapping and decided that Patricia was worth more investigation, but not physical at this stage as she might well turn out to be worthwhile. Anyway, having a DI with an OBE as a friend would bound to be advantageous at some point or other along the line.

Participants in the office party at Christmas time quite often wake up the following morning with regrets. Typically, in the construction industry the innocent slap-and-tickle at the outset ends up with someone's other half disappearing off with somebody else's; all with the help of self-service alcohol from a table set to one side. In government circles, fluted glasses of orange juice or cheap champagne are served from a silver platter by a waiter as one walks in the room.

Superintendent Tonybee made it quite clear that he expected Patricia to attend. She had done so twice in previous years when she had not been a decorated officer, but now that she was among the more notable echelons of the force, her absence would be noted. Gone were the days when the entire division would look forward to a packed disco in the canteen during the week leading up to Christmas. Nowadays the rank and file only attended with their wives and partners if it didn't clash with family life. Despite a tight budget, Tonybee wanted to retain the annual Christmas 'do', which, on a social scale, slotted in somewhere between the two extremes. To save precious pennies, he had downgraded it and hired a room in the Vine pub just round the corner from Berkshire police headquarters. He'd been told it would have the appropriate atmosphere and a TV channel with music. It wasn't supposed to be an alcohol-fuelled event, but the up-and-coming newcomers in the force usually managed to upset someone or other during the latter stages of the proceedings. The old cry of 'somebody call the police' was met with a howl of derision and 'we are the police'.

Having already paid her respects to Tonybee and other higher-ranking officers, about halfway through the evening before the volume became too loud, Patricia was thinking of leaving when she spotted Justin saunter in. Walking in front of the big screen and side speakers that were well past their best, she immediately made a beeline, meeting him at the bar. She had mainly been talking to another inspector in the drugs squad and was becoming bored.

"I see we've got the usual suspects in tonight," remarked Justin with a slightly raised voice; he had to, to be heard over a burst of laughter.

"Yes. It's DC Flanders holding court again."

He followed her nod and saw a circular group of males at the other end of the bar. "No wonder old Tonybee hires this place out... he'd never allow that kind of language in his station."

This was the fifth time they had met outside working constraints in a few short weeks, and everything seemed to be gelling. "Another wine?"

"I've had three already... but as it's Christmas. Only one though."

Once the barman had obliged, Justin motioned, "Over there?"

Wending their way towards a quieter corner, they overheard one officer in a group patting himself on the back for catching the local flasher 'Bill' again. "This time he had an actual camera flash gun strapped round his middle, so that when he opened his old man's coat... it flashed..." Although a relaxed atmosphere, conversations naturally gravitated to what was going on in the world of crime.

Once ensconced at a high-level table, Justin asked, "Have you ever come across Bill?"

"Only once. He thought I was worth flashing."

"He's quite right. I'm surprised *The Sun* haven't been in

touch with you to pose for page three yet."

"Don't be daft, I'm no model."

"But you are. Haven't you noticed how people look at you as you pass them by? You turn heads."

Patricia thought about this for a moment, recognising more of his flattery. He had been sincere all along the line and from the look on his face, this was no exception. "I'm just lucky, that's all."

"Maybe, but it's your natural beauty that attracts men."

"Is that what attracted you when we first met?" She tested him just a little.

"Hardly. It was nearly pitch black out there and if you remember, one needed an umbrella to keep the rain out of our eyes."

They looked directly at each other across the table. Patricia was totally infatuated with him and thinking that she would pose for him, if only he would ask her. She thought of a way of prompting him. "So, ought I to pose for you in my uniform?"

"For me, any pose from you would do, but your uniform's a bit formal. Besides which, there's already one of you with your medal hanging up in the corridor."

"Oh God, not that one again. Makes me look old with that hat, and my eyes... they're nearly black."

"Well, if you want me to take a better photo, I'll have to dig out my digital Nikon."

She realised he had somehow turned the tables on her, and now it would be her doing the asking. She decided not to give in – just yet. "One with a big telephoto lens I presume." She was referring to his role as a security cum surveillance officer, but hinting that the size of his equipment might also be in the equation. Coming from her, it was a bold comment, and with the innuendo came a little tension. She sipped pensively from her wine glass watching the look on his face.

"Oh no. It was just a quality present from my parents last birthday. It replaced the one they gave me for my eighteenth." He laughed. "I'd dropped the old one in the Thames photographing off the back of a boat." Justin knew exactly what she was referring to, and decided it would be more fun if he played the innocent, just for the moment anyway.

"What were you photographing?"

"Fish."

"Fish?"

"Yes, fish." He watched her blink and frown at the same time.

"I didn't know there were any fish in the Thames, and anyway, how can you take photos of a fish from a boat when they're underwater?"

"Technically speaking, you're correct. There aren't... they were porpoises which are mammals."

"What, porpoises up the Thames?"

"Yes, a whole pod of them breaching. My girlfriend at the time had been over to New England earlier that year to watch whales breaching and had heard that there was a group of porpoises that had got lost in the Thames. She asked me if I'd like to help her and her friends try to guide them back to sea."

"And did you? Manage to save them, I mean."

"Oh yes. Well, most of them. Some just beached themselves and eventually died in the mud, but with the help of another two boats we managed to corral most of them and whoosh them back down the estuary."

"And then you dropped your camera."

"No, not then. It was as we were disembarking onto a jetty. She was posing on the slimy algae boards but slipped, and in my haste to save her from dropping into the mud, I dropped the camera."

"So now you've got a new one. Do you use it much?"

"Now and again. It's good for long distance shots."

"How about close-ups?" She moved closer to him over the tabletop.

"Those too."

"Does it have a good zoom?"

They were less than a foot apart. "That depends upon what I'm zooming in to."

"How about someone this close?" There. She'd done it. Virtually asked him to photograph her, but she didn't care anymore. She wouldn't have noticed if the entire room had gathered round.

Justin took his time answering and spoke slowly. "The subject would have to be a beautiful lady with a gorgeous smile, have the right light on her, and be willing to strike the right pose in front of the director. Do you think the subject might want that?"

It was music to her ears and she was buzzing with excitement. "I can think of one subject who might be willing."

They held each other's gazes, but it was Justin who broke the magic moment. He straightened up. "Right then. I'll just go and get Brenda over there."

The surprise was total and caught Patricia mid-spell. She'd even started to wonder who the hell Brenda was, and then remembered. He had an innocent look on his face and it took her a couple of seconds to realise.

"Oh, you beast. How could you?"

His infectious smile was back again. "Well, I had to try. Do you know if Brenda is up for it?"

"What?"

He'd caught her off balance again. "You know. Big Brenda... the one with the..." he shaped his hands in front of him.

"Oh, stop it." She was laughing now too. "You know nothing about Brenda... anyway... you couldn't handle her."

"You're right there. Not my type."

Patricia had had enough. "Come on then, am I your right type?"

"I don't know. I haven't seen you pose yet."

***

Half an hour later she turned the key to her front door. Justin stood behind her with his hands round her waist, tickling her midriff. "Let's start by getting you out of these wet clothes."

"At least wait until we get inside." She had forgotten her coat again. Her jacket wasn't really in need of drying out and it was a bit of a lame excuse, but she played ball while Justin put his photo bag down on the hallway floor. "When you picked up your camera, was your lodger in?"

"No. But I don't keep tabs on her and she could return at any minute."

"You know, you haven't told me a thing about her." Patricia took the opportunity to probe a little. "After all, she may be your secret wife in hiding."

Justin laughed at the suggestion. "She's an air hostess with British Airways. Her name's Janie and she comes and goes at all hours which is why we're here rather than mine."

She kicked off her shoes. "Well, what pose would you like me in? Anything particular I should wear?"

He took her in his arms and they kissed gently, mouth to mouth. "How about your nurse's uniform?"

"You're dreadful." She whacked him playfully on his chest. "I haven't got a nurse's uniform... but I might have something better. Go and set up in the living room and get us some drinks. I'll be back in a few minutes."

Even with the overhead and wall lights on, it was a little dim and he would need the flashgun to obtain quality shots. He was hoping more than wondering what she would appear in, and looked around to find the best spot. There on a side table next to the sofa was a half-knitted green and yellow jumper; it covered most of a newspaper crossword and he moved it slightly to make way for a leg of his collapsible tripod. While waiting for her, he surveyed the snug room and could understand why she would feel so comfortable in it. He looked down at the carpet and thick rug that covered three-quarters of it and decided he ought to remove his shoes; not just out of cleanliness, but to make them both feel at ease a little more when she did appear. Bending down to place his shoes to one side, a change in the light made him look up. He nearly gasped.

She stood in the doorway wearing a black silky dressing gown tied across her middle with a neat bow. One hand was on her extended hip while the other tousled her hair as she leant against the jamb. "Will this do?"

All sorts of thoughts went through his head. Would it do... would it do? It was bloody marvellous. Perfect. An angelic face and... and... he was initially speechless.

"Well, if you don't approve, how about this?" She extended a shapely leg and ran her foot up the other one, showing ample inner thigh.

He held his hand out and gathered his wits. "Don't move... just don't move." He went behind his camera and went to look through the viewfinder, but stopped at her next comment.

"That won't do you any good," she laughed. "Not unless you take the lens cap off first."

He slowed down and tried to remember what settings he ought to use. "Just testing." He flicked the switch on the flashgun as he turned the small knob to auto, glanced at the small screen that framed most of her and pressed the button.

"OK. Now, how about this?" She placed her feet together, stretched her arms diagonally away from her and leaned forward as though taking a bow, but with her head looking straight into the lens. Her smile was what stood out the most.

"Very nice," he said appreciatively as he clicked twice, but the second time the flash hadn't charged quickly enough to go off. "Hang on a sec while I check something." He attended to the camera to see if its battery was still good and to see if the first shots had come out OK. When he looked up with his finger on the button, she had fully opened her gown at arm's length to reveal her naked body except for a set of white underwear. With the black background of the gown, her bra and panties highlighted her very shapely figure. And not just any old bra either as it lifted her cleavage to show off to the maximum.

Justin just about had the presence of mind to press the button; once. He gulped.

"How about now?" She had raised her arms like Batman and spread her legs apart; starfish style.

He was beginning to feel the heat but waited until the flash had charged before taking another shot.

"Beats the hell out of a nurse, don't you think." She lowered her arms, reached for her glass of red on the sideboard and drank nearly half of it. "Well, what other poses does my director desire?"

"How about a sideways one without your gown and you looking over your shoulder at me?" He was thinking of making best use of her figure, and watched as it glided to the floor.

"No, I've got a better idea." She stood square onto the camera, unclasped her bra at the front but kept the half-cups covering her nipples. "Is this sexy enough for you?" She pouted her lips.

No sooner had Justin snapped away than she pulled back her bra revealing the most gorgeous pair of orbs he had ever seen. "How about these then?" Momentarily her arms and bra halves were out wide, but before the flash had a chance to recharge, she closed them again and fastened the two halves.

"That's not fair," retorted Justin as he straightened up.

She turned around and leaned over presenting her bottom to the camera. "This will have to do instead."

"Not as nice a view but it certainly shows you've got some cheek."

She gave him a seductive look and collected her gown before standing up. "Come with me."

Justin wasn't quite sure what was going to happen next, but he followed her into the bedroom just as she turned off the light.

"Now it's my turn," he heard her say.

They made love for the first time together.

***

The problems of Northern Ireland were of such importance that the Secretary of State held a permanent position on the Cabinet; a position recommended by the prime minister and appointed by the Queen. It necessitated a chamber in the

Palace of Westminster all by itself; although from the size of room, one would hardly call it a chamber.

As that Secretary of State, Maurice Hamilton was one of an elite few who had access to virtually any part of the House of Commons at any time, but this morning, there was only one place he was heading. He stormed through doors as he wended his way to what he considered to be his own personal chamber, ignoring the occasional polite 'good morning, minister' from some of those he passed. To his mind, there was absolutely nothing good about this morning. As he approached the final door to his own office, he shouted, "Lloyd!"

The bespectacled Clarence McCorley Lloyd had an anteroom off Hamilton's office and was opening the dividing door in an instant. He had learned from the outset not to keep his master waiting and immediately went to take his coat. Whereas ministers were appointed to certain positions and rarely remained in that department longer than two years, Lloyd was a career civil servant and had seen various politicians with their differing opinions come and go. He was a little past middle age, with a grown-up family, and had quietly risen to the rank of assistant private secretary to whoever had been appointed to the Northern Ireland office. He didn't agree with Hamilton's methods but it was not his remit to question them or the reasoning behind those decisions. In secret, he detested the man but never let his feelings show; that would have been most unprofessional. On the rare occasion when he did agree with Hamilton, he would do his very best to expedite whatever was necessary, but in the main he would find some legitimate reason to elongate the process's passage through the fine grinding wheels of the service. His immediate superior, Mr Cummings, was the permanent private secretary who tried to keep away from Hamilton as much as he could and left as much as possible for Lloyd to sort out.

"Good morning, minister," Lloyd always greeted Hamilton irrespective of the weather.

"Tommyrot. It's another foul day out there." He shrugged out of his damp coat leaving Lloyd to hang it on the coat stand. "Have you seen today's papers?" He did his best to slam a copy of *The Times* on his desk. "Well, have you?"

Lloyd had but didn't get a chance to reply, and in any case he recognised a rhetorical question when he heard one.

"The headline might as well have read 'Hamilton fucks-up' but thank God they're not allowed to print that. And that bollock-head of an editor I was with last night totally ignored me. That's what really gets my goat. Bloody typical of the press. You tell them one thing and they go and print something totally different. And where did he get the idea from anyway? I tell you, there's a bloody mole inside this department and when I find out who it is, I'll have his balls."

He'd spent the previous evening with one of the better-known Fleet Street newspaper editors in one of the parliamentary snooker rooms, and despite them both knowing that they needed to be circumspect with what they said, it still took the best part of three frames to say what could normally be said in a few minutes. Hamilton was by far the better player and even managed a break of over fifty, but erred on purpose on two occasions just to pressurise his opponent. He loved snooker and saw it as an ideal opportunity to cheat when he could. One of his favourite methods was to deduct a score rather than add, or add two instead of one to his. Even so, he really was rather good at the game.

Lloyd had experienced these rants from Hamilton on several occasions and wisely waited until he had vented his anger by busying himself preparing the usual coffee from the sideboard. He placed the cup and saucer on his desk. In the past that would be the end of his tirade, but not on this occasion.

"Why should we appease those Fenian bastards? All they do is cry to the rest of the world about being hard done by when we come up with an idea to suit everybody, no: correct that... when I come up with an idea to suit everybody, and the bloody papers believe them. I never said we'd support the abortion initiative." He rounded on Lloyd with an accusing finger. "But someone in this department... and only yesterday mind you... has told someone in the press that we would. That was supposed to be kept back until the conference next month and now we're back to square one. I've put my reputation on the line for this one and it's not going to reflect well on the government either if it goes tits-up." He looked down at Lloyd who did his best to keep his feelings to himself and continued. "Someone's been eavesdropping and this time I want to know who."

"That'll be a job for the security section, minister."

Hamilton was about to retort when he realised that Lloyd was correct. He strode round to the high-back chair behind his desk, looked at it for a moment and then sat down hard on it. "Well get Postles in here, and I mean now. I want this resolved."

"I think you will find that Mr Postles is on annual leave until the end of the month, but I will go and enquire who's standing in for him while he's away."

"Yes, do it." He clenched his teeth in frustration. "Now, what else have we got to attend to today?"

Lloyd pointed out the half-a-dozen folders on Hamilton's desk. "They're in chronological order, but from the third one down you'll see that you have a working lunch appointment with a delegation from the IFPO which you really cannot defer again."

"Who the hell is the IFPO? No stop. I can guess the first part. Irish... yes?"

"It stands for the Irish Fish Producers' Organisation, minister."

"Oh that lot again. Right. While I go through these, you scuttle off and get whoever was in charge of security yesterday up here."

Lloyd retreated to his own office which was little bigger than a den insulated from the outside world with wall-to-wall shelves of soundproof books and files. He knew exactly who he was going to call in Mr Postles' absence and briefly wondered if he wasn't putting too much on Sergeant Crawford's plate, but as it was he who was on duty at the time, he had little compunction.

Just over an hour later, Justin Crawford knocked on Lloyd's door and entered without waiting for a response. "Morning, Lloyd. What's up?" Everyone referred to Lloyd by his surname.

"Good morning, Justin." The two of them got on well.

"He's got a bit of a bee in his bonnet this morning, only this time it's more of a wasp, and it's coming your way. And to boot, he's not very happy about it."

"The usual?"

"More or less. It's about how yesterday's confidential meeting got leaked to the press and I think what really irks him is that it only took a few hours. Have you seen this morning's newspapers?"

"Not yet. Haven't had time. What do they say?"

"Have a look." Lloyd handed him a copy of *The Times*. "Third paragraph down says it's from a government source and as far as I know, apart from the four of you, only you and your sidekick Davey were with him last night." He waited for Justin to read the relevant passages, looked down at his desk phone and saw that a light had gone out on it. "He's just got off the phone, so you'd better go in. Come on."

Lloyd opened the door, announced Justin, and stood to one side to let him pass before returning to his own desk.

Hamilton surveyed Justin, as a cat might watch a mouse before pouncing, and was about to lambast him when another thought came into his mind. If he did find something worthwhile, he would want Justin's cooperation and rather than have to wring it out of him. He could make him stand in front of his desk like a naughty schoolboy and tell him how worthless he was for letting this kind of information slip, or take the other approach of getting him on his side. Unusually for him, he chose the latter.

"Crawford, isn't it? Do sit down, please." He pointed to one of two comfortable chairs off to one side and waited until Justin was looking directly at him. "You're more of an expert at this sort of thing, so tell me how we're going to stop these leaks. I'm particularly concerned about what I said in confidence last night, and as you were there with your machine, I hope you can shed some light on the matter. I take it you've seen today's *Times*?"

"Only the front page, and before you ask, no I haven't had a chance to go through last might's recording." It was extremely rare that anyone ever had to listen to a recording and when they did, it seldom revealed anything relevant.

Hamilton was impressed that Justin was ahead of the game. "Well, when you get the chance, just make sure it wasn't me eh? Now, these other characters with me last night, apart from Andrew from *The Times*, there's only David Walters,

Cornelius Ransome and Conor Coe who were present." He was looking down the list he had scribbled on a scrap of paper. "I don't trust any of the buggers which is why I made sure I was circumspect, but someone's got hold of the wrong end of the stick and told the press the complete opposite." He let Justin briefly mull on that. "And in order to get into the papers by this morning means that someone must have been very quick off the mark. "How do you suppose that came about?"

"I'm not sure minister, but if what you say is true, perhaps it came from another source."

"I am the only source and you don't get things done in this world by telling all and sundry what you're about to do in advance... it'd get scuppered before it left the room." Hamilton was itching to thump the table with his fist, but kept his temper – just. "And talking of which, the only times I've mentioned our real proposals have been in this room."

"Has the PM been advised?"

"Of course he's been advised..." Hamilton stopped and widened his eyes. "Oh bollocks... no... he wouldn't... unless... what about his lackey?"

The two men looked at each other, not daring to ask or answer the obvious questions.

Hamilton broke the silence, talking to himself as much as Justin. "Where do we go from here?"

"Well the usual course is to inaugurate an investigation."

"Don't be absurd. Any investigation would be carried out by in-house intelligence and they report directly to the PM, and if there is a rat they'd tell him one thing and me another. No, we can't use them."

"How about an independent enquiry by an outside firm? That's been done before."

Hamilton's eyes narrowed. "That's against the rules, and anyway, word is bound to get out somewhere along the line. It always does. No. This requires tact. I can't be found to have started an enquiry all by myself and have people running around asking questions without further questions coming back at me. 'Who started this?' 'Why are you asking?' etc. etc. Not only will the finger be pointed at me, but whoever's responsible for this leak will know I'm after them."

"With respect minister, they already know you're after them."

"And why would they know that?" Hamilton frowned.

"Simply that you'd be bound to know there was a leak after today's headlines, and that you're bound to wonder where they got their information from."

"Ummm. You're right... so, whatever we do, it must be circumspect. They'll be looking out for us. Any suggestions?"

"This sounds to me more like detective work... picking through half-truths and rumours."

"Can you do it?"

"Nooooo... I'm no detective. I wouldn't know where to start."

"Do you know any detectives... ones you can trust, I mean? After all, you are a policeman working out of a county headquarters and you must come across them from time to time."

"Oh certainly, there's plenty of detectives, but they're mostly local chaps. You know, have their own snouts and guard their manors jealously and ergo a measured amount of corruption, so it follows that trust is a bit on the short side."

"Well something's got to be done." Hamilton narrowed his eyes as a thought struck him. "I suppose it's useless asking if it's you?"

Justin wondered why Hamilton hadn't considered this before. "Totally useless and for two reasons."

The two of them squared up to each other with unblinking eyes across the desk.

"Go on."

"In the first place I'm not always the one on duty when the leaks occur and on previous occasions those leaks have usually been sanctioned either by you or the PM's office. In the second place, I think you'll find that the press had already gone to print by the time last night's meeting was over; that was well past midnight."

The way that Justin presented the facts was music to Hamilton's ears. Here at last was a man he might be able to trust, particularly as he had precious few around him that he could. He opened his top right-hand drawer and placed a worn leather-bound book briefly on his desk before picking it up again. He'd used this ploy before and found that it had worked. He stood up and walked round to stand directly in front of Justin, offering it between them. "This is a copy of a Presbyterian bible handed down to me; it's been in our family for generations and is a faithful companion." He paused to let the gravity of the situation sink in. "There's either a traitor in my office or you'll swear on the Bible that it's not you." He was doing what he did best; cornering people so that they had no way out.

To Justin, the inference was clear. If he didn't swear, then he'd be out of his job before he'd even left the chair he was sitting in. If he did, he was committing himself to servitude of someone who he was not particular fond of. He consciously didn't flinch, nor fidget, but locked his eyes on Hamilton's. As intended, he felt cornered.

He didn't have to stretch his arm out far to lay his hand

on the bible. "You have my word."

Hamilton kept the book and his eyes steady for a moment before turning to place it back in his top drawer. He sat down again. "Right then. You find us a trusty detective and bring him to me, but not here. You pick a suitable location away from the prying eyes of the press. If he does find our traitor, not only will I make it worth his while, but I expect there'll be a gong in it for him as well. You can work alongside him but only you report to me because it would raise some eyebrows if I was seen meeting with a stranger to this Palace on a regular basis. As Mr Postles seems to have eavesdroppers everywhere, even on our private phones and computers, you'll be the liaison chap. OK?"

It made sense to Justin. "Just two questions at this point. We'll need a decent slush fund if you don't want this traced."

"How much?"

"As we're talking about the higher elements of government, it'll need to be decent. Say fifty grand to start with."

"That much, eh?"

"At least. These people are probably employed by those in high office and won't want to reveal anything unless it's worth their while. Very worthwhile. On second thoughts, make that a hundred grand."

Hamilton frowned. "I'll have to conceal that amount of cash."

"From what I've gathered, your family's fairly wealthy. Say you've bought a boat in Spain, vintage wine from South Africa or the like. Just so long as you can justify it when it comes to the crunch. I'll get hold of a briefcase similar to yours."

Hamilton considered Justin's comments and smiled; it was the first time he had seen him do so. "Just make certain that we can keep tabs on that money. We might be able to put the recipient at... shall we say... a disadvantage. A bit of leverage applied in the right place at the right time goes a long way. Second question?"

"I presume you won't want Lloyd in on this, so I'll have to find a way to bypass him. I'll catch up with you when I'm on your normal security detail, but don't be surprised if you feel someone brush up against you out of the blue. It might be me passing a message."

"You presume correctly... but please don't pick my wallet when I'm not looking. I know how adept you chaps are at that sort of thing. Oh, and er... I'm off to the English National Opera House tomorrow night. I'll arrange an extra ticket."

Justin stood up to go out via Lloyd's office and wondered momentarily if he ought to offer Hamilton his hand to shake, just like conspirators; but at the last second didn't. He was about to turn the door handle, when Hamilton added in a soft voice. "Considering the bollocking I've just given you, you'd better look a little crestfallen as you pass through Lloyd's office. We wouldn't want him getting the wrong idea, would we?"

Justin shook his head in acknowledgement and turned the handle, mentally preparing himself for questioning by a curious Lloyd.

Justin sat at the steering wheel in his car staring at a blank concrete wall in the underground car park only three minutes' walk away and wondered how he had got himself entangled with Hamilton. Joining the diplomatic service when he did as one of many minions ought not to have been this complicated, but now he was in the midst of a conspiracy, and he didn't like it one little bit. He'd been perfectly happy doing what he had been doing while earning a reasonable salary along with it, and he shook his head in disbelief that somehow he had been coerced into spearheading a witch hunt. He really wasn't concentrating on the drive back to Maidenhead, but at some point or other along the M4 motorway, he ceased thinking about what had just happened and bent his mind to the future. He mentally prioritised what he needed to do, realising his first hurdle was to find an honest detective. The obvious answer came as such a surprise that he nearly missed his turn-off, and he wondered if he dared involve Patricia, but he could think of nobody else; well, perhaps detective sergeant Williams, but he was a bit too old school and probably wouldn't have the necessary computer skills that would be called for.

The risks were clear. Involving Patricia meant jeopardising their relationship which had by now developed into something well past casual over the past year. They had even talked about moving in with each other and only a few days earlier, he had made up his mind to propose to her the next time they had a long weekend together. The old adage of not mixing business with pleasure crossed his mind, but then again, the two of them working together would more likely produce results. On the other hand, if everything went wrong, they might both be out of a job, even separated. He called her on his mobile and said he'd meet her at her place after work that evening.

She opened her door with that lovely smile. He didn't say a word as he squeezed past her, went to the kitchen, poured out a glass of her favourite wine for her, took her by the elbow and set her down at her end of the sofa next to her knitting; he sat facing her at the opposite end. Her smile had been replaced by a natural look of concern, but even so it took nearly a full minute before he spoke. He had had precious little time to imagine all sorts of consequences and in the end gave up trying to envisage any of them. He would put it to her as an equal, not a lover.

By the time he had finished, her glass was half empty. She hadn't interrupted him but had listened as though hearing a confession, all the while exercising her analytical mind. "I'm not sure it's me you ought to be asking. Trying to figure... shall we say... the conventions that go with ministerial operations will take a while, because that's where I'd need to start. Who he meets, talks to, likes, dislikes and that's before I delve into motives..."

"You would have one advantage and starting point."

She raised an eyebrow without having to ask what it was.

"The Irish. And I believe you already know some of the locals who regularly come and go from here to the West End."

She was about to ask how he knew that, but it took her the briefest moment to remember that that was part of his job. "Shit. This is big, isn't it?"

Justin nodded. "I think I'll join you in a drink now."

It took them the best part of three hours thrashing out theories and methodology, but it wasn't until they had made love and were lying in bed that she said she'd do it.

As an afterthought, Justin added, "Just make sure you find something on Hamilton himself, because he's a sly bugger and will use you until he thinks you're useless and then he'll spit you out and leave you to shrivel up under the spotlights of the press."

"You said he promised a gong, but I've already got one of those."

"That won't protect you. You'll have to find something else... and it's usually the people higher up the food chain who can help you the most. Who put you up for you OBE?"

"That was Kerry Terringford and she's since been

promoted to the top job of assistant commissioner. You're right, I'll keep that up my sleeve. In fact just the other day I received a reminder that all medal-holders are due to attend a photoshoot soon, so that'll give me an excuse to get in touch with her again."

"When was the last time you visited the opera?"

Chapter 7

Treachery

Hamilton was over the moon as he looked up at it out of the side window of his limousine taking him back to his London apartment. It reminded him of the thoughts those generals must have had back in the Napoleonic days after a victorious day's battle, followed by an evening of self-indulgence. He patted the knee of the woman sitting next to him.

His business in the parliamentary chamber could not have gone better and his speech had received approval from nearly all sides of the House; he'd even received a pat on the back from one of the opposition on his way back through the lobby. With time to spare around midday, he phoned one of the up-and-coming lobbyists who had been trying to obtain a position on his staff. He had a permanent suite booked in the Marriott hotel directly across the river and had thoroughly enjoyed her company in bed, leaving her with deluded aspirations. Returning to his office, good news followed good news and he surprised Lloyd by wishing him a 'good evening' as he swept through the door without closing it. The rear door of the waiting car was opened for him by his chauffeur as he approached, but Justin intercepted him a few feet from it.

"Minister." Justin kept it formal under the scrutiny of others as he had done so many times before. "When we arrive at the opera house, just wait until I give the all-clear before getting out." Hardly audible he added, "You'll be meeting your detective there."

He knew that his security detail, one of whom was Justin on this occasion, would be following in the car behind as his Daimler swept along Whitehall towards Trafalgar Square and he wondered what sort of man Justin had found for him. He wasn't particularly interested in the opera but the lady from the EEC fisheries ministry had insisted on being taken to the English National Opera House where 'The Barber of Seville' was being performed. He was greatly looking forward to what he called 'afters' and would invite her back to his suite at the Marriot for canapés. Two conquests in one day was a bit of a rarity for him, but he still felt that his manhood was quite up to the task and he relished the challenge. He knew she wasn't the world's greatest beauty, but she had a wonderful bust and knew how to flaunt it. He hoped she would be wearing some sort of eye-catching plunge dress to help take his mind off what might well turn out to be an average performance on stage. Then he remembered... she liked to be called Katka.

The curtain to the second-floor box was pulled back for him by the second security man as he approached. "Two ladies for you tonight, minister." He kept a deadpan expression.

He paused. "Two?"

"Yes sir."

He briefly paused but continued and saw that indeed there were two beautiful women seated each side of the vacant cushioned chair, clearly reserved for him. They both turned as he entered the box overlooking the stage. He instantly recognised Katka on the right and was delighted to see that her low-cut dress was all he could have desired, took her raised hand, and lightly kissed her on it. "My dear, how delightful to be adorned by your presence again, but I am

afraid your attractive companion has me at a disadvantage."
Hamilton certainly knew how to impress when the need arose.
The prospect of having to entertain two women on the same
night... well... that would almost be a first. "I take it you two
ladies are acquainted with each other?"

Patricia had taken the time to be well dressed for the
occasion, but without being overly noticeable, and had been
forewarned by Justin as to his guile. She was not exactly up
on the etiquette of either meeting a minister of the Crown for
the first time, nor conversant with opera, although she had
been to one before, in the stalls. "Minister. Please allow me
to introduce myself as Patricia Eyethorne. Mr Crawford felt
it might be better if someone of the opposite sex accompany
you in the box tonight. He felt that this evening, a little extra
security would not go amiss and that I could advise you on
certain matters... that is, if you have the time."

She was as guarded as she could be, choosing her words
with the care they deserved in the presence of another.

Hamilton immediately realised that it was Justin who
had foisted this woman on him and at first he had trouble
pigeonholing her. A woman, not a man. But what a beauty.
Especially in comparison to Katka's mediocre looks. Right
now, whether or not she was up to the task of finding his
traitor almost came second to her attractiveness. As he took
his seat, the curtain behind them was drawn closed and he
realised he faced a quandary. He really needed to talk to both
women separately; one from a diplomatic aspect and 'afters',
the other without raising any suspicions. He decided he might
be able to dispense with the security business during the
interval, so concentrated on the usual small talk with Katka.
Just as the overture was about to begin, he turned to Patricia
and told her that Katka would be absent during the interval.

The heavy stage curtains met in the middle indicating that the fifteen-minute interval was available for those wanting refreshments or to visit the washrooms. "Katka my dear, much as I adore your company, can you give me a few minutes alone with my other guest?"

"Of course, Maurice." She flashed a smile at him and left clutching her small matching handbag.

Waiting for her to disappear through the curtains, he turned to Patricia. "So, you're my detective are you? Somehow you look familiar to me, or is it that you have the face that fits all seasons?"

She turned square on to him and wasn't going to waste valuable time bandying trivialities. "Probably the latter but I have been in the papers. I understand you want me to dig out a mole in your office without anyone else finding out, and in particular connected to your latest initiative. I'm going to have to ask you some very direct questions, and unless you give me your fullest answers, I won't be able to help. I'll also need access to files and pertinent correspondence, and to do that I'll need your authority as, say, a researcher. I'll need to interview those close to you and some that appear unconnected. Initially I'll concentrate on whatever is current." She leaned down to her handbag and handed him a sealed envelope. "Here's a list of items and documents I'll need immediately, and that includes you being able to clear things with my super at Maidenhead, because otherwise he'll be wondering why I'm not at my desk."

"Crawford wasn't wrong when he said you were efficient. You get straight to the point. I have to emphasise that the Commons security jealously guard their own, and sooner or later, they're going to ask questions, so just be ready for them. Mr Postles can be a very spikey character." Hamilton had opened the envelope and was perusing the one-page list and was taken aback with the last item. He laughed. "This'll really put Lloyd's nose out of joint."

"Lloyds?"

"Lloyd is my assistant in the adjacent room and he's going to suspect all sorts." He folded the piece of paper, put it back in the envelope and placed it in his inside jacket pocket. "Nobody normally gets to see me except through him."

She mused over his last comment for a moment. "Then we're going to have to come up with a secondary means of meeting regularly other than the occasional visit to the opera or in your office, which we have to assume is bugged."

He blinked at her suggestion of bugging. "You're right. I have a suite at the Marriott; number 314." Even as he said it, his thoughts turned to how he might be able to bed the lovely creature in front of him, who now sat like she was posing. He began to see her in a different light, literally, as the background illumination haloed her angelic visage, and he wondered how long it would take before she surrendered. "I assume you can start tomorrow morning?"

"Better make it first thing Monday. I've a few items that can't wait and need to be cleared up over the weekend. Anyway, a Monday morning is a natural time for a new researcher to start isn't it, so if you don't mind?" She stood up.

"You're not staying for the second half?" For the first time he saw her full shapely figure and would have licked his lips if it hadn't given away his desires.

"I've also some groundwork to do before the trail goes cold. Good night, minister. Oh, I presume you do want me to refer to you as minister?"

"Yes. That would be best, for the time being." He lustily watched her depart.

Being the first time in ages travelling to and from London, it had taken her longer than expected to commute back to Maidenhead via the Circle Line underground and Paddington station, but with a sense of relief, she let herself in through her front door. She half expected to find Justin sat on her sofa, but then she remembered that whenever he could, he dedicated Monday evenings to cricket practice; he wouldn't be back until after nine. She opened her laptop after plugging it in for a recharge, sat at her end of the sofa and forlornly looked at her knitting on the side table, wondering when she'd next get the chance to do the next bit. She'd spent the entire day in Hamilton's office logging and transferring data and would now have the chance to start making some sense of it all.

It was nearer ten when a sweaty Justin gently woke her by nudging her knee, first making sure that her laptop wasn't going to fall to the floor. "Hello square-eyes."

It hadn't been long since she had dozed off and seeing Justin's figure standing over her invoked instant happiness, but she took in his comment anyway and rubbed her eyes. "Do I really look that bad?"

He didn't comment but walked away into the kitchen and returned a minute later with a half-glass of wine which he handed to her.

"Not too bad then if it's only half a glass?"

He waited until she was about to take the first sip. "Well, how was it in Hamilton's hallowed chamber of horrors and did you manage to upset Lloyd?"

She reacted by truncating her sip. "Upset's hardly the adjective I would use to describe his reaction when I first walked in the door... more like apoplectic." She went on to describe how he had firstly tried to bar her from Hamilton's office and then started laying down rules and it was only when she called Hamilton on her mobile and handed it to him that he grudgingly gave way, all the while still telling her what she was and wasn't allowed to do. Hamilton was away and she had had a blazing row with Lloyd over whether or not the communicating door could be closed. Despite her getting her own way, he managed to find constant reasons to come and go, all the while trying to look over her shoulder at what she was doing. Around midday, Lloyd had called in his superior, Hamilton's permanent private secretary, to try to gain some sort of authority back, but that too had failed. "I don't know if he's more frightened of Hamilton or what I might find out about him, but what I've gleaned so far is that everything Hamilton says or does goes through him."

"So he's got access to everything sensitive then."

She nodded with the glass at her lips. "I naturally started alphabetically, and you should have seen the look on his face when I asked for the files on the Abortion Initiative. His entire demeanour reeked of conspiracy and I caught him trying to smuggle some papers from Hamilton's desk back into his office and we had another stand-up row. At this early stage, I don't know if he's being genuinely protective of Hamilton or if he's trying to hide something, but I've got a hunch it's the latter. I suspect that by tomorrow, anything relevant will have been removed which is why I'd photoed as much as I could today. And by the way... my square eyes match yours... have you seen yourself in the mirror?" she giggled. "Did you have a mudslinging contest?"

Justin frowned in jest. "No... I bloody fell over in the only muddy patch for miles around. I'm sure Soapy hit the ball in that direction on purpose. I'm off for a quick shower."

When he returned with just a towel round his middle, Patricia had her head resting on the back of the sofa with her eyes closed, but he interrupted her train of thought anyway. "Getting anywhere?"

"Not yet, but Hamilton's back tomorrow and once I've questioned him about a few things... oh, I don't know. It's a bit early yet."

Justin took the opportunity. "How about we go away next weekend, not this one but the one after? I've a friend who's got a cottage not far from The Mumbles in South Wales right on the coast and he said I could use it anytime when he's not there. He's in Spain at the moment so I know it's free." He could see her thinking. "Come on. By then you'll need a break."

"I thought you were committed to cricket in the season?"

"That one's been cancelled, I found out tonight, and anyway, that's just about the only free weekend I've got off this summer." He sat down close on the sofa, and distracted her by locking her eyes while he sneaked his hand onto her knee and squeezed gently.

"OK... OK. You've made your point. I'll come." She laughed and moved her knee before her reflexes had no other option. "Now bugger off while I finish tying up some loose ends."

***

Patricia had carried out her virtual audit of Hamilton's affairs over the next few days. She had been working at her small desk in Hamilton's office since before six in the morning one day the following week when in Hamilton's burst in. "Lloyd." He ignored her.

There was no need for the coat removal ceremony as the weather was being unusually kind for a change, and he sat down at the same time as Lloyd appeared with the usual armful of folders. "Good morning, minister."

"You've been a naughty boy." He waited to make Lloyd uncomfortable. "I told you to provide Miss Eyethorne here with every assistance, but as we now know you didn't and I gather you still aren't. Why not?"

"Minister..."

Lloyd came out with a plethora of excuses which Hamilton truncated. "In future you do what I say and not what you think is best for me. OK? Now, what's on today other than the environmentalists that I already know about?"

Once Lloyd had finished and retreated back to his own office, Hamilton turned to Patricia. "And how are you getting on today, my dear?" His friendly tone reflected his increasing desire to get as close as possible to her. It was becoming an obsession and he realised he would have to do something about it soon.

She gave him a summary of what she had been doing then bought her laptop over to his desk so that he could see the screen; she stood bent over to one side. Despite her explanation, Hamilton was immediately distracted by the low cut of her blouse that hung down to reveal her lacy bra and cleavage. He found that he couldn't concentrate while she was in that position and shifted in his seat a little to get a better view. He only vaguely picked up on what she was saying while the rest of his mind tried not to drag his thoughts away from the gorgeous body so close to him. He realised she had stopped speaking.

"Can you say that last bit again?"

She pointed to the far right of the screen, accidentally

displaying a little more of her pendulous bosom. It wasn't that she dressed nearly provocatively on purpose, but Hamilton was now totally incapable of thinking about anything else other than lust. He nodded his head in agreement backing it up with an "ummm" and an "I see".

The spell was broken by the buzzing of his intercom on his desk; it was Lloyd. "Mr Postles is here to see you, minister. Shall I send him in?"

He dragged himself back to reality. "Yes." He addressed Patricia. "You'd better make yourself scarce. Go and find a coffee or something and act like a junior." Even after all these years, he couldn't help using the old school expression.

Patricia folded up her laptop and made for the door to the corridor just as Mr Postles entered the room via the communicating door; their eyes briefly met.

Not many people wear a waistcoat these days, but Mr Postles proudly wore one. He wasn't yet a portly gentleman but somehow it gave him an air of authority; which is exactly what he had and wanted to portray. He seldom ventured near the corridors of power, preferring to carry out his exacting occupation as head of security from his own chamber in the Palace of Westminster; or as the general public called it, the Houses of Parliament.

Few in the Palace knew anything about Mr Postles' private life; that he was married with a loving wife and three grown-up children, only one of which was still living at home, nor that he had three sisters and an extended family. However, most knew of his reputation as a stickler for behaviour and old-fashioned correctness; woe betide anyone who crossed the line. In his own mind, standards were there to be kept, and on the odd occasion when he had had to intercede, he would quite rightly belittle the offender, whether they were a cabinet minister or a lowly backbencher. He was one of those whose bark was as vicious as his bite. The mere rumour that Mr Postles was on the warpath would have MPs scurrying to display their innocence in the opposite direction. He wasn't a vindictive man; he just wanted to do his very best to uphold parliamentary standards, which was why he needed to visit Maurice Hamilton.

"Good morning, minister. I hope you can spare me a few minutes of your valuable time. May I sit down?" It was his way of saying that it was his own time that was valuable and that he had as long as it would take to say what he was going to say, regardless.

He crossed his legs at the ankle and arched his fingers as his elbows rested on the arms of the leather chair. "Just make sure your intercom is off, please, as we don't want the whole world to know about our conversation." He watched Hamilton's eyes flick towards his desk.

"How can I help you today, Mr Postles?"

"It's about your new research assistant. I've received a notification from both your secretaries, Lloyd and Mr Cummings, that you have recently engaged her services. I'm here to tell you that she is not a researcher, and may be here in another guise. At your initial request we issued her with a pass after carrying out our usual security checks and found, shall we say, some anomalies."

"Go on," feigned Hamilton. He suspected what was coming and had half prepared himself.

"My department performs its duties thoroughly by making sure that those who are there to protect ministers of the Crown, such as yourself, from assassination attempts and the like, are themselves sound. We do our utmost to ensure that foreign powers, as well as home-grown disgruntled maniacs are not trying to infiltrate our system of government and that takes time-consuming and painstaking investigation. What you may not be aware of is that we have to delve into those people's private lives, often very deeply." Mr Postles held up his hand towards Hamilton. "Don't worry minister, it's not you I'm referring to... I already know enough about you not to have any worries on that front." Mr Postles was an excellent liar; he knew all about Hamilton's extra-marital affairs. "What does concern me is why you have chosen to engage the services of one Detective Inspector Patricia Eyethorne OBE... you do know she's a detective inspector, don't you?"

"Of course... that's why she's here. Because she's a detective."

"Can I ask what she is trying to detect for you, minister? We have our own specialised in-house detectives who are most capable and have already been screened, so you have to forgive my curiosity in wondering why you have bought in an outsider."

"As usual Mr Postles, you have hit the nail on the head. It's exactly because she's an outsider with fresh ideas that she is more likely to be able to obtain a result."

"And what result are you expecting?"

Hamilton once again feigned his answer. "I've got her looking into the ins and outs of the Abortion Initiative and to come up with an alternative strategy, because at the moment, we're deadlocked."

"Surely this ought to be a task for the policymakers, not a detective?" Mr Postles kept a straight face but from the tone of his voice, he was sneering.

"I'm afraid you're wrong there. We've been at this for months now, years even if you consider the papal decrees from the introduction of the pill way back in the seventies, and we're still not much further down the line. No. What this needs is someone totally unconnected with either the constraints of politics or the Catholic church, to trawl through reams of papal edicts and the like, and to find a way through. A loophole if you like."

It was very rare that Mr Postles was caught wrong-footed but what Hamilton had just said did exactly that. He considered this for a moment, and on balance had to concede that Hamilton had a point. With Eire being predominantly Catholic and a mix of both Protestants and Catholics in Northern Ireland, apart from other political issues, the one of abortion was very sensitive and a constant cause of unrest. It was one of the lynchpins that dissidents could pick up on and validate their more violent actions in pursuit of a united Ireland. Hamilton might have had the right idea in obtaining the services of a complete outsider, but Mr Postles wasn't going to let him off the hook quite that easily.

"Your actions in search of a solution are commendable, but parliamentary procedures dictate that any appointments are first cleared by my department. If you had come to me with your choice of personnel, it would have spared some embarrassment." He leaned forward to emphasis his next point. "I gather she's been asking some rather awkward questions of others in your name, and quite rightly, those complainants have been putting me on the spot. Am I to say that we've sanctioned her position or that she's merely acting on your behalf? You see my predicament, don't you? It sets an example for others and before we know it, we'll have all and sundry running around." He hardened the tone of his voice, his bark. "You've put the entire security department at odds with every other department and not just here. There's Whitehall to consider, even No10, and when the PM's office finds out, I'm afraid it'll be you who has to be partially responsible for the next terror attack." He decided it was time to twist the knife. "You see, people are at their weakest when it comes to sex, and we all know how appealing the likes of Miss Eyethorne are, don't we?" He was letting Hamilton know that he knew about his sexual exploits and inferring that there was some connection with Patricia Eyethorne.

Hamilton was starting to quail and tried to deflect the wrath of Mr Postles. "You said you found some anomalies. I thought she was regarded as a bit of a paragon?"

"She is indeed, but nobody's perfect. Why did you choose her?"

"Through one of your security chaps." Hamilton had no qualms about naming Justin Crawford, but hoped that by not revealing how he had come by her might keep the waters muddied enough.

"Oh, you mean Mr Crawford."

By not being completely open, Hamilton realised that he had just been spotlighted. It was an easy trap that he had fallen into, and he realised that Mr Postles now knew that he was not being completely open.

"That's right. Mr Crawford. Why, is there a problem?"

"There might be." He waited for any sort of reaction but none was forthcoming. "You do know that she's the darling of the Police Federation and is instantly recognisable by the press? Is that why you hired her? To raise your own profile? Or is there another reason that I don't know about?"

"All I did was mention to Crawford if he knew of anybody who might be able to help... I mean, I wasn't expecting a detective of her standing, but he said she was available."

Mr Postles eyed him with suspicion, knowing that he was

hiding something, but he couldn't put his finger on it; not yet anyway. He suspected Hamilton's story and probed further. "That's a bit of an odd thing to do... asking one of the lackeys if they might know of someone of sufficient intellect to carry out a delicate task? An academic might have been a better choice, wouldn't you say?"

"I needed someone with an enquiring mind... someone who wouldn't be afraid of asking awkward questions, and who better to ask those questions than someone who is used to asking them?" It was a bit of a weak story, but Hamilton was feeling cornered and had to somehow justify his decision. He then remembered that Mr Postles had raised an issue and jumped at the chance of terminating the line of query. "You were saying something about an anomaly."

"Ummmm. You won't know about this, but Crawford and Eyethorne look like becoming a permanent item."

He blinked in genuine surprise. "An item?"

"Yes... They've been living together for a while now and we've come to the conclusion that they intend to stay that way."

At first, Hamilton didn't understand the significance, but then he thought back to when he had asked Crawford if he had known any detectives and been given a rather non-committal answer. Crawford had lied to him. Eyethorne had lied to him when he had asked her how well she knew Crawford. They had his untraceable hundred-thousand pounds and were pretending to track down a spy, when all along it was them. Crawford was in the ideal position to be privy to his confidential conversations and had obviously made full use of the recorded conversations. What a fool he had been. It was sheer betrayal and in his eyes, one of the cardinal sins that deserved full retribution. He could see how they would work together. He would pass on confidential information to any one of his contacts and get handsomely paid in cash, and then let Eyethorne know what was happening so that she didn't go anywhere near revealing their skullduggery. He almost admired their affrontery. He would have his vengeance, but right now he needed to mollify the man sitting in front of him, who he now considered to be on his side.

Mr Postles could almost see the cogs going round, but what he didn't know was that they were going in a different direction to what he thought. "If I were you, I'd reappraise Miss Eyethorne's appointment."

"You mean sack her?"

"Certainly. And before she puts any more noses out of joint. See what she's produced so far and tell her that you now have enough to be getting on with. Return her to Maidenhead where, by all accounts, she was performing a sterling service. In other words, give her a pat on the back, because I'm sure the public don't want to see a decorated rising star fall from grace so young." He leaned back in his chair and watched Hamilton frown. "I'll also need your assurance that if you find you have the need for another research assistant in the future, that you'll come to me first."

Hamilton was frantically thinking how he was going to get his money back and how to get his revenge on the young couple. He resorted to his military training; one problem at a time and concentrated on the former. He would make them pay at his leisure. Looking at Mr Postles gave him an idea; he would need his help and changed the tone of his demeanour. "Yes, my sincerest apologies for any embarrassment I may have caused and of course you're right. An academic would be far more suitable and I'll consider carefully any suggestion you may have on that front. I really am very sorry, but give me a couple of days regarding Miss Eyethorne, will you?"

"Well, just so long as you do get rid of her, I won't need to call on you again, will I?" he lowered his hands to the arms of the chair in preparation to rise.

Hamilton stopped him. "Just before you go, you know you said you sometimes need to delve deeply into peoples' personal lives... well, I have an inkling that our young lovebirds may be up to something."

Mr Postles relaxed his arm muscles. He was intrigued. "Go on."

Hamilton tried to play the innocent party as carefully as he could, knowing that just one slip in front of this very astute man may give the game away. "It's probably nothing, but since you mentioned that they are living together, it's crossed my mind that they may be thinking of going it alone; setting up their own agency. It's just the odd whispered word here and there over the phone that I've caught, but I thought it might be something you may be interested in."

It was Mr Postles' turn to frown. "I find that hard to believe. Crawford's got an exemplary record and every three months we carry out in-depth revisions. In fact, if my memory serves me correctly, his was done only a fortnight or so ago. As for Miss Eyethorne, we don't really have much interest in the numerous detectives around the country, but because of her relationship with him, we carried out a level two check and she came out clean as a whistle. If they are colluding to go into business together, it's a very recent decision."

"Is it worth checking again?"

Mr Postles tapped one of his middle fingers on the arm; it was his way of helping himself to think. "Ummmm. Probably. I'll think about it."

"Just the other day I overheard Crawford saying something

about working from his home computer. Could he actually do that from his house?"

"In theory, yes. All he'd need is a phone line and a computer; and his own two feet of course... I'll look into it." He looked at his wristwatch and rose.

"You will? In that case can I ask that as the pair of them have been working so close to me that you make me privy to anything you might find?" He could see Mr Postles about to waver at his suggestion. "You may find something that could cause me embarrassment and ergo, reflect badly on the service."

Mr Postles looked down on Hamilton and saw worry in the man's face. He wasn't concerned with Hamilton's position, but if the Civil Service were to suffer because of his simple oversight, it could reflect badly on him, however minor. He had his own reputation to uphold. "Leave it to me. Good day, minister."

Hamilton closed his eyes in relief as the door closed, leaving him alone with his thoughts. He prayed that Mr Postles' investigations would reveal where his hundred grand had gone; and soon. With gritted teeth and rising blood pressure, he cursed himself for being so blind to the pair of them. The bastards had made a mockery of him and he would make them pay. Northern Ireland could wait.

Mr Postles was the epitome of efficiency. He was returning to his security centre but had hardly taken three paces from Hamilton's office before he was on his mobile phone arranging an investigation into Crawford and Eyethorne. He doubted that anything untoward would be found but by acting straight away, he could quickly satisfy himself that it was Hamilton's imagination that was awry and could put the issue behind him and move on to more important items.

The sun hadn't even reached its zenith when a British Telecom van parked up in the street several yards away from Justin's rented abode. One of the two operatives, both dressed in BT's overalls, alighted and set up a mobile barrier round a manhole in the pavement. The other, clipboard in hand, walked down the short path to Justin's neighbouring property, and knocked on the front door. A bleary eyed man dressed in boxer shorts and t-shirt opened the door. "Can I help you?"

"I'm from BT and carrying out a survey to install our new super-fast fibre optic for broadband in the area." He waved his bogus identity badge in front of the sleepy-looking individual. "Now, let's see." He pretended to look down a list on his clipboard. "You must be a Mr Crawford. Yes?"

"No, I'm Mr Norris. Mr Crawford's next door." He looked to his left.

"Oh, I'm sorry to trouble you... you're on my other list, but while I'm here, perhaps you'd like to know that we're planning to install fibre over the next few months and we are asking if you would take this up if it were available."

At the mention of super-fast and fibre, Mr Norris started to wake up after his night shift. "Of course we would, but at the right price."

"Oh, the installation is free, but it's the connection that costs, and that'll be in our brochure." He handed one over. "We're checking for current speeds in the road today. Do you know if Mr Crawford's in?"

Mr Norris looked up and down the street. "His car's not parked where it usually is so he's probably at work. Do you want me to take a brochure for him?"

"No that's all right, sir. Sorry to trouble you."

Mr Norris glanced at the departing man, then the

brochure, thought nothing more about the visit, closed his door and went back to bed.

The operative whistled as he walked down the adjacent path, fingering a picklock in his pouch as he approached Crawford's front door. He received a brief nod from his colleague who was pretending to busy himself. Their superior had told them that Crawford would be out, but to take the usual precautions. Once inside, he located the computer, switched it on and plugged in a lead from his disguised clipboard which doubled up as a hard drive. Within a few minutes, he and his colleague had packed up and were on their way back to London.

Hamilton was just walking away from one of the division lobbies after a late afternoon vote in the chamber and looking forward to his next paramour, when he was intercepted by a younger man who introduced himself as one of Mr Postles' aides.

"Mr Postles sends his apologies for not seeing you himself, but asked me to hand you this envelope." A buff A5-sized envelope passed between them. "He suggests you may find its contents useful leverage."

Half-squinting an eye at the smartly dressed man, he wondered what might be in it, and diplomatically asked. "Do you know what's in it?"

"No minister."

"Very good then. Be sure to thank Mr Postles for me." Even though he was itching to find out, he decided not to open it there and then, but wait until he had returned to his office.

"Lloyd. Get Mrs Reddison on the phone and tell her I'll meet her as arranged at nine o'clock." He closed the communicating door, sat down at his desk and retrieved his letter opener. At first he couldn't believe his eyes. Not just one but several colour photographs of a scantily dressed Miss Eyethorne in a series of seductive poses. He looked through them three times before reading Mr Postles' note clipped to the top one.

'*Thought this may come in handy for you in case she proves awkward. P*'

He looked over the photos again and stared at them in disbelief. He laid them out side by side and ogled her magnificent body, appreciating the way she was showing it off, and not caring that he was committing most of the seven deadly sins. He looked closely at one particular shot; just over Miss Eyethorne's shoulder was a wall-mounted photograph with Crawford in it and it struck him that these photos must have been on his computer. He started to guffaw and formulate plans on how he would use them. This was a godsend of all godsends. He turned over Mr Postles' note to see if there was any mention of unusual amounts of money, but the page was blank. He sat back in his chair and roared with laughter. "*Habeo eos*" With his head back he cried out loud. He remembered a Latin quote from one of the Caesars. "I have them... I have them... and by the balls," he added.

A concerned Lloyd burst in but stopped by the doorway. "Is everything alright, minister?" He hadn't heard such sounds ever coming from Hamilton's direction before.

"Alright... alright?... nothing could be more right. What are you looking at? Do you need to go to Specsavers or something?" He saw Lloyd craning his neck trying to see what was on his desk.

Lloyd averted his gaze and thought to himself, 'There's nothing wrong with my eyesight when I'm wearing glasses.' He hadn't had time to put them on. "Er, Mrs Reddison confirms nine o'clock this evening, minister."

"Very good, now close the door behind you." He returned to the photographs, leaning back and clasping his hands behind his head, smiling while he dreamed of more ways of exacting an excruciating revenge. Oh, but this was going to be the best yet. Something made him look at his watch and he reluctantly dragged himself away from his cerebral thoughts to attend to this evening's forthcoming pleasure. He opened a file and briefly scanned its contents as he would need to be pre-armed when he met Mrs Reddison. It dawned on him that he really wouldn't be that interested in the Anglo-Irish schools exchange programme that he knew she wanted to talk about. He was bound to be distracted, but he had to make the effort. All day, he had been looking forward to the afters in the Marriott and would half-promise her some sort of action in exchange for sexual favours.

He carefully put the photographs back in the envelope and placed them in his briefcase. He certainly didn't want Lloyd, or anyone else, finding them. He suspected Lloyd had a key to his desk drawers, but had kept his suspicions to himself.

***

"Looks like it might be Lloyd then," said Justin in between a mouthful of noodles from the Chinese takeaway that they were sharing.

"Just a few things to double check with the Registry Office and others in the morning, because it looks like someone changed his name when he was hardly out of his nappies." She played the fingers of her left hand over her laptop while hovering a forkful in mid-air with her right. "According to parliamentary records, his full name is Clarence McCorley

Lloyd, born in Liverpool 1970 to a Michael and Colleen McCorley, but it looks like someone's added the Lloyd part. I won't be able to ascertain that unless I can access the parish registers."

"Just because someone's changed a name doesn't make them a criminal."

"Of course it doesn't, but there are too many other irregularities and when you add them all up, the straw that broke the camel's back becomes a hay bale. I'll give you an example of one. I managed to grease the palm of a *Guardian* columnist... I might add that it took quite a lot of greasing." She looked at Justin with sincerity, indicating that Hamilton's slush fund now had a decent dent in it. "And when I mentioned that recent leak about the Power Sharing Assembly had come from within Hamilton's department, he opened up just enough to implicate Lloyd. Well, not just an implication and he wouldn't name any names because he didn't know any, but he said the photocopy had been handed to him by someone matching Lloyd's description. Another few grand and I'm sure when I show him a photograph, he'll confirm it's Lloyd."

Justin carried on eating.

"I've checked the timing and it matches. Then there are other dealings he's had with the same man which coincide, and that's not all. There are other similar unexplained instances and not just while Hamilton's been the Northern Ireland secretary; before him as well. The finger is definitely pointing at Lloyd, but this last abnormality to do with his name change is a bit of a mystery. Coupled with other trivialities, there's definitely something not quite right about Lloyd." She took a small mouthful. "I also managed to track down Lloyd's retired predecessor, but I didn't need to offer him anything because he hadn't a kind word to say about him. He's a staunch kind of fellow with old-fashioned British values; you know the sort, but get this. He told me that while he was the Northern Ireland assistant, Lloyd's job now, he was constantly being offered money or luxury holidays and the like to divulge privileged information. He said he'd warned Lloyd about the problem when he handed over the reins and do you know what Lloyd said to him?"

"I can guess, but go on."

"Something along the lines of it being the best gravy train in the British Isles where one feathers one's own pocket as much as one can. Can you believe it?"

"Doesn't surprise me, but by and large we're not a corrupt nation... not when you compare us to some of the African states, but I suppose just about everybody's got their price."

Patricia stopped munching and looked earnestly at Justin. "Even us?"

Justin mirrored Patricia's actions and thought about it, considering that the bulk of Hamilton's fund was in their hands. "Suppose that wasn't a hundred grand he'd given us, but a million... more if you like. What then?" He resumed his forkwork.

"I can't see it making a difference. Just because the amount is greater doesn't make it more tempting, especially when you compare our relatively tiny amount to what those in government are handling every day."

"You're now going down the route of when is enough, enough? I believe it was the Duke of Wellington who came up with the phrase 'power corrupts but absolute power corrupts absolutely'. Don't we already have enough? You and me?"

"Are you testing me, Mr Crawford?" If she'd worn glasses she would have been looking over them after sliding them down her nose, but there was humour in her voice.

"Why not? It's not a hypothetical question." He kept a straight face.

"Ummmmm. This time it's a hundred, next time a million. Ohhhhhh I see where you're going with this." She sat up straight, discarding her laptop onto the floor. "This time it's Hamilton and while we give him a legitimate result, we tell him we've used up all of the hundred grand he gave us. Word will get round that it was us... well me actually who succeeded, and we approach another minister for our modest fee. The greater the leak, the greater the fee. Is that it?"

Justin was intrigued by her suggestions as he hadn't projected his thoughts down that route. "Go on."

"And once we've exposed a couple of culprits, we'll have established ourselves as reputable mole-hunters, can set up on our own and say goodbye to our nine-to-fives."

"Nine-to-five, that's a joke. I can't remember the last time I had such social hours... and by the way, that goes for you too."

"You know what I mean."

"I do, but the question still stands. Are we also corruptible? Once you've satisfied Hamilton's curiosity, do we hand back the balance or keep a little for ourselves? Out-of-pocket expenses and the like. Take your journey up to Liverpool tomorrow and consider how much reimbursement you need, and by how much do you round that figure up?"

"I don't see why it shouldn't be any different to how I submit my expenses at the moment, except I wouldn't have the police inspectorate all over me half the time."

Justin scraped the last of the sweet and sour sauce up with a prawn cracker. "So, we play a straight bat."

"We play a straight bat as you put it."

"I'm so glad we agree. Do you reckon you can tie it all

together before the weekend because I've booked us that cottage in South Wales?"

It was Patricia's turn to delay a response while she munched through a portion of shredded chilli beef. "Ought to... depends on how long I'm in Liverpool and then at the Government General Register Office just up the road in Southport. Probably best if I go up the day before, because otherwise I can't see myself getting back until past midnight. And that's if the bloody train guards aren't on strike again. Oh sod it... I'll drive."

"Just make sure you don't lock yourself out this time."

She balled up the paper bag the takeaway had come in, threw it at him and missed.

Justin's heart was singing. He'd have liked to have proposed to her somewhere exotic like the Maldives, but the dunes around The Mumbles would have to do.

Chapter 8

Swings and roundabouts

Not sulking but ruminating; that was the best way to describe Hamilton's mood, yet nobody but him could tell the real difference. Even his wife had cast a second quizzical look at him over the breakfast table but she knew better than to ask as she was just as likely to get the usual dismissive brush-off. It wasn't at all out of the norm that he had a lot on his mind, but she detected a change in his way he answered her questions about the day's business ahead. A slight inflection at the end of an answer instead of a gruff bark and the way he pondered a little longer than before. She wouldn't have said he was happy, yet there was a definite optimistic air about him.

Across the table, Hamilton surprised himself by beheading his first egg with rare accuracy while listening to both the BBC news on Radio 4 and his wife at the same time. He had formulated a plan that would enable him to retrieve his money by enlisting the unwitting help of Crawford. He would pit the two lovebirds against each other, ruining their little scheme, and hopefully the rest of their lives at the same time. Including how to bed the gorgeous Miss Eyethorne. Encompassing it into the overall plan had been a bit tricky, and there were still a few details to finalise, but what had started out as a bonus, now became an integral part of the scheme. He paused one of his marmite soldiers in mid-air as he pictured another piece of the jigsaw falling into place. Oh, but he was so looking forward to this one, probably his best scheme yet, and he could almost see her now, squirming – not just mentally, but physically also. She'd be his catch of the day.

He realised his wife had asked him a question and, as on previous occasions when he had been miles away in thought, he had had to ask her to repeat herself. Once again he dragged himself away in order to provide her with a satisfactory answer. He quite liked his wife and was most grateful for her diligence in maintaining the image as the mother of a utopian English family; not just for the sake of his career, but also for her kudos and position in society. Their two younger sons were well on their way to becoming adults, boarding at Harrow school and just beginning to make names for themselves. And to the outside world, they enjoyed a healthy family lifestyle. He suspected his wife knew about his extra-marital affairs, but had so far not mentioned or confronted him about them. After all, it would only end in divorce and bring her privileged position to an early end. On the odd occasion when he had bothered to think about it, he too wondered if she had indulged herself with the opposite sex, but quickly dismissed whatever the outcome might have been for the simple reason that the answer was irrelevant to him. They both enjoyed an easy relationship with each other on the basic principle of not upsetting the apple cart. What they didn't know about each other's lives wouldn't hurt them, but they were certainly wary of the frequent questions raised by the media, and in particular, the left-wing press.

The cogs continued to turn in Hamilton's head as he savoured the last of his breakfast; and he once again treated the entire operation as a military manoeuvre by always keeping the objective at the foremost of each step while calculating the odds on alternatives. He just happened to catch the time with a passing middle-distance glimpse of the kitchen clock and wrenched himself away from the future and back to the present. Wiping the crumbs away from his mouth with his napkin, he resolved to affect the first part of his plan the following morning, regardless of whether or not Miss Eyethorne had uncovered any suspects. It was too late today to do so, and anyway, he still had a couple of minor loose ends to tie up and a phone call to make. His wife noticed the spring in his step as he headed for the door and wondered what had happened to make him happy as he gave her a quick peck on her cheek on the way out.

***

Two hundred miles away not too far north of Liverpool, Patricia Eyethorne replaced the heavy register back on the metal shelf, and paused for a moment before heading back to the terminal linked to the central computer. She just needed to cross-reference one more item to satisfy herself that her conclusions were correct. It would provide her and Hamilton with almost irrefutable proof. She had been rather surprised that Mr Postles' department hadn't picked up the basic anomaly, but then again, it had been before Mr Postles had taken charge and his predecessor had obviously not had as firm a grip; or maybe it had just been one of those oversights in an under-strength department. At the back of her mind, she wondered if the registrar himself had been complicit, but that investigation could wait for another day.

Less than two hours later, having completed her investigations earlier than expected, she too had a spring in her step as she made her way back to her car.

It promised to be another hot airless day in London and Patricia had dressed accordingly by putting on a semi-see-through pink blouse and lightweight grey knee-length skirt. Picking up her briefcase and donning a navy blue jacket, she had looked at herself in the mirror on the way out, satisfying herself that it concealed her bra straps. She had hoped that by removing her jacket and breathing in to stretch the thin fabric she would distract the person she was meeting just enough. She now sat at a high table sipping orange juice in a café, just off the Strand, waiting for him. He looked his dapper self as he walked through the door, and she didn't need to beckon him over as they made eye contact straight away, but he looked around automatically before joining her on the stool opposite.

"I ordered you some Perrier." She nodded towards an ice-cold glass on the table.

"Thanks." He immediately took a sip. "But I don't know why you asked to meet because I've nothing more to add."

"Oh I think you have. Just one more little detail. That is unless there's more you haven't told me about." She picked out a small envelope from her jacket pocket before removing it and draping it over the empty stool next to her. She watched his eyes briefly flick towards her cleavage as she straightened up, and smiled to herself knowing that her distraction was working. She extracted a photograph of Lloyd and slowly turned it round. "I need to know if this is the man you met." She could tell from his reaction that she was correct.

"No, that's not anyone I've seen before." With shifty eyes, he took a bigger sip from his glass.

She held his gaze for a moment. "Might there be some inducement I could offer you? Some grand gesture perhaps?" She emphasised the word 'grand'.

He gave a short nervous laugh, but then frowned. "Even

if I could confirm that it's the same man, it would need to be a decent gesture, and I think that might be too steep for your pocket."

"You don't know how deep my pockets are." She breathed in and caught him eyeing up her chest.

"If there were several gestures, I might be able to recall a name to the face."

"Gestures are symbolic and often come to nothing, but I think you'll find that what I have in my briefcase represents reality." She watched him fiddle with his glass, knowing that she had him hooked. She leaned forward, resting her bosom on the table. "Perhaps two gestures?"

His lips moved with indecision as he was having trouble concentrating on what exactly was on offer, but decided it might be worth a punt. He was well aware of whom she was but wanted her to instigate the offer, otherwise it might be himself who could be charged with bribery if this was a set-up. He phrased his words carefully. "You're being rather *ten*acious." He accentuated the 'ten' part, indicating that he expected ten-thousand pounds.

"On the contrary. That's only half useful." She hoped five thousand would be enough.

He looked around, averting his eyes from her provocative figure and giving himself time to think. "Have you seen *The Full Monty*... the film I mean?"

"Go on."

"It was rated fifteen to protect the children, when it could have quite easily been an eighteen. And for eighteen, one would expect The Full Monty." He'd upped the ante to eighteen thousand and indicated that there was more than just confirmation of the name to go with the face.

Patricia sat back, knowing that she had a maximum of

twenty thousand with her. She considered his analogy. "I've also seen the film *Ten* when the star ended up disillusioned, and I'm not sure I'd be impressed enough either."

"Was that rated eighteen or fifteen?"

"Had it been released today, probably not even a twelve."

He fiddled with his glass again while considering that twelve grand would come in very handy right now. It was more than he had hoped for. "I believe we've settled on fifteen then."

"Fifteen it is, but I need The Full Monty first otherwise the rating's going to go down."

"All non-attributable, right?"

"Right." She retrieved her notebook from her case and, unseen by the man from *The Guardian*, switched on her voice recorder.

"Well..."

Less than an hour later, she sat alone on a bench, riverside of Victoria Embankment overlooking the Thames, going over her notes of what the man from *The Guardian* had said. Even though he was a well-known and well-connected figure in the world of journalism, she still had to consider the validity of what he had related, but in hindsight it all made sense now. Her dilemma was how much ought she to tell Hamilton, because what she had been told was probably worth well in excess of fifteen thousand. Coupled with her first encounter with the man, he was now richer by twenty-thousand pounds; all in cash. He had given names, times, dates and links that went far beyond Hamilton's sphere of influence, and even hinted that there might be more.

She made up her mind and decided to divulge only the relevant parts to Hamilton and keep the rest for further investigation and a possible approach to Mr Postles. By retaining certain elements of information, it might be the perfect platform from which to launch her own agency; but that was jumping the gun, because right now, she needed to concentrate on Hamilton's brief. She took a leaf out of her notebook, wrote two words on it and put it in her pocket.

Bypassing Lloyd's office as she had done so before, she walked into Hamilton's office mid-morning to find him crouched over his desk, pen in hand. He looked up. "Aaaaaah, there you are." She wasn't to know the reason for the look on his face.

"Good morning, minister," she replied in a flat tone. She sat her laptop down, extracted the piece of paper from her pocket and quietly placed it face up on his desk.

Hamilton read: *'Office bugged.'* He looked up at her in surprise. This didn't change his overall plan but he needed to adjust it, and quickly too, because what he was going to say to her would have to be outside the confines of his walls. He pressed the button on his intercom. "Come in."

Lloyd was through the door in a flash. "Miss Eyethorne and I have a matter to attend to elsewhere. Where and when is my next appointment?"

"Three o'clock in room 404. You're attending an inter-departmental meeting on communication protocols between Northern and Southern Ireland, minister."

He looked at his watch as he rose. "Right then. Get everything together and put it on my desk. I'll be back before then."

"Minister, before you go in, you'll need time to peruse the proposed amendments from the Home Office, released just a few minutes ago."

"Right." He indicated that Patricia should follow him

as he strode out of the door with a small portfolio in hand. He didn't like having to change plans, and he had one or two contingencies up his sleeve for the whole operation, but this was not one of them. This was unexpected. He put the horrifying thought that everything he had been saying in his office had been overheard by someone else; that would have to be dealt with later. Right now he would need to bring the entire plan forward by some hours.

They strode side by side down the corridors of power. "We need a safe place to talk," he said quietly.

"Coffee shop?"

"Too risky and too many eavesdroppers. We can do better than that and I know just the place." He opened his phone and spoke to his driver. As they emerged from the lift in the underground car park, he saw his chauffeur holding the nearest rear door open and had the car running. He also spotted his security detail sitting in the car behind and saw that one of them was Justin Crawford; he frowned as he considered the proximity of Miss Eyethorne's partner, but dismissed it as inconsequential. It would make no difference. "Say nothing in the car," he added as they neared.

Some five minutes later he opened the door to his suite in the Marriott hotel and ushered her in through its lobby. "Make yourself at home and take your jacket off, I'll just be a moment."

She'd never been in the converted County Hall building that was now mainly a Marriott hotel and was a little awed by its grandeur, but nevertheless, was instinctively drawn to one of the windows overlooking the Thames. Almost directly across Westminster Bridge stood the Houses of Parliament, anchored at the nearer end by Elizabeth Tower which housed Big Ben. It was arguably one of the most iconic worldwide sights that one could look at for hours, and she felt privileged to have been given the opportunity. She saw a group of tourists disembark from a river boat onto the pier opposite and watched them as they milled around in typical fashion with their cameras. The red buses traversing Westminster Bridge, the stalls selling British paraphernalia, black cabs, small sail boats, and off to her right was the massive London Eye wheeling gently round: it all added up to a stunning scene in the sunshine, but she'd often seen it before from different angles and turned to look round the room with a critical eye.

It was a very well-appointed spacious room with modern decor and plush furnishings of settees and chairs, but the hanging abstract paintings weren't to her taste and she grimaced at one of them. She had entered through one of the three doors. Hearing Hamilton's footfalls in the background of one of them, she turned her attention to the rest of the room. A chess board on a tasteful stand stood in one corner next to a mounted cello and bow, and a few feet away on a large wooden desk was a framed photograph of Hamilton shaking hands with an army general; she recognised the face but couldn't put a name to him. A telephone off to one side of the desk, and on the other, Newton's cradle sat at the back next to a Rubik's cube, adjacent to a set of poker dice, and in front by a writing pad, an oversized antique-looking letter opener. One of the top drawers was ajar and purely out of curiosity, she hooked a finger and opened it a couple of inches, paused, and then another few inches. On top of some papers was a pistol and a half-full box of ammunition. Her policing instincts were immediately heightened, and she wondered if he had a licence for such an unusual weapon.

Returning the drawer to it previous position, she looked to her right to see if she had been observed and wondered what secrets the other drawers held. A little nervously but inquisitively, she slid open the other top drawer and unsurprisingly saw a sheaf of papers clipped together. She kinked her head to one side and started reading through the top A4-sized spreadsheet wondering if it was personal or government related. In the left-hand column was a list of names, in the next were comments and in the last ones were dates, times, and numbers. She cocked an ear, checking to hear what Hamilton was doing, and lifted the top page to reveal other similar pages, and then it struck her that all the names were female. She looked more closely at the top page, attempting to interpret, and one name immediately stuck out. Katka. She mentally checked the date when she had met her at the opera which coincided with the date next to her name and thought it was the same. With apprehension, she read the comment *'frigid, but stayed the course'*. She looked at other comments and was stunned at some of them. Across from Penelope O was *'stunning boobs, lousy lay'*. Another *'thunder thighs'*.

At first it was just shock, and she cringed at the thought of what kind of person Hamilton really was, but before closing the drawer quietly, she cast her eyes down the final column; they were scores out of ten. She turned her back on the secrets within the desk, seeking a more kindly view like the one outside, but put her hand to her mouth in horror as she felt the hairs on the back of her neck stand up. Was she to be his next conquest?

Her first instinct was to run and get away from him and she took an instinctive pace towards the door; but then stopped herself. Frantically thinking what she ought to do in the decreasing time available, she took a deep breath and put a hand out against the desk to steady herself, and then hurriedly withdrew it. She closed her eyes and with another breath calmed down. Thinking... thinking. As a policewoman, and an inspector at that, she had received training for this kind of thing and she reminded herself that this was the sort of situation that she ought to be able to control. She opened her eyes and walked over to look out of the window, hoping for inspiration.

Maybe he had only bought her here to discuss their arrangement, because twenty minutes ago they were in his office, and he certainly had been surprised at her revelation regarding the bug. On the other hand he may have planned to bring her here all along, but at another time. Yet ever since she had met him, he had been nothing but polite to her and perhaps she ought to leave his private life out of the possibilities that were going through her head. There was no way he could know that she now knew his secret... or maybe he had been keeping an eye on her the whole time. She looked over towards the door where kitchen noises were coming from, but could see no evidence of him peering through it, and returned her gaze to the Thames. She decided to keep an open mind, give him the information he had asked for, and leave straight after, but if he tried anything on... well... she would just have to face up to that.

She turned as she heard Hamilton entering the room and noted that he had removed his tie and jacket. He held out a tumbler of whiskey as he neared. "I hope you like your scotch with just an ice cube. Here, come and sit down. One gets used to the view. Magnificent isn't it?" He patted the cushion on the large sofa next to him as he seated himself with crossed legs at one end. In the hot weather, he had taken off his jacket and tie and sat looking up at her, but her suspicious instincts were on high alert; the room was air-conditioned. Was this

his plan to get her half drunk, relaxed and uninhibited before inviting her into his bedroom? He was much larger than she was, and she wondered if she would be able to fend him off if he forced himself on her.

Once she had sat down next to him as far away as practical without arousing suspicion, and before she had a chance to get comfortable, she saw him rest an arm on the sofa half-behind her. His relaxed pose did nothing to allay her fears.

"Now my dear, tell me what you've found out, but let's start with this bug first. How can you be sure without first sweeping the room with some electronic device or other? Mr Postles' brigade would have found it, wouldn't they?"

She took a small sip from the tumbler, more to whet her mouth than anything else, but she was glad of its warmth as it trickled down her gullet. "I'm not certain it is bugged, but one of my reliable contacts who I was with just this morning, thought that it was." She had to be careful about how much she revealed, otherwise she would have no cards left in her hand to play after the dust from this episode had settled. "The obvious place is in your intercom, as any bug detector wouldn't be able to find anything out of the ordinary in among all the other wires and stuff in there, and the only real way to find out is by taking it apart."

He mulled over this for a moment. "How about my phone or house... or any one of the cars?"

"He didn't say anything about them but he was pretty certain about your office."

"Ummmmm. I'll have to be more careful what I say in there from now on. Well done, but now tell me that you've discovered who the turncoat is."

She leaned forward to place her tumbler on the low-level coffee table in front of them, unintentionally affording

Hamilton a decent view of her cleavage. He briefly forgot what he had just asked and admired her bust again. The analogy of *'Pinky and Perky'* sprang to mind, but then she was talking again.

She started by explaining the difficulties she had encountered when interviewing civil servants within the Houses of Parliament and how uncooperative they had been, but had gleaned a direction of inquiry from off-hand comments. In her capacity as a detective, she had learned that one errant word here or there, or a sudden shifting of the eyes when replying to a question, would be enough to make one consider the reasons for the misdirection. When all those errant words and eye shifts started to point down the same path, it was logical to follow it. Marrying up suppositions with hard facts had been almost impossible, as anything recorded or archived had already been vetted and altered to suit the necessary circumstances. However, some background lower-grade material had not been through the vetting process, and that had provided her with enough facts to proceed to the next step.

She continued explanations and mentioned some of her interviewees by name, but realising that she was 'laying it on a bit thick' – probably partially stalling for time – decided it was time to reveal who Hamilton's mole was. "So it all boils down to one person." She took a bigger sip from her glass.

"And who's that?"

"It's your own secretary... Lloyd."

He guffawed and nearly chocked on his swig of scotch. "Lloyd!" It got him thinking. "I know he can be a bit sneaky at times, but aren't all of his ilk? Oh come on, those bunch of busybodies in the civil service are all the same, but to purposely leak information to the press without some sort of authorisation, well… that's another kettle of fish. It's too obvious and too easy to be found out and anyway, he wouldn't dare."

"Bear with me on this one, because that's not all. Did you know he had a name change when he was young?"

"That doesn't prove anything. Many people have name changes."

"Not when they are five years old."

"So?"

"He was too young to realise that he could even think about changing his name, which means that someone changed it for him."

"Go on." Now she had his concentrated attention, whereas before he had been rather dismissive.

She didn't need to consult her notebook as the facts were well etched in her mind. "On his real birth certificate it shows him as being named 'Liam McCorley Alloyd', born to Gerald and Sian Alloyd in County Armagh on the second of January 1970. Somewhere around seventy-five, not only was his name changed to Clarence McCorley Lloyd but his date of birth had been altered to the twenty-second of December 1970. If you write down the numbers 2-1-70, it's easy enough to change to 22-12-70, and at a glance it's easy to miss when set out that way. What's more is that he was supposedly born in Liverpool. Now we all know that there's a large Irish community in Liverpool because it's an easy crossing across the Irish Sea, and that the workforce there is predominantly Irish, but they have infiltrated every aspect of society including the town hall where the registrar's office is located. From dustmen to traffic wardens, publicans to undertakers… registrars to priests."

She watched him trying to make the link between the last two, even three.

"It wouldn't take much for them to collude, especially if they had the same ideals at heart."

He was making the string-ends meet. "OK, so someone's changed his birthday etcetera and he now works under me, but that doesn't mean he still has links to the Republicans, does it?"

"It does when you ask yourself the question: why did someone go to all the trouble of disguising who he really was? Remember, in the seventies there was all sorts of unrest in Northern Ireland and…"

"You don't have to remind me because I was there," he tersely responded.

"I know because I've looked up your records. You were off chasing the small fry while there were others after the hierarchy, and you wouldn't have known what else was going on other than in your own theatre of operations. In the background, there must have been those who were thinking long term and I believe it was they who instigated Lloyd's insertion into the government."

"If only you could prove that," he said smugly.

"All but."

"Really?"

"Not actual proof, but everything I've found out clearly indicates Lloyd is the culprit, and when you think about it, if there was a bug in your office, who better than Lloyd to monitor it. There's also a man who I managed to track down and who positively identified him as being the one handing over classified information, but there's no way he'll ever testify to that. He wants to remain anonymous and will refute any allegations to the contrary."

While Hamilton thought about her conclusions, she added, "And this goes back to about the time when Lloyd joined the civil service as a junior clerk. I have times, dates and some locations... there really isn't any room for doubt."

Whiskey in hand, he stood up and walked a couple of paces to look out of the window; he didn't need the distraction of Miss Eyethorne this very instance; later maybe. It was indeed the result he had been looking for and was pissed off that the security service under Mr Postles' keen eye had not either found it, or if they had, not pointed it out. Could it be that it had been purposefully overlooked? That was a question for another day, because now he had the perfect opportunity to put pressure on Lloyd. He could visualise it... confronting Lloyd and having him wriggle like a worm on a hook. He would, of course, need the detailed information that Miss Eyethorne had, otherwise Lloyd would blankly deny everything and then he would be the one looking foolish. Taking a long pull from his tumbler, he decided he would need time later to think this through, but in the meantime he needed to get what Miss Eyethorne had on Lloyd.

He was about to turn round when another thought struck him. She had provided him with a result yet that was at odds with what Mr Postles had said. But then again, she may have prejudiced her information so as to deflect suspicion from herself and Crawford. He would certainly need to carefully consider who was deceiving who. He looked at his empty glass and was about to go and get a refill when he realised that she hadn't mentioned anything about his hundred thousand. Was the information she had just given him worth a hundred thousand? There was a lot to think about, because he was rather surprised that she had actually found his mole, and he may have to change his approach to her; but just a little. He watched a bus going over Westminster Bridge and on the side of it was an attractive woman showing off her legs, advertising a brand of stocking, and his thoughts turned to what he had planned.

"Another whiskey?" He didn't wait for her reply, but deftly collected her tumbler as he passed the table en route to his cocktail cabinet in the lobby.

She hadn't finished the one she had, but had little choice and thought she could always not finish it.

He returned and handed back her glass, but instead of sitting, chose to stand across the table from her. "Naturally, you have all this written down somewhere?"

Taking a small sip, she shifted position. "Not all of it as I haven't had a chance to compile it properly yet. I've only just come from meeting my last contact, but I can put it on a memory stick for you once I've collated today's results, and can let you have it Monday."

He was so looking forward to bedding her that day and expected her to take extreme umbrage at what he had planned to do. But on the other hand, she would be more unlikely to cooperate in handing over the information afterwards and with a silent curse realised he would have to wait until she was ready. "Can you not let me have it tomorrow?"

"Sorry, but I've got the weekend booked and it's something I can't put off."

He cursed again. Apart from the delay, he had assured Mr Postles that her employment would cease, but perhaps she need not visit the House again. He would need a little tact. "You probably won't know this, but you've been ruffling a few feathers among our civil service colleagues, and they didn't like it; not one little bit. I've been asked to revoke your pass and can't get it extended beyond today, so if we meet back here Monday morning... make that noon as I've a constituency meeting first thing. But there remains just one thing... have you spent all of my money?"

She'd been expecting this question and still had not made up her mind, because in the back of it, she was still trying to get to grips with the list she had discovered. She had come prepared to state the true balance, less a few disbursements, but if he was the philanderer she suspected he was, didn't he deserve all he got? She decided that it would be inappropriate to deduct funds as his personal life was irrelevant to the matter in hand and would put that argument to Justin over the weekend in Wales. "There's well over half left and I'll bring it with me on Monday."

She felt a sense of relief getting that one out of the way; at least for now.

"From what you've told me I've a lot to think about, so it's probably best if we do pick up again on Monday. I'll have made my decision as to what to do about Lloyd by then, but if you do come across anything useful over the weekend, you'll let me know, won't you?"

"Of course." She rose and collected her jacket draped over the back of a wooden chair.

Hamilton ushered her out through the lobby, smiled and opened the door for her. "See you Monday then."

She waited until she was in the lift before letting her breath out fully.

Chapter 9

Sheer delight

"What a wonderful little cottage, even though it feels a little damp," Patricia added to her comments about how it was just as well Justin knew where he was going. "And almost in the middle of nowhere. Oh…what's over there?" she said, pointing at the roof of the only other visible building a quarter of a mile away.

He rested his hands on her shoulders from behind and kissed the nape of her neck. "That my love is the beauty of this place. It's only a stone's throw away from The Mumbles Cricket Clubhouse."

She turned. "Oh you men are incorrigible. You mean to tell me your friend bought this place so that he could come all the way to the back-end of beyond just to play cricket?"

"Oh no, not just cricket." He pivoted her to look out of the other window. "You see that path over there? That leads to Hairpin Cove."

"And what happens at Hairpin Cove?" she asked sceptically.

"It's a gorgeous secluded bay where one can go beach casting and if you like I'll take you there."

"You know I can't fish."

"There's an added bonus."

"Ok… let me guess… after you've caught your fish, you

get to eat them... right?"

He laughed. "Not unless you gut them and cook them first, you don't." He looked up at the sky. "It'll be a nice surprise for you, I promise, and as it's a lovely evening, why don't we start straight away? In any case, I could do with stretching my legs."

It had taken the best part of Saturday to drive down the M4 from Maidenhead to the south coast of Wales, past Cardiff and Swansea and eventually to the remote headland. The unusually fine British summer, now well into autumn, was coming to an end, or so the weatherman on the radio had said, and Justin hoped it would last; at least until the end of the night.

Hand in hand they walked down the narrowing path, hedged in by sheep-filled fields until they rounded a thicket and stopped on a rocky outcrop. "This is as far as we can go down here, but look."

She could hardly fail to miss it. Nearly two-hundred feet below down an almost sheer cliff was the sea. Way off to the left in the haze were the ugly urban sprawls of Swansea and Port Talbot with their towering chimneys from the steel works, but to the right and in total contrast was miles of unspoiled coastline.

"What's that place?" Shielding her eyes, she pointed directly away from them.

"That's Somerset and Devon."

"I never realised how wide it was. This is the River Severn, isn't it?"

"It's not officially the Severn until you reach the bridge we came over a few hours ago. This is the Bristol Channel, and just about as far as you can see off to the right is the Atlantic Ocean."

"It's beautiful."

"I told you you wouldn't be disappointed, but wait a couple of minutes and you might be able to see the sun setting into the water. Keep looking closely."

While she peered into the distant horizon with the gentle breeze wafting through her hair, Justin knelt down on one knee, retrieved the small box in his pocket which he opened, held out, and waited.

He didn't say a word as she turned and looked down; he didn't need to.

It took nearly a full minute before small tears began to well up in her eyes and she had to wipe them away to peer at the ring which looked like it had two diamonds either side of an oblong stone mounted on it. "Are you going to ask me or not?" There was a hint of joy and laughter in her voice.

He kept her waiting as he grinned back, watching the setting sun gradually changing the hue on her beautiful face, but he couldn't maintain the impasse any longer. He had prepared a few words to go with his marriage proposal, but they seemed inadequate, and he felt his heart thumping as he asked the inevitable question. "Patricia. Will you marry me... for better or for worse?"

Her initial instinct was to say yes immediately, but she played his game by cocking her head to one side and compressing her lips as though in thought. Before the tears of joy became overwhelming, she knelt down on both knees as close to him as possible with the boxed ring between them. "Of course I will, you silly sausage."

They kissed deeply, savouring each other, and when they finally pulled apart, she added, "On one condition."

He raised an inquisitive eyebrow.

"That you make love to me now. Right here, right now."

Once again, he kept her waiting, but when he did speak, it made sense. "Can we do it on the grass over there, because this rock is knackering my knee?"

They both blurted out laughing.

The name of the outcrop was Rams Tor, and it was living up to its name.

Chapter 10

To do unto others

It was taking them ages to return to Maidenhead because there'd been a crash on the M4 – what the police nowadays describe as 'an incident' rather than 'an accident' – and on top of that, Sunday night traffic was worse than usual due to the spray thrown up by other vehicles. Summer had come to an abrupt end with the arrival of a storm; the weatherman had certainly got it right this time.

"I'm seeing Hamilton tomorrow, hopefully for the last time," she said after turning down the radio a little.

"You found his mole then?"

They'd spent the entire weekend walking along coastal paths, across fields and visiting coffee shops during the day, and making love whenever they were up to it at night. The peace and quiet coupled with their betrothal had been an idyllic occasion to forget all about London. Thoughts about their diaries, friends, careers and all that went with the Monday to Friday dogma, had been forgotten, but now that they were nearing the capital, and with Monday morning just a few hours away, they had to discuss Hamilton.

"I was right. It is Lloyd, but he's just the tip of the iceberg and with a bit more digging, I'm sure I can come up with a whole plethora of networks; all hidden beneath the surface."

"What was Hamilton's reaction when you told him?"

"I think he was genuinely shocked." She decided not to tell him about where she had told him, nor what else she had found in his apartment. Not yet anyway, because that would require an entire evening's discussion. She certainly didn't want to spoil the last part of their wonderful weekend. "But I've got to return his money and told him that there was less than half, so how much do we return to him? I thought we ought to keep five hundred for our own expenses. What do you think?"

"You mean your own expenses, not mine? All I did was act as intermediary, but that sounds fair to me."

"You haven't moved it from your gun cupboard, have you?" She was referring to where they had stored the surplus.

"No. You know where the keys are."

A thought crossed her mind. "We'd better pray we haven't been burgled while we've been away, otherwise we'd need to tell him that we spent the whole lot."

"Don't even go there. How much have you spent?"

"All in all, twenty-eight thousand, plus our five hundred. Twenty on one chap alone, but well worth it I'd say."

"I hope he sees it that way as well."

***

The blustery storm had passed overnight leaving a windy, but dry autumnal day, and she dressed accordingly, putting on a thicker blouse and longer skirt. She'd have to wait until next year before getting her summer frocks out again. She'd got up early and completed her compilation onto a memory stick, but before closing down her laptop, found another stick, making a second copy which she put in a drawer; just in case. Her meeting with Hamilton ought not to take too long.

She phoned her superintendent to say that her secondment was coming to an end and that she would be back on normal duties the next morning.

It turned out that she was quite right to delay her return to Maidenhead police station until the following day, because she had to wait in the lobby of the Marriott until nearly one o'clock before he arrived; Justin wasn't on duty and she wondered what he was doing right now.

"Come on up," he said tersely as he walked smartly towards the lift. "Bloody party officials." He added as the lift doors closed. She correctly surmised that he wasn't in the best of moods, and followed him and his security man down the corridor to his apartment. "Wait downstairs for me, I may be a while. Now come in my dear."

"Pour me a scotch and while you're at it, help yourself." He disappeared, presumably into one of the bedrooms.

Two iced whiskies in hand, one far smaller than the other, she walked through the living room to the same coffee table, making a detour close to his desk and noted that all drawers were in exactly the same position as they had been before the weekend. When he appeared a few minutes later, she saw that he had changed into something akin to a quilted smoking jacket and looked in a far better mood.

"Here, let me have that." He held his hand out for the tumbler and downed most of it in one gulp. She wondered if he'd had time to savour it. "That's better. Now, let's get down to business and first things first. Is that my money in your bag there?"

He hadn't even asked her to sit down. "All that's left... seventy-one thousand five-hundred pounds... I kept five hundred for my own costs." She took out a buff envelope and handed it to him. She wasn't to know it, but he was stunned. Stunned at the sum she had just mentioned, because he expected her to say a far smaller amount, if anything.

He finished his glass and swapped it for the envelope. "Here, get me another, will you, while I check it."

Returning from the lobby, she saw him closing one of the lower desk drawers. He didn't have the envelope in his hand any longer and supposed that he'd put it in there.

He didn't waste any time. "And have you the information that this has cost me?"

She was prepared and had the small memory stick easily to hand from her bag. "All ready for you. All you need to do is plug it in." She held it up.

He peered at it before taking it from her. "And you're sure that everything I need to nail him is on here?"

"Oh yes, and I've even prepared a chart that cross references his comings and goings for you. I think you will find it easy to use."

He placed it in his pocket, beamed at her, took another slug of scotch and put his tumbler down. "Well done my dear, and now let me congratulate you properly."

Before she knew it, he had put his arm round her shoulder and was walking her out of the room, into the lobby and through an open door into one of the bedrooms. She didn't know if he was being sincere or if he had something else in mind, and she mentally prepared herself for whatever might come next. What did come next was a complete shock. He had gently guided her in front of him and as she crossed the threshold of the bedroom, saw he had laid out what looked like photographs on the king size bed. Inquisitively but with automation, taking two more paces forward, she instantly recognised the photos of her in a series of provocative poses.

Flashes of thought as to how and where he had got hold of

them, why he had laid them out on the bottom of the bed, but more urgently, what were his intentions. She was dumbstruck until she heard him close the door.

"You really are a most attractive girl and I would hate to see your... shall we say... talents... wasted on the general public."

There was no response from her, so he continued. "You do see what I'm getting at don't you?" He wasn't sure that she did and added, "I'd much rather you wasted them on me."

She was still trying to fathom how he had obtained the photographs, but now focused on what he was implying. If she had got it right, he was proposing that they should have sex, otherwise he would release the compromising photographs to the press who would, no doubt, pay handsomely.

Making up her mind quickly, because she had to, she picked up one of the photos and turned slowly to see him beaming at her; he reminded her of the condescending grins on Laurel and Hardy's faces. Inwardly she was cringing, but she managed to keep a straight face. "I suppose you would like me to start by posing... like this?"

"Oh I am so glad that we have an understanding."

Somehow she found time to reflect that he now had a grin akin to that of the Cheshire Cat from *Alice in Wonderland*, and oh, how he was lapping it up. She forced a smile back at him, putting him at ease, then raised the photograph facing towards him under her chin with both hands, so that he would be able to imagine what was to come next. She spent the valuable few seconds envisaging various scenarios and hoped that what she had in mind would work out all right in the end. "Here, hold this." After turning it back round again, she held out the photograph for him to take, freeing up her hands, but giving him a distraction.

Slowly, she unbuttoned her jacket and laid it neatly over the arms of a nearby chair, turned square on to him, breathed in to stretch the fabric of her blouse, then out again and started with the buttons from the top. She followed his eyes as he watched her fingers undo each one on their way down until they reached her skirt. She untucked the remaining material and finished the last two buttons, then delicately undid the cuffs, before removing it and dropping it to one side on the floor. Putting her arms behind her to release the skirt clasp and zip, only accentuated the thrust of her breasts still restrained within her bra, and she saw where his eyes were focused as she let it slip to the floor. She thought it best to keep her shoes on. Her underwear wasn't especially provocative, but it had the predicted effect on Hamilton, as she mimicked her pose in the photograph – starfish style.

"Now it's your turn." She kept her legs apart but rested her hands on her hips as though daring him to do so.

Once he'd recovered from his gawping at her perfect body, he dropped the photograph, untied his jacket and in his now flustered state, undressed down to his underpants. She could see his expectant member bulging, and for a briefest of moments, wondered if she could go through with it. He stood there waiting for her to make the next move, and to add to his excitement, she seductively licked her lips.

"You like games, don't you?"

He nodded.

"Let's try Simon says."

He hadn't played the game of copying another person's movements since his school days and certainly none of his other conquests had been so suggestive in their foreplay. He forced out an "OK."

She was making this up as she went along, but started

by putting her legs together and placing her hands over her breasts. He naturally followed. She then stretched her arms out wide and watched him do likewise, noting that his bulge had got bigger and that a small wet patch had appeared on his briefs. She returned to her legs apart pose, put her arms behind her back, thrust her boobs forward and craned her neck. Their heads were now only a couple of feet apart and she pouted her lips. "Close your eyes."

He immediately obeyed.

She took one pace back and with all her might, swung the toe of her right foot directly into his groin.

Instantly his eyes opened wide and his hands whipped round to his nether regions, but he didn't, or rather couldn't, put his legs together. All she needed to do was take her time stepping to one side to let him topple forward until his chin came into contact the soft edge of the bed, and she guessed he had been holding in his breath, because his wheeze went on for some time as he ended up on the carpet.

As he struggled for breath, she lifted one leg over him so that she was directly astride of his prone body, put her hand back on her hips again, and looked down at the pathetic form beneath her. His mouth was open as he tried to suck in more air, and the veins on the side of his neck obtruded. Wondering if he was going to be able to pay attention and knowing that she was still being provocative, she leaned over him so that her restrained boobs were as close as they could be without touching him. His eyes were screwed tightly shut. "Open your eyes."

With difficulty he did so, and couldn't help but see the enhanced cleavage between her breasts and quickly closed them again.

"Open your bloody eyes." Her command was obeyed.

"If I ever catch you trying to pull a stunt like that again,

I'll bloody castrate you." Even her sharp voice made him wince. "And as for those photos, if they ever get out, I'll say that you were blackmailing me."

He firmly shut his eyes. She stood and kicked him in the side, not too far from his manhood. "Look at me when I'm talking to you." He opened them smartly again, hoping to avoid another encounter with her shoe.

"We do understand each other, don't we?" She used his expression.

Lying on the floor and hardly capable of thought, all he could do was nod, but it wasn't enough for her, so she kicked him again, and this time a bit harder, and in closer to his groin. He let out an unusually higher pitched scream in agony.

"Don't we?" She raised her voice so that there was no doubt.

"Yes." It was a plea more than anything else and she could see it in his eyes.

Not caring if he was looking at her, she dressed in front of him and collected all the photographs, before smoothing her skirt. She was about to leave when a thought brought a smile to her face. She activated the camera on her phone and pointed it at him. "Say cheese." She said gleefully, but he wasn't looking.

His breathing was beginning to return to something like normal as he watched her head for the doorway out of the corner of his eye; she turned in it and looked back at him briefly before disappearing through it. Exiting from the lift on the ground floor, she forced a smile at his security detail sitting in one of the chairs and walked, probably a little too fast, towards the outside, turned left away from the giant Ferris wheel of the London Eye and sought out one of the benches against the concrete wall of the riverbank. A couple of student types sat at the other end jabbering away in some sort of Eurasian language she couldn't understand, and at last she felt a bit safer.

Head bowed and supported by her right hand, she closed her eyes, recounting her experience with Hamilton, but after a short while opened them and saw that her left hand was shaking. She sat upright without focusing on anything particular and realised that her whole body was now reacting to the entire encounter, and it made her feel a little sick. She started questioning herself. Had she done the right thing by knackering him, or should she have knuckled under? Had there been an alternative and what might it have been? There hadn't even been any negotiation. He had reeled her into his world like a hooked fish; and she had ended up in his lair and, like a cornered animal, finally lashed out. No, not quite like a cornered animal, because she had used her intellect to escape. But now she had an enemy, and not just any enemy. Not only was he one of the most powerful men in the country, but now, probably vindictive as well. Oh God, but what had she done? Kicking someone in the balls was one thing, but if that person happened to be a minister of the Crown, one would be wise to consider emigrating in short order. At the very least, she could expect to lose her job and all the benefits that went with it, and OH NO… Justin; he'd be moved on as well. Both of their reputations would be ruined. When they came to arrest her for assault, it would probably be useless to claim that he had been trying to rape her since it would simply be her word against his. All she had were a few irrelevant photographs, but she could hardly produce them, and anyway, they would be to her own detriment. She doubted that her threat to castrate him would be sufficient to prevent him from pursuing her demise, but she did have the photograph she had taken which might help if it came to it. She would need someone to speak up for her, but once the word got out, there would be few who would be willing to risk their own reputations. She had no friends in high places, but would Justin know someone? She needed to speak to him and reached for her phone.

She couldn't remember what his schedule was that day, and as she heard the first of the ring tones had a sudden inspiration and pressed the stop button. There was that list of sexual conquests in his top drawer. She immediately kicked herself for not remembering it before she had left Hamilton's apartment. She should have taken copies of it on her phone. Now if she could somehow get hold of that, it would be real leverage and provide an adequate form of protection from whatever Hamilton might want to put their way.

She phoned Justin again. "Bloody Hamilton..." And started to tell him what happened. When she came to the part about the photographs on display at the end of the bed, he stopped her and asked her to repeat. Once she had finished with a truncated version, and Justin had had a chance to take it all in, he told her to meet him at The Queens off Kilburn High Road. "It's somewhere out of the way where we can talk without the risk of being overheard."

She remembered he wasn't going to be on duty until tomorrow. "Half an hour?"

"Make it forty-five."

"See you there."

Justin was waiting for her at one of the tables in the fairly busy pub; it was still the back-end of lunchtime. He had a glass of red wine waiting for her and rose to give her a long hug as she neared. She clung on to him and he could feel the tension in her before they separated.

"You OK?"

"Just about." They sat and she took a swig from the glass.

"Tell me again what actually happened... it's OK, you can talk safely. I've looked around and there's no one suspicious here."

"Oh God. It was horrible." This time she started right from the beginning when she had first met Hamilton at the opera, trying not to leave anything out but mainly omitting Lloyd's involvement and instead concentrating on her encounters with Hamilton. She had had time to think on her way to The Queens Arms and recounted the whole story as if giving a statement, knowing that Justin would appraise the situation in a professional capacity and wouldn't want too much conjecture.

He interrupted her. "Where are the photographs now?"

"I've got them here, but he's bound to have copies. And anyway, they're from a digital source so can be replicated at any time."

When it came to the part about her actually kicking him between his legs, he stopped her again. "Now that you've calmed down a bit, think back and tell me what it felt like."

In thought, she closed her eyes, gently biting her bottom lip, and upon opening them replied, "Now that you mention it, it felt good. Yes, really good. It was like a kind of release. What are you smiling at?"

He sat back in his chair. "I only wish I had been there to witness it. That's all."

Those few words and his demeanour did more to help her relax than anything else, and she felt some of her anxiety dissipate. She gave a short burst of burst of laughter. "Oh, but you certainly know how to make a girl feel happy." She reached out her hand and put it on his. "Thank you."

"Well, when things start getting tough and your whole world looks like it's going tits-up, it helps to remember the highs, so just cling to that thought the next time you come across a sticky patch."

"We're in a sticky patch right now and no end of thinking about how good it felt is going to make any of it go away."

"You're right there, but tell me more about this list you found. Can you remember any of the names on it?"

"Uhnuh." She was sipping. "Only one; the woman at the opera."

"That's not enough." Justin was pensive, and reached for his phone. "I've an idea." She watched him scroll through various icons until he opened a page. "Hamilton's due in the Commons for a vote this evening, and I doubt he'll be allowed to miss it as it's crucial, so he won't be at his apartment. The concierges know me well enough to let me in, and if the list is still there, I can photo it. I'll tell them I've been sent to fetch something; I had to do it once before, so there's no reason why they won't give me a key. Now, once we have that list and let him know we have it, he won't dare touch us."

She thought about his proposal for a few seconds. "You sure? After all, it'll be me he'll be after, not so much you."

"He'll be after the both of us, so don't even think that it's just about you. He's a spiteful bugger and he'll utilise anything he can to get his own back and that means using me to get at you. In any case, I want to find out how he got hold of those photos from my computer, but that's another matter, so leave that to me; it can wait. The most important thing right now is to protect you."

He automatically looked around to see if anyone was taking any interest in them and was about to dismiss the occupants of the pub, when he spotted a woman sitting on her own. He blinked and glanced elsewhere before briefly returning a surreptitious look at her again. Patricia was used to seeing him look around and thought nothing of it. Outwardly, especially in front of Patricia, he was sanguine, but inwardly he was seething. Not only had Hamilton tried to rape his brand-new fiancée, but he had somehow hacked into his computer and stolen personal data. Those photographs were not the only intimate details he had on disc. Certainly he had followed the advice provided by the security officer when he had first been enrolled into the diplomatic service, but inevitably there were other private items that he really didn't want known. And then there was the issue of why Hamilton had taken the decision to have his computer hacked. He was unlikely to be able to do it himself so would have instructed a specialist; and not just any specialist either. It was as though Hamilton had maliciously gone out of his way to ruin his life, and that of Patricia's. He would have to do something about Hamilton, but right now his priority was to ensure his wife-to-be wasn't going to be pilloried by the press and the public, lose her job, probably lose her self-esteem with it, and end up as an unemployable has-been. Worse than that, Hamilton could find a way to reciprocate what she had done to him and have her physically disfigured for life; even murdered if he was desperate.

Such were his inner thoughts and he was only half-listening to Patricia as she described Hamilton's unsubtle approach to her on his sofa. He happened to glance at the woman across the room, thinking how ungainly she was, but an alarm bell in his head started as he wondered why she had gone out of her way to disguise her beauty. Not only was she wearing a wig, but why go out with such crooked glasses? Why not straighten them up? The only people who went out purposefully looking like that were those who didn't want to be recognised. He kept half an eye on her as Patricia had stopped speaking.

"It's probably best if you returned to your post in Maidenhead. When are you due back there?"

"I phoned the super this morning and told him I'd be there tomorrow. Why?"

"I'm just thinking of how best to keep you out of Hamilton's reaches in the meantime, because it'll probably take just one word from him and you'll be transferred to Land's End or somewhere remote like that. Why don't you go home, stay incommunicado, and wait for my call? Probably late tonight"

"Do you really think he'd do something like that?"

Justin thought about it for a moment. "Maybe not straight away, but he's known for his vindictive qualities and is bound to plan his revenge in his own good time. Which is why we're going to need that list."

"Yes, I've been thinking about that. What he's done isn't illegal and he could claim that it's someone else's, or even planted to discredit him."

"Not if I can track down some of those names. Here hang on a moment... move to your left a little... I want to take your photograph."

"What?" With all the talk about sensitive photographs, she was incredulous.

"Just a little to your left, and smile." He pointed his phone above her right shoulder and pressed the button several times.

"What on earth are you doing?" She hadn't smiled.

"Don't look round, but there's someone I'm uncomfortable with sitting three tables behind you. I've just taken their photo because she's been joined by someone whose face rings a bell." He put his phone back down on the table. "I'll have a look through the records when I get time."

"Someone I might know?"

"Unlikely… can't pigeonhole him, but there's something familiar about him. Anyway, that can wait."

She had finished her wine. "Think I'll have a soak in the bath. After that episode, I feel rather dirty."

He was about to say that he preferred her that way, but under the circumstances, thought better of it.

It took Hamilton well over ten minutes to get to his feet, and that was after crawling to the en suite and levering himself up by grabbing hold of the heated chrome towel rail attached to the wall. "Shit," he swore gently as he burnt his hand, and transferred his other one to the side of the bath, on which he now perched delicately with his wedding tackle dangling over the edge. He winced as he explored his nether regions with one hand while making sure that the back end of his buttocks didn't slip off the bath. Looking into the wall-mounted mirror behind the basin, he saw a sorry old man. He was only in his fifties, but the man looking back at him with tousled hair and ashen face looked more like seventy. "Bloody woman… aaaaaargh." His hand had found a sensitive spot. He grabbed the round stand-alone mirror and angled it between his legs to see if there was any permanent damage, but couldn't see anything. He looked at his 'old chap' which was now shrivelled up in protective mode and breathed a sigh of relief; at least he wasn't bleeding.

It was painful to stand even half doubled-over but he managed it and took an exploratory step, then another, all the while holding onto the basin surround. "Bastard of a woman." He continued to mutter oaths as he tentatively took more steps, making sure he emulated a rider just out of the saddle after three long days.

Sitting on the edge of his bed while gently kneading his groin area, he changed his contemplation from his own physical injuries to the matter of recovery. He'd never experienced such agony in his whole life, not even when he had broken both tibia and fibula while on exercise. That had taken months to properly heal, but now he didn't have the luxury of being absent from government for any significant length of time. He couldn't remember exactly what time he was due where later that day, but recalled that he had a couple of appointments prior to a late vote in the House. He needed to get back to his office and gingerly stood to see how far he could walk without the aid of a piece of furniture. Slowly at first, the more he walked the easier it became, but he definitely needed to keep his legs splayed a little too much to go unnoticed, so he practised standing fully upright; it hurt, but it would have to do. Getting dressed was agonising when it came to putting his legs through his underpants, especially when they came into contact with his bruised region, but he endured and finished after far too long.

Just movement was making it easier, but the dull ache wasn't going away and, if anything, was getting worse. He coughed lightly and immediately regretted it as it sent a lance of pain from his groin up to the base of his neck. "Fucking woman," he swore as he bent over to tie his shoelaces with difficulty, and continued to mentally curse her. He'd attend to her once he had today's business out of the way and make her life a misery.

***

It was getting on for midnight when Justin let himself in

through Patricia's front door and found her asleep in her favourite seat; he assumed she'd been waiting up for him. He blew gently into her face, then a little harder and watched her surface from reverie. He smiled as she opened her eyes and uncurled herself.

"Hello gorgeous."

"What time is it?" she asked through bleary eyes.

"Time for you to go to bed."

Emergence from a somnolent state didn't take long, but she still rubbed her eyes, and once finished, sat up and asked the inevitable. "Did you get it?"

Justin knew she would never have gone straight to bed without knowing; it was his own way of teasing her. "I got it alright… and more."

"Go on. Tell me all." She was still shaking off her nap, but he had her full attention.

"The concierge gave me the key so getting in was easy, and I found the list in the drawer you described and photoed it." He produced three phones from his pocket; she recognised only his. "I bought a pair of pay-as-you-go phones, one for you, the other for me and I've already plumbed in their numbers on each." He passed the beige one over to her. "Now we each have an untraceable copy and can contact each other without looking over our shoulders."

He could see her thinking and saved her the time. "Look… if Hamilton's going to come after us, the last thing we need is someone hacking into our conversations and knowing what we know. A copy of the list, which by the way was two-and-a-half pages long, is on each phone, not on my original, and we really don't want to download it onto either of our computers, or any other computer for that matter. It's got to remain untraceable, so tuck it away somewhere safe for the time being because it's your insurance policy."

"OK, I'm with you on that one, but how are you going to let Hamilton know?"

"Now, here's the best part." He ignored her. "When I went back to my office, I managed to correlate some of the names and dates with his itinerary and found enough of them to put faces to those names, so now we know who they are and how to get in touch with them if necessary. There's two in particular that if it got out would cause a dreadful stink."

"Go on, who are they?" Patricia was definitely perking up.

He kept her waiting. "If I said to you Lady Abergail, would that ring a bell?"

"Lady Abergail... Lady Abergail... What, the daughter of the Earl of Stafford?"

"The very same."

"And the other?"

"Well, I'm not sure I can tell you that as it probably comes under the Official Secrets Act."

"Come on, you big git. We've gone this far so you might as well tell me. In any case, I've got the list as well and could look her up."

"Not this one you couldn't. Not even on your police computer."

Patricia purposefully looked sadly glum. "Not even for little old me?"

"Maybe later... if the going gets tough."

"OK, but you still haven't told me how you're going to tell Hamilton."

Justin produced a slim white envelope in a transparent plastic bag and placed it on the table. "I photocopied the list and added a typed sheet of paper which anonymously says something along the lines of ensuring your well-being... mine as well. I'm on duty tomorrow morning from six and quite simply I'll slip it into his chauffeur's pocket first thing. Oh don't worry about it not being found in time because it'll be sticking out of his pocket, and Hamilton picks up on things like that. Even if he doesn't, it's not going to be long before his chauffeur finds it and hands it to him. He'll naturally suspect that you are its author, but he won't dare say a thing."

"Ohhhhh, he'll definitely suspect me, but won't he wonder how it got there and assume it was via you? He'll reason it out, won't he."

"He probably will, but without any fingerprints on it, he won't be able to prove anything. I'll be wearing gossamer gloves when I take it out of the plastic bag."

"You seem to have thought of everything."

"Not quite." He waited to see if her detective mind could work out what he was referring to, but when nothing was forthcoming, he continued. "There's still the matter of how Hamilton got those photos off my computer... They're still on there and even if I wipe them now, whoever downloaded them, will have digital copies, because they either used a stick, hacked in through the internet or broke into it. That's what really galls me... Some individual prying into my private life."

"Shit... How are you going to trace them?"

"I'm going to have to confront Hamilton and if he starts playing silly buggers, then I'll finish off what you didn't. Minister or not, I'll bloody castrate him if I have to; even if it costs me my career."

"You know, you don't have to do this for me."

"It's not just you. State secrets and security is one thing, but when it comes to someone abusing their position, to my mind they're a real disgrace. They think they're untouchable and can do what they like, but let me tell you, he's not going to like what I'm going do to him. People like that deserve what they get."

Patricia had never seen Justin angry before and it frightened her. His raised hairline and clenched teeth accentuating his jawline, and with wide eyes staring straight ahead, she knew he meant what he said. She felt she ought to try to temper any rash action he was thinking of taking. "You're going to have to make sure nobody's within earshot when you confront him."

"I know, I know. I'm just trying to figure out where and when, because the shithead's rarely alone. He seldom goes home to his family, and when he's in his London apartment, he's got some wretched tart or other with him." Justin had calmed down a little as he trawled through when best to catch him alone. Being one of his security guards certainly placed him in the perfect position, but there was no doubt in his own mind that he would have to be very careful indeed; it would take a degree of planning to choose the right moment.

"Are you going to delete those photos?"

"Tonight." Her question distracted him from his thoughts and he relaxed a little, but looked at his watch. "Anyway, why would I need photographs to remind me of you when you're right here?" He even managed a smile.

"Well, we can't stay up all night and I need more sleep, so I'm off to bed. I've to have an early start tomorrow and no doubt my desk will be piled high." He rose at the same time and they cuddled in the middle of the living room.

She was about to close her bedroom door, when she turned. "By the way, did you see the pistol in one of his drawers?"

"Pistol?" He looked genuinely shocked.

Then she remembered that she hadn't told him about it. "Yes, in the other top drawer, but I didn't have time to see any

227

markings on it."

"You're sure it was a real pistol and not a toy?"

"Well... I'm not sure, but there was a box of ammunition next to it, so I assumed it was real."

"Shit. I wish you had told me that before because I could have noted the serial numbers. If it was real, he would have to have a licence for it otherwise it's an imprisonable offence, even for a minister of the Crown. And he should have it in an approved locked cabinet, like mine, not kicking around in a drawer for anyone to get hold of."

Yawning, she eyed up her bed just wanting to absorb what he had told her as she drifted off to sleep.

On the other side of the door, Justin waited a few seconds before smiling to himself because he was now sure that he had convinced Patricia that he hadn't found Hamilton's pistol. Walking the short distance back to his own abode, he mulled over his now numerous options. Once Hamilton opened the envelope, he was bound to check his top drawer to see if the copied list was actually the same, and would realise that whoever had taken that photo, may also have discovered his pistol. He would be faced with the prospect of being blackmailed not just over the list, but also the missing firearm. Justin chuckled, because he had already checked up on Hamilton's licence online, via a colleague's secure computer in his office. Apart from various shotguns that were registered at his country home, there was no mention of a pistol, and in any case, a pistol of that calibre had been outlawed several years ago; especially as its serial number had been erased. He hypothesised that Hamilton had purloined it during his tour of duty in Northern Ireland and had kept it all these years.

He had some homework yet to do and would need time on a computer, but not his home one as he suspected whatever keystrokes he made might be monitored. His duty tomorrow was from six in the morning until six in the evening, so he decided to catch three hours sleep before visiting a twenty-four-hour internet café he knew of in Wembley, off route. He'd need to be on his guard from now on because once Hamilton opened that envelope, he didn't know what he might be capable of and he'd have to keep a sharp eye out for tails, and constantly be looking over his shoulder until the matter was resolved. He was trained to be observant for exactly that kind of activity, and would use that training to protect himself as well as Patricia, but if he suspected Hamilton's hand in anything detrimental to either of them... well, he still had his gun. It was well hidden under a neighbour's garden shed and would stay that way if it was needed.

Justin had watched the chauffeur discover the envelope and hand it to Hamilton as he got in the back of the car, and could only assume he had opened it – from his perspective in the car behind, he couldn't see. Throughout the day, he had had plenty of thinking time, waiting in and around the security car as Hamilton visited this person and that at various locations around London, including lunch at The Ivy not far from Covent Garden. They had never made eye contact, even when they had been only a few feet apart. Frustratingly, while on duty, he wasn't allowed to use his phone for personal calls or to trawl the internet, and was itching to speak to Patricia to see how she was coping on her first day back at work. When his relief replaced him at six o'clock, he immediately phoned her mobile, but had to leave a message, so returned to his office where he logged on to his security computer, completed his day's tasks and turned his attention to the face he thought he had recognised from the day before in the pub.

Downloading the man's image from his phone, it didn't take long before 'Doris', as they affectionately called the information bank, came up with a match. Aiden went under several surnames, the most probable being Walsh, but they were mostly all irrelevant which was why Doris didn't list just one; but what she did list was a plethora of crimes and suspected involvements in various nefarious activities. In the light of what Patricia had found out about Lloyd, he virtually ignored the basic information about his parents, place and suspected date of birth etc., but concentrated on recent activities, of which there were few. Further down the page was a list of known associates and he was surprised to see that some of the names had been given codes. 'Annie A' and 'Terry X' were two of them with notations against them warning about their secret status. He naturally clicked on the icons in turn and as he did so, they became highlighted in red and ceased to function. He stopped after the second, not wanting to enrage Doris with a third red background, and theorised that they ought to remain unknown; at least to someone of his own paygrade.

He quickly moved onto the next pages which contained operatives' detailed reports on each incident; mainly in Northern Ireland. Dates of alleged involvement in gunrunning, extortion and kidnapping were among some of the offences, but perversely murder was not included, and he arrived at the conclusion that Aiden was one of the Irish Republican Army's backroom boys who got others to do all the dirty work. In other words, he had stayed under the radar just enough not to be detained on sight. Aiden's whereabouts was currently unknown but what sparked Justin's interest was that the last entry was made only two months ago. It stated that Aiden's activities had moved away from Ireland and that he was probably living somewhere in north London and working with others in one, two or even three cells. The officer concluded that Aiden was most likely acting as a liaison between them and the IRA hierarchy, and that a concerted offensive was likely to be targeted against the latest power-sharing proposal in the near future. What really got Justin's attention was that a copy of this memo had been circulated to all the relevant departments, including Hamilton's; but he had never seen it. This was exactly the type of information he and the others on the team ought to have known about.

He checked the date of circulation and cross-referenced it against the Northern Ireland's database, specifically the section that was relevant to his security department, and looked for clues as to why it had never reached them. Hamilton's department was certainly on the circulation list and he looked down to see who the recipients were... and stopped at CML; short for Clarence McCorley Lloyd.

'Christ' he thought to himself. Somewhere down the line, Lloyd and Aiden must have been in contact with each other. He sat back in his chair and contemplated the ramifications, then sat forward again and wondered if he ought to go through the recipients again, noting whose initials corresponded with names. It would take some time to obtain official clearance to check everyone and follow through to the respective departments to see if the memo had been delivered to the right people, and although he knew he wasn't supposed to go poking around, felt that there was justification. Then the thought occurred to him that this was exactly what Patricia had been referring to when she had said that Lloyd was just the tip of the iceberg.

His concentration was broken by the ringing of his phone. It was Patricia on the old mobile phone. "Can you talk?"

Justin glanced up from his desk and looked around the almost empty room from the reflections in the windows. He hadn't realised how long he had spent on the computer and saw that it showed nearly nine o'clock. "Yeah, fine."

"I've been burgled."

"What?"

"I've been burgled." She repeated the comment as though it was a perfectly natural daily occurrence such as signing for mail from the postman.

Initially, Justin felt real chagrin that it had happened to his fiancée, but it didn't stop there. Once he had got over the surprise, anger and thoughts of retribution started to supplant his normally clinical logic. "Can you tell what's been taken?"

"Not yet 'cos the place is a bit of a mess."

"I suppose you've called the station?"

"That's my next call and I'll get the forensic boys over here in the morning."

"Ummmmm, probably not worth it. I'll bet a pound to a penny they won't find any fingerprints." He was thinking that this couldn't be a coincidence. "It's bound to be connected with Hamilton."

"Now hold on a minute. Just because we're mixed up with him doesn't automatically mean it's him."

"Well, it's your manor and you should know most of the local criminals, so ask yourself this. Is it likely that one of them would target your flat and if the answer is no, then we have to assume it's linked to Hamilton."

There was silence at the other end of the phone, so he continued. "I'm just about finished here so I'll be over in about forty-five minutes."

"OK, see you then."

The light traffic at that time of the evening meant he

was there sooner, and as he walked through the door into her living room, he found her sitting on the floor trying to untangle strands of wool.

"The bastards ruined my scarf."

It was the look on her face that portrayed how upset she was. Justin felt anger rising again but managed to keep control. "What's missing?"

"Not much as far as I can tell, but they took my grandmother's jewellery box and an old school journal that was underneath it."

"Valuable?"

"Ummm, one item was probably worth two or three grand. A charm bracelet."

"How did they get in?"

"Oh the usual. Jemmied the window and forced its lock." She motioned with her head in the direction of the bay windows.

"What about your laptop?"

"No, I had that with me, and before you ask, if they were after that, they wouldn't have broken in while I was at work." She too had been thinking the same as Justin, after his computer had been hacked.

"Maybe they didn't know that you didn't have a desktop or even some sort of interlinked tablet."

"Maybe, but at the moment I can think of only one local crook who specialises in stolen goods – Tom and I'll catch up with him tomorrow. There's also a jewellery fence I can put the squeeze on." She looked up at him. "Only when I've had words with them will we know."

He held his hand out to help her up and saw the dampness in her eyes. He took her in his arms. "Listen, don't let it worry you tonight, because you're coming over to my place. OK?"

"OK."

Justin was again constrained by his duties and was chomping at the bit to access the internet, but he dared not jeopardise his position of being close to Hamilton. He was surprised that Hamilton had not found a way of having him moved to another position, but sitting in the security car outside one of the government offices in Whitehall, he had plenty of thinking time, and a nasty thought suddenly occurred to him. Perhaps it was Hamilton who was keeping him close. Could it have been that the note he had left was having its desired effect or did Hamilton have his own agenda? It was worrying. Hamilton probably knew that Justin wasn't allowed to make private calls or access the internet while on duty and thus be hamstrung; maybe that was his way of limiting his movements?

His relief arrived just before six o'clock. Making sure he was out of sight of any security cameras, of which there were dozens in that vicinity, he phoned Patricia. "What have you found?"

He heard her exhale. "You're right... there were no fingerprints or any DNA left behind and I also discovered that they took my old mobile phone from one of the drawers. And before you ask, no there was nothing on it worth keeping."

"How about your burglar and fence?"

"Haaa. That was a result. Pure coincidence. It transpires that he had just raided Clarkson's house the same night and we caught him red-handed with a bag of loot this morning. You should have seen his face when we woke him; he couldn't believe that we were on to him so quickly. So, he had to freely admit that he was at Clarkson's but emphatically denied that he had been anywhere near mine. Better still, and keep this to yourself, we're carrying out a sting on his fence tomorrow.

The only trouble is that I hope the press don't get a whiff of this before we can nab him as well. On the upside, once we do, it'll be us who are contacting the press and yes... I'll probably be in the limelight again."

"That's brilliant news and I'm really pleased for you. Make the most of it while you can. Yet another feather in your cap and I suppose your super's impressed, what with you being back at work again for just one day."

"Hey... I'm the girl with the golden touch. More fortune and glory... well maybe not fortune," she said gleefully. "How's your day been?"

"Oh, I've had plenty of time to go over everything, languishing in the passenger seat of a car all day, but now that you've told me that, there's no doubt that Hamilton's had a hand in your break-in. What time are you getting home?"

"Funnily enough, I'm just about finished here, so in about an hour or so."

"See you at yours with fish and chips tonight? I'll pick it up on the way. Do you want a wally?"

"Great. Oh, by the way, we've just had another circular reminding us about terrorist activities, only this one had a photograph of that chap in the pub and I've got to acknowledge receipt of it. Won't take me long."

As they munched their way through the encrusted cod and soggy chips, they discussed the ins and outs of what Hamilton was doing, more than Patricia's coup.

"Bloody Hamilton's up to something, I can smell it. He purposefully avoids eye contact with me, whereas before, he would visually check with me and the others, to see if the coast was clear. Right now, we're in no man's land and that envelope I gave him won't last forever, because he'll find a way round it. I reckon it's just a matter of time before he makes a move. So the question is, do we make our move first?"

Finishing up her chips, she wiped the excess ketchup from her lips with the paper towel and was about to make her own suggestion when there was a knock at the door. They naturally looked at each other quizzically.

"Expecting anyone?" he asked.

"Probably just some Jehovah's Witness, I'll get it."

Justin couldn't hear what was being said as he dipped the last of his chips into the small pot of ketchup, and then scrunched up the plain white papers that their takeaway had come in. He saw Patricia closing the front door as he walked through to the kitchen towards the bin in the corner. "Who was that?" he asked nonchalantly over his shoulder. When he did turn round, he saw her standing in the doorway with compressed lips.

"That was our venerated superintendent... Arthur Tonybee." There was a tone of sarcasm in her voice. "He'd come to tell me personally that I won't be needed tomorrow morning when we arrest Cliff the Fence as he would be taking direct charge of the operation himself. Gave me a story about how the station needed someone with a higher profile than me fronting the event, and that the press would be sympathetic if a more senior officer was charge. It's bullshit and he knows it. He just wants his face in the papers instead of mine."

Justin thought about this for a moment. "Are you sure that's his real reason? After all, you're the highest profile officer in the station by far. He hasn't got an OBE, nor has he appeared on the front pages of the national press. And anyway, supers don't do arrests. That's normally done by inspectors or sergeants, and it's they who give the interviews. He's just a glorified office manager."

"What are you getting at here?"

"Call me suspicious, but I detect Hamilton's hand in this. If he's thinking of revenge and any kind of character assassination, the last thing he'd want is your profile raised any further by way of more front-page news, and Clarkson definitely warrants front-page news."

She nibbled her bottom lip for a moment, turned and disappeared into the living room; Justin followed. "What are you doing?"

"I'm phoning Rudi, the deputy super, because he knows more what's going on than Tonybee. You do know why they call him The Buzz, don't you?"

He clearly didn't.

"It's because he's about as irritating as a half-a-bee in your ear." She put her phone up to her own ear. "His first name's Arthur... Arthur Tonybee... 'arf-a-bee?"

"What makes you think Rudi will tell you anything?"

She briefly glared at him, wondering whether or not to tell him one of her little secrets. "If you must know, it's because he's got a crush on me, and yes, I did date him for a short while. Rudi, good evening..." Her tone changed.

Justin listened to one side of the conversation, getting the gist of it and watched her take the occasional step round the coffee table. He cringed as she buttered him up with her dulcet tones but eventually she said good night.

"Well?"

"Ummmmm, can't be sure, but it sounds like too much of a coincidence. Rudi said that only this afternoon a diktat had come down from the Home Office that all station commanders in the London area – and that includes our own super – should temporarily include themselves in the role of arresting officers as a training exercise. Apparently to 'broaden their horizons and integrate more fully with the rank and file, thus boosting morale'. What do you think?"

"And this just came down this afternoon, did it?"

"Yes."

"I think it stinks."

"Yeah, Rudi had the same impression as well as it was effective immediately. He said he'd heard of it happening once before but usually these type of changes are notified well in advance so that rotas and timetable can be adjusted to suit."

"It's Hamilton using the old boy network. I'll bet you he's had a word with his mate the Home Secretary; they're pretty pally you know. Yes… now it all makes sense." Justin looked like he had had one of those light-bulb moments. "He was visiting the Home Office this morning and I should know because I was waiting outside for the best part of half an hour. Oh the bastard. He's trying to make it look like it didn't come from him when all the while he's manipulating the system to suit his own ends – again. Next thing you know and we'll both be out of a job and probably arrested on some trumped-up charge. He'll think of something nasty, of that I'm sure. Right that's it. I'm having it out with him first thing in the morning. I'll tell him we're going to circulate a copy of his list of whores."

Justin was enraged to the point of apoplectic seizure and to Patricia's mind, not thinking clearly. She went and stood directly in front of him. "Now hang on a moment and think calmly… I've an idea. No, two ideas."

Justin was fuming, but at her close proximity and her big round eyes, he did as she suggested. He calmed down. "Go on."

"You mentioned character assassination. Well, I've a way round that. All the super said was that I wasn't to be part of the operation tomorrow morning, but there's nothing to stop me holding my own press interview and giving my version of the arrest, is there?" It was as much a rhetorical statement as a question. "Our burglar's due to meet with Cliff the Fence at nine o'clock tomorrow morning in The Market and if I tell our local *Maidenhead Advertiser* chap to meet me just round the corner, he'll have the drop on the nationals and he'll be able to sell it to them – complete with yours truly in glorious technicolour. It keeps me in the public limelight and will hopefully counter any malicious gossip that Hamilton might be trying to put my way. And it'll keep Terry happy at the same time."

"Terry?"

"He's the press chap from the *Maidenhead Advertiser*. He and I talk to each other all the time." She saw Justin working his way through the scenario. "What do you think? It might even make the BBC news."

"It's a high-risk strategy because it'll put Tonybee's nose well out of joint and you might not be his golden girl for the foreseeable future."

"Maybe, but everyone thinks he's not going to be in that job for much longer anyway, so that doesn't matter."

"OK. I'll go along with that, but you mentioned a second idea."

"Ummmmm. I'm not sure you're going to like it and I need another glass of wine first."

They settled down on the sofa.

"I need to ask you a few questions first." She was fiddling with her phone.

"Go on."

"You know that chap you took a photo of in the pub the other day. Is this him?" She turned her phone round so that he could see her screen.

"Yes, that's him. His first name's Aiden, but we're not sure of his surname. Why."

"He's that chap in our circular we received today. What can you tell me about him?"

Justin pursed his lips and drew breath. "Now you're getting into the realms of national security." He got up, turned on the TV and motioned with his head that they should go outside.

The drizzle was definitely chilling so they both put on coats and, standing in the lee of the building, Justin told her what he had gathered from Doris.

"I was hoping you would say something like that because he's the answer to our prayers."

"How do you mean?"

"You said the report stated that there's something in the air about an operation to stop the latest power-sharing proposal. What do you suppose that means?"

"It normally means that there's about to be some serious disruption in the form of an attack on the mainland such as a bomb in the centre of London. Something that catches the headlines around the world like that bomb in the Baltic Exchange a few decades ago, or an attack on one of the royals." Justin was back to his normal self.

"Would that also include an attempt on the life of one of Her Majesty's ministers?" She had already guessed the answer, but was leading Justin.

If Justin had been about to drink from a full pint of beer, most of it would have ended up on the floor. He was initially dumbstruck at the suggestion. "Bloody hell, it most certainly would." He blurted out, "Ahhhh, I see what you are getting at. Jesus, but you've got a contorted mind. If you're thinking what I'm thinking…"

They peered at each other in the evening gloom, trying to extrapolate various outcomes.

Patricia spoke first. "Should we even be thinking of this?"

"OK, if Aiden and his IRA mob are going to try to murder Hamilton anyway, why not help them by giving them a free hand. Is that what you're saying?"

"Not quite. I'm saying let's find out what their plans are, let them have a go at Hamilton, but arrest them just before they do. Hamilton won't be able to touch us as we've saved his life, the power-sharing initiative gets to go ahead, nobody gets murdered and that way we both come out of this whiter than white. We'll both be promoted, decorated – again in my case – and live happily ever after. How about that?"

He gave a half-chuckle. "You make it sound so simple, and that I like but for one thing." He made her wait a few seconds and she didn't even need to ask the simple question. "How the hell am I going to find out what they're up to? There's the full might of the secret services of Great Britain trying to find out what's being plotted, and you want little old me to find out all by myself."

"Why not start by contacting the officer who made his report on Aiden's location? And then there's that girl who he was meeting in the pub. Did you manage to get her photograph?"

"Do you know, I never thought of that; I was concentrating on Aiden." He retrieved his phone from his pocket and tapped on the photograph icon, illuminating both of their faces. "There she is. I thought there was something odd about her at the time, but it didn't sink in when Aiden turned up. Look, you can just about see she's wearing a wig." They both peered at the small screen which now had reflective tiny rain bubbles on it. "Isn't she? This is no good. It's too small to get enough detail, but I'll tell you what, I'll run her through our computer before I go on duty tomorrow morning and see if Doris can't play with her."

"I'll tell you what else," volunteered Patricia. "As you'll be tied up all day, I'll get one of our crime prevention officers to visit The Queens on the pretence of carrying out a community check, and trawl through their security camera discs. He could also ask the staff if they're familiar with them, how often they frequent the pub, if they know if they're local, etc."

"OK, but as long as he's experienced enough not to put them on alert." He rubbed his unshaven chin in thought. "Maybe they do meet on a regular basis and if they do…" he left the comment unfinished."

"Can we go back in now? I'm getting cold."

"Yes, but just one thing. This sounds like a dangerous game we're about to play and the IRA don't take kindly to one of their own being taken out. If we do manage it, he'd be the catch of the day, and when this is all over, we may have to emigrate."

"Well, I'll look forward to emigrating with you then." She pecked him on his cheek.

Chapter 11

Trembling leaf

A typical crime prevention officer used to be someone appointed from the ranks of the force who carried an air of reliability; someone past middle age and someone who looked like they knew what they were talking about. Someone the public thought they could trust and discuss their problems with. Despite Constable Sarah Pindage looking more or less reliable, she was not archetypal, which was why Detective Inspector Eyethorne has chosen her to visit The Queens Arms. Certainly, she was one of the team that visited local businesses and encouraged them how to be more vigilant, and when it came to securing their own premises, she knew her onions, but she was nowhere near retiring age. She was rather drab-looking and hardly worthy of a glance in any high street. She rarely dressed in her uniform when visiting shopkeepers as that immediately tended to put some of them off and today was one of those days.

Plastic cup of tea in one hand and a sandwich in the other, she walked up to the inspector's desk and stood adjacent to her. They knew each other just about well enough to be on first-name terms.

"I wouldn't eat there if it were free. Easy Dough across the street's much better." She placed her cup on a corner of the desk and waved her thick sandwich.

Patricia looked up from her paperwork to glance briefly at the time on her computer screen. "You're back early... how did it go?"

Sarah swallowed the mouthful of ham and cheese in her mouth. "It's a joke down there. Apart from the padlocks on the gate at the back to stop the locals walking off with empty beer barrels and the old brass bolts on the two front doors, all they've got is a knackered old Yale on the door to their flat above. They've got a mangy old collie dog who's more likely to lick you to death than bark. There's a rusty inoperative alarm system on the outside that's home to a wasps' nest and the wiring looks like it was ripped out years ago."

"What about their CCTV?"

"Haaa! What CCTV? They've got a couple of dummy casings inside and defunct cameras above each door as you go in. Anyway, the governor reckons his biggest problem is the staff, not the locals." She took a half-bite from the rest of her sandwich.

"So nothing on video?"

"About the only thing you'll catch on video down there is triple-rated from under the counter."

"Anything about the locals?"

"Now that was difficult and I had to invent some cock-and-bull story about us receiving rumours about a local gang who were going about raiding pubs, and that their MO was to pose as customers leading up to an actual burglary. That's not so far-fetched as there was a firm doing more or less that a few years back. Anyway, I mentioned what you told me about a woman wearing a wig and guess what? He remembered her. Said that he didn't think she was capable as she was rather gawky and in any case, she wouldn't have got far as she had a permanent limp. Reckons she lives across the road next to

244

the Islamic Centre in the block of flats there as he saw her crossing the main road the other week."

"Did he mention anything about her boyfriend?"

"Naah nothing other than he drank Guinness and that she was a V&T girl. She was particular about her vodka but not bothered about her tonic."

"Regulars?"

"Not what you and I would call regulars, just occasional."

"Right, here's what I want you to do. We need to find out where they both live, so we'll do the usual leaflet scene. Print off a thousand or so A5 leaflets decrying the evils of drink and that Christ is our saviour or something like that, and start handing them out in that vicinity. That way nobody will query why you're hanging around there. If you spot either of them, you can follow them and pretend to be posting them through letterboxes. Take the new chap with you, he ought to fit in from what I've heard of his accent... what's his name?"

"Willy."

"Go on."

"Constable Mark Williams, but everyone calls him Willy."

"OK, take Willy, but keep a tight leash on him. I really don't want our suspects knowing that we're on to them."

"And exactly what are they suspected of?"

Patricia turned to her computer and retrieved both the circular about Aiden and a photograph of her; Pindage positioned herself for a better look. "We suspect he's IRA but keep that to yourself for the time being. So far, we haven't a clue as to who she is, so if you get the chance, see if you can find out. If she's hanging about with him, there'll be a connection."

Pindage thought about this for a moment. "This could take days, and we can't keep handing out leaflets for more than two or three, and the landlord did say that he thought they met in the evenings rather than during the daytime. Besides which, I've got my own schedule."

"You'll only need a day or so, as if they do live nearby, one or other of them is bound to return home at some point."

"Just one other minor point, Guv... this is definitely out of our manor, isn't it? So what happens if the local factory spot us?"

"Use your initiative and if it all goes tits-up, refer back to me. OK?"

"Whatever you say, Guv. When do you want us to start?"

"This afternoon if you can get hold of Willy."

"No problem. He's waiting on me anyway." She stuffed the last of her sandwich in her mouth and wandered off but Patricia called her back.

"This is important Sarah." She didn't often call her inferiors by their first names but felt that the situation warranted it. "Let me know the minute, day or night, if you find her. OK?"

"Right, Guv."

Patricia was nearly right; it took less than a day. Constable Pindage phoned late the same afternoon. "She lives just round the corner at number 12 Greville Place; Flat 5b on the ground floor. Clocked her coming back. But Guv... you ought to know she's probably getting ready to move out."

"How did you find that out?"

"I didn't, but she went shopping and came back with two medium-sized suitcases and they sounded empty to me as she wheeled them over the blind cobbles, so she's either going on holiday or getting ready to do a runner. I reckon it's the latter because you don't take two suitcases on holiday, what with the price of extra luggage on a plane these days."

Patricia had been hoping for early news, but not quite this

early, and had not prepared herself for the good news quite so soon. "Are you there now?"

"Yeah, just outside her flat and running out of leaflets. Don't worry, she can't see us as it's dark now."

"Make sure you keep it that way and stay put until I get to you." She rang off, looked at the time hoping it was past six o' clock and saw that there was another forty minutes to go before she could call Justin. She decided that there was just time to finish up what she was doing and get to Constable Pindage's location before Justin was available on his phone.

Traffic was grinding its usual way through the suburbs of west London and as she was nearing The Queens, her phone private rang; it was Justin. "Any news?"

"You're not going to believe this but..." She briefly told Justin the news.

"Right, I'll be with you as soon as I can, oh... and err... make sure you cover all exits. We don't want her disappearing out the back door while we're watching the front."

Patricia found Constables Pindage and Willy hiding from the chilly damp weather in their car by the crossroads. She immediately sent Willy off to scout around for a rear entrance to the block of flats and replaced him in the warm front seat.

"You can see her bedroom window from here; ground floor, third from the right. Net curtains are slightly ajar."

"How do you know it's her *bedroom* window?"

"I don't, but I reckon it is because I saw her shadow undressing and most people don't get undressed in their living rooms. That's probably the one on the side facing over there." She pointed. "Guv... are we on overtime now?"

"Both of you, but not for much longer as I'm expecting... back-up." Patricia was now wondering if she ought to keep the two constables on for a while longer, but if either of them saw her with Justin, then natural curiosity might start unnecessary conjecture. She made up her mind. "As soon as it does, you can both go, and I'll see you in the morning. Any sign of her fella?"

"No, just the normal type of person who you'd expect to be coming and going from a block of flats but I reckon one of them on the first floor's a knocking shop. You can just see the top of her front door through the commonway window up there. While we've been sitting here, regular as clockwork every twenty minutes, different blokes come and go and we've been guessing which one's coming in." She looked at the clock on the dashboard. "I reckon there ought to be a changeover in about five minutes, so see if you can guess who."

They sat in silence and listened to the rain drumming on the roof for all of three minutes before the door to the first-floor flat opened. As the man exited the block, they watched another approach; Sarah turned on the windscreen wipers for a better look. "That one, now watch the door upstairs open in about... ten seconds."

It opened and closed.

"It can't be only one girl, can it?" commented Sarah with wonder in her voice. "If it is, then she's raking it in. Probably fifty quid a go, and that's two hundred an hour. Even if there's two of them, that's still loads more than I'm earning."

Patricia pondered the question before looking across at Sarah, who she found looking back at her. "More than I'm earning as well."

It took another couple of thinking minutes, during which time Patricia asked herself if it was more than a local whorehouse. Drugs perhaps? "Tell you what... once my back-up has arrived, wait for another couple of chaps to exit and follow the next. See where he takes you, because the timing

248

is too regular for a sex shop. Tell me what you find in the morning."

"OK Guv."

Patricia's phone buzzed from an incoming text. 'Where are you?'

"Right, he's here, so you and Willy stay put for a while." She got out of the car and walked diagonally over the crossroads, spotting Justin standing by a post box. He walked away when he was sure that he had been seen and she followed him to his car a short distance away; still within sight of the block of flats, but from a different perspective. Once ensconced in the passenger seat she gave him a truncated version of how the woman had been found and pointed to Willy off to their left; he looked wet and miserable.

"Brilliant idea of yours to get the ground troops running around, but he does stick out like a sore thumb." Justin was referring to Willy, as nobody in their right mind would be hanging around as he was in the rain. He didn't even look like he was waiting for a taxi.

"More likely to be arrested for loitering without intent. I'll go and have a word." Patricia got out of the car, trotted over to Willy, spoke to him briefly before circuitously making her way back to Justin's car. "I told him to keep dry in the other car. Now, tell me what we do from here."

"I've been thinking about that and wondering how she communicates with Aiden, so follow my logic on this. It's probably not on a regular basis so it has to be by mobile, Blackberry or something encrypted, and even then that'll be kept to a minimum, so it's no use calling up a mobile tracking van as it might be days before they text each other. We can't just go knocking on her door as she'll clam up, so we need to get her away from her flat. I reckon we slip this note under her door." Justin produced a folded slip of paper.

It said: 'Queens Now.'

He continued. "We know they meet at The Queens Arms and that they obviously consider that a safe place to go, so why not? Other than accosting her on the street in broad daylight, I can't think of any other way. Can you?"

She nibbled her bottom lip in thought. "And then what? Anyway, we might be sitting there like lemons until closing time, while she legs it."

"No. She won't do that... not if she's smart... and we do think she is smart; certainly enough to disguise herself. So she'll come to one of two conclusions. One that Aiden's been compromised and that another in their group is trying to get hold of her, but that's rather unlikely; or two, that us security types have cottoned on to her and want a discreet word. She won't run because she'll realise that she's being watched and we'd just pick her up somewhere along the line. And then there's the curiosity aspect... she'll want to know who's keeping tabs on her and what sort of threat they pose. Find out what we know etc. She's bound to want to know one way or the other, and in answer to your second question, we try to convince her that you and I are for real."

Patricia had put her finger to her mouth to get a better purchase on a loose piece of skin on her inner lip. "And how do we do that? She'll want some sort of proof that we're not part of an elaborate scheme to flush out the rest of her cell."

"I'm still working on that one, but in the meantime, get your chap to slip this note under her door, and make sure she hears him doing it. Then get them to stay put and observe just in case she does run. See you in the pub."

"I've just thought of a third conclusion." She watched Justin's hand hover beside the door handle.

"Go on." He didn't turn to look at her.

"There could be a third, or even a fourth member in their cell."

Now Justin turned. "In that case she's even more likely to turn-up, isn't she?"

Apart from a noisy bunch of after-work types crowded round one end of the bar with the men centring their attention on the lone female in their group, there was a mixture of a few locals and a couple of passers-by. Patricia had ironically chosen the same table that Aiden and Erica had sat at before while Justin stood at the bar; he returned with three drinks.

"You're optimistic, aren't you?" Patricia indicated to the third as he sat down.

"I'm guessing she'll want Grey Goose and Tonic and anyway, it's another hint for her that we know more about her than she thinks we know, so let's try to keep it like that. If you get the chance and she's carrying a handbag like she was the other day, see if you can get a peek inside it."

She gave him a half-sideways look as if to say 'you'll be lucky'. "Fat chance." She reached for her glass, but Justin stopped her hand before it reached it.

"Why do you think I've given you a wine glass like that?"

Patricia now noticed that instead of red wine, it was clear and absolutely full to the brim with ice cubes, and it took her a moment to work it out. "Ahhhhhh, you want me to spill it. Looks like water. Is it?"

He nodded.

"And it's water because...?

"I'll let you work that one out for yourself, but I'll give you a clue... there's three reasons, well four actually if you count the glass." He let her mull and watched her reasoning.

"What's the fourth... something to do with the ice?"

He nodded again. After nearly a minute she gave up. "Tell me you swine, or I'll make sure it gets tipped over you."

He was grinning. "OK, OK. When she reads that note, she'll probably spend a few minutes working out if it is safe or not to come to The Queens and continue to do so while she's putting on her disguise, which by the way, she'll need to do in any event. She's probably well-practised at it, so it won't take her too long. If she's careful, she'll walk down to the main road and scout round the pub looking for any sort of a trap, and when she discovers there isn't one, she'll walk through one of the two doors and look around. You're facing one door, and I the other, so when she does come in, we need to beckon her over. OK? By the time she sits down, the ice in your glass will have melted enough so at the slightest touch, it will naturally trickle a little over the side, making the side slippery and hence, your accidental spillage. Look, you can see how it's already condensing on the outside."

"You're rather devious, aren't you? But come on then, have you thought of a way of convincing her of our dilemma?"

"I can't think of any actual proof that would convince her, but there's ways of phrasing things so that they appear to be proof, so follow my lead and let's see where they take us." He looked at his watch. "Oughtn't to be very long now. By the way, you haven't told me about Cliff. How did that go?"

"Oops. In all the excitement of finding our golden girl, I'd forgotten about that, and that was only a few hours ago. Went like clockwork, but none of my items were found, so that implicates Hamilton, or at least someone else. Doesn't it? Don't look now but I think she's just walked in the door behind you."

A disguised Erica started taking a few nervous steps

towards the bar when she spotted Patricia holding up a glass with one hand and a bottle of tonic with the other. The gesture was clear enough for her to realise that an invitation was being offered and she angled her way over to the spare chair and sat down. Justin smiled, noting that the zip on her cheap handbag wasn't fully closed, but it stayed firmly on her lap.

Nothing was said for a few seconds as the two parties looked between themselves for some sort of reaction, but it was Erica who spoke first. "Give me one good reason why I shouldn't just walk out of here."

Justin still held his smile. "Free vodka and tonic. Grey Goose alright?"

She returned his gaze with unwavering eyes and he added "Please don't let it go to waste, because neither Patricia nor I drink vodka."

Still no reaction from Erica with her steady stare, so he relaxed a little more by leaning further back on his chair, hoping to ease the tension between them. He indicated with his eyes on her drink. "The very least you can do is listen while you drink."

After a few seconds pause, she looked across at Patricia who inclined her head a fraction as if to say 'why not?'.

"OK then. I'm listening." She didn't touch the vodka but did ease herself so that her back rested on the chair support.

Justin still wasn't sure how this was going to go, and while the initial persuasion for her to stay had been going on, he had tried not to look as though he was inspecting her disguise – which he had been. He decided that there was a rather beautiful woman underneath. "I believe we have a mutual interest in someone."

His comment was met with a blank stare, and he decided that she was good at masking her feelings which would make it more difficult for him to read. He had no option than to come straight out with it. "Hamilton."

The very slightest of a hardening of her eyes told him an awful lot.

"Hamilton? I don't think I know any Hamiltons." Now she reached for her glass and added the tonic, which in Justin's mind revealed that she did. He opted to continue playing the game softly.

"Maurice Hamilton MP, often called Bloody Hamilton because of his reputation for leaving a bloody mess behind him wherever he goes. The press love him because he's such a juicy target to write about and he frequently courts controversy when on TV.

"Oh yes, I've heard about that Hamilton. Who hasn't?"

"Some would say that he's a possible candidate to be the next prime minister, but equally there's others who would prefer to see him dead... very much a Marmite man. You either love him or hate him." Justin watched a pair of newcomers enter the pub but decided they posed no threat.

As Erica sipped from her glass, Patricia added, "We're not really into Marmite ourselves."

Justin decided that now was the time to dip a toe in the water. "Do you like Marmite?"

"I thought I was just going to listen. Not answer any questions."

Fair enough, thought Justin, so he tried a different tack. "Let me put it this way. Patricia and I have recently come across a batch of bad Marmite which is proving rather difficult to keep down, and we're afraid that unless we find some sort of cure, it might turn out to be terminal. As far as we know, there's no known antidote, but we're on the lookout for someone who may be able to point us in the right direction.

Of course, if you're not the person we've been seeking, we'll just have to carry on looking for those who think they might have the answer, but on the other hand, we'd hate to interfere with your own, shall we say... observations."

"We think we can help each other, is what Justin is trying to say," Patricia volunteered.

Erica made sure her reactions were minimal as she weighed up the consequences of either agreeing or disagreeing with the Marmite analogy. "If you tell me a little more about your experiences, I might be in a better position to see if I can help, but that might depend upon this being an industrial or personal issue."

A wave of relief swept over Justin as he had managed to get some kind of response, but with her obvious referral to the security forces he decided to hide the truth and not mention their involvement; at least not yet. At this early stage, he reckoned that if she had the slightest whiff of establishment involvement, she would walk out. "Oh, this is definitely personal."

Watched closely by the other two, Erica stalled for time by gently revolving her glass round until the lemon lined up closest to her, all the while furiously wondering if the unknown couple sitting at the same table were genuine. Then she remembered that not only did they know where she was staying but also had a V&T waiting for her. She needed to find out how they knew these things, and at the moment, her only reasoning led her to conclude that they must be associated with English security. But what branch? She briefly thought about looking around to see if there were any others in the pub, but then thought the better of it, because by doing so, it might well alert them to what she was thinking. And running away was certainly one of her options, but if only she could find out who they were, so she decided to play their game and see where it went.

"OK." Taking a leaf out of Aiden's book, she retrieved some coins from her purse in her handbag, stood up and shovelled a few into the jukebox, pressed several random buttons and sat back down. What she didn't see was Patricia taking a photograph of her half-open handbag while she was doing that. Once the music started, she said, "I might be able to offer you some advice for your Marmite problem, but I certainly wouldn't help just anyone. Who are you?"

Patricia beat Justin to it because she knew Erica would pose the question sooner or later. "We're private detectives but you won't find us in Yellow Pages as we don't advertise. Justin and I have been running our own business for a while now and rely on word of mouth, rather than carry out those assignments that run-of-the-mill agencies do. There's only the two of us and we specialise in having noteworthy clients with... unusual problems." She was looking at Justin who cottoned on as quickly as she had hoped, and he took up the reins.

"Yes, and now we've found ourselves holding the wrong end of the stick, so to speak, and think that you too are on the same end as us."

Erica had unshakable belief in herself, Aiden and their cause, and was totally unconvinced of Justin's last statement; she tried her best not to let it show. "Uhuh. I thought you had the smell of police about you. So how did you find me and where do I fit in?"

"Through Hamilton," answered Justin before Patricia could.

"Hamilton." She did her best to sound surprised. "I don't have anything in common with him, and why should I?"

"But you do, whether or not you know it." He was disappointed that she remained emotionless at this last comment and now had no choice other to carry on. "You see... he engaged us to investigate certain parts of his personal life... what exactly we can't tell you for obvious reasons, but along the line we came across a link with someone you know; hence the connection to you. As you can imagine, after that it wasn't too difficult to trace you to your flat."

It was Patricia's turn to try and keep a straight face, as she knew what was coming next from Erica.

Erica still felt secure enough. "You'll have to do better than that, because anyone could make up such a story. Who's this mysterious link and what have they got to do with me?"

Justin and Patricia looked at each other and she nodded. Justin had had a glimmer of an idea that he had been pursuing for some time, and now it was materialising even as he spoke. "Hamilton asked us to find someone who was passing information from his Northern Ireland office and it turned out to be a right royal leak; not just from his office, but from other government offices as well. Sure, there'll always be those who leak information both officially and unofficially, but when those leaks start impacting on what one really doesn't want made public knowledge, or even passed onto one's opponents without your own knowledge, then it starts to become a serious matter. In this instance, we found Hamilton's mole and when we told him who it was, his whole attitude towards us changed."

He paused to sip his soda water and Patricia interjected as she could see where Justin was going with this one. "It was as though he hadn't wanted us to actually find the mole for him."

"That's right, and when we dug deeper, it became a

possibility that he had been trying to sabotage his own peace initiative through his own fictitious mole. He had been creating false information from what others were led to believe were from untraceable sources, but all the while, they came from him. A double mole if you like. The problem from our perspective was that we found a real mole, and together with their associates, they added up to quite an anthill. When we told Hamilton, he shut us down immediately."

"You'll have to excuse Justin's turn of phrase as he tends to get carried away sometimes. Moles and ants don't really begin to describe the nest of vipers we found." Patricia thought it best to add to the analogies as a way of giving Justin more thinking time. He was clearly muddying the waters by trying to disguise part of the truth with lies.

"Now who's getting carried away?"

"This is all very interesting, but I still don't see what it's got to do with me."

"I'm coming to that, but you need some of the background so that you'll believe us when I tell you the connection."

"Well, who is it then?" Erica reached for her drink.

"I can't give you the name of the mole inside Hamilton's office, but he led us to a man known as Aiden."

Try as she did, Erica struggled to finish swallowing her small mouthful, and her reaction was not missed by the other two. At that moment, she knew that they knew that she had a connection with Aiden, and that it would be no good denying it now. Neither of them spoke but watched as she slowly replaced her glass on the table. She had never thought for one moment that anyone would be able to trace either her or Aiden, but these two sleuths had managed to find her and possibly Aiden as well. She had irregularly moved from rented flat to rented flat across London these past few years;

never leaving a forwarding address and keeping very much to herself. So how had they found her? She inwardly cringed at the prospect of them knowing about their plans to assassinate Hamilton, and realised she had to discover if they also knew. Please, please, please. She thought to herself. Not when we are so close. She looked down at her hand and saw that she was shaking a little; like a trembling leaf. Was it anger or anxiety she was now experiencing? She couldn't tell, but she did her best to regain control of herself and concentrate on the matter in hand.

"I know of an Aiden, but…"

"The same one you met in here the other day," interjected Justin before she had a chance to say something along the lines of not having seen him for months. "You see, we found out that he's planning to have a go at Hamilton and we're here to… offer our assistance."

"You what?" A stunned Erica looked quizzically from Justin to Patricia.

"That's right." Patricia felt it was her turn to back up Justin. "Because having found his real mole, Hamilton's putting the squeeze on us. He doesn't want us revealing what we know to anyone else."

Erica's mind was in turmoil, struggling to understand complete opposites. First she had suspected some sort of trap, then that she would be bullied into revealing her associates' names and coerced into cooperating with her enemies, and finally threatened with arrest and imprisonment; none which had materialised. In fact, quite the contrary. They knew far too much for comfort, but surely they couldn't have found out about the Rubik's cube? Could they? It had to be some sort of trap.

She swigged most of her drink. "Naah. You're joking.

This is a set-up." She decided to bluff it out. "Just because you saw me with someone you thought to be called Aiden doesn't mean I'm involved with whatever he's up to. You're fishing for vague pieces of a jigsaw without a picture to help you, and you think I'm involved. Well, think again because I've got plenty of friends and Aiden just happens to be one of them. And anyway, why should I help you when all you're doing is accusing me of some sort of conspiracy? If Hamilton's got some sort of beef with you, then you can sort it out, but without me. I don't want to get involved with whatever's going on. OK?"

She finished her drink and made to leave.

"There's more… if you'll stay and listen." Justin leaned over and put his hand gently on her arm. She paused.

Erica thought about this for a moment and realised she would have to stay if she wanted to find out what they knew. "OK… but I'll have another first."

"I'll get them." Patricia had not touched her drink and easily slopped her glass over the table so that most of the water ran towards Erica and dripped down towards her feet. "Oh rats."

Erica left her handbag on the table to free up her hands which she used to smartly shove her chair back a foot or so to avoid her feet getting wet, but there was no opportunity for either of the other two to have a look inside.

"You're the unlucky one today," piped up Justin. "She usually does that to me."

"I'll get a bar towel while I'm at it. Same again?" Patricia didn't wait for an answer.

When Erica had finished re-positioning herself and Patricia had given them a towel to mop up with, Justin took the opportunity to get an aside in. "Why the disguise, because it doesn't do you justice?"

Surprised at Justin's comment, Erica slowed her domestic mopping up operation, but recognised that it was a clever question. She couldn't admit it was to evade CCTV, so she'd have to make something up; it was going to be a half-truth anyway. "There was a man I was seeing a while ago and he turned out to be the violent type, but when I confronted him with being an active member of the English Defence League, he hit me – several times. I had to move flats but he was the stalking type, so that's when I started wearing glasses and this wig. When I saw your note under my door, I wondered if he had managed to find me again."

Not bad for a spur of the moment reply, thought Justin. And she's quick.

Once Patricia was re-seated, Justin continued. "We have another problem in that Hamilton's trying to blackmail us. It's not the first time he's tried it on because that's been just one of his methods of clawing his way into the position of power that he now enjoys. As a minister of the Crown he now has even greater power and he appears to be abusing it to a full extent."

'He's always abused his position,' thought Erica, but she wasn't going to tell them how she knew that. "Are you going to tell me that he's got something on you?"

"Ashamedly yes, because we didn't see it coming. He managed to get one of his chaps to hack into our computer and steal our client list, and he's now threatening to release sensitive information to the security services. This would not only be more than awkward for us, but also of great embarrassment to them. Normally if they were run-of-the-mill people it wouldn't matter too much, but when they are notable clients, many of whom move in government circles...

well, you can see where this might end up. One or two are the kind of people who you wouldn't want to meet down a dark alley, but there are those who are rather influential and more likely than not, able to have us locked away for life on trumped-up charges – even murdered if it came to it, just because of the sensitive information we have."

"That still doesn't prove anything. You could be making this all up."

Justin produced one of his phones and found Hamilton's list of conquered women. He adjusted the screen so that the reference to their sexual scores was off the edge, shifted his chair a little, turned the phone round so that Erica could see and held it there for a few seconds. He knew he'd have to be very careful what was visible and once he saw her focusing on names, slowly scrolled down. He saw her eyes widen and her body stiffen when it came to Lady Abergail. "You know her then?" It was just as well that he didn't need to scroll much further as there was one particular name he didn't want her to see.

'Shit.' Erica was horrified at what else this pair of detectives had discovered. 'They must know almost everything and they're only one or two steps away from finding out about the cube.'

"I suppose it's a waste of time asking how you know Lady Abergail?"

There was no way she was going to divulge that and instead, keeping a straight face, took a pull of her vodka.

"OK then, but all these people on that list are going to be in Hamilton's pocket, and we're going to have to emigrate to Guatemala… unless we can find some way of stopping him. And we think you and your friend Aiden may be in a position to do just that."

"Now hold on a minute. Just because I know Aiden

doesn't mean I'm involved with whatever he's up to. He's someone I met a few years..."

Justin moved his head suddenly closer. "Let me tell you a bit about Aiden, and if any of it sounds familiar, please stop me." He started to recite what he had memorised without revealing where the information had come from. "You see, we know Hamilton's his target, but what we don't know is how or when."

"What we particularly need to know is when, because if we can stall him long enough, hopefully he won't be in a position to blackmail us anymore," added Patricia.

"We won't be able to say anything because that would indicate our culpability and it therefore follows that neither your name nor Aiden's will ever get mentioned. This is strictly off the record."

They gave her some time to think about this, but then Patricia blurted out. "For God's sake, the bastard tried to rape me." It was a heartfelt plea.

She gave a savage look towards Patricia, understanding what she must have gone through. More than anything else, she wanted her revenge on Hamilton, but unless she started to play ball with the couple in front of her, it looked like they might well interfere with Aiden's carefully laid plans. They had still not given her any proof, but they'd found out just about everything else except for the cube, so she had to surmise that sooner or later they might well do. Aiden... he was the key as he always had been, and it crossed her mind that perhaps she ought to tell him. But then again, knowing what kind of a single-minded person he was, he would just as likely dispose of her down one of those dark alleys himself. What a cleft stick she was caught in. If she told them nothing, they might find out about the cube, but if she confirmed what they already knew and misdirected them with a few twisted facts, Aiden's plan still ought to succeed.

"For ages Aiden's had all sorts of designs to disrupt the Irish power-sharing issue by any means possible, but every time he'd get close to whatever he'd been scheming, somehow it always fell apart. Hamilton's office isn't the only organisation that has leaks, you know, and he once told me that someone he'd known since his youth had betrayed them; grassed on one of their own... and he's not been heard of since. I've always known he's had connections with the IRA but I haven't probed for obvious reasons, and I don't want to start now. This time he told me that nobody else knows what he's doing, other than it's likely to be around the new year and before the power-sharing agreement comes another step closer to reality." Erica had done her best to sound sincere, knowing that she was being closely scrutinised. "There's nothing much more to add really."

Justin wanted a little more convincing. "So what were you and Aiden discussing over lunch the other day and how did you contact each other?"

His mention of her recent lunchtime nearly caught her out as she wasn't expecting to have been seen that day. She wondered how much more these two knew and how long they had had her under surveillance.

"Oh, he just phoned me out of the blue and suggested we meet here. It's as good a place as any, and he knows I live nearby, and before you ask, no, it's not a regular event. We were just catching up and I naturally asked him what he was up to these days... that's when he mentioned that he had something in the pipeline for the new year, but no mention of Hamilton. It could be anyone he's after."

"I don't suppose you could arrange another meeting, but

this time include us?"

"No way…" she retorted, thinking furiously now. "For starters, I never contact him, it's always the other way round, and even if I did, he'd smell a rat. Then, he'd suspect something was amiss coming so soon after our lunch, and in any case, I think he said he was going up North for a while… but I can't remember where."

Both Justin and Patricia were suspicious of her statement about them contacting each other, but to them, this was almost a predictable response.

Patricia decided to divert the conversation away from this aspect. "So, what's your connection with Lady Abergail?"

Erica was suddenly on safer ground. "Hardly any connection at all. I was at a wine bar in the West End not so long ago and came across Lady Abergail. She was celebrating with a few of her friends, and once I got talking to her, helped myself to a bit of free champagne. Better than this stuff." She finished her vodka and looked at her watch and rose. "So you see, I've not been much help at all really. I must go."

"One more thing." Justin stalled her, fearful that they might never see her again. "We really are sincere about helping, so if you think we can, here's my number." He was writing the number of his private phone on the back of a beer mat as he spoke.

She nearly didn't take it, but then had second thoughts. "You know where to find me."

They waited for her to disappear through the door to the main road. "I need a proper drink." Patricia made for the bar and when she returned, Justin was catching up on his phone. "She was lying through her back teeth."

"So were we, but wouldn't you if you'd been caught out like that? There's bound to be elements of truth in what she said and all we've got to do is separate fact from fiction. Time to bring your detecting skills to bear."

She nibbled at her bottom lip for a moment or two. "She was too nonchalant about her relationship with him, so let's assume she's closer to Aiden than she was letting on, and if so, she'd be holding back any vital information. For example, she said that he'd gone up north somewhere, inferring that he was now out of contact, but that wouldn't stop them contacting each other. Even if you're on the other side of the world, you can still phone someone day or night. And then there's that cock-and-bull story about wearing a wig etcetera, and from what Sarah told me about her suitcases, she's up to no good."

"Sarah?"

"Oh sorry, I forgot to mention that one of my constables spotted her with new empty suitcases this afternoon."

"Oh bugger... that means she's on the move."

They both realised it at the same time as they looked into each other's eyes. "That'll be tonight then," said Justin.

"I would if I was her, and I'd be packing right now." Patricia got her phone out. "Hope we're not too late... I'm ringing Sarah."

Justin left her to it while he visited the toilet, mainly to take the opportunity to see if there were any spurious characters hanging about; there weren't. When he returned, Patricia was ringing off.

"They were just about to leave, but she confirmed that our target had returned and I told her to stay put, but to follow if she left. She's dispatched Willy to peek into her window to see if she's packing."

"Willy?"

Her phone rang. "Thanks. Stay there."

"Sarah says she's packing, so it'll be a simple case of just following, but I can't keep those two on all night."

Justin thought about the dilemma. "How long would it take you to pack... assuming you're in a hurry and there's not too much stuff?"

"In an emergency, about ten minutes. Especially if I didn't have to put on make-up or a disguise. She's already wearing those."

"Well, that leaves us with less than five. Do we know if she's got a car?"

"No."

"Let's guess she hasn't got a car because otherwise she'd have to register it etcetera and provide an address, all of which is traceable, and I'm guessing again that she doesn't want that. So she'll be on foot."

"And if she's on foot, she'll probably head for the station... or the underground. Both are just round the corner, so she won't be using a taxi."

"And that means we've got to follow her on foot, but you and I will be recognised, so we've got to get Sarah and Willy to do the donkey work. We can follow at a distance... you on foot well behind the other two, and me by car. Give Sarah a ring and get her up to speed, and for God's sake tell them to be circumspect. Probably best if you stay here until we know which direction she's taking."

Patricia was already dialling Sarah as Justin left, and he had been in his car for less than a minute when Erica emerged wheeling two brown nondescript suitcases. He watched the two plain-clothed constables wait until she had rounded the corner before getting out of Sarah's car and following; he also followed on foot to see which station they was headed for. "She's going for the tube, so you can pick them up as they pass. That's the Bakerloo line, isn't it?"

"Yeah… I'll let you know if it's north or south."

He returned to his car and waited for Patricia's call. "She's waiting on the south platform. I'll let you know where she gets off."

Justin headed for Paddington station, then along the Edgware Road towards Marylebone and down to Charing Cross in response to Patricia's occasional calls. He strategically parked up illegally on Victoria Embankment in familiar territory waiting for her next call, realising that she may have had problems with getting a phone signal in some of the deeper tunnels of the underground, and when she did ring, he immediately set off to cross the Thames over Waterloo Bridge.

"Looks like she's headed for Elephant and Castle. Oh, this is going to be fun," commented Patricia sarcastically. "That's the end of the line, so she's either meeting someone or is going to disappear into one of the blocks of high-rise flats. Shit."

Justin had to wait at a set of roadwork lights but wasn't worried as he was only a few minutes away. She rang. "Meet me in St George's Road a couple of hundred yards from the big roundabout."

When she got in his car, his first question was, "OK, where are they?"

"Looks like she's found somewhere to shack up behind that deli over there, down Garden Row. I'm waiting for Sarah…" Her phone rang.

"Well done to you both. Now get yourselves back home and, before you ask, I'll sort your overtime."

She put her head back on the headrest and closed her eyes for a moment. Justin waited. "Third flat on the first floor. They reckon she's alone." She hadn't opened her eyes. "So now what do we do?"

"Now, we go home."

Chapter 12

Dogs don't bark just because they're mad

In his office, Hamilton had been automatically signing a seemingly endless pile of Christmas cards while reading a report delivered by a committee convened months ago by his predecessor. It was a boring document about a proposed change to how government officers were to be elected at local level and he wasn't really concentrating on it. Fortunately, someone had circled the pertinent parts in pencil and he'd occasionally add his own comments with his fountain pen. In between these menial tasks, his thoughts kept wandering back to Crawford and his bitch Eyethorne, and what to do about them. Crawford was easy to deal with, as a word in the right ear to ostensibly promote him would turn out to be a god-forsaken posting somewhere near the Falkland Islands; that would split them up for starters.

But his prime target was a different kettle of fish. He was still a little baffled as to how she had managed to get hold of his prized list, which was now securely under lock and key in his safe, and surmised that she must have rifled through his drawers while he was... OH, the bloody ignominy of it. But how had she known it was there in the first place? BITCH was too kind a description. His conundrum was simple. How to corner someone who appeared to be whiter than white? He drew analogies with some of those disgraced politicians from earlier administrations who had fallen foul of the press. Everyone's got dirt on them from their past, so it was surely just a matter of finding it, but Mr Postles and his department would have made sure she was 'clean', so that left him with only one option. He would have to do his own dirty work and naturally, it would have to be unattributable to him.

He spotted a spelling mistake and frantically crossed it through and replaced it with the word 'IDIOT', and turned the page while wondering why someone would spell the word 'trap' with two Ps. He turned it back again. That was it. He'd set a trap for her, and soon. But Christmas was just round the corner with the parliamentary recess looming and he wondered if he could squeeze it in. He'd already had quiet words with his colleague in the Home Office about her, so could hardly ask another favour there, and still she had managed to steal the limelight. He glanced down at the floor next to his bin where he'd scrunched up the newspaper bearing the story about her arrest of Clarkson's burglar. It hadn't been important enough to make the front pages, but it was still a smack in his face.

Trawling through his classical learnings, he penned a scrawly list of the seven deadly sins on his blotter. Lust, which he bracketed with the word sex, Gluttony, Greed, Wrath, Sloth, Pride and Envy. He put an 'x' next to the first three and then two others next to Envy and Sloth, leaving Wrath and Pride. Wrath would come later, which meant that Pride would be his primary method of skullduggery. Yes... that was it... she took great pride in her job of upholding the law, so he would need to bait a juicy trap.

He continued signing his Christmas cards, occasionally looking down at his list, all the while mulling over what he could possibly use as bait and how to snare her. He paused at Greed, again wondering if money would attract her. OF

COURSE. He still had seventy-odd-thousand pounds in an envelope she had returned to him and there would bound to be some of her fingerprints on some of the notes. Certainly she had returned a large portion of his original stake but he wondered how much of it she had really kept for herself. He smugly reflected that it would be a high price to pay, but worth it. He could buy himself another yacht with that sort of money; well, a bit of a yacht anyway. It got him thinking about what else one could buy with seventy thousand. What might she buy with seventy thousand, illegally? His pen hovered over his list and he dotted out most of his 'x's. Drugs.

He abhorred those who sold and used the likes of heroin and cocaine, especially that sweet sickly stench of cannabis he had rarely come across. If he could have his way, all drugs would be classified as Class A and the dealers locked up for life. Oh, wouldn't that be just perfect. If he could set up a trap where she was found in possession of seventy-thousand quid and a stash of drugs... He chortled to himself, but then stopped suddenly. He hadn't the first idea as to how to get hold of any drugs, let alone several grands worth. Deep in thought, he savagely scrawled another couple of cards. He wondered if any drugs came across from Northern Ireland, and if so, he could quite simply enquire within his own department without raising any eyebrows or involving his colleagues from other departments.

His pen hovered over a jolly-looking Santa with a sack-full as he recalled that there'd been a crackdown on drug smuggling with the inauguration of a new sniffer-dog section in Belfast last month, and it would only be natural for him to follow it up. Getting hold of whatever had been confiscated would have to be played by ear, and he was a little uncomfortable with going into a situation without one of his contingencies, but he'd think of one. He wondered if he ought to take some of that seventy grand with him, because everybody had their price. Except THE BITCH and her sidekick.

Once he'd got the stuff back to his apartment, he'd need to set up a sting operation, and another thought entered his head. If he could somehow link in an Irish connection, he would come out of this not only smelling of roses, but sate his appetite for revenge. Oh, but this was getting better by the minute.

He looked at his diminishing pile of cards to sign with glee, reached for the intercom button but hovered his finger over it as another thought entered his head. Lloyd. He was up to no good, so he could be the Patsy if it all went tits-up. He pressed down on the switch. "Lloyd, we're off to Northern Ireland."

***

Alarm bells were ringing in Patricia's ears, but try as she might she couldn't get out of the fire station. She dragged herself away from her nightmare, opened her eyes and reached across her bed to thump the bloody machine into silence. She'd gone to sleep thinking about how they were going to be able to find Aiden through Erica, and before drifting off, had vaguely concluded that they'd have to follow her 24/7 all the way up to and including New Year's Eve. It just wasn't possible without a lot more manpower, so they'd have to find another way.

Going through her morning routine and having let her subconscious ferret around while she was asleep, she virtually slept-walked into the bathroom and considered what Erica had said the previous day. New Year... New Year... Why New Year? Could it be New Year's Eve... Day, or even into the new year? But she didn't think the Irish Assembly issue was being addressed by parliament until March. Or was it April? Certainly not December or January. So she was lying about that as well, and if not then, when? Brushing her teeth in the mirror, she applied her detecting skills by posing the question that if she'd been caught unawares, what would she have answered if she'd have wanted to put someone off the trail. The obvious answer was sooner rather than later. She stopped her brush stroke mid swing and looked herself in the eyes. Christmas was just round the corner. Bloody hell, they were going to try to assassinate Hamilton at Christmas... Eve or Day? She spat out the toothpaste and glugged a beaker full of water round her mouth. That would certainly grab the headlines. Day, she decided, because that was when the security services would be at their most vulnerable, and because nobody with forethought would choose the 24th when you could do it on the 25th. Christmas Day it would be then.

She wandered into the kitchen, flicked on the kettle and nonchalantly looked out of the window to see if it was raining again, but it was still too dark to see anything other than the rain spots on the window. Darkness hid many things, including assassins, so it would either take place early in the morning, say around seven-thirty or about four o'clock in the afternoon; both times when visibility was at its most awkward. Just enough light to see, but not enough to clearly identify someone.

The next question was 'how?', and she went through the IRA's stock tactics. Not that she was any sort of expert, but she thought that handguns and shotguns were at the top of the list, followed by bombs. Knifing was probably out because one would have to get so close that his bodyguard might well intervene, and that bodyguard night well be Justin. She made a mental note to ask him what his rota was. She dismissed poisoning and returned to the first three options which would depend upon where.

Cup in hand, she robotically returned to her bedroom to get dressed, posing the question of where Hamilton would be on Christmas Day, because that would surely govern the method of his murder. Like the rest of the country, he'd most likely be at home with his family. She didn't know where he lived when he wasn't at his apartment, but it wouldn't be in London; would it? She'd have to ask Justin. And if he was ensconced in his home with his family somewhere in the countryside, then perhaps Aiden would need to use a sniper's rifle, because getting a bomb past security on Christmas Day would stand a good chance of discovery. Wondering where he lived, she pictured a stately home down a driveway bordered by mown lawns and manicured hedging leading to a gravelled parking area in front, but then altered the image to something smaller. Perhaps a Victorian mansion on the outskirts of a village, or... Wherever he lived, it wouldn't be run-of-the-mill and would likely be a little remote. That would fit in with the need for a sniper's rifle.

Other types of firearms would need close proximity to the target, but it could be a bomb of some sort. But how to deliver a bomb on Christmas Day? All the delivery companies had to give their staff a holiday, so it wouldn't come via them, and likewise for a food delivery parcel. A taxi perhaps or a chauffeur-driven government car... someone he was expecting. Might he have bought his wife a new car for Christmas and if so could Aiden have intercepted its delivery and planted a bomb in it? How about a new horse box, if she was into equestrian activities? Or even a horse... no, that was just too ridiculous, but an exploding horse would certainly be a first.

Returning to the sniper's rifle theory, she wondered just how close Aiden would need to be and... Oh, she was going round in circles. She stopped her conjecture and retrieved her calf-length leather boots by the front door.

Peering through a smeary windscreen as the drizzle and darkness did their best to hinder her commute down the half-lit roads, she still managed to mull over Aiden's two options. Rifle or bomb? Sitting in her parked car with the engine running outside of the police station, she finally decided it was fifty-fifty, but those odds would probably alter after speaking to Justin. She looked at her watch and rang him, and for a good five minutes he listened to her reasoning. He told her that Hamilton lived with his wife and children in a large detached house with grounds on the edge of a village not too far from Worcester.

"Getting hold of a decent sniper's rifle wouldn't be too difficult these days, but Aiden would have to be trained to carry out such a shot. And not just trained because he'd have to keep his eye in, and doing that is rather difficult without being discovered in the UK. Sure, there are some ranges dotted around but they're monitored. He could always hide in the remoteness of the Moors or even the Scottish Highlands, but he'd be running a risk at this time of year as deer stalkers are about."

"Erica did say he was going 'up North' didn't she, and if he's practising in the middle of nowhere, he may well be out of phone range."

"Not every night he wouldn't as he'd need to put his head down somewhere warm like a B&B or a pub, so I think we can discount that as a reason."

The phones went quiet for a few seconds as they both had the same idea at the same time, but Patricia got hers in first.

"What if he's using a professional? Someone from outside?"

"Yes, I've just had the same thought myself. It's unlikely, but let me think about that one. Let's get back to your bomb theory, because that's a real possibility."

They batted a few ideas back and forth and Justin hypothesised. "If the bomb isn't to be delivered on Christmas Day, then it must already be in transit; it might even be there already."

"Oh God, this is getting messy, because you and I can't just waltz into Hamilton's office and tell him he needs to call the bomb squad in to check out his home. He certainly won't believe me and he's unlikely to believe you. He'll think it's some sort of revenge conspiracy to screw up his Christmas, and if nothing is found we'll have more than egg on our faces."

"Then we'll just have to keep tags on Erica and hope that she leads us to Aiden, because that's the only way we're going to find him."

Patricia cringed at the thought of having to allocate enough personnel for a round-the-clock surveillance operation. "I can't do that. I don't have the authority... and even if I did, there's not enough officers willing to work overtime on the run-up to Christmas. Besides which, it's well out of my area. Isn't there a way of tracking her phone?"

"Of course there is, but for that we'd need to make this an official investigation because I too don't have the authority. I'd have to go to my boss, who may well have to go to his boss with a target of this importance."

She faltered before answering. "But that'll open up what we've been up to, won't it?"

"More than likely."

Again the phones went quiet while they both thought about the consequences. Patricia broke the silence. "Look,

276

Christmas Day's a week away, so give me a day or so to come up with something. I've an idea but I haven't thought it fully through yet. I'll let you know."

"OK, but bear in mind that we may already be too late."

"I know, I know. Speak to you later." She was about to ring off. "Oh by the way, you did say you had this Christmas off, didn't you?

"Luck of the draw and it's been confirmed I've got three days off this year, but that's not to say that I won't be called if there's some other emergency."

"At least that's some good news. Bye."

She sat in her car thinking through her idea of getting Constable Pindage to carry out one of her normal crime prevention exercises, but Elephant and Castle was across the other side of London on the south side of the Thames, and probably well over thirty miles away. It was certainly out of her area and entirely unjustifiable should she be challenged by another police authority; probably in The Met's jurisdiction she thought.

But all Sarah would be able to do would be observe and follow, and even if she managed to get Willy on board, the three of them wouldn't be able to watch Erica twenty-four hours a day. Maybe they didn't have to, because Erica would be sleeping at night and this didn't need to be a full twenty-four hours surveillance operation. She decided that if Erica and Aiden were going to meet, it would be during daylight hours; perhaps between eight o'clock in the morning and up to about ten o'clock at night. Not that there was much daylight at this time of year, but she had to narrow down the number of hours somehow, and it would only be for the next day or so, because after that it would probably be too late anyway. And she still had to convince Sarah and Willy to play ball, so she locked her car and went inside the police station.

It all boiled down to where Aiden was and what method of assassination he was going to use. She automatically acknowledged a 'good morning' from one of her colleagues as she walked along the carpeted corridors, but was concentrating on what he might be doing. Either a bomb or a rifle would probably best be prepared away from London, so perhaps after all, it might be a complete waste of time following Erica, but they had to try on the off chance. Perhaps if they could find Aiden's location, that may provide some sort of indication as to how he intended to carry it out. Too many ifs and buts.

Where the bloody hell was Aiden?

Chapter 13

Dead men don't know when the lights go out

Carl was on his second free pint in his favourite corner of The Cobblers, having earned them by swapping the empty barrels for full ones. Unusually he'd been asked to do so on a Wednesday due to a special brewery delivery on the run-up to Christmas. He looked a little ruefully into the depths of the murky beer. Rueful because he would no longer enjoy Alistair's company and occasional free pint because yesterday had been his funeral. As an ex-Union shop steward and Presbyterian, many of his work colleagues had been given the afternoon off to attend the service at the new crematorium. It wasn't that new but it was certainly an improvement on the old cramped one, and the chapel was full with standing room only at the back. Alistair had been a popular man and one by one they filed past his grieving widow offering condolences. Afterwards, gathering round the sandwich and beer-bottle laden tables in the adjacent church hall, the talk had started off mainly about Alistair and how could he have been so foolish to take a shortcut home across the railway lines and get run over on the level crossing. He had been hit by a van and it was being hypothesised that the driver would never have noticed the bump over the rails and body. The autopsy had not revealed more than the normal amount of alcohol one would expect to find in a man on his way home from the

Comrades Club, and witnesses had stated that he hadn't had more than three or four pints, his usual.

But Carl was ready to put thoughts of his passing behind him and stared into the middle-distance, wondering how the heels on Gwen's shoes were. He downed the last of his pint and decided to have a third in memory of Alistair; he paid for that one.

Twenty minutes later he said goodnight to the landlady and started the relatively short walk back to his flat. As usual, it was raining; not heavily as it had been recently, but enough to make one blink from the frequent windy droplets. As usual that time of night, nobody was about and he half-stepped off the pavement and went to cross the unlit road when he heard a car from behind. Turning to make sure he wouldn't step out in front of it, he was surprised to see that it was just a few feet away, accelerating and driving directly at him. Despite his best efforts, there was no way he could avoid being hit by its front bumper. He felt a shooting pain as one of the wheels drove over his leg, and as his body went down, his head banged violently against tarmac. Dazed, he watched the out-of-focus car reverse towards him, quickly recoiled his legs and rolled out of the way with inches to spare. He was trying to understand why someone would do such a thing, when he saw a man get out of the car and walk towards him. He had trouble seeing the man's face as the rain peppered directly into his line of sight, and he wondered if he was going to be offered a hand up. Instead, he watched the man's boot make contact with his arm that was half-across his body, and felt another sharp pain. He instinctively bought his other arm across to shield that side of his body as another kick landed. And then another on his ribcage.

Stunned as he was, he realised that unless he did

something very quickly, he wouldn't last long, and with an effort, watched for the next kick. When it did start to come, he grabbed hold of it with his good arm, yanked and twisted it as hard as he could. He was not a violent man but had once nearly been on the receiving end one Saturday afternoon after a Rangers football match. He knew that 'putting the boot in' was a favourite pastime of the thugs that frequented the football stadiums in Scotland, just so that they could get their own kicks out of their miserable lives.

Still in the prone position, he knew he could not stay down while his assailant got up to give him another kicking, so he struggled to his feet and nearly fell over from the agony that shot up his leg. In the gloom and the vague illumination from the car's headlights, he looked down on the man who he now saw was dressed in a long dark overcoat; but he still couldn't see his face as it rested on the kerb. Now he was angry, because for no apparent reason, this man had just tried to kill him, but rather than put his own boot in, he stood over him with the rain dribbling down his face, waiting for some movement from his attacker. He wanted to look him in the eye and see what kind of person was picking on him. He rubbed his arm and after a minute, decided that the man had been knocked unconscious by hitting his head on the kerbstone. He nudged him tentatively with his foot and stepped back half a pace, wary that he may be feigning or have a knife hidden under his coat.

There was no reaction. "Get up you bugger." He waited; ready. "Come on you shithead or I really will thump you." He gave another not so gentle shove with his foot but again nothing.

He went closer and, grabbing the man's arm, dragged him around so that he could see his face and what he saw shocked him. It looked as if the lower part of his face had been stoved in by someone using a sledgehammer as the jaw was at the same odd angle as his nose; all covered in blood that the rain now helped to wash away. Not that he was trained in first aid in any way, but he went to feel for the man's pulse by putting his fingers on his neck; he'd seen people do that in films. It was then that he realised that the man's neck must be broken as the head lolled unnaturally to one side.

He was dead and he had just killed him. He couldn't believe what had just happened. Not noticing that the rain was becoming heavier and that the car's windscreen wipers were still going, he stood there looking down on his first real dead person. It took him a couple of minutes to start wondering what he ought to do next and he looked around to see if there was anyone else about; nobody. The nearest streetlight was over a hundred yards away, not too far from The Cobblers, and in the other direction were rows of terraced houses with hardly a light showing as far as he could see. He contemplated continuing walking home and leaving the man lying dead in the gutter, but that was not his nature. This would have to be reported to the police, so he wandered slowly back towards The Cobblers, and started to wonder why that man had just tried to kill him.

When he told the landlady, the first thing she did was draw him a pint of heavy and place it on the bar in front of him; she noticed that, unsurprisingly, he was not quite his usual self. Only after that did she phone for the police. The first to arrive was a lone constable some ten minutes later, and after a couple of questions directed at Carl, he went off to see the body for himself. Death by violence was not common in that part of Scotland, but even so, the public often had a tendency to overstate, which was why only one policeman was initially allocated. But soon after, it seemed as though the entire police station had descended upon The Cobblers, along with two ambulances and even a fire engine; and the inevitable crowd materialised out of nowhere.

Much to the delight of the landlady, The Cobblers became the temporary incident room, and she dug her husband out from in front of his football on the TV. She was looking forward to taking more money tonight than in an entire week.

Officialdom was well out of Carl's experience and he was first questioned by a uniformed sergeant, who handed him over to a plain clothes detective, who asked him the same questions and then marched him down the street to where the man still lay. Carl repeated his story and pointed out one or two things including the tyre mark on his trousers, while a police photographer flashed away. On the other side of the cones and barrier tape that now surrounded the scene, was an army of medical types itching to get at the body and somehow a local newspaper photographer managed to get round the barrier and blind Carl with his own flashgun.

"Bugger off, Norman," said Detective Inspector Mcleash, and the reporter sulked away into the shadows after taking another couple of snaps.

"And you say you've never seen this man before?" It was a repeated rhetorical question, but he was looking closely for an out-of-place reaction from Carl. Very difficult considering the number of stroboscopic roof lights from various vehicles that now blocked the street.

Carl repeated his innocence and several other questions but eventually it seemed as though Mcleash was satisfied. "I'll need a statement from you, so we can either go down the station now or first thing in the morning."

"I'm working tomorrow, so can we do it now?"

"Right. Hang on there a minute and I'll get one of the constables to drive you there. I'll follow on once I've tidied things up here. Ahhhh... here's the doctor, so I won't be too long."

Carl hadn't been in a police car before; come to that, it was his first time in any car, and he had to be shown how to put the seat belt on. It was gone midnight by the time he was given a lift back to his flat, and getting undressed, he inspected his very sore leg. Seeing little more than a slight abrasion, he thought nothing of it, so went to bed still wondering why.

At his desk late the following morning, Mcleash took his fingers out of his ears when the fire alarm bells stopped making their weekly practice din. It didn't matter that he had worked there for years, and it didn't make any difference that they lasted only twenty seconds, but every week he somehow forgot that at eleven o'clock on a Thursday, the bloody fire alarm system regularly sounded off. And every week he cursed the bloody health and safety gits; as did most others who worked there, similarly ignoring the racket.

Now that he had two free hands, he attended to his computer and opened the file from the Procurator Fiscal, commonly known as the coroner, that had just been emailed. Skipping the first page that contained no useful information whatsoever, he looked for a name. 'Unknown.' All the other information was there. Sex, age, height, weight, cause of death, etc., and everything else on the report tallied with what Carl had attested to the previous night. He looked further down the report for the list of items found with the dead man and other than what he had been wearing, he was a little disappointed to see that there were only two items: a mobile phone and a comb. No wallet and no cash. There were no tattoos, but there was significant old scarring to his back and the coroner had hypothesised that this may have been caused by something akin to a whip or a cane in the man's youth. The slight traces of common dust under his fingernails didn't provide any clues either.

He enjoyed mysteries, which was one of the reasons why he had joined up in the first place, but he hadn't come across one where the victim had next to nothing to identify him. Knowing that the phone would probably provide the answer, he reached for his desk phone and was about to ring the coroner's office when he spotted one of his colleagues holding a plastic bag heading his way.

"Compliments of the coroner," said the officer as he dumped the bag on his desk. "He thought you might like this."

"So he's turned into a mind reader as well, has he?"

"He wouldn't bother reading my mind, but it was sent over just a few minutes ago. Do we know who he was?" The officer was obviously referring to the dead man.

"Not yet, but this'll give us a clue." Mcleash looked at the report and saw that it had already been fingerprinted. He opened the bag, took out the ordinary-looking phone and pressed the on button. Disappointingly, the screen came to life and revealed a keypad, requiring a passcode.

"Shit. Here, send this off to boffin branch and see what they can do with it." He didn't watch the officer depart but returned to the coroner's report to see if there was anything he had missed, such as traces of alcohol, drugs, medication or smoking, but there was nothing. Certainly he'd had cases where the deceased had initially been unidentified, usually on a Saturday night after a Rangers match, and he was also used to waiting for someone to come forward from Missing Persons within a day or so, but this man didn't fit into that category.

For a start, it wasn't a weekend when Rangers were playing at home, and this chap was dressed in expensive clothes. Smiling to himself, he concluded that he definitely wasn't a Rangers supporter. This man looked like he was from a reasonably well-off background who'd got lost, but what was he doing in that neighbourhood at that time of night? Visiting someone perhaps? As things stood at the moment, only his phone would be able to provide a clue, but with Christmas just round the corner, he doubted he'd hear back from the technical section until the new year.

He turned again to the docket on the vehicle: a run-of-the-mill three-year-old Ford Mondeo which was registered to a private address in Birmingham, and that would be his next line of enquiry. But the baffling part was that there was no paperwork, no discarded pieces of paper, coins, maps or other paraphernalia usually found in the average car. It was as if it had just been thoroughly valeted. Nor had it been reported as being stolen according to the Police National Database. It was as though the man had purposefully gone out of his way to make any sort of identification difficult, and that was intriguing in itself. He sent an email to the West Midlands Police based in Birmingham requesting that they make local enquiries of the owner, but once again, he'd be lucky to hear from them within a week or so.

Posting a photograph and details the man on Missing Persons might end up being the quickest method after all, and with the usual local problems connected with the run-up to Christmas, he decided to do just that. It meant spending over quarter of an hour on the computer inputting the necessary data and having the file on his desk collecting dust until he was identified, but he'd at least start the ball rolling.

***

Over four hundred miles away, tucked away in an alley across from Erica's flat, Constable Pindage was cold and wet because she didn't have the luxury of a car and the coffee shop didn't provide a direct line of sight. She'd had more than enough coffee anyway and had had to visit the shop's toilet three times already. She was miserable as well because it was a boring job and it was getting dark; she was beginning to regret offering her services to Inspector Eyethorne. She looked at her watch again, wishing the minute hand would go faster, but it oughtn't be long now before she would be relieved. Her surveillance of Erica's front door from a hundred yards away had been uneventful, except for a troupe of colourful West African ladies who had decided to practise their noisy dance routine in the walkway right next to her. Trying to stay inconspicuous, she had temporarily moved further down until they disappeared into a back door of the community centre.

Patricia tapped her on the shoulder a little before four o'clock just as it started to rain again, and she nearly jumped out of her skin. "Anything?"

"Nothing, but I went past her window an hour or so ago and heard her telly was on and she hasn't come out since. Willy said she'd not moved this morning, so I reckon she's staying put; at least until this evening." She inferred that it was now up to her replacement. "Can I go home now, Guv, because I'm really cold?" she pleaded.

"Thanks Sarah, and thank Willy for me as well."

"See you in the morning, Guv." She headed off towards Elephant and Castle tube station rather than catch a bus, knowing that it would be considerably warmer in the underground; it was quicker anyway.

Some four hours later and despite being kitted out in her warmest clothes, Patricia knew how Sarah had felt as she too headed for the tube. It was a long time since she had carried out the menial task of watching and waiting, and without the distractions of her desk, she initially had plenty of thinking time. Justin had phoned soon after six and they had batted a couple of ideas around, deferring final decisions until they met up later. With the onset of the numbing cold that slows the mind, her thoughts had ground to a halt, and it wasn't until she had warmed up somewhere around South Kensington that she felt her judgement return to normal.

Walking through her front door, she immediately detected the welcoming aroma of fish and chips, and knew Justin had anticipated her arrival time perfectly. He also had a glass of wine waiting for her, and other than a greeting of 'hello gorgeous' as she went to sit down, said nothing until she had had a few mouthfuls. "She's still ensconced in her flat then."

"I've been thinking about that and I reckon she's waiting for something or someone, and that Aiden's told her not to move until that something or someone happens."

"What's your reasoning behind that?" He watched her peel off a crispy bit of batter with her fingers before putting it in her mouth and enjoying it to the full.

"If you haven't got a job, where's your money coming from?" She didn't wait for his response but continued. "And if you've no regular income, then you'll be being paid by someone, and I reckon that'll be Aiden; probably from IRA funds. So when he says 'stay put' she does just that, and when he says 'jump', she jumps." She paused chewing and looked him straight in the eye. "She could be our assassin, not Aiden."

He masticated both his piece of cod as well as her hypothesis. "You could be right, as his docket portrays him as being a thinker rather than a doer and he might well get her to do the dirty work rather than risk his own hide, so I'll go along with that for the time being. What else led you to that?"

"Look... we can't find Aiden and we really don't know what he's up to and he could still yet be our killer, but we do know... sorry... suspect she's up to her neck in whatever's being planned. What we do know is that she's desperately trying to keep out of sight and to my mind, that's exactly what a pre-meditated murderer would do; right up to the last moment."

"OK, but we still can't rule out the possibility of Aiden being there on the final act, can we? So what are you proposing?"

"I don't think we can wait any longer... we've got to tell Special Branch... because you and I aren't exactly endowed with the necessary manpower to either carry out a search for Aiden or keep a watch on Erica. If I'm right, there's only a few days left."

He swallowed. "And if you're wrong?"

"If I'm wrong, then we'll just have to live with it, but at least we'll have clear consciences; Hamilton or no."

"They'll need a report from both of us."

"I know."

"And they'll need to know everything."

"Yes."

"I mean everything including Hamilton's attempted rape, because once they start digging, they'll find it all."

"You don't have to bloody remind me," she retorted angrily, but then softened her tone. "Look, we either stand back and do nothing because there's nothing else we can do, or, alert Special Branch and let them take it from here. Do you know anyone from SB?"

"I used to but he emigrated... we were in the same training class together. I'd need to go through official channels by taking it to my commander. How about you?"

"I've thought of that. If I take it to my Super Tonybee, he'll just tell me to send my report in with the weekly updates, but if I time it right when he's out of the office, as he frequently is, then I can take it to his deputy, Rudi. Now he's just the sort of man who is able to pick up on the urgency and forward it on to the right department straight away. Come to think of it, I believe he mentioned his brother was with Special Branch... or was it his cousin? I can't remember, but someone in his family is connected with the security services."

"Wouldn't this best be done together rather than separately?" He scrumped up his fish and chips wrapper. "And as you've been working directly under Hamilton in his office, I suggest you do the initial running and I'll join you when we're both called in. Between the two of us, we ought to be able to convince them that the threat is real and not just a wild goose chase."

She thought about this while screwing up her own wrapper and placing it next to his. "OK then. I'll get my report done in the morning as I've had a long day and need to get some shut-eye first. You'd best get your report ready tonight because you won't have a chance tomorrow."

"I know." He got up, taking the wrappers into the kitchen. "I'll wait to hear from you."

They said their goodnights.

Chapter 14

Trouble
(Friday 22nd December)

Having arrived at her desk even earlier than normal to write up a report in an acceptable format, Patricia was grateful that she hadn't had the distraction of her colleagues or been pestered by any phone calls and urgent emails. But now the day's business began to intrude and she struggled to complete the final pages. Just when she thought she was nearing the end, she remembered yet another item that she had omitted, and had to go back to make adjustments. She realised that from the complexity of the case that she'd need to write a precis at the end; just to make certain that the reader appreciated the gravity of the matter.

She looked up from her screen and groaned as she spied one of Tonybee's favourites heading her way.

"The super wants to see you."

"OK. Won't be long." She returned to her screen.

"He said now as it's urgent."

"It's always fucking urgent." She really wanted to finish her report before becoming distracted by what would probably turn out to be another tedious investigation. "Sorry... it's Stoner, isn't it?" She had trouble recalling his name straight off. She was aware that she may have offended him when all he was doing was relaying a message.

"Constable David Stoner, ma'am."

"Tell him I'll just be a minute." She inwardly groaned as her computer pinged yet another email to her inbox. "Bollocks." She swore out loud realising that she'd never be able to complete her report until she had dealt with Tonybee. Stoner was hovering. "OK, OK, I'm coming now." She pressed the save button and minimised.

She knocked on Superintendent Arthur Tonybee's door before entering without waiting for a response. She hadn't been this close to him without his hat on for several weeks, and she saw a man whose hair was far more grey than black. To her mind, it only went to emphasise the need for his retirement, but in the meantime he was her superior and someone who needed to be obeyed if she wanted to keep her job; which she did. She assumed he would be admonishing her for her transgression with the press's coverage of the Clarkson jewellery theft and decided to use her charm as she had done so in the past.

She stood directly in front of his desk and with a cheerful bounce in her voice she said. "Good morning, sir."

"Errrr, yes good morning Inspector and thank you for coming straight up, because I expect you've got a lot on your plate right now." He was from the formal school and still addressed people by their rank. "It's always busy on the lead-up to Christmas isn't it."

"There's always a lot on my plate, sir." She decided to respond to his formality knowing that it wouldn't aggravate him. She waited for him to continue, but instead he was looking down at pieces of paper in front of him on his desk, and he made her wait.

Eventually he looked up and addressed her. "We've had an unusual tip-off and it directly involves you. I suppose it's because your name's more noticeable than others due to your frequent appearance in the papers, but I'm not going to admonish you for that." He briefly smiled at her, obviously referring to her recent transgression. "Not only are you capable of carrying out this task, but you've actually been demanded, and I'm attaching a pair of officers just to make sure things go smoothly."

She interpreted his last comment as him having to comply by the book. He momentarily looked down at the papers again, but then continued. "Apparently there's a shipment of cocaine that's due to be exchanged in the Marsh Lane car park at midnight tonight. It's really annoying because it's this sort of thing that goes on right under our noses, and these dealers don't seem to pay us any regard."

She knew the site next to the river well, as it wasn't far from one of the temporary travellers' sites. Everybody blamed the local pikeys for the plethora of burglaries and petty theft that went on in the area, and with good reason. It was a notorious location for late-night sexual activities and drug taking, and she had in fact made one of her first arrests there. Worryingly, it was only a few minutes away from where she lived.

"A request for me sir?"

"Yes. It seems our anonymous informant owes you a favour." He looked down again. "Here we are... the note finishes off saying... 'now we're evens, sweetie'. Any ideas who it might be?" He peered at her.

She was totally wrong-footed by his question. "Er... not off the top of my head, but if I could study the whole note, it might give me a clue."

Tonybee considered her request for a moment before handing over the two-sided note. "You'll see it stipulates you and you alone must arrive at Marsh Lane on foot precisely at midnight and I've already issued the necessary instructions that you're to meet Sergeant Chilvers and Constable Seaford, both whom you know, just down the road from there at eleven forty-five. I can't have you exposed to criminal types all alone in the middle of nowhere, A: because it's not safe, and B: you may well need back-up if you're to make arrests. Here's a copy of the operational orders." He handed her a sheaf of papers in a transparent plastic folder.

She hadn't quite finished reading the note and would need to re-read it without the distraction of Tonybee. "How was the note delivered?"

"It aaaar... I'm not really sure. It came up with my other post. Hang on a moment, I'll ask the desk sergeant." He picked up his desk phone.

While he was enquiring, Patricia started to re-read the handwriting on what looked like the sort of stationery paper one would pick up from a newsagents; no clues there then. It wasn't dated nor was there any indication as to an address, but it had been folded at some point. She sniffed it without any conclusions and then held it up to the light but there was no watermark. She looked closer and there in the background was perhaps the faintest hint of other writing, typical of a biro indenting through the previous page of the pad. She studied the top edge and detected miniscule traces of the glue that would have held this page to the rest of the pad. She smiled to herself and decided not to mention that to Tonybee.

It was a rather condescending letter but the instructions were clear. There would be a grey minivan parked in the Marsh Lane car park with a bag of uncut cocaine under the passenger seat. A lone recipient would appear at midnight and drive it away. It was suspected that the van would be kept under surveillance up to the point when it was driven away to make sure that it wasn't stolen, which was why only one person could approach. If more than one person approached, the watchers would drive the car away themselves. The author refused to provide their name, preferring anonymity, but felt that their civic duty was to report such a significant criminal transgression to the authorities. As Detective Inspector Eyethorne had shown decency when arresting their sibling, they appreciated that the favour ought to be returned.

She was trying to recall who had a brother or sister, when Tonybee interrupted her thoughts.

"It came by first-class post and the envelope's being retrieved from the bin and will be here any minute. Now that you've read it, have you any clues such as who's got a brother who's been put away recently?"

"I'll have to check that, sir, but they could be referring to their sister." She didn't want to remind him that his sexist view had precluded all females, but was happy that she had done so.

"Yes, of course. Possibly a sister as well." He responded to a knock at the door and in walked a constable bearing an envelope in a plastic bag. "I suppose this has been handled by half the staff down there, has it?"

This was the first time that the young constable had been told to visit the superintendent's office, and he was quite naturally a little awed. "I dunno, sir. All I was told was to bring this up to you."

"OK." He waited until the door closed again. "Here, have a look." He held it up for Patricia who peered at it through the cellophane.

"I'll need to get this and the note down to forensics for fingerprinting, but I'll photocopy it first if that's OK with you, sir." She went to leave.

"Just one other thing. In case you are wondering why I have allocated just two other officers, and you'll realise this when you come to think of it, it's because that car park's down a dead end road and there's only one way in and out. Besides which, staff are hard to come by at this time of year, but those two are good officers and ought to suffice."

On her way back down from the fourth floor to her desk, she pictured the car park and recalled that she had had to get wet when making that arrest all those years ago. It was bordered by the river on the far side.

Sitting in front of her computer, she toyed with the idea of playing a pencil over the raised indentations on the note which, in theory, ought to bring out what had been written on the previous page, but instead decided to take it directly to forensics; just in case it didn't work. Fortunately, she got on well with them and they promised to let her have the results that same afternoon.

It was getting on for mid-morning by the time she got back to finishing her report on the threat to Hamilton, and needing to refresh her memory, she looked up the electronic circular she had shown Constable Pindage a few days earlier, just to make certain she had her facts straight. Her jaw nearly hit her desk when the page re-directed her to 'Missing Persons' and it took her a minute after reading through it for the reality to sink in.

They'd futilely been following Erica in the forlorn hope of tracking down Aiden, when all along, he'd been in Clydebank. And now he was a cadaver in Clydebank. She wondered what the hell he had been doing there and started to hypothesise but almost immediately gave up. She spotted the link on the page to Detective Inspector Mcleash and instead of emailing him, picked up the phone.

It was a fairly broad Glaswegian accent that greeted her. "Mcleash."

"DI Eyethorne, Maidenhead." They were both the same rank doing more or less the same job in different parts of the country and further introductions at that level were unnecessary.

"Now correct me if I'm wrong, but isn't that somewhere in London?"

"You're not wrong, but we're just outside of London and not connected to The Met." Everyone referred to The Metropolitan Police simply as 'The Met'.

"Well in that case, I'll be happy to help a fellow officer from just outside of London." He had a slightly sarcastic tone to his voice, and indeed it was his own way of getting through the day.

"That male you posted on 'Missing Persons', yesterday at twelve-fifteen." She had to look at the screen to verify the time. "We think his name might be Aiden Walsh." She automatically used the 'we' as though it was an official investigation and thought nothing of it.

He leant back on his sprung-loaded chair. "And what leads you to that conclusion, may I ask?"

On the spur of the moment she decided to keep things simple. "He's just someone we've been looking for in connection to a crime prevention case, and I only spotted that you'd posted his details a few minutes ago."

"You've been looking for him for long then?"

"A few days. Why?"

He considered replying 'just curious', but knew that this would just raise her level of inquisitiveness, when what he was really trying to do was to find out more about this chap in the morgue. What he didn't want was someone from London stealing his limelight; if there was any to be had, and a woman at that. "Oh, we don't often get a response this quickly. That's all." He knew there was much more to it than that, but wasn't letting on; not just yet anyway.

She needed to know a lot more. "How did he die?"

Mcleash leant forward and repeated as best he could what the coroner had written. "It says here that he died from a basilar skull fracture leading to intraparenchymal haemorrhaging." Smiling, he leant back again, knowing what was coming next.

"What's that in English?"

"He bashed his head on the kerb and it stoved his head in."

People didn't just bash their heads on kerbs, and especially people like Aiden. "And how did he manage to do that?" She felt as though she was trying to get blood out of a stone the way the conversation was going, so added. "You see, we don't think he was an alcoholic and that sounds like an injury someone would get coming out of a club after hours."

"Oh aye, you're right there. According to our coroner, there was no alcohol in his bloodstream and he wasn't on drugs either." He realised that if she was any sort of decent detective he would have to let her know as she would find out anyway. "It seems he and another chap had an altercation outside a pub, and he definitely came off worse."

Patricia had hurriedly suspected that there must have been at least one other person involved with his death, and now Mcleash had confirmed it. "Do you have the perpetrator in custody?"

"Oh no. He's a local chap and claims he's never set eyes on our dead person before. I believe him too." He could almost hear the cogs going round in her head down the phone line and waited to hear if she would ask what he thought she would ask next. He had to wait several seconds.

"Aiden Walsh. Was he carrying any weapons?"

He was pleased with himself, and inwardly acknowledged that she was quick. Now that he had established that he wasn't talking to just another copper trying to shuffle paperwork from one tray to another, he decided to help her a bit. More to the point, he recognised that the woman on the other end of the line wasn't from the press. "No, nothing more dangerous than a comb. By the way, you're the second person to ask me that today. I had Special Branch on the phone just before you rang and they're sending someone up from your neck of the woods tomorrow. Want to inspect the body etcetera, so it looks like we have somebody of interest in our morgue here. Can I ask exactly what your interest in him is?"

She was still rather stunned, hardly daring to believe that it was Aiden lying in his own freezer drawer up there and presumed that Special Branch wanted to make their own confirmation; they probably had to as he was on one of the wanted lists. It was just as well she and Justin hadn't presented their reports, as they would have been laughed out of the room, but she too had to make certain, because if it wasn't Aiden, then their own conclusions still needed to be seriously considered. There was only one way to be sure. "Have you anyone to identify the body? Because if not, then we do."

"Ahhhhh, next of kin?"

"I'm afraid not, but someone who was close to him. Look, can I bring them up to see you this afternoon, and I'll explain more then?"

Mcleash half-huffed loud enough for Patricia to hear. "He must be mighty important if you want to see him that quickly, and by the sound of it, you want to get here before the Special Branch chap... Am I correct?"

"Yes inspector." There was no point in disguising the fact that she wanted to beat Special Branch; it was like waving a red flag to a bull. Anyway, she needed to be back in time for her midnight operation. She looked at the clock on her screen and hoped there was enough time to do both. Timing would be very tight if she was to collect Erica, catch a flight to Glasgow and return in time to be at Marsh Lane by eleven forty-five, just under fourteen hours. "Can I get back to you in a few minutes?" She needed to check flight times, then all she had to do was get half across London and persuade Erica to go with her.

***

Erica was bored of sitting around watching daytime TV, but knowing that revenge was just round the corner after all these years, she had decided to endure her self-inflicted solitude; at least until she met Eamon at Gatwick. The last thing she needed right now was to be recognised by some smart bloody CCTV system. Certainly her disguise ought to fool general cameras, but she had read that some had facial recognition technology and it wasn't worth the risk. She'd already decided to alter her appearance further for the meeting with Eamon and was confident that she would be just another figure in their lenses. Other than going over in her mind how the simple transfer would take place, the only other thing rattling around in her head was how those two sleuths had found her. She still couldn't believe that they had traced her through Aiden, but there was no other explanation that made sense. And then there was their story about a double mole in Hamilton's office which didn't make sense either. She'd gleaned from Aiden that there was one mole, but a double mole? It was too incredible to believe, but the mere fact that they had found her, knew where she met and even knew what her favourite vodka was, lent enough credibility to their stories for her to consider that what else they had told her was also true.

She wondered why Aiden hadn't rung her yet to confirm her meeting with Eamon, and was itching to hear from him. She'd already made her own mind up that if he hadn't called her by the time she needed to leave, she would still go and collect the package from Eamon at the Holiday Inn. She presumed he had chosen the Gatwick hotel rather than Heathrow one because of the flight timings and anyway, Gatwick was just that little bit further outside London and not frequented by the press as much.

For the umpteenth time she looked rather forlornly at her phone, willing it to light up and ring, but it didn't even bother to look back at her. He was also supposed to be telling her where she would meet Chloe to hand over Hamilton's Christmas present, but she had that one covered herself as she'd already decided to visit her in her apartment if her nightclub plan failed. They might even manage an evening out; or in if she was alone and could be persuaded to share her bed again.

"Oh come on Aiden, fucking ring me." She swore at her plugged-in phone as she jumped up from the sofa and went towards the kitchen to make yet another cup of coffee, and then swore again as she remembered that she was out of milk. She diverted to the bedroom and donned her disguise, deciding to try out her face-altering appendages. The fatter and longer nose took a little time to fit, her eyebrows took on a puffy appearance and the small piece of foam she wedged between her lower teeth and cheek made her almost unrecognisable. She checked herself in the mirror against the passport photo, the new one that Aiden had supplied her with, and nodded in satisfaction at the similarity. There was a knock on the door and she stopped mid-stride into the living room, but then continued. Probably one of the local do-gooders again who would rattle their charity collection box for the homeless at Christmas, but when she opened it and saw Patricia standing there... well, she was rooted to the spot and speechless.

She didn't really take in that Patricia looked around furtively before walking through the door, but couldn't help notice her go to the living room window, raise a part of the net curtain enough to peer outside for a moment, before turning to address her.

"Sorry that you're not expecting me, but something's cropped up and I really need your help in a hurry." She feigned being a little breathless. She'd also feigned being followed.

Erica could hardly believe her eyes. "How the fuck did you find me?"

"It's a long story and we haven't got enough time for me to tell you straight away, but I promise I will. En route."

"En route?"

"Yes. To the airport. Our flight leaves in an hour and a half."

"What?"

"We're going to Glasgow."

"Eh?" She was incredulous and stood there with an open mouth but remembered to keep the piece of foam in place with her tongue. "Why the fuck should I go to Glasgow with you?"

"Because that's where Aiden is. Look, please get you stuff together otherwise we'll miss our flight and I'll explain as we go."

"No way." She moved so that the sofa was defensively

between them. "And why should I want to meet with Aiden, and in Glasgow of all places?"

Patricia had imagined that confronting Erica like this would probably go the way it was going, but there was no other way given the time available. She had envisaged her initial refusal but kept her bombshell until this moment. "So that you can identify his body."

"His body?" she almost screamed.

"I'm afraid so. He was killed by someone, but we're not sure if it was murder. Look, please get ready and don't forget your passport. You might need this as well." She picked up Erica's phone, unplugged it and handed it to her."

"No... I'm not friggin' going anywhere with you."

"I really think you have to, because you might be next," she lied. She also saw Erica trying to figure out what on earth was happening, but couldn't wait for her to start asking awkward questions. "If you get on the train with me now, I promise I'll tell you, but it has to be right now." She prayed that Erica would be desperate to know.

Her head was in a whirl as she started to take in what Patricia was saying. Aiden dead? Surely it wasn't true? Aiden was too canny. But he hadn't phoned. She could feel her shakes coming on again, because life without Aiden... Oh no, please don't let it be true, but she knew she had to see for herself. Then she started worrying about going through airport security and having to test out her passport and disguise.

Patricia played her last card by going over to the window again and looking out.

"Who's out there?" asked a very worried Erica.

"I've told you, there's no time to explain." She picked up Erica's handbag and held it out. "Anything else you need?"

"You'll tell me everything?"

"As much as I can."

"And we'll be back tonight?"

"Yes. Now come on."

It clinched it. Erica reached for her coat that was lying on the floor and prepared herself for seeing Aiden for the last time.

Patricia had flinched at the timing. Even though there was a virtual shuttle flight service to and from Glasgow, it went out of Gatwick not Heathrow, but then she realised that it would be far easier than she first thought; Elephant and Castle was more or less en route to Gatwick, and the timing of the flights gelled quite nicely to be back on time. She had spoken at length to Mcleash while on the underground and had arranged that he should meet them at the airport. It wasn't that he was at a loose end as he had enough to deal with, but once he had looked her up on the internet and realised she had a relatively high profile, he knew that by association his career stood a good chance of enhancement.

On the half-hour train journey from London Bridge to Gatwick, Patricia had kept her promise to Erica, but omitted as much as she could. Her wariness of Erica as the possible assassin was based on the principle that if Aiden was indeed dead, then who else might it be. Whatever else, she was still a link. There was of course the possibility that the threat had vanished now that Aiden was dead, but her instincts told her otherwise.

At that time of the day outside of rush hour, the train was only half full, so being overheard was not an issue. Erica posed questions here and there and finally said, "Come on then, how did you find me?"

Patricia did her best not to sound too condescending. "It

was a matter of following you on the underground."

"But I was looking all the time and neither you nor Justin were there."

"Oh, we were there alright and please don't ask me to elaborate. Allow me to keep one or two trade secrets to myself."

Conversation ceased while the train boomed through a tunnel, and when it emerged, Erica had more questions; some rather uncomfortable but Patricia managed to steer her away just enough. Erica had niggling doubts but couldn't put her finger on anything specific. To her mind, everything Patricia was telling her appeared to be true but proof would come in the form of Aiden – if indeed it was Aiden. All this was happening a little too quickly for her to logically think it through, but she was beginning to query one or two aspects. Just before they arrived at Gatwick, a question to which she already suspected the answer, entered her head. "You said I might be next. Any idea who's after me?"

Patricia was ready for this one. "That'll depend firstly on you positively identifying the body as Aiden's, and secondly his method of demise which we can find about from the policeman we're meeting."

"We're meeting a policeman?" she asked with concern.

"Oh yes, it's routine and there's no secret about it. And talking of secrets, when we get there don't be surprised if they address me as Inspector." She reached into her jacket pocket. "Look... I even have a fake warrant card." She saw the worried look on Erica's face and explained further. "You see, to get the cooperation we need, I phoned ahead and impersonated an inspector from Thames Valley Police. It covers such a large area and has so many stations, it's unlikely that anyone checking will be able to confirm if I even exist."

The train ground to a halt and she rose. "And now you know another of my little secrets."

Erica was full of questions during the brief flight and while Patricia answered them without revealing her own true persona, in turn, she had her own questions for Erica. By the time they landed, neither of them was any more trustful of the other than they had been at the outset. At the first opportunity, Erica had removed the foam from her mouth, and then replaced it for the benefit of the security cameras as they disembarked.

"Have you lived your entire life in a disguise?" she asked as they walked towards the pick-up area, but when Erica didn't answer she added, "OK then, are you going to live the rest of your life like that?"

Erica pulled up suddenly. Patricia did likewise and turned to face her.

"Look. I'm here to identify someone, nothing else. OK? I don't want you or anyone else prying into my private life and I don't want to know you when we're finished here. So when we're done, I'm going straight back to my flat and you can bloody well fuck off and leave me alone. I don't care if there's someone trying to find me because after this, I'm going to disappear for good, so don't bother trying to get to know me better." She stormed off in the direction of the exit, leaving Patricia behind for the moment. Thirty feet later she stopped, turned and shouted back, "You fucking coming?"

Only a couple of passers-by bothered to glance in her direction at the foul language; after all, this was Glasgow where swearing was second nature.

From the outset, Mcleash felt the tension between the two women as he drove them the short distance to the morgue and didn't bother with small talk. Other than to ascertain who

Erica was, very little was said right up to the moment when the curtain was drawn back to reveal Aiden's body.

Erica was acutely aware that her reactions were being studied and managed to maintain a perfect deadpan face. The usual pedantic identifying questions were asked, but she had had enough.

"That's him. Alright. Can we go now?" She walked away without waiting for any kind of reply.

"She's not very happy," remarked Patricia.

"Live people identifying dead people rarely are."

"No, I mean she's not very happy about being dragged all the way up here to Glasgow. I think she'd already resigned herself to Aiden's death, and I also think she knows a lot more than she's telling."

"What do you want to do about it?" Mcleash was curious from a professional point of view.

"Look, if it's OK with you, we'll pack her off back to the airport and then you and I can go to your station and have a chat about it. She'll be on the next flight in about an hour and I'll catch the last one later tonight. How does that sound?"

"That's fine by me."

"Can we first make sure she gets on the London flight and I'll arrange for someone to meet her at the other end?"

"That's also fine by me." It was pretty much what he wanted, but it didn't turn out exactly like that; he took her instead to The Hungry Horse.

"This looks like an interesting station," she commented as they drew into the pub car park.

"And a better one as well… at least on this occasion."

"I'm sure you'll tell me more inside."

As they waited for their soft drinks at the bar, he continued, "I don't know how you operate south of the wall, but up here, if you come into our station, you'll need to be signed in, and I'm guessing that you don't want Special Branch knowing that you've been here. Then even if your presence didn't get noticed by Special Branch, the lads in the station could hardly fail to notice you, tongues would wag and I'd never hear the end of it; professionally of course."

"Of course," she agreed.

"But then there's a couple of desperate unmarried types in there who would stop at nothing if they thought it was going to get them anywhere; unprofessionally of course."

She looked at him without speaking, wondering if he was making this up or trying to make a pass at her.

"Besides which, it's warmer in here." He turned away to pay for the round, but the comment surprised her as she didn't think it was warm in there at all. She decided he wasn't making a pass.

They took their drinks over to a table in one of the corners away from twitching ears and she watched him awkwardly dig his phone out of his pocket before he sat down.

"You have to be a bit careful round here." He indicated to his phone while waving it in his right hand just above the table. "In the wrong street in town it feels like an academy for pickpockets. My third one this year." He placed it on the table right in front of him. "But it ought to be safe enough in here."

She saw a middle-aged handsome-ish man who didn't look particularly haggard, but had a slightly weather-beaten look about him. Not just his face but also the clothes he wore as well. She hardly heard what he was saying as he remarked on the criminal elements of society in Clydebank and decided that he didn't seem to be stressed in any way. Somehow he exuded confidence. And then she realised he had asked her a question.

"Do you want to go first or shall I?"

"I think it'll be quicker if you go first."

He did and it was quick, because from his perspective, it was reasonably straight forward. All except for the part as to why it appeared that Aiden had purposefully tried to run over a complete stranger.

When it came to Patricia's turn, initially he struggled to see what the connection was. Justin, Hamilton, Lloyd, eventually Aiden and Erica. She left out Hamilton's attempted rape and a few other details she considered irrelevant, and it took her quite a while before he started to cross-question her. She finished up by giving him the reason why she wanted to make sure it was Aiden before Special Branch got a look-in. "Good as they are, if we present our report to the wrong man, he might not grasp the urgency of it in time, or worse still, not act on it until it's too late. Especially with Christmastime distractions. So you can see why we're eager to be sure of our facts so that we can ram the point home. Anyway, we don't want someone else stealing all our hard work."

"In other words, you want the credit for it," he quickly interjected.

"If you like, yes. And why not? I'm sure you've been in a similar position when someone from another division has stolen a case from you through no fault of your own."

"Aye, you're right there... and it sticks in the craw."

They looked at each other knowingly.

"So I'll help you as much as I can as I've no axe to grind on this one and plenty of other cases I can be getting on with. Dead terrorists I can do without on the run-up to Christmas."

"Your time's much appreciated, but tell me about the chap who got run down. Over the phone you said you believed him. Why?"

"There was no connection, no motive and he's as clean as a whistle. Local chap, works down the docks, just on his way back home from the pub where he was changing barrels that night, and when I interviewed him, he was dead straight. Not one of your shifty types, if you know what I mean. Despite being run over, he didn't even want to go to hospital." He lightly chuckled.

"What, no injuries at all?"

"Only a slight bump on his head and a grazed shin where the wheels had run over it."

"Is he a relative of Schwarzenegger by any chance?"

"Unlikely. He's not ugly enough for that, but he's probably about the same size, bigger perhaps."

"Any chance he's with the local bully boys?"

"Na. Look, I've a copy of his statement here. Why don't you go through it while I take a jimmy?" He thumbed his phone a few times until he found it and handed it to her. "Oh and there's also the report from traffic there as well. No skid marks indicating that he didn't use the brakes."

When he returned he saw that she had finished reading it; it wasn't very long.

She handed over his phone. "Let's get back to Aiden and ask ourselves why he would want to take out a nobody. You haven't read Aiden's dossier and don't know what a scheming shit he is, but we have and I can assure you he must have had a reason and I'll bet you it'll be something to do with Northern Ireland. Does Carl have any political affiliations and if so, are they in any way linked to the IRA?"

"None that I'm aware of and he doesn't seem the type. Keeps his head down. You can see from the question I asked him on page 2 that he's a member of the Union, but you try getting a job in the docks without being a Union member. It'd be worse than wearing the wrong colour scarf at the wrong end at a Rangers match. You wouldn't last five minutes."

"Do we know if the Union has any Irish association?"

"That sort of question is outside of my remit. More of a Special Branch issue, which may be one of the reasons why they want to see for themselves."

"Yes, you're right. I suppose there's no news on the car, is there?"

"Too early. Probably stolen and the owner's on holiday and we won't know until West Midlands Police track him down."

"What about Aiden's phone?"

"Still waiting for Beth the boffin to come back to me on that one. The last I heard was that she was struggling to open it, but give her a chance. She's the kind of woman who can open oysters with her teeth."

She laughed at the analogy. "Well, until we know about the car and his phone, that brings us back to Carl again, doesn't it?"

Mcleash broke the silence that had appeared out of nowhere. "I know what you want to do and I've no objection." He looked at his watch. "You're about to ask me if you can speak to Carl. Oh don't worry, as I said before, I've no axe to grind and I won't take offence if you think I may have missed something. This is the kind of mystery I like to be in on at ground level, so why don't we drink up and I'll take you to him. He'll be at home now... or down The Cobblers."

Patricia looked at her watch and noted that she'd be able to speak to Justin shortly and get him to arrange for Erica's arrest before she disappeared forever. "You know, this may sound a bit old-fashioned, but thank you for being so helpful."

"When it comes to you writing up your report, just

remember who bought you a round of drinks." He was smiling.

A second knock on the door of 79 Whitecrook Street and an ageing lady answered by opening the front door. "He's upstairs on the right, Flat C." She didn't wait for them to even enter before disappearing back into her own flat, so they followed her instructions; knocking on the door with the letter C painted on it.

Carl filled the doorway and silently gazed at them.

"Hello Carl. This is a colleague of mine from down London way and she'd like a word with you."

He looked down on Patricia and after a pause, took a step back and let them both in. Mcleash made the more formal introductions once they were inside the now cramped living room that doubled-up for dining and watching TV. There was just one wooden chair in front of the two uneven tables that abutted each other along one wall, and on them were the tools of Carl's trade as well as numerous models in varying stages of construction. Mcleash had seen it once before but still felt a little empathy with Patricia as she looked around the room at little trinkets and not-so-little replicas. Mainly of boats and the paraphernalia that went with them and she was tempted to touch an unusual-looking copper rose and stem that was somehow attached by nothing to the wall. It was beautiful and delicate, but the thorn on it warned anybody of the dangers of trying to pluck it. After gazing round the room, she looked up at the ceiling from which other models were suspended. To her, it was like walking into a living museum; one for the living, not the dead. She bent down to the table to inspect what looked like a railway station scene and saw that the two-inch high stationmaster had a little boy by the ear while waving his green flag. It was so surreal that it started to suck her into the story behind his actions. What had the lad been doing and how had the stationmaster caught him? He was obviously waving the all-clear flag to an imaginary train at the same time. And then she noticed a tiny whistle in his mouth. It wasn't made of the same substance that he was made of, and looking even closer, she saw that his lips were slightly pursed to hold the whistle. WOW. This was a work of art.

She straightened up and had to crane her neck to look Carl in the eye. "That's a wonderful piece of work, but where's the rest of it?"

She was surprised at the gentleness of his voice when he did reply. "Oh, that's for George down the road. He and his son have a train set in their attic and they asked me to build a station for them. This half will be done once I've put the brass leaf on the top steps."

She just had to have a look again and noticed that the steps appeared to emanate from underneath, while not actually doing so.

"And you do this in your spare time? All these models?" Her comment was rhetorical but posed so that it still required an answer.

"Oh yes. People come to me all the time with bits and pieces, but if there's nothing to be done, I just start making something."

"Why?"

"Why?" he repeated. "Well, I've nothing else to do when I'm not down the docks and I thought I'd make something."

Patricia was trying to get to the bottom of his thinking. Anyone who was worthwhile had a hobby and this was obviously Carl's, but he was so good at it. "Is all of your work local?"

"Mainly contacts from friends down the docks."

"Anyone in particular from outside the dock?" She looked over at Mcleash and felt a little embarrassed as she was probably asking the exact same questions he had been posed a few days earlier.

"Mrs Harbel wanted some wooden butterflies for her shopfront and I made those out of American black walnut; at least I think it's walnut, not too sure. Look, here's the piece it came from." He bent down under the table and produced a scrap of timber half the size of a cricket bat without the handle. "Found it sticking out of a pallet."

She realised that she would not get anywhere asking about individual pieces as they were probably all genuine cases in their own right, but had to try to establish any sort of link between Aiden and this man. There just had to be something.

"I was going to ask if you've made anything unusual lately, but I see most things in here are unusual." She glanced at a pair of ships dividers that had been etched onto another small piece of wood.

"Not to me, they're not," replied Carl.

"Well, let me put it another way. There's something you must have made for someone who knew the man who tried to run you down. Now, can you think of who or what that might be?" She stood directly in front of him wanting to look into his eyes when he replied.

In thought, he cocked his head slightly. "I really can't think of anything I've made that would upset anyone. All I do is pick up scraps of wood and metal and turn them into shapes. I see the grain on a piece of wood and I see a face. I mould it so that it brings out its features and with a bit of the right polish and a decent cloth, I like to bring knots of wood to life." He reached up with his arm a little and pointed at the figurehead on a ship. "She's called Iris after the Greek goddess of rainbows because this ship makes rainbows as it sails into the setting sun. She's one of my favourites." He was smiling at the figurehead.

Patricia looked at Mcleash who shrugged his shoulders indicating that he too had hit the same brick wall. She decided to change tack. "Carl, have you ever been to Ireland?"

"No."

"Where have you been, Carl?"

"When, this year?"

"Yes, this year, or last."

He had to think about that one. "Nowhere, just here."

"Have you got a passport."

"Why do I want a passport when I'm not going anywhere?"

Patricia was becoming frustrated. "Well, you must have a bank account."

"Oh yes. I've got one of those."

"Can I see your statements?"

Carl dipped his head, then opened a drawer of the dresser, produced a folder and handed it over. Mcleash looked over Patricia's shoulder as she leafed through the few pages. There were only regular entries of his salary and rent withdrawal. With no passport, driving licence, TV licence, or the need for any other type of licence, and coupled with his almost reclusive lifestyle, this ought to have meant that there would be some indication somewhere along the line that could be easily picked up on. She reminded herself that Aiden had a definite reason for trying to murder Carl and concluded that she wasn't looking in the right place or asking the right question. "Do you mind if we have a look around?"

"Fine."

They didn't need to carry out a deep search as Carl led a

neat lifestyle. He wasn't OCD, just neat, and they soon found themselves back in the living room where they started. There was nothing out of place. Almost absentmindedly, Mcleash picked up the Rubik's cube that was sitting on the edge of the nearest table. "Are you one of those who can do this then?"

"No. I just make replicas."

"Why would you want to make a replica when it must be cheaper to buy one?" It was a valid point and one that bought a frown to his forehead.

"Mr Gowern wanted one made out of metal, so I used that one as a pattern."

"Oh." Mcleash felt a little silly asking a question which had such an obvious answer, and he quickly replaced it on the table.

"He was very pleased with it. And I repaired his wife's stiletto shortly before he passed away. She was pleased with that as well."

Patricia could see that they were not going to gain anything further by staying any longer, and saying so to Carl, they thanked him and left. Mcleash started his car to warm it up and they sat there, each lost in their own thoughts for a few moments.

Patricia broke the silence first. "You're right. He's totally innocent isn't he, even if he doesn't know that he's got a link to Aiden."

"Aye. A gentle giant with not much more than two brass farthings to rub together, but I'll tell you what… he's probably more content in his life than I'll ever be. Just look at what he's got. OK, you and I have both got jobs and pensions, but I've got the responsibilities of a family, a mortgage, and a superintendent who wants the impossible. He's got his own little world which he controls at his own pace and is behoven to no one. Now, where might you stand in all of this, eh? Would you rather be me or him?"

"Right now, I'd settle for a whisper of a hint as to his connection, because I'm as certain as I can be that Aiden was here just to silence Carl."

"Why?"

She looked inquisitively at him across the interior lighting.

"Why are you so certain?" he repeated.

"Because when we asked Erica where Aiden was, she said she didn't know, but then she mentioned something about him being out of phone contact 'up North'. And this is definitely up North."

"How long ago was this?"

"Only three or four days ago. Why?"

"Just posing the question because we had an unusual death here a couple of weeks back. Nothing suspicious, just unusual, and I was wondering how long Aiden had been up here. See if there's some sort of link there, but I doubt it. The man's funeral was last week and he's well and truly in the ground now."

"Keep wondering, because we don't know how long Aiden was up here for. Any other unusual activities?"

"Ooch, not unusual, as quite a few crimes come under that category. There was another hit-and-run the other day, not more than a mile from where Aiden's body was found, but that was on the main road, and anyway, we think we know who did that. We just can't find him, but he'll pop up probably in one of the cells over Christmas. That's not unusual in itself, but having three similar car-related incidents in two weeks, now that's unusual."

"What about the second unusual one?"

"Oh that was only an OAP taking a shortcut home across

the railway lines and he managed to get run over by a van on the level crossing of all places. Not by a train, mind you, as one would think, but a van. The driver didn't stop but it's not surprising as that's a bumpy crossing just there. He probably didn't even notice he'd run over anyone on a dark night."

"Was the van driver local?" she asked, expecting the answer.

"Nay. Normally the CCTV would have picked up the incident but the control box for the cameras had been vandalised the day before, so we've no footage and no way of tracing the van."

"How do you know it was a van?"

Mcleash had to think about that one for a moment. "I think that was the conclusion of the report. You see, as the incident occurred on Scottish Rail's property, British Transport Police handled it, and I only mentioned it because it was one of three hit-and-runs in a fairly short space of time."

"I'd say that qualifies it as being unusual. Any chance you can get a copy of that report?"

"Every chance as it's still fairly fresh. But that's more of a coincidence than anything else. OK, I know that coincidences sometimes add up, but these three really are random and only two of them stand a chance of being connected."

"Without anything else unusual to go on, and with very little effort, it'll be worth eliminating the possibility, wouldn't it?" She was being thorough." How soon can you get that report?"

"It'll take a day or two but I ought to be able to email it over to you before Christmas."

The mention of Christmas made Patricia look at her watch and she saw it was about to turn six o'clock. Time to phone Justin, but first she needed to conclude matters with

Mcleash. Her return flight wasn't for another hour or so and the airport wasn't far away and while he drove her there, she went over the timing in her mind. The flight would land her back at Gatwick about nine-thirty, allow an hour and a half plus to get through the airport and across London, ten minutes changing and freshening up in her flat, ten minutes to Maidenhead police station to pick up a few bits 'n' pieces, and that would leave her at least fifteen minutes to get to Marsh Lane. Perfect. She'd have time for a nap on the flight.

Justin rang as she was thanking Mcleash kerbside at Glasgow airport.

"Glasgow's a bit wet, but then I gather it often is."

"What of interest in Glasgow?"

"Aiden."

"You've found him?"

She told him of the day's events as she walked over to the machine and managed to multi-task her way through the check-in icons while still speaking to him.

"Erica ought to be landing about now, so can you arrange to have her picked up and detained when she gets to her flat?"

"I presume you want her arrested on a terrorism charge so that we can keep her in over Christmas?"

"Section 3 of the 2019 counter-terrorism act allows us to do just that under 'obtaining information' etcetera. I think you'll find that it updates the 2000 act, but best to have a look just to make sure she can't get bail."

"Do you want me to use my authority or will you want to use yours?"

"Keep it simple and use yours. I tell you, if we lose her this time, she'll disappear forever and we'll never get to the bottom of it until it's too late. I don't know how many more disguises she's got but her latest one'll fool most people."

"I'll get on it right away then and let you know. See you later."

"Probably not as I've got an operation on at midnight, oh and you'll love this… it's just round the corner from where we live in Marsh Lane."

"Have fun, you busy bee."

***

Erica hardly took in her journey back to London as her thoughts were quite naturally centred on Aiden. She kept going through in her mind what the assistant at the morgue had read out from the file when she had asked how he had died – 'A diffuse axonal injury leading to fatal edema of the occipital lobe' – and when she had asked for that to be translated, he told her. Asking to see the injury at the back of his head, the assistant had replied that that would be pointless as there was virtually nothing to see because death had been instant and there had been no time for any swelling or discolouration to set in. Her few other questions had been politely answered but when she had asked to see his personal effects, Mcleash had told her that they would be released to her after the inquest, and no, a mobile phone hadn't been found on him.

Her foremost thought was that someone had murdered Aiden quite simply because he wasn't the kind of man who would go tripping over kerbs; not even in the middle of the night. And those bastards, being the embodiment of the establishment, were lying because he always had a mobile on him; sometimes two or three.

She hardly took in that Patricia was dropping her off at the airport rather than catching the same flight, and in fact nearly missed the call during her wait on one of the ergonomically designed 'comfortable' seats in the waiting lounge. Unbeknownst to her, she had been overlooked by Patricia until she had gone through to the embarkation lounge. Her thoughts had centred around what had happened to Aiden and she remembered him saying that a certain person wouldn't be around for much longer. Who was this man and had they had a fight? Was he the one Aiden had described as having an extraordinary skill and did that skill include murdering people? A horrific thought entered her head. If this man had murdered Aiden, was she his next target? Perhaps Patricia was right and there really was someone out there hunting her down. She looked up and around from her seat trying to see if anyone was taking interest in her, but instantly discarded the idea. An airport with all its CCTV would not be a good place to carry out a murder. Where then? Probably not on the flight or at Gatwick either... it would have to be back at her rented flat when she would be alone.

"Shit." Her loud expletive made a passing couple look at her briefly. She realised she wouldn't be able to return to her flat and wouldn't be able to retrieve any of her luggage. She looked at her watch, got up and headed for the few shops to re-stock. What a stroke of luck. As she approached Boots the Chemist, there was a woman attending to a stall outside, and that stall sold wigs. Perhaps she could turn this to her advantage after all. If she could disguise herself enough, she may be able to see who was waiting for her at her flat without being seen. There would still be enough time before meeting Eamon at Gatwick later that night.

***

"Shit." Patricia swore but not so loudly that anyone paid

much attention.

"I know what you mean." A stranger in the form of a middle-aged man standing next to her commented. "I do this run all the time and it's always the last flight of the day that gets delayed."

"Why this one?"

"If you wait a few minutes, there'll be an announcement over the loudspeaker and I'll bet you it'll say one of two things. Either it'll be a baggage breakdown or a technical issue with the plane. Never what the real reason is."

"How do you know what the real reason is?"

"Because I work in the industry as a logistics manager for this and other airports." He held out his hand. "Len Robinson."

After the usual Anglo-Saxon hesitation, she took his hand and introduced herself without providing him with her occupation. "Come on then, what's the real reason and how long a delay will it be?" They both moved away from the ticketing machine and made way for others to discover that they too would be delayed back to Gatwick.

"In answer to your first question, it's because of the French air traffic controllers and as to your second question, on average about fifteen minutes."

She half-laughed. "How on earth can the French traffic controllers be responsible for Scottish airspace? They're miles away in the other direction."

Len was smug, having hooked a beautiful woman. This ploy had worked before and although he was happily married, he would sometimes take the opportunity to 'play away' as he called it when the chance came. Despite his occasional unfaithfulness, he was very good at his job and knew what he was talking about. "Sliders." He gave a knowing nod to his head.

"Sliders. OK I give up, what are sliders and what have they got to do with airplanes?"

"Think back to when you were a child and had a toy where you had to move squares around in a square frame. To complete the picture you had to move an individual square to make space for the next so that you could move another into the right position and so forth until you had a complete picture the right way round."

From the look on her face, he knew she remembered. He went on to explain that aircraft worked on the same principle when it came to short haul, and that right now their aircraft was probably on its way from Bordeaux or Marseilles, not Heathrow. The French air traffic controllers changed shifts just about the same time that their aircraft was about to take off and hence the delay while they re-affirmed the status of certain itineraries. "They're about as pedantic as ours, but better safe than sorry, eh?"

A bing-bong sounded and announced that their flight was indeed delayed due to a shortage of baggage ramps.

"See what I mean? Don't worry about being late though, because the captain usually puts his foot down once we're in the air and we arrive only a few minutes late." His congeniality was contagious, but Patricia was practically immune. She was looking forwards to a few minutes' shut-eye and hoped that Len wasn't going to try to pester her on the flight.

Even with the captain's help, they landed nearly fifteen minutes later than scheduled, but then had to wait longer than normal as the disembarkation ramp decided it wasn't going to play ball on this particular night. Keeping an eye on the time, Patricia was aware that she was fast running out of it if she was to make her rendezvous at a quarter to midnight, and considered going straight there if she had to. She phoned Justin as the ramp behaved.

"I'm back on the ground at Gatwick. How's things with Erica?"

"We're still waiting."

"What? At her flat?"

"Yes. The team's staked out on both access points and I'm in a car across the road with Byron, but she hasn't shown up yet. I reckon she's done a runner because if she was on that flight, even a cripple in a wheelchair would have been here by now."

"Oh no. Shit." She looked at her watch and had to agree with his assessment.

"I was waiting to hear from you first before grabbing her belongings. We don't need a warrant as this comes under the anti-terrorism laws. What do you think?" He could hear her hurrying down the concourse towards the station.

"Go for it. There might be a clue in that lot somewhere. Listen, I've really got to dash. Talk to you later." She broke into a run as she spotted the train timetable display. If she could make this train into London, then she wouldn't have to rush later.

"Shit," she cursed as it pulled out.

***

Erica smiled to herself in her comfortable window seat as she watched Patricia hopelessly running down the platform after the departing train. It didn't matter that Aiden was dead and it didn't matter that she no longer had someone to guide her, because what he had put into motion all those months ago was now unstoppable. She clutched her bag on the seat next to her closer, knowing that the Rubik's cube in it would soon be on the last leg of its journey, and briefly mused over Eamon's surprise at her appearance. The look on his face as he finally recognised her under her disguise had been priceless, but she had kept a stern face, considering it to have been more professional. Certainly, she had been tempted to share a drink at the bar with him, but instead opted to make the transfer of the cube as quick as possible, and hence make the train she was now on, up to London.

She started to bend her thoughts to meeting Chloe tomorrow, and had to decide where she was going to stay the next few nights. There had always been a couple of options, sometimes more, depending upon her activities at the time, but now she had to decide if she was going to try to seduce Chloe or not. She plumped for The Royal Lancaster opposite Hyde Park because of its handy location, and gave Liam a ring. He was one of the concierges whom she and Aiden had got to know well and once again, she was not disappointed. He couldn't offer her a suite as they were nearly full on the lead-up to Christmas, but did have a deluxe to offer her, and yes, she was welcome for longer than two nights if she wanted. She knew what his usual fee was and didn't object because she liked him; and he was quite handsome. She closed her eyes as the train rattled through a tunnel, smug in the knowledge that she was outsmarting the powers that protected Hamilton.

***

Now one of the bloody trains was running late and going slow because of something on the line, and Patricia was becoming anxious. She started to think about what reason she would have to give to Tonybee in the morning for not following operational orders and she shuddered at what he was going to say about her end-of-month expenses. She could see his expression now 'two return flights to Glasgow...'. At Victoria, she caught the District Line to Chiswick Park as she had parked her car in the local police station on the way down, and it was only a hop, skip and a jump from there onto the M4 and Maidenhead. Due to the very light traffic on the motorway out of London, she actually made up some of the time she had lost earlier, but not enough to make any real difference. Now, only a few minutes behind her schedule, she ran into her flat to change underwear and into something warmer before driving over to Maidenhead police station to collect her set of handcuffs and radio. A quick glance at her watch confirmed that she would just make it in time and then she went back out to the car.

"Shit." She fumbled in her pockets. "Shit shit shit." She looked at her keys hanging from the ignition switch. "Aaaaaaaaaaaargh! Shit!" She looked round but this time there was no Justin to help her out, so instead ran back inside the station to see if anyone knew how to break into a Vauxhall Astra. Approaching midnight, the place was nearly deserted with neither the duty sergeant nor the constable manning the radio able to leave their posts. The canteen was empty, but she came across Willy who was just on his way back out, having arrested a couple for dogging in the High Street, ironically on the steps of the magistrate's courts where they would be appearing the following morning.

"Willy. Please tell me you can break into an Astra." She almost pinned him against the wall.

"What model?"

"Errrr, a five-year-old fourteen hundred diesel."

"Simple. Why?"

She grabbed him by the collar in desperation. "Because I need you to break into mine so I can get my keys and I need it done now."

"OK, OK. Just show me where." He was a little bemused.

Five minutes later the lock clicked. Patricia grabbed him roughly by the collar again and violently kissed him before jumping into her car and driving off. Willy stood there and watched her drive a little recklessly out of the station gates and onto the deserted roads. She knew it was now midnight and that Marsh Lane was at least ten minutes away but she prayed that Messrs Chilvers and Seaford had somehow managed to arrest the drug dealer. "SHIT," she swore as she turned into one of the narrow back streets off the one-way system. A six-foot barrier with large white letters on a bright red background stated that the road was closed, and she somehow noted that it was all the fault of the local gas company. Not being able to take her shortcut would add another few minutes onto her journey and sure enough, by the time she arrived at Marsh Lane Car Park it was twenty past twelve.

The stroboscopic effects from the blue and red lights of half-a-dozen police cars made it difficult to see exactly who was who, and it was only when she had walked almost right up to the river's edge and turned, that she could make out an officer with pips on his shoulders. He was talking to Sergeant Chilvers; Constable Seaford waited in the background. Surveying the scene by shielding her eyes, she saw several plain clothes officers huddled in two groups either side of the minivan that had all its doors open. She reflected that it was her who was supposed to be in charge of this operation and in her absence, another senior officer had stepped in, and from his uniform, he appeared to be an inspector. She didn't recognise him but approached him from his line of sight so that he had a chance to see her.

"Ahhhhhhhh, there you are." He pointed with his head towards Messrs Chilvers and Seaford. "According to your two chaps here you're supposed to be running this operation. I take it you are Inspector Eyethorne?" His sarcastic tone put the emphasis on the 'are' part and he was clearly going to enjoy her tardiness to the full. She decided to push back as he was the same rank as herself; and anyway, this was her patch not his.

"In my division it's customary for a visiting officer to announce themselves before barging in on someone else's case."

"Yes, you're quite right, but in this instance I think you'll find that I have jurisdiction here. Not only was I on time, but I'm here to investigate you."

"Me?" She was incredulous.

"If you really are Inspector Eyethorne, then yes, you."

"Why are you investigating me and you still have not told me who you are?"

"Ummmm, well, that might depend on why you're late."

"Well I'm certainly not going to tell someone who's rude enough not to tell me who they are."

"Yes, I see your point. Very well. I'm Inspector Dewbury of the drugs squad and yes we do still work out of Pimlico. Now tell me what you know about this car." He looked over at the grey minivan.

It took nearly five minutes of Dewbury's questions and Patricia's answers before he was satisfied that somewhere along the line, someone had made a mistake. His tone changed. "Well, we can't just leave government property lying about, can we?"

"Government property?" Patricia queried, wondering

exactly what he was referring to.

"Yes. We traced the registration plates to a government administrative department in central London, and by the look of it, I'd say it was normally used for document transfer etcetera. In fact, there's still a few boxes of blank paper in the back."

"What about the drugs?"

"Oh we're pretty sure it's cocaine, but only lab analysis will tell us how pure it is and possibly where it came from. By the way, I'd like to call past and pick up that letter your super received. I presume you still have it?"

"No problem. I asked our forensic department to give it the once over, but they should have finished earlier today."

A plain clothes offer approached them with a brown envelope. "We've dusted it down for prints but what do you want to do with this, Guv? There's the best part of ten grand in it."

Dewbury took it off the officer. "I'll take that." He was about to put it in his coat pocket when he saw Patricia staring at it. "And why might this interest you?"

The first thought that entered her head was how alike the envelope was to one that she had given Hamilton, but it was difficult to tell in the dark with flashing lights. Her second thought was that all buff envelopes of that size would naturally look alike, and the third thought was more of a question. Should she bring Hamilton to the attention of Dewbury? "Let me see that."

Watching her reactions carefully, he handed the envelope over to her. She knew instantly that it was the same one, but nevertheless, she took it towards the headlight of one of the cars where she could study it in greater detail under the plain whiter light. It also gave her a few more seconds thinking time. A letter opener had been used on one end of it, and inside there were two bundles of fifty-pound notes, still elastic banded together with the same colour and type that she herself had used. Hamilton.

Maurice bloody Hamilton. She was fuming and her thought process went into overdrive. What the fuck was he up to now? And then it dawned on her that all this had been a set-up just to put her off his scent. No, not just that. It was meant to entrap her. Had she not been late and had... one thought after another. The shithead of a bastard.

She turned back to Dewbury and put on an innocent expression and with a smile announced, "Just wondering what ten grand looks like."

Dewbury suddenly realised that although he and his team were quite used to seeing envelopes with wads of cash in, to an inspector from outside of the drugs squad, it would come as a novelty.

The last thing she remembered seeing was 02.31 on her bedside alarm clock.

Chapter 15

Gibbons
(Saturday 23rd December)

The four hours' sleep Patricia had managed showed in her bathroom mirror. Conversely and oblivious to Patricia's midnight escapade, Justin had enjoyed another night of banking sleep. His phone beeped at him with a message from her and he rang her straight back and, after the brief usual morning greeting, asked how last night went.

"Poxy Hamilton…" She told him exactly what she thought in no uncertain terms and gave him a truncated version of last night's goings-on. "Listen, no matter what, we've got to meet up tonight and resolve things, because I can't go on having to look over my shoulder the whole time. And by the way, neither can you."

"No problem. My three-day break starts at six o'clock tonight and coupled with the Christmas holidays, means I've got over a week free. How about I book us a table somewhere to celebrate?"

She was about to reply that she didn't feel much like celebrating in either a pub or a restaurant, but then gave in to her needs. "OK, but make sure you keep an eagle eye on the bastard today, and see if you can't find out what he's up to next. Does Hamilton know you'll be off for over a week?"

"Um…. unlikely but all he has to do is ask and he

might not even realise I'm not there tomorrow. Remember, yesterday was the last day that Parliament was sitting before the Christmas recess and today I'm guarding him at his house near Worcester. From now on until the new year, it'll be family and friends time, but in his case I expect he'll find enough time to bed a mistress or two in his London apartment."

"Do you know what his next official appointments are? We really do need to keep tabs on him."

"I know of one and I'll find out about any others. Regarding my report, mine's finished and I emailed it over to you last night. Oh, it doesn't matter if any of Hamilton's lackeys hack it because it's about to come out into the open anyway and once you've had a chance to finish yours, you can forward it to Commander Stanley Gibbons at Special Branch. I've come across him before and he's got a reputation of getting things done quickly. His email and contact details are in the link I've sent you."

"After all my running around yesterday, I need to add to mine and tweak the penultimate part. With any luck I might be able to get that done this morning before Tonybee finds me something else to do. Oh and I've got to see forensics about... Look, I've got a whole lot on and I'll tell you all about it later. See you tonight about seven-thirty."

"One other thing that I'm feeling a little guilty about."

"Go on."

"If I hadn't been with Hamilton the whole day, we could have picked up Erica at Gatwick instead of having to wait for her to not even show up at her flat. I reckon that's why Hamilton is keeping me on and making sure I haven't time enough to put any sort of spanner in his works."

"That makes sense, but until we have enough proof of his actions and resolved his possible assassination problem, you're in the best position, even though you won't be with him over the next few days. Your privileged position as one of the bodyguards of a minister of the Crown means that when you say something, you're more likely to be listened to. So stay put, for both our sakes."

"You're the boss." He loved her when she put into words what he was thinking.

It was only when she mouse-nudged her computer on her desk into life that she took in that it was a Saturday, and despite the warm central heating system, she gave an involuntary shiver. Outside through the window the non-existent dawn confirmed the onset of winter. Automatically, she plugged in both of her phones for a recharge.

Before knuckling down to complete her report, she was glad to see a big sealed envelope from forensics in her in-tray. She opened it and retrieved the two-sided note in a plastic bag and the report that went with it, all the while praying that it contained something useful. Attached to the back of the report was a copy of what the ever-so-feint imprinted writing was, and this had been translated into text on a fresh page. It stated that at least two different notations were on it and the doodling was inconclusive. The first in the top left-hand corner was the day before yesterday's date, but the second was in a much bigger scrawl and was a registration number that had been partially doodled with. At the bottom of the page was a badly drawn arrow, the type that could have been used by Indians chasing cowboys. The report itself was largely irrelevant as it described the notepaper, guessed the demographic of the author etc., but as she put it to one side, an alarm bell rang in her head. She re-read both the note and the imprinted page, but nothing sprang to mind immediately, but there was something that was causing her to feel uneasy, yet she couldn't put her finger on it right now. Coffee. Perhaps if she had a cup of coffee it might help… but it didn't.

She groaned at the number of emails that had come in in her absence and was about to ignore all of them so that she could finish her report when she spotted one from Clydeside police – Mcleash. It was the report on one of the hit-and-runs he had promised her, and she wanted to eliminate this from her thoughts and consign it to her mental irrelevant box. The attached report was in a standard format although there were a few differences. Being of Scottish origin there was a sub-report from the procurator fiscal instead of a coroner with references to the Sheriff's office, but by and large it was clear that Mr Gowern had been hit by an anonymous van or small lorry and had most probably died instantly. She routinely turned a page to an attached appendix and while her hand hovered the mouse over the red 'x' top right of the screen in readiness to move on, she stopped. She could hardly believe what she was reading. It was a report from one of the Transport Police officers stating that the metal CCTV control boxes hadn't just been vandalised, but professionally broken into and that the relevant circuit panels tampered with enough to disrupt the signal feed that same day. Whoever had done this had known exactly how to disable the cameras both sides of the track. The reporting officer had added his own codicil suggesting that this had possibly been carried out by an ex-rail employee who regularly jumped the signal lights and that any further investigation ought to focus on this aspect. She went back and re-read his passage on the tampering facet. If true, then whoever had run over poor old Mr Gowern had not wanted to be caught doing so, and it therefore followed that this was a murder case. Mr Gowern… Gowern… Gowern… she'd heard that name before… but where?

She picked up the phone hoping that Mcleash was up and about this early. He was, and after thanking him for his email, bought the appendix to his attention.

"I know," he said casually. "But I thought you'd like to read it for yourself." It was another of his methods of testing his contemporary and he was glad that she had picked up on it so quickly. To his mind, some officers would not have bothered reading any appendix and consign such report to the 'finished with' box. Inspector Eyethorne went up another notch in his estimation.

"I take it you're treating this as a murder case now?"

"Oh aye, but there's very little to go on. The man had no contacts with any gangs so we can rule that one out, he had no debts to speak of, no offspring, no will, and just the standard union life assurance policy that'll pay almost bugger all to his widow. There's no motive anywhere as far as I can tell, but I've yet to pursue a couple of lines of enquiry, so don't give up hope yet."

"Mr Gowern's murderer. He would have had motive."

"Definitely, and you've hit the nail on the head, but which would you prefer? Your chicken or your egg? Find the motive and we might find our murderer and vice versa."

"I'm sure I've heard his name before, but I can't place him right now. Any thoughts?"

"You're asking if I can trace a man called Smith," he chuckled down the line. "There's any number of Gowerns up here. We've even got a Constable Gowern working around here somewhere and there's probably a clan of McGowerns running around in taxis somewhere else, so don't be surprised if you've seen or heard that name before."

"What's his wife think?"

"Listen, while I'll help you all I can, I've got other fish to fry. Leave this one with me and when I get the chance to ask her a few questions once she's over the death of her husband, I'll let you know."

"Sorry, I ought to have been a little more sensitive."

"Apology accepted. Now if you would like to leave this one to me, I'll wish you a good day." He hung up.

She chewed her lip realising that she had been a little too pushy by asking a fellow officer miles away in another division to investigate the way she would have done. It was his patch and his rules applied; not hers.

She went to save the procurator fiscal's report but realised she wasn't sure where to file it, but then made up her mind. She was confident that somehow there was a link to Aiden and Erica, so it went into a related sub-folder. Gowern... Gowern. She gave up trying to force her memory and instead sent Mcleash a diplomatic thank you email. Within a few seconds he replied and asked if she could bring a friend with her next time, because their office novice was lacking decent female company. That bought a smile to her face.

She hurried to finish her report, looked at Justin's link telling her how to get hold of Commander Gibbons, and despite it being a Saturday, phoned to make an appointment. She could tell that her call was automatically transferred and whether it was her well-known name or just plain old luck she never knew, but she was told by the person on the other end of the phone that he would be free to meet her at twelve noon today at Scotland Yard, and yes it was the new one on Victoria Embankment on the other side of the river to the London Eye. It was a little early to leave but she knew that if she didn't leave now, sooner or later Tonybee was bound to ask for her. She downloaded the reports onto a memory stick, grabbed her phones, laptop, other paraphernalia and left. If she wasn't in the building, then she wouldn't have to answer any awkward questions.

With the weather taking a turn for the worse, she was about to grab a taxi to the train station, when she gratefully accepted a lift from one of the patrol cars on their way out of the compound; the cheery constable telling her that the trains to Paddington left about every twenty minutes, so she ought not to get too cold. She made good use of the overground train journey by firstly looking up Stanley Gibbons on the internet and found precious little about him, and then by writing a brief report on the previous night's fiasco but there was no way she could disguise that fact that she was late on the scene. It got her thinking about why the drugs squad had been so heavy handed over what would normally be a provincial incident and handled pretty much as Tonybee had set out in his operations dossier. And why had Dewbury been told to target her specifically, and... hang on a minute, didn't he say that the minivan was government? Hamilton was government. Number plate... the number doodled one was the same as the van in the car park. And then it all clicked into place. Realising that the only reason why she had not picked up on it before was because of her tiredness and she rubbed her brow trying to recognise how she was actually faring up. Coupled with the envelope of cash, the whole episode reeked of Hamilton's skullduggery, and had she been on time, then Dewbury might well have had justification in arresting her as the suspected drug dealer. Being arrested and consequentially suspended while a lengthy tribunal investigated, would have been Hamilton's perfect method of sidelining her, while he considered how else to destroy her reputation and career. Justin was right... the man had to go.

So now she was faced with a dilemma. If she managed to

persuade Commander Gibbons that the threat was real, he would take the appropriate measure to ensure Hamilton's well-being. On the other hand, if she presented their reports in such a way as to sound a little vague, and the commander decided not to take any action, then perhaps he would survive to see in another new year and be free to pursue his vendetta against her and Justin. By the time the train pulled into Paddington, she had made her mind up. A real first-class bastard he might be, but it went against the grain to allow terrorism to succeed. She would convey their fears to Commander Gibbons in the strongest possible way and have to find another method of neutralising Hamilton.

Over the decades, Special Branch had morphed and merged with other state security services and was now officially the Counter Terrorism Command. Everyone still called it Special Branch as it was easier and one didn't become a commander by just waiting to be promoted; one had to be special to earn that rank. Nearer fifty than forty, Commander Stanley Gibbons looked even more youthful, but that only helped to wrong-foot those who had not come across him before. Other than his razor-sharp mind, he was the epitome of a middle-aged man, and he didn't rise out of his chair when Patricia was shown into his rather small office that overlooked the Thames Embankment from the second floor. Having refreshed his memory by reading her file, he wasn't surprised that she was exactly on time; he expected nothing less.

The introductions were brief, mainly because Patricia nervously followed his lead. She wasn't used to being this close to those who wielded great amounts of power on a day-to-day basis, but his tone was pleasant enough, and after sitting down upright on the only other chair in the room, felt a little more at ease.

"And how can I help the infamous Patricia Eyethorne today?"

She was already opening up her laptop which she had primed while waiting in an anteroom, and went to place it in front of him on his desk.

"No."

She stopped.

"In words of three syllables and in less than one minute, I want you to tell me."

It took her five seconds to decide that this man really did cut straight to the bone and that she ought to do likewise. "Maurice bloody Hamilton's going to be assassinated on Christmas Day."

She didn't know this man or anything about him, but what little she had gleaned so far helped her square up to him. His reaction, or rather lack of it, was all that she expected.

"I like someone who puts their neck on the block and you've just done that." His deadpan face didn't reveal his thoughts. "And I suppose you're now going to present me with your evidence."

"Is there any other way?" she asked.

"Not really, but you can always tell me rather than just sit there while I trawl through what is probably a politically correct and methodical report that could probably be condensed to one paragraph."

"Two." She went along with his terse attitude.

"Two what?"

"Two reports." She then regretted being so blunt and quickly picked up on the fact that he wanted to be told something rather than having to read it. "And we both agree that there's an IRA link to his assassination in three days' time."

"Who and how?"

"That's why I'm here. We're close but not quite close enough. We think it'll be a bomb at his house but we don't know how it's going to be delivered. Our only link has disappeared and to make matters far more difficult, Hamilton's out to get us."

"Ummmmmm. I come across as many death threats to Hamilton as I do for the rest of the Cabinet put together. One might be forgiven for assuming that this is because of the Northern Ireland office that he holds and the violence that goes with it. One might just as well conclude that it is because he is rather good at upsetting most of the people he comes across and that he is who he is. Coupling these two factors together by themselves would account for ninety per cent of those who would wish him permanently removed from his current position. The other ten per cent are represented by a certain cross-section of society wanting him dead because of his extreme right-wing views that he is always keen to air. All in all, it's rather surprising that the man's still alive really." He smiled for the first time. "This brings me to my point that he somehow manages to stay alive by removing his enemies first, and that if you consider yourself as one of his enemies, then I'm not certain I really ought to be standing next to you when he takes aim."

Patricia was quick to pick up on what he was telling her. "No, you've got this the wrong way round. I'm not here to ask for your help. That's just a bonus. I'm here to offer ours. Even though he's the most obnoxious person I've ever come across and I wish all manner of ills on him, that still doesn't justify standing back and letting someone murder him, especially if that person is a terrorist."

"How very honest of you. You appear to be one of those

whose moral compass is firmly fixed in the right direction." He was very pleased that she had not risen to his comments about self-preservation but instead had focused on Hamilton's predicament. Most others he knew would have grasped at the chance of assistance from him, but this woman had kept her gaze firmly fixed on the objective, almost disregarding her own safety. "Very well then, tell me more."

At the end of her report she had compressed the essence of it into bullet points and with a prompt from her laptop, she rattled them off. When she finished, she realised with horror that she hadn't even read Justin's report and prayed that it corresponded to hers.

"So no actual proof then," he replied.

"One defines proof as being irrefutable, or in the case of a jury, beyond reasonable doubt. In this instance we're somewhere between the two."

"From your point of view."

"From our point of view," she corrected. "But there's two of us with the same opinion."

He scrutinised her, trying to read into her mind. Her face was towards the window and the weak winter daylight helped just enough to clear away the few remaining shadows cast by the overhead lights. He liked what he saw, but he reminded himself that he wasn't trying to quantify her beauty, but instead assess if she was being desperate or honest. He decided it was the latter. "And you'd like to make it three, eh?"

She was beginning to become a little irked by his probing comments and questions, but maintained her composure. "I think you'll find I've already answered that one. I'm here to help you, not the other way round."

"And it certainly wouldn't do your career any harm if you were proved correct, would it?" He sat passively looking directly at her. "You see, I'm trying to put myself in your shoes and I ask the question 'how can I dig myself out of this trap that I've built for myself'. I know, I'll involve the Special Branch and see if they can find out what I cannot, and as a bonus, Hamilton is warned off my fiancée and me. Let's get them to do the dirty work. How does that sound to you?"

She struggled to understand why he was querying her evidence and her ethos at the same time. This was a man that Justin said was just the right person, yet here he was, belittling almost everything she was saying. Yet she detected that something was not quite right from the tone of his voice... or was it in his body language. He'd hardly moved an inch since she had walked in. Perhaps the truth was in his eyes and returning his level stare, she thought she felt not a battle of wills, but a battle of truths. That was it... he was goading her. Another test perhaps? She decided to join in his game and with a big smile replied. "Sounds perfect to me. When can you start?"

Her response nearly caught him out and she thought she saw the hint of a flicker of his eyelids. "Touché. I must say you do seem to be able to pick up on the salient issues rather quickly. OK then. Now that we've got that out of the way I think we can agree that your assessment is made for all the right reasons and not one of personal gain. That goes for both of you. I've known about your fiancé before you two became an item, and far from it for me to cast judgement, I think you've got a bright future together. Oh, and my congratulations by the way." He smiled again. "Now, to business."

The speed which he covered what he wanted to say kept her mind racing and reacting. She didn't have too much trouble keeping up with him.

He continued. "I agree from what you have just told me

that there's a risk, but it's my job to decide how great that risk is and what counter measures to take, if any. There's a small army of analysts and their computers hidden away in a building somewhere up the M1 and if we give them your report, the system will take a few nanoseconds to probably dismiss the whole thing. As the saying goes, 'to err is human but it takes a computer to really fuck it up'. That's why us humans have noses, and right now my nose tells me that you're probably right. There's not much smoke and even less fire, but I think you're onto something because I've received snippets of information from elsewhere that point in Hamilton's direction. By the way, did you know that that's the way all the best schemes start off? No smoke, but all fire? Rumours and enthusiasm come before action. Tell me a little more about Erica."

He leaned back in his chair, arching his fingers in front of him, while Patricia described Erica's reactions in detail when they had met her in the pub. He led her step by step through certain passages again, asking an occasional question, before moving onto Aiden. "Did you see her reaction when she saw Aiden's body?"

"She kept a straight face, so nothing there, but she was positive it was him."

"Not too positive?"

"How do you mean?"

"Well, when someone's expecting bad news and you actually tell them, their reaction is totally different than if they hadn't been forewarned. Think back to when you first told her about Aiden and try to picture her that very instant. And not just her face either. Did she stiffen or twitch in any way?"

She recalled Erica in her flat when she had told her about Aiden and vaguely remembered her doing a bit of shouting. "I think she was genuinely shocked and now I think about it, she really wasn't prepared for his death right up until the point in the morgue when she saw his body. I reckon she thought that was Aiden, and I too am convinced. But if in doubt, you can always ask your man who's up there today."

"We've got a man up there now?" He blinked.

"Yup."

"And how did you find that out?"

She was about to tell him that she'd heard it from Mcleash, and then thought the better of it. "You forget that I'm a detective and that it's my job to find out relevant things." She asked herself if he knew that there was one of their operatives in Glasgow looking over Aiden's dead body to confirm it was actually him, and then half a second later realised that he really hadn't been told. She did her best, which was good enough, to disguise what she knew from him.

He extended one arm and pressed his intercom button. "Inchcombe."

Three seconds later and a man's voice replied, "Sir."

"Who have we got in Glasgow right now identifying the Irishman?"

"That'll be Weston, sir."

"Get him to contact me asap, will you?"

"Yes sir."

He flicked a switch off and stared at Patricia. "We may as well have official confirmation, and now that you seem to have worked your way into our own investigation… no… let me rephrase that. You seem to have taken over our investigation, you may as well read our file on Aiden Mullhagity." He opened a drawer on his left and produced a large buff folder which he placed on his desk within reach of Patricia. "That's our hard file and I'll get someone to give you a digital copy, but while we're waiting for Weston to report back, you might as well read it... but don't take too long, will you?" He was telling her to cast her eyes over the salient points and read the detail later.

Glued on the inside of the cover on the left was a page of basic information on the subject. She worked out that Aiden Mullhagity would have been in his mid-fifties, that his mother came from the county town of Sligo and that his father was unknown; there was an asterisk indicating that there was further information on this matter elsewhere in the folder. She noticed that in fact there were quite a lot of asterisks on that page, all referring to the appendices that were treasury-tagged together on the right-hand side. In the box headed 'Activities' was the notation 'B4', so she found appendix B4 logically between B3 and B5 which listed his suspected involvement in noteworthy occurrences. These numerous events were also listed and cross-referenced to other files. She returned to the first page and looked up the C4 appendix on 'Known Associates' and ran her finger down the long list. She didn't recognise any of them, but stopped at one particular name halfway down. Shocked, she looked up at the commander and saw him staring directly at her.

"Hamilton."

He just nodded back at her revelation.

"He knew Hamilton." She returned to the file to see if there was any more information on his association with Hamilton.

"Don't bother looking because it's been removed, and anyway, ever since he's been a minister, it's been a state secret."

Nibbling her bottom lip, she felt her process of working it all out was going far too slowly, but she got there in the end. The mere fact that Gibbons had Aiden's folder immediately to hand meant that he already knew he had died and it followed that he would have known about one of his operatives visiting Glasgow today. Had his intercom conversation with Inch... what's-his-name been a charade for her benefit, because she was now convinced that he knew she would be calling on him. Not necessarily today, but it went a long way to explaining how she had made her appointment to see him so quickly. Rather than telling her, he was pointing her in the right direction and letting her discover for herself that there had been a link in the past between Aiden and Hamilton. The way he was going about this felt like she was being tested again, but to what end, she asked herself. She concluded that this man would be almost impossible to work with as it seemed that he would query every aspect of everything and everybody. That being the case, she made her mind up to be more cautious when around Gibbons and to make sure of her facts rather than believe what he told her.

"I take it there's no chance of my seeing that particular report?"

"And why do you assume that?"

"You said it yourself that it's a state secret."

"I see from your own file that you've already signed the Official Secrets Act, but you'll appreciate that there's varying levels of secrecy within it. Not even I am allowed access to some of the more sensitive ones, but I'm pleased to say that I'm one of those who does have the authority to decide who gets to see this particular one."

The slim folder he produced from the same drawer as earlier was dark green and once again he proffered it for her.

"Go and find a comfortable chair in the other room and once you've read it, we'll carry on our discussion in a few minutes. Oh and errrr, no sneaky photographs."

Patricia sat on the rather uncomfortable chesterfield sofa as it was the more spacious and read a dispassionate report that seemed to have been made quite some time ago. In fact, it had mainly been written some thirty years ago by, she presumed, a military intelligence officer, and it referred to a particular set of liaisons between Captain Maurice Hamilton and Aiden Mullhagity. While it was clear that the MI officer had been keeping a discreet eye on Mullhagity, there was some criticism of the way that Hamilton carried out his methods of contact with him – via a young woman. Not only was the introduction of a third party who would be privy to whatever information was being passed against all security protocols, but also that Hamilton often donned civilian dress, rather than his uniform, when meeting with the said girl. As a serving officer of a front-line battalion, he should never have been allowed to expose himself to the dangers of being either kidnapped or shot, outside of the security of the barracks, yet frequently he did so without his commanding officer's knowledge. Hamilton had obviously used his position of authority and threatened the sentries with any kind of repercussion if they reported his passing through the security barriers, both on his way out and return, often in the wee hours.

As a result of these clandestine meetings, some minor players within the IRA had been interned and Hamilton had been credited. The MI officer conjected that Hamilton was being supplied with information via the female intermediary, but could not see any evidence of what he was bribing Aiden with, and therefore assumed that blackmail was being used. He also conjected that Hamilton and the female were having an affair, but try as he might, he could not find out anything about her; not her name, where she came from. Nothing. He could not afford to dig too deeply as otherwise his own cover might well have been blown, so he let matters drift as the information coming through this particular channel, while of low quality, was still worthwhile. Right up to the point when a senior Loyalist was murdered, ostensibly by his own supporters.

The information had come through in the usual way – Aiden, through the female, then onto Hamilton who had passed it onto his liaison officer who dutifully passed it onto Military Intelligence who issued instructions for their man to verify what was alleged. Somewhere in the chain, word had made its way back to the IRA who engineered an assassination made to look like the Loyalist had really been an informant and therefore killed by his own people. In reality, Aiden had been instrumental in setting up a network over several months to establish his source of information as being accurate and had sacrificed several youths just to take down the Loyalist. He had used the female, Hamilton and Military Intelligence to do exactly that, but the MI officer never found that out.

Questions were naturally asked, and, in search of the truth, Hamilton made one of his forays outside of the barracks one night to visit the female at her flat. He found her in her own bed with her throat cut and quickly retraced his steps. Aiden had been waiting in the shadows for exactly this moment, and had photographed Hamilton leaving; his black and white snapshot was then posted to Hamilton's commanding officer. Aiden delivered a copy of that same photograph to the IRA hierarchy who used it to whip up more sentiment with their sympathisers, by claiming that the Brits were now using their own nefarious methods to murder innocent women.

Aiden had engineered the entire episode to get rid of the Loyalist and to make it look like it was Hamilton who had carried out the murder. It had been the perfect opportunity for him to worm his way into the decision-making circle of the IRA while setting friends against friends among his enemies.

While the MI officer was oblivious to the underlying reasons why Aiden had murdered the girl, his report agreed that it was prudent for the news of the 'sudden death' of a young girl to be kept quiet and away from the press. He diplomatically concluded that there had been a plot to try to tarnish the reputation of a serving officer by Aiden Mullhagity.

Patricia re-read some of the report again, this time between the lines, trying to get to grips with both Hamilton's and Aiden's reasons. Similar to the MI officer, she wasn't to know what was behind Aiden's actions, but she could guess part of it. As for Hamilton, she questioned why he had struck up a relationship with the young girl in the first place, and concluded that somehow it had been Aiden's doing. She felt as though she was being dragged into a world of skullduggery and didn't like it one little bit. Why and who was doing what to whom and in which order. She considered that if she could establish events in chronological order, then she might stand a chance. People react to what others do in different ways, but it is that reaction that exposes the rationality of an individual. She started making a note of dates on her phone.

Casting her eye through the pages of the folder before closing it, she spotted a small crucifix-shaped asterisk next to the first mention of the young girl, and queried herself as to why she hadn't seen it before. She rifled through the rest of the folder but couldn't find any reference to it, but did note that she hadn't been named.

She felt a little like a schoolgirl reporting back to her form teacher as she once again sat in front of Gibbons. He'd just asked her for her conclusions.

"It confirms to me that Aiden had certainly been one of the IRA's top planners for some time, and if that really is him lying on a slab in Glasgow, then we have a chance of laying a few ghosts to rest. I believe that's for your department to deal with." It was a cheeky comment, but she felt that it was warranted. She continued. "Did Hamilton ever find out about Mullhagity, and if so, when?"

"Do you know, I've never asked myself that question. I expect he was told shortly after. Why?"

"I'm trying to establish if there was anything further between the two of them thirty years ago, because there appears to be so now, so if I can find out what, then we might stand a chance of finding out what Mullhagity was planning for Christmas."

"Fair comment. Anything else?"

"What's the reference to the young girl and did anyone ever find out why she was murdered?"

"Ahhhhhhhh. I was hoping you wouldn't ask such a question, because you may have just hit the nail on the head. However, I am afraid I am not at liberty to discuss that particular aspect."

To Patricia, it was like getting the answer right and then being told by the headmaster that it was really wrong. Two and two does not make four. "Well then, am I wasting my time here?" She had come to Special Branch half expecting to be turned away in any case, and certainly not allowed access to sensitive information, but this was turning out to be more than just pertinent; it was possibly the key to the entire affair.

"No, your time here has not been wasted because you have discovered that Mullhagity and Hamilton have, correction... had an association that goes back some thirty years. To find out what the content of that association was, is now up to you to find out by other methods. I am not allowed to help you on this matter. That said… I am also not allowed to deny anything either."

She was about to ask how he would suggest she went about that, but paused. It must have been something in the tone of his voice, because it certainly wasn't in his body language. Was he really asking her to guess? The pair of them sat there looking at each other; he waiting for her to make the next move, while she was considering the similarity to 'twenty questions'.

She started. "The young girl wasn't named in that report. I presume that was because her name was a closely guarded secret… which means that whoever wrote that report knew this and had been directed not to mention her by name. We don't know who cut her throat, only suspect… If it was Hamilton, then he would have presumed that she was working for the IRA and he would have naturally wanted to cover his tracks. But it wasn't him because that's not his style. So we suspect it was Mullhagity as it was he who circulated photographs. We also think it was him otherwise the person writing the report would have named her. And finally, it is highly unlikely that MI would have arranged to have her murdered as she was passing information to Hamilton, not Mullhagity… ahhhhh. She was passing the wrong information to Mullhagity. Oh… I see now, Hamilton had been forewarned before he got to his posting that there would be someone on the outside able to pass on information to him, and that's why he was nipping out of a night time to meet her."

Gibbons sat there motionless listening to her logic.

"The murder of the Loyalist must been the catalyst… the timing fits perfectly… but that indicates that she knew what Mullhagity was going to do... and that means that they knew each other. He wouldn't have told just anybody... she would have needed to be either entirely trustworthy or... a member of his own family... no wait a minute. That's a bit weak. Something else must have happened for him to have murdered her... and the only thing I can think of is that he had been ordered to do so by the IRA. That would prove his loyalty to them. But then that means that the IRA knew who she really was and that someone had told them."

She looked him square in the eyes. "That's why you cannot discuss it because that informant is still around today... and quite possibly part of today's government... Oh my God, it's not Hamilton is it?"

"I cannot confirm or deny anything."

"That's more his style... getting his enemies to murder his enemies... but why would he?" She started to chew her lower lip. "Let me think now."

"Hamilton only went back there to check if she had been murdered because he had been told that that's where he would find her... and there's only one person who would have known that. The murderer. Mullhagity. That means Hamilton and Mullhagity were somehow in direct contact with each other. Oh and I suspect that Hamilton and the girl must have been quite intimately engrossed with each other considering the level of information coming through for a senior Loyalist to have been murdered." She frowned in thought. "I wonder if the two of them were lovers. That in itself would have been sufficient for Mullhagity had he known. Hang on a minute... maybe he did know... Oh, now I'm going round in circles. Without knowing who the girl was, I'm not going to be able to get any further."

Up to that point, although she had mainly been looking

at Gibbons, she had not been focusing on him, but she did so now. "How did I do?"

"Your hypothesis would make any professor proud, but... it's still only a hypothesis." He opened his arms, spreading his fingers as if to reinforce what he had just said.

"I don't suppose it's any good me asking to know the identity of that young girl? You know... old-fashioned cooperation etcetera. The sort of stuff that keeps the old boy network alive and the country safe."

"Ummmmm, there may be a chance. I'm seeing a certain person first thing Monday morning and I'll pose the question."

"Well, to help you pose the right question, do you think it would help if that person knew we have Hamilton's list of prominent females?"

Gibbons narrowed his eyes. "Are you threatening in some way?"

Patricia was ready. "Me... no. Wouldn't dream of it."

Gibbons instantly recognised that she meant quite the opposite and his estimation of her went up another half-notch. It was the timing of her delivery as well as the way she said it. "In that case, there's little more for us to discuss on that subject, is there? I take it you've got a copy of your report, so please be kind enough to leave it with me. I'll go through it over the weekend. OK?"

She retrieved a memory stick and put it on his desk. "I presume that means you don't want us to pursue this until you've confirmation that it is actually Mullhagity in Glasgow?"

"While you were reading that report, our man confirmed that the body is indeed Aiden Mullhagity, so all that remains is to locate his girlfriend and find out what they planned. You said she uses disguises, so that's going to make it more difficult, unless she pokes her head right in front of a camera and she's unlikely to do that."

"Our experience has taught us that she's a natural at keeping away from surveillance, but nobody's perfect. We found her latest flat but now that she's disappeared and left her stuff behind, only indicates that she knew she'd been rumbled and that she's most likely gone into hiding somewhere until this is all over. Hence my request to come and see you today instead of waiting until Monday. We don't know where to start looking and haven't the manpower nor the amount of surveillance that you have."

"I see your point, and I can see no reason why we shouldn't help locate her. In that case, let's go back to basics and through this logically. Where would you go if you were a fox and the hounds were on your trail?"

"I'd go to ground."

"And where's that? Ignore Ireland for a minute because she'll want to see this operation go through first so she's unlikely to risk going through any sort of security gate until after Christmas. She'd become too visible to the security services."

"OK… I'd go back to familiar territory… an Irish quarter."

"Very good, so that's where we'd start looking. But then ask yourself where she is heading and when… and we know the answer to that, don't we?"

Patricia appreciated the way he was leading her. "I'm not sure that we do, because if it is a bomb, then she doesn't need to be near it to detonate it."

"Quite right, but she still needs to get it delivered to him, doesn't she? So somewhere along the line, there'll be some sort of link. Find that link and you'll probably find her and the bomb. I take it you've left me with some decent photographs of her?" He had picked up the memory stick.

"Several."

"Good, then we'll begin our end while you go off and trawl through whatever information you've got again to try and find that link. Here's my number so you can keep directly in touch with me." He handed her a business card as a way of saying that their meeting was over.

He waited a minute before getting up from his chair and walking over to the Georgian-style window, then watched her walk down the path towards Thames Embankment. He mused that she had been a complete breath of fresh air. Not only the way she had held herself, but also her attitude. He wondered if one day a woman like her, maybe even her, would be sitting in his chair doing his job.

He pressed an intercom button on his desk. "Inchcombe." He waited the usual few seconds before hearing, "Sir."

"Send an IT man in here would you? I need some photographs to compare with, and then summon our duty VT chap who handles cameras in the Portobello Road and Kilburn areas."

Sitting back down, he put away the files he had got out for Patricia's benefit, leaving his desk clear, but from another drawer he lifted out a dark red folder, opened it and closed it again, just to make sure it was still there. He wondered if Patricia would ever find out that the murdered girl was Aiden's niece and that Hamilton had indeed been having a sexual relationship with her.

***

Erica spread out and luxuriated under the duvet of the king-size bed, having enjoyed a hot bath with complimentary salts in The Lancaster. Although the room had a view of the

Serpentine in Hyde Park opposite, the short daylight hours only offered a decent glimpse when the sun was out, but that didn't concern her one little bit. She'd had a busy day and now there was time enough for a late afternoon nap before tonight's appointment with Chloe. As she drifted off with a smile on her face, she reflected on the afternoon's romp with Liam and wondered how many other women he swapped for rooms on a regular basis. Probably not so many, as he had seemed quite desperate, but she felt no guilt as she had teased him right up to the very last second.

Phoning Chloe earlier in the afternoon, she pictured her in an ebullient mood as she announced that a group of them were dining at Rules in Covent Garden before moving onto Peacocks Nightclub just off Regents Street around midnight. She was delighted to hear that Erica would be joining them but could they please stay off the Handgrenades this time? She didn't know if Abergail would be there as she'd heard that she was going out with someone who owned a casino. After some casual chat about gambling, Erica lied about having bought a new dress and had been invited out to some mysterious island in the Indian Ocean for Christmas by a young maharaja. She'd tell Chloe all about it later.

She had fervently prayed that the credit card that Aiden had given her still worked when she visited the first of several trendy stores down the Kings Road and when she found that it still did, put the worries of the past couple of days well behind her. For once in her life, she didn't have Aiden looking over her shoulder, but even so, she was quite sanguine when it came to looking good rather than only pleasing herself. There was no faking the expensive clothes and jewellery this time. Along with a roll of sellotape, she also picked up some expensive-looking Christmas wrapping paper together with bows and tags.

As the revellers of the last Saturday night before Christmas in London started to get going, she sat by the window next to the dresser and as a precaution donned a pair of rubber gloves before removing the cube from its paper bag. She had not really thought about a Rubik's cube before tonight and had not even handled one up to now. Carefully, she laid it towards one edge of the wrapping paper and as prettily as possible turned it into an innocent Christmas present by adding a green bow and gift tag. Rattling the biro between her teeth, she wondered what to write, and decided on 'For all those hours of fun xxxx Santa'. That ought to infuriate his wife if she ever got to read it. She couldn't risk taking it with her tonight so put it in the room safe before returning to the window chair. She fetched the photograph of her father from her bag and indulged herself by running her fingers over the smooth surface. "Just a couple of days more and I'll get him for you." She shut her eyes and held it to her cheek.

Moving over to the bed to paint her finger and toenails, she turned on the TV to help pass the time. Halfway through the news, the presenter announced that the police were looking for a woman in connection with the disappearance of a man. Her heart missed a beat when she casually looked up and saw a photograph of herself and Aiden. She couldn't believe it. No one appeared on the national news unless it was important, and she didn't think that they were important. And then she thought about it a little more. They must be considered important and there must have been a request, or even a demand by a senior policeman for any kind of announcement and it therefore followed that they knew about her and Aiden. Hamilton. It had to have come from bloody Hamilton as he certainly carried enough clout to get it on TV.

She hurriedly finished off her nails, blowing on them and wishing the varnish would dry quicker, and then slowed down as she realised that there was no need to panic. She'd been in her room for several hours and if they knew where she was, they'd have arrested her by now. And there was no way they could know about the cube... unless Eamon had told someone... or someone higher up the chain, but that someone would have to be pretty senior and that in itself would probably be newsworthy. All that mattered now was to get the cube to Chloe who would naturally include it with any other gifts she may be giving to the Hamiltons, and with any luck, that would probably be tomorrow; Christmas Eve at the latest. She wondered if the Hamiltons were the kind of family who opened their presents on Christmas Eve or waited until Christmas Day, but then she didn't care because it really didn't matter. Blowing on her fingernails for the final time, she eyed up her disguise on the sideboard and the dress that was hanging up, and relished the onset of the night. She wanted to keep a close watch on Chloe as she needed to know where she was going to be in the morning and it would be so much simpler if there was no boyfriend involved. She convinced herself that that was the real reason why she was going to corner Chloe herself. Had Aiden been about, he would have probably told her not to waste time and money and instead deliver the cube to her in the morning. But he was no longer in charge, she was, and she was bloody well going to enjoy herself tonight.

***

For some reason, Justin had picked up their evening's takeaway from the local Thai restaurant, when Patricia had been looking forward to a Chinese.

"What's a… Goong Phad Phak when it's at home anyway? It's wonderful," she asked reading from the receipt.

"Something with mango and sweetcorn, I think."

"And I can't even pronounce this one, but I can taste the ginger in it."

Justin sucked the end of a noodle into his mouth. "They use a lot of ginger and several other exotic ingredients. You'll know when you find one of the tree caterpillars, because it complements the ginger nicely." His nonchalant tone suggested he was being serious.

She immediately stopped munching mid-chew and through half a mouthful responded. "Caterpillars?"

"Oh yes." He pointed his chop sticks to the left-hand side of her plate. "If you don't want that one, I'll have it."

She looked down but failed to see anything resembling a caterpillar, then realised he was up to his usual tricks. She decided to try and get her own back and poking around with her own chopsticks, declared, "Oh no you don't. Are they supposed to still be moving?"

He may have choked had he not just swallowed. Their eyes briefly met over their plates before they continued eating, when the phone rang; she answered it.

"Right sir. Straight away."

"The station?"

"Yes. Tonight's duty officer has just been run over by a drunk driver and Tonybee's asked me to step in for tonight. GOD this is the last thing I need right now." She swore.

"Finish your food first. You can't operate without a decent meal inside you and we'll just have to discuss today's events in the morning."

"Tomorrow afternoon more like."

Chapter 16

No trespassing without permission
(Sunday 24th December)

Erica found herself being chatted up by a suave-looking eastern European who kept fidgeting with his Rolex; not looking at it, just fidgeting. Humorously, she wondered if he was doing that to make sure it was still there. The situation suited her fine, as while he vainly kept talking about the wonders of his family's vineyard and castle in Bulgaria, she was able to glance over his shoulder in the direction of Chloe who at the moment was low-level seated on the far side of the dance floor. She really didn't want to become involved with her circle of friends and their irrelevant chatter right now; on another occasion maybe, as it would probably have provided her with handy links. She would wait until the party thinned out a little when she would get more of a chance to steer the conversation in the direction she wanted.

She guessed that Gregou wanted her to ask him about his watch which she dutifully did and out came another long story about how cheaply he had managed to buy it while he flashed it prominently between them. It was obviously an important status symbol to him and rather than look at her own far more delicate watch, she easily saw that it was approaching three o'clock. With a change of music on the dance floor which saw couples start to pair up for more intimacy, she felt it wouldn't be long before her opportunity would come, so she excused herself from his company. She visited the ladies to make sure she was comfortable, checked that she still looked the part and then made her way over to Chloe who was now standing with her back to the dance floor and talking to one of her friends who looked like she was preparing to leave.

She got as close as she dared and then said in her ear. "You're lucky they don't serve Handgrenades here after one o'clock."

Chloe whipped round with a genuine smile on her face and hugged Erica like a long-lost sister. "Handgrenades... who needs Handgrenades... we've moved on to Stingers. Here, try a sip." One of her girlfriends joined them as she leaned down to the table, picked-up a bowl-shaped glass with the usual cocktail accountments poking out of it and guided the straw to Erica's lips. Waiting for a few seconds she eagerly asked, "Well... what do you think? Oh... you've changed your hair." She was like a child waiting for approval, and Erica obliged.

"I think it ought to do your libido a world of good... but I wouldn't want to overdo it."

Chloe turned to her friends, introduced Erica and told them of her approval of their latest discovery, but one of them with rather bleary eyes remained seated. "Here, I must tell you about Michaela's latest find." Michaela was the tall blonde standing between them. "She's going to be taking one of the leading roles in Edgar's next film and she's off to the Austrian Alps in the new year. Where are you going, Micky?"

The conversation batted to and fro while Erica did her best to look as though she was enjoying the 'Stinger' which, she was informed, was a mixture of Bas Armagnac and crème de menthe, frothed with soda water. In truth, it was quite pleasant but inevitably quite potent and wanting to remain on the sober side, managed to mistakenly lose her glass among some others on the table. Somewhere along the line, Erica established that Chloe would be at her flat until lunchtime when she would be leaving for her uncle's house in the Cotswolds via the Hamiltons'.

"Oh in that case I wonder if you can do me a favour? I bought a lovely little something for Maurice, but I'm on a midday flight out of Heathrow tomorrow... off to an island in the Indian Ocean somewhere... but it was so last minute and I've run out of time to get it to him. Could I drop it round to you en route to the airport?"

"I'd be delighted. Go on, tell me... what is it and how big is it?

"Oh that'd be telling and I certainly don't want his wife accidentally finding out early." She patted Chloe on her shoulder and moved closer to her ear. "Don't worry about the size... it's a lovely little item and very light. Just something he'll be able to enjoy on the day, if you know what I mean." As she backed off, she winked.

Chloe wasn't too certain what she meant by 'if you know what I mean', but felt she had to acknowledge that she did by opening her mouth a little and formed the word 'Oh'. Before she knew it, Erica had taken her by the hand and led her to the dance floor and, mingling with other couples, found that she had to involuntarily mimic her movements. Their bodies weren't that close to each other at the outset of the melodic saxophone, but as the track progressed, Chloe found that she needed to respond to Erica's lead and realised that she was actually enjoying herself, and embraced more closely. 'Let them talk' she thought about her friends who would no doubt wonder what her sexual orientation was.

From Erica's point of view, it was an unexpected tinge

of guilt that had urged her to lead Chloe into the cavorting throng. Realising that a totally innocent Chloe was likely to be one of the first to be aggressively questioned after the demise of the Hamilton family members and quite probably accused of complicity, felt that she ought to say goodbye in her own fashion. Hugging her by using her left hand to cover her right buttock so that their hips touched, it was a pleasure to lead Chloe in an entwined gyrating rhythm usually reserved for lovers. With her right hand stroking the nape of her neck, it was easy to guide her head so that there was no other option than to look each other directly in the eyes, and tilting her own head a little, she parted her lips and was glad to see Chloe respond. They kissed; their tongues tentatively exploring one another's. This was certainly trespassing, initially without permission, but they were now both on the fringes of the social control that decent society demanded, and delved deeply into each other.

The spell lasted until the music changed and Erica was mature enough not to hold hands on their way off the dance floor. All bar one of their friends seemed not to have noticed their intimacy, but Michaela was looking at Chloe in an appreciative way as they approached the table. "No wonder you asked your new friend along. Tell me more about her."

Remembering to set her alarm first, it was gone five when Erica's head hit the pillow. Spreading out across the wide bed before drifting off to sleep, she wondered if Chloe and Michaela would be enjoying each other's company.

***

Some thirty miles away and about the same time that Erica was going to bed, something had woken Patricia. Half-asleep, she got out of bed and padded off to visit the toilet, desperately trying her hardest not to wake up, but when she did return to the comfort of her duvet, found that her mind was going over a myriad of snippets from the past few days. Huffing, she turned over but it was no good, so she lay on her back with her eyes closed and let her mind wander among the imaginary white fluffy clouds, each one a different snippet. She was no analyst, but recognised that her unconscious self had been putting bits 'n' pieces through her mill while she was asleep and now she tried to grasp what it had come up with. Half-drifting back off to sleep she started to go over the awkward incident with the drugs squad and wondered how Inspector Dewbury had received his information. If she could establish its origin and how it had been passed down to him, then that might provide her with information about Hamilton's connection – if any. It would be mighty difficult to establish that he had anything to do with it, but she'd have a good go. Then another cloud came into view and this one was wondering how and where had Hamilton got hold of the stuff. Dewbury had asked for a copy of the letter that had arrived on Tonybee's desk, so that gave her the perfect reason for contacting him first thing. She hoped he would be working around Christmastime.

She started to doze off with a glimmer of a smile on her face but the clouds kept coming. Evoking a slightly happier time, one reminded her of Mcleash's ironic sense of humour. All coppers have their own sense of humour, and she genuinely enjoyed Mcleash's because it didn't involve belittling anyone. Report... he said something about forwarding a report on the old man run over on that level crossing and she started to go through the one he had already emailed, then remembered that she had been trying to find some sort of link with the name of ... of... of... Gowern. That's right... Alistair Gowern, that poor old age pensioner who wouldn't have known what had hit him on his way back home. Not even recorded on camera because they had been vandalised... no wait a minute, the report said professionally vandalised... didn't it? The cloud started turning black because nobody puts CCTV out of action unless they don't want to be seen, and from the far end of the cumulus came the suggestion that whoever was driving that van had run over Alsitair Gowern on purpose. The first person to spring to mind was Aiden who had come to a sticky end trying to run over what's-his-name.... Carl... Carl... Jenkins... no. Carl Jenkinson.

Despite it being pitch black, she instantly opened her eyes wide because she remembered that Carl had also mentioned that one of his contacts was a Mr Gowern. She felt the nape of her neck crawl with the certainty that she had just put a link into place, despite Mcleash's warning about yet another man called Smith. She would need to check reports and statements to verify her suspicions, but it was too much of a coincidence. Sleep was now impossible, so she got up and dressed in preparation of going to the station, regardless that it was very early. She hoped that with any luck, she'd be able to discuss something a little more concrete with Justin when he woke up. On the short drive to Maidenhead, she mulled over the one thing that still did not gel, and that was the connection between Aiden and Carl, and try as she might, there was nothing obvious. She must have missed something because as far as she could see the only common factor between the two men was that they both knew Alistair Gowern. Carl would have known him as a shop steward and there was unlikely to be any suspicious activity there, but why should Gowern have known someone of the likes of Aiden? Perhaps there really was a funding issue with Union monies ending up in a terrorist's pocket?

This time, she remembered to take her car keys into the building with her, reminding herself to buy a bigger key ring and fob so that she wouldn't be able to leave them in the ignition. Surprisingly, she wasn't the only one in the almost deserted police station at that time of the morning and came across Sarah Pindage and Willy on their way out; both were carrying what looked like loaded sports bags, one with wheels it was so large. Glancing at the wall clock and seeing that it was a little past six-thirty, she asked, "Where are you two off to at this time of the morning?"

"Town Market in The Parade, Guv. We've got to set up our dummy pitch before the others get pole position. Last shopping day before Christmas and it'll be booming, so we've a good chance of catching other stockholders selling hooky gear and grabbing a few passing dippers while we're at it."

"Dippers... you mean pickpockets?"

"Yeah. Also, we've come up with a great idea."

She nodded her head down at their bags and Willy obliged by momentarily hefted the lighter one a few inches higher.

"Go on," Patricia curiously enquired.

"You remember that sex shop we raided back in the spring and found boxes of illegal DVDs... well we also found boxes of eyemasks, whips, stays, blow-ups, etc., but best of all velcro handcuffs, all of which we confiscated as evidence. Now that the court case is over and the owner's in prison, it's all been earmarked for disposal, so we thought we'd make good use of it before it gets chucked out."

"Yeah," interjected Willy. "And I've even found some unusual x-rated Christmas wrapping paper that kind of gives the game away, and it'll be a laugh to see who's going to buy that sort of thing. We've even got a side-bet going as to who buys more toys... men or women."

"Don't worry about us making a profit, Guv... that's guaranteed... we're going to donate all funds received to The Blue Lamp Foundation... you know... the police charity. We reckon there's going to be over a thousand quid by the time we finish today as well as a few dodgy characters in the cells tonight, and lots of lovely contacts. Here, I didn't think you were supposed to be on duty today? Had I known, I'd have let you know what we're up to earlier."

"I'm not. Just tying a few loose ends together, but have fun with your stall today." She went to let them pass by standing to one side but then pensively stopped. "If you're intending to arrest as many as you think, how are just the two of you going to do that without letting the whole world know who and what you are?"

"Oh that's the beauty of it. Either Willy or I, depending upon the 'customer', will demonstrate the ease of working the velcro handcuffs and lead them round the corner to a lock-up where we'll have an arresting officer and a van ready; Sergeant Shahman'll be in charge of that lot. The idea's that we tell 'em the good stuff's in a van just round the corner. When it's full, he'll deposit them back here and return for more... simples Come on, I don't want to miss our pitch. See you later, Guv."

Patricia smiled as they left, musing that Willy was in good hands when it came to solid training. By selling previously seized goods, it was perhaps a little on the grey side of legality, but by utilising the sex aspect, they had the perfect tool. After all, who was going to admit being hoodwinked into being persuaded to wearing furry handcuffs in broad daylight? They might even be pink ones. She laughed as she made her way to her desk reflecting that it lifted the spirits to see the likes of Pindage and Willy using their initiative. She half thought of asking Sarah to put some of that Christmas wrapping to one side for her, but immediately dismissed the idea as otherwise word might get round the station what kind of present she was buying for her fiancé. Now that would be embarrassing.

Her computer behaved on start-up and as she nestled herself in her chair more comfortably, had the feeling that the day's omens were working on her side for a change. Even if she had previously downloaded files, she wanted to see if Mcleash had added anything, despite it being rather early, so wasn't disappointed when she found nothing new. Mcleash was allowed to have what he needed at his fingertips on his phone, so why couldn't she? Anyway, she hadn't downloaded what she wasn't allowed to. She refreshed her memory from the reports he had sent and then re-read the one on the vandalised CCTV boxes from the transport police. It was only the engineer's opinion, but he/she had been quite clear about it. Only someone with a working knowledge of electronic wiring would have known what to do as it had been the shared power supply to the governing printed circuit board that had been disconnected. Further, the locked waterproof cabinet had not been forced, indicating that it had been 'picked'.

This last part was just too much of a coincidence. Someone had certainly tampered with the recording system so that their deeds would go unseen, and that someone had to be Aiden; it fitted his MO. For less than a minute, she pursued the idea that someone else had been responsible for de-activating the CCTV and the closest she could come up with was a train driver, or someone crossing illegally. To eliminate any other possibilities, she'd have to contact British Transport Police and ask if any other cameras along that stretch had been disabled and if, as she suspected, that answer was 'no', then she could cease any conjecture that it was anyone else but Aiden.

She asked herself again what possible reason would Alistair Gowern have to contact Aiden. His file said that although he was one of the more influential Union officials in the dockyard, he wasn't considered extreme, and in any case, he had retired not so long ago, and was now virtually powerless. She conjected that Aiden had been smuggling in arms, drugs, people, or whatever through the dock and that Gowern had been his link; turning a blind eye or even assisting, but that didn't stack-up as if he had received any recompense, it certainly didn't show up in his bank account. He didn't take lavish holidays or have any yachts stashed away and neither did his wife, so how come they knew each other? Perhaps he had a big envelope of cash under the mattress but if he had, then his wife didn't know about it, otherwise she'd be sunning herself somewhere an awful lot warmer than Glasgow.

Wondering why he would have crossed the railway line at that point she looked at google maps, located where he had lived and started to hypothesise. The more she looked the more she frowned. Certainly, there were a few shops and pubs on the other side of the line, but there were closer ones on the same side as his house. Curiosity aroused, she carried out a similar exercise from Carl's aspect and found that they both lived and worked on the same side of the line. She started marking way points depicting where events had happened, sat back looking at the aerial area and eventually determined that Gowern had no reason whatsoever to cross the railway line – that is unless he was up to no good and she couldn't imagine that.

There was now no doubt in her mind that Alistair Gowern had been murdered by Aiden on that level crossing, and the question was had they met there or had Aiden coerced him to meet at that location. Perhaps Aiden had already killed him and dumped the body on the line hoping that a train would destroy… no, the BTP report stated that there had been signs of him being hit by a van, and anyway, leaving a loose end like hoping a train would finish off the evidence was not Aiden's style. Gowern had been lured to meet Aiden at the crossing and then run over by him.

All she needed now was a motive, but obtaining that would definitely be a challenge with both the victim and the perpetrator dead. Yet it was one that had to be found if she was to get any further with the imminent assassination attempt on Hamilton.

Looking round to make sure nobody was overseeing her, she downloaded all relevant files onto yet another memory stick, and reckoned they had until the end of the day to either find Erica or an answer to the conundrum themselves. A trawl through and response to the emails she hadn't attended to yesterday and then out of the station before Tonybee discovered that she was actually at her desk, but it seemed to take her ages and was well past nine o' clock before she managed to log off and exit the station. She sent Justin a text saying she'd be back in an hour.

She decided to take a circuitous route home and parked up not far from The Parade. She sauntered into the market area like any of the other Christmas shoppers, positioned herself inside a shop so that she could watch Sarah and Willy through the glass without being seen herself. It must have been sheer luck because within a few minutes she watched Sarah suspiciously lead a couple of chaps round the back of the adjacent tent, presumably to where Sergeant Shahman was waiting. Repositioning herself, she watched as the guilty pair were ushered into the arresting van. God, but it was such a simple idea and for the first time in a few days, laughed out loud.

The smell of Justin's freshly brewed coffee hit her senses as she walked through the front door.

"Good timing. I've got eggs and dippers nearly ready."

She laughed aloud again.

Justin stopped in his tracks. "What... all I said is that it's nearly ready."

"It's just that you mentioned dippers."

A totally blank look was on his face. "So what's so funny about dippers? All they are is toast, butter and Marmite."

She felt mirth running away with her emotions and had a fit of the giggles. When she calmed down, she told him that she would explain about dippers over breakfast.

She turned the radio up so that it would interfere with any would-be eavesdropper, plugged the memory stick into Justin's laptop and, pointing it in his direction, watched his eyes flit from page to page in between dippers, egg and coffee. Cleanly shaven, he looked perfect to her and she wondered how she looked to him. She mused that whereas she had had a rather busy schedule running around half the country, by comparison he had had a relatively leisurely time of it. She hoped his fresher mind might be able to pick up on something she had missed. She hadn't added any of her conclusions and waited to see if he would come up with the same answers as she had.

He finished chewing and sipped at his cup. "Mcleash seems a competent chap, but it's a shame he hasn't offered any information on... Mr Gowern's wife." He had to adjust the screen to pick out the pensioner's name.

"I know. I was told to mind my own business when I touched on that subject, but he's quite right, so I left him to tell me when he's ready."

"Any mileage in that?"

"No. He's straight. I think he was just being a bit more sensitive with the deceased's partner, that's all."

Justin scrolled, and after a while noted, "There must me some sort of connection between the three of them. Aiden, Gowern and Jenkinson, even if the sole survivor doesn't know it."

"Mullhagity."

He looked up. "Eh?"

"Mullhagity. That's Aiden's real name."

"That was one of the several names mentioned in the security report. How did you arrive at that name?"

She told him the majority of what she and Commander Gibbons had discussed. Midway through, Justin got up and walked out into the corridor and back again, deep in thought and still listening. "You have been a busy bee. No wonder we missed Erica with all that's been going on." Hold on a mo, I'm just going to visit the loo,"

Patricia understood this to mean that he needed more thinking time, and as far as she was concerned, he could take as long as he wanted. She'd been racking her own brains for hours, whereas Justin had only had a few minutes to take it all in.

Even before he appeared, with a raised voice he asked, "Do we know if Gowern and Jenkinson were pally with each other?"

"Not according to Mcleash. One was an influential Union man, the other a labourer."

"Because there was something that drew Aiden up there." He walked back into the room, looking even fresher, and addressed the picture of a canal boat on the wall. "And that something was common to both Gowern and Jenkinson, so what do we know that they had in common? Other than the obvious employment aspect."

Patricia broke the silence first. "All I can think of is that they both knew Aiden."

He spun round. "No. Wrong. Never assume. That's the classic misdirection step that is rather basic when it comes to accurate assessment. I'll give you an easy example. We both know each other and have common friends, but what if I wanted something from you that you didn't know much about... You'd go and ask someone. Let's call him number three. And if number three didn't know either, they'd go and ask someone else, number four. Four would tell three who would tell you, and you would tell me. Anybody wanting to know how I found out whatever it is I asked about in the first place could come to a conclusion that I knew number four, when in fact I wouldn't know him from Adam."

He waited for the imaginary link to get firmly set in her own mind. "So if we progress with that principle in mind, it brings us to the conclusion... that..."

"That Aiden knew both of them," Patricia interrupted cheekily.

"OK.... OK. That doesn't get us any further, so let's look at it from the perspectives of the other two. Carl first, non-alphabetically. He obviously knew Gowern through the Union, but not necessarily Aiden. Even though Aiden knew him, it wasn't reciprocal, which means that the link has to be Gowern and not Carl. OK so far?"

She nodded.

"Now let's try that the other way round. Gowern knew Carl Union-wise, and vice versa, and also had to know Aiden, as otherwise how was he to know where and when to meet Aiden. Those two definitely knew each other, therefore the link between Carl and Aiden has to be Gowern." He started pacing again. "So somehow he and Gowern became pally. He may have used blackmail or bunged him a few quid that wouldn't show up anywhere, that doesn't matter. What does matter is that Gowern put Aiden onto Carl... now why?"

He stopped pacing and looked at Patricia who had been ticking things off on her fingers. "What did Carl have that Gowern didn't? Perhaps there was another link that we haven't even discovered yet? No, wait a minute." He went back to his laptop and flicked a few pages away and focused. "Here it is, Carl and Gowern used to drink in the same pub... The Cobblers Arms... outside where Aiden was killed... that's this side of the railway line and a natural social point, but there must also have been a comrade's club or union bar... no that's no good because Aiden wouldn't have been allowed in. Go back a step." He was talking out loud to the canal boat again. "Aiden tried to run Carl over outside The Cobblers to prevent him from talking to anyone and the fact that it backfired is irrelevant, so that means Carl had a secret that Aiden was willing to risk everything for... and if Aiden was really trying to cover his tracks, he'd want to eliminate both of them." He turned back to Patricia more slowly this time. "So what is it that Carl knows or has, that is worth two men's lives? That's the crux of it and once we find that out, we're nearly there."

Patricia hoped that Justin's logic was the direction they wanted to go, otherwise they'd be going down another dead end, and told him as much.

"But that's how we work thing out isn't it? A process of elimination, otherwise we're just led by what the enemy wants us to think."

"You're quite right, and from what we both know about Aiden, that's his speciality. So, I'll go along with your reasoning as it appears to be the only way forward at the moment."

"Right then. When you visited Carl with Mcleash, what was it that struck you most? Go through what you actually did there."

She closed her eyes and tried to replay it in her own mind. She pictured herself walking through his door behind Mcleash and... "His models... they were all over the room, some hung from the ceiling. One particular model of a railway platform with a man holding a boy by his ear..."

"Was there a level crossing there?" asked Justin.

She still had her eyes firmly shut, but shook her head. "Not that I saw... it stood alone on his table... then there was a ship, an old sailing ship that he particularly liked. He went on about the figurehead being the goddess of something or other... I can't remember what."

"OK. Go on."

"Then we asked him about bank statements but nothing stood out, and then I had a look over the rest of his rather small flat and it was all very neat... and then Carl said something about repairing something for Gowern's wife... Mcleash fiddled with a Rubik's cube... and we left." She opened her eyes and focused on Justin who was looking down on her.

"God but you're beautiful when you're dreaming."

It took her all of one second to retort with a big smile. "I'm beautiful all the time, thank you very much. Did you listen to a word I said?"

"Oh yes. Carl's into models, big time. So, we can conclude that Aiden wanted some sort of model from Carl... yes?"

"OK... I'll go along with that," she said hesitantly.

"So all we've got to do is find out what kind of model it was that Aiden wanted, and we can progress from there."

"But where does Gowern fit in?"

"He's the cut-out."

"Cut-out?" She frowned a little.

"Yes. Basic espionage stuff. If you're passing something down the line you use one, two, three or more cut-outs depending upon the sensitivity of the information. That way if the message is intercepted, the first knows nothing about the last or even who or where the end user is. It protects those at either end of the chain, and in this case, that'll be Aiden. And if one wants to make sure that there's no possible link from one cut-out to another, you just eliminate one of the links."

"And to be sure, Aiden tried to take both of them out." She was rather pleased that she managed to state the obvious before Justin.

"So what you've got to do now is get hold of Carl and question him about what he was making for Alistair Gowern, who in turn would have passed whatever it was onto Aiden." He looked at his watch. "I'll bet you the dockyard is shut so he ought to be able to answer his phone."

"I don't think he has a phone."

With a groan, Justin's face expressed what he was thinking. Patricia continued.

"But maybe Mcleash will answer his." She reached for her pay-as-you-go mobile.

He looked at his watch. "Let's hope so. Oi... use..." He got up and took her phone out of her hand and whispered in her ear. "Use your normal phone."

She mouthed an 'Oh' and swapped them. She put her actions down to tiredness.

While she spoke to Mcleash, Justin cleared away the plates, occasionally glancing in her direction, and when she finished, she came and cuddled him. "Good and bad news. Well, not too bad. Mcleash says he'll ask Carl nicely, what with it being Christmas and all that. The bad news is that he was just on his way to church and that he wouldn't get round to it until this afternoon and if Carl was out, then it would have to wait until tomorrow."

"Is that the bad news?"

"Errrr, not quite all of it. You see, his fee for doing this on a Sunday is a bottle of Scotland's finest."

"Oh that's no problem."

"No problem, but it'll cost because he wants a twenty-one-year-old single malt Glenfiddich."

"And that's expensive?"

She nodded. "Bloody expensive. I should know because it was one of my friend's father's favourites."

"Riiiiight. Leave that one to me. I know a man who can help. Did you tell him why we want him to specifically ask Carl about models?"

"Oh yes and he totally understood. He said he'd also ask the Lord's help when on his knees in about half an hour."

"Is he a bit of a religious nut?" Scepticism was beginning to creep into Justin's assessment of Mcleash.

"Noooo." She gave a short laugh. "He told me it would give him something else to pray for while kneeling next to his wife. I think it is she who drags him along to church on a Sunday.

"Right then. In the meantime, we can concentrate our pagan brainpower on two things. One, if it really is some sort of exploding model, how it's going to reach Hamilton, and two, even though Gibbons said he was going to try to trace Erica, we can always lend a hand."

"We might be too late already."

"We might, but we have to assume that thing's going to explode on Christmas Day, and we're not doing anything else in the meantime. Are we?"

"Do you want to work on the delivery first?"

Justin frowned. "You just said delivery... it might be as simple as that... it might be delivered by courier."

"Or the postman," volunteered Patricia.

Initially they both cheered up at the prospect of discovery, but Justin kyboshed it. "Nooooo, none of those will wash. Everything that goes into that house is run through a scanner and when the dog's about, it'll pick up the scent of explosives. One of us chaps usually opens anything larger than a flat envelope, so you can bet your bottom dollar that Aiden will have known that and come up with another way of circumventing the process."

"So how about if Hamilton himself brings it into the house. I assume he doesn't get scanned every time does he? Even his wife or kids. What about them?"

"Now you're onto something." He clicked his fingers and waved the index in Patricia's general direction. "Keep talking."

"Welllll, it wouldn't need to be very large..."

"Like a model," interrupted Justin in a lightbulb moment.

"Yes. A model." She jumped to her feet. "And one disguising a bomb, but unless Hamilton brings it in through his own front door, it won't get past security. So either he or one of his family is going to bring a model bomb home."

"Only a thought, but the classic mistake can often be overlooking the simplest idea, and in this case if someone wanted to get something past security such as a bomb, then make it look like a bomb. Only you make it so that it sticks out like a sore thumb so nobody would dream of it being that obvious. Believe me, it can work. Only last year down at the Channel Tunnel someone was transporting crates of plastic toy hand grenades; realistic too as they had been 3D printed with all working parts. One of the chaps was a bit of a model nut and decided to take one apart by unscrewing the base, and guess what popped out? Grains of explosive. It wasn't heavy enough to make a big difference overall and would normally have been overlooked, so let's assume that all models, however big or small, are capable of exploding."

"Right then, back to Carl. How about this." She started to tick off things on her fingers. "Aiden gives Gowern the model job and he passes it onto Carl..."

"We still haven't established how Aiden and Gowern knew each other."

"Oh shit... we haven't, have we." She started to nibble her lower lip. "Can we skip that for the moment, because there must be some sort of connection somewhere that we just haven't been able to put our fingers on yet?"

"Go on then."

"So Carl's got this order from Gowern but doesn't know it's for Aiden. He makes the model and tells Gowern that it's ready and gives it to him. Aiden comes up from London, collects it and to cover his tracks, murders Gowern, and then, going on your theory of security, he wants to double-up on his tracks and knock-off Carl. Only Carl's a bit of a tough nut and doesn't die from being runover and instead clobbers Aiden so hard, he accidently kills him. Believe me when I say Carl could do something like this. He's a real hulk of a man."

"I'm sorry, I can't go along with that because Aiden had nothing on him that was remotely illegal, let alone an exploding model."

"That's because he'd already got rid of it." She played her fingers over the laptop. "Here we go... look at the time difference between Gowern's death and Aiden's. "If I'm right, Aiden had been to Clydeside to collect his model, and while he was up there planned and murdered Gowern. He then came back down South and handed it over to her, but with nothing much else to do, he went back up to take care of the final link – Carl. He wouldn't have risked two deaths with the same MO in the same week, otherwise eyebrows may have been raised, which is why he had to leave a bit of a gap."

"I'll grant you that's feasible, but where had Erica hidden it? Where was the model when you dragged her up to Clydeside? Unless she'd already delivered it to Hamilton... no that doesn't make sense... maybe she'd passed it onto to someone else... someone else we don't know about."

"What? Another cut-out?"

"Why not? Remember Aiden was very devious and would have thought nothing of getting someone else to do his dirty work."

"She could be passing it along as we speak." Patricia's tone of voice lowered a little. "And if it's a bomb, it needn't be very large, so she could have had it in her bag up to Scotland and back."

"And that explains why she didn't need to return to the rented flat in Elephant and Castle. She went straight on to somewhere else."

Patricia started to wag her finger at Justin. "Hang on a moment. Something that Gibbons said to me just before I left... where a fox would go when the hounds were after it and the answer is 'to ground'. So where's Erica's 'ground'?"

"I'd say it was where we first found her near Kilburn High Road. That's a prominent Irish quarter."

"Noooo. Too obvious and she'd not risk going back there, especially after being found there before."

"Yes, you're right. Neither would I. So where would you go?"

She nibbled her lip briefly. "That's what we've got to leave for Gibbons to find out because he's the only one who can authorise a digital facial search on the scale that we need. So, let's focus on this model. Perhaps we can go at it from that angle." A frown crossed her face. "I'll need to be quite specific when updating Mcleash and I wouldn't be surprised if he demands more credit when this is all over."

"Give it to him because from what you've told me, he's earned it, Correction... is earning it. But I disagree with standing back and waiting for someone else to find a needle in a hay stack called Erica. She must have other links. People she's got to know... not necessarily well and certainly not too well, but well enough to receive help when asked for. She's Irish so there's bound to be some sort of family connection somewhere along the line." He half-laughed as he knew what was rhetorically coming next. "When's the last time you came across an Irishman who wasn't related to someone on their rugby team or had a cousin who lived down the road in the next village?" he asked with a raised eyebrow. "Let's follow that and see where it gets us."

"What... follow the yellow brick road?"

"OK, OK, sorry about the pun but you must see what I'm getting at. Who do you know who's a general know-it-all?"

"Oh that's easy... Ernie the barber. You can't stop him talking once he gets going."

He looked at her for a moment without saying anything but encouraging her to continue.

She opened her mouth in comprehension. "Well... there's also Sheila who's got her own mobile all-day breakfast bar just off the Heathrow ring road, then there's Jim the driving instructor... OK, OK, I'll make a few calls."

Justin was holding his hands up in mock surrender.

"While you're doing that, I'll get in touch with a couple of my colleagues who may be able to point us in the right direction and once we've given yon Scotsman a chance to get out of church, you contact him. And also tell him if we've discovered anything more by then." He moved closer to her and whispered in her ear. "Come on, let's go down the pub."

Patricia frowned for all of three seconds before realising that it would be a better place to start talking to other people on the phone from. No hidden microphones.

***

Erica was sure her mobile alarm didn't sound like that, and it took her just a moment after surfacing from her somnolent state in the luxurious bed to realise that it was the bedside phone. She picked it up without answering.

"Erica... it's Liam. Listen, there's been a copper round asking if anyone looking like you has checked-in and it was pure luck that it was me who he asked rather than Andy; he's my boss and usually handles questions like that but he'd popped out for a quick fag."

"You sure it's me he was looking for?"

"Oh yes. He had some sort of photofit programme on his phone and he flicked it about to show different angles but it was definitely you he was looking for. He also checked the register on the computer and downloaded it but as you're not on that, you're OK."

Initially the news stunned her but then galvanised her into sitting up on the bed. "How long ago was this and has he gone?"

"He left about ten minutes ago... I couldn't phone you before as I had to attend to this American couple." Liam's tone was apologetic.

"And no sign of any other rozzers?"

"No. He was the only one."

She clenched her teeth in thought. "Are you sure he was a policeman?"

"Oh yes... you can tell them a mile off. He even smelt like one."

Just for a moment she thought of asking him more questions but then thought better of it. "Thanks Liam... I owe you."

"Errrr, I'm off duty later this afternoon... can I come up and see you?"

She immediately knew that he wanted to screw her, reckoning that he'd earned it, and why not. "Fine, but give me a ring first." She put the phone down before he had a chance to say anything that might make her change her mind, and as she did so, felt an instinctive urge between her thighs.

She hurriedly dressed after using the minimum of make-up, casually walked down the corridor, passing an argumentative couple on their way back from breakfast, got into the service lift and exited the rear of the hotel onto Lancaster Terrace. She knew there were no CCTVs just there but was careful not to stray into range of the ones just round the corner on Bayswater Road. Nevertheless, and just in case someone was being observant, she kept her head down, changed her gait slightly and wandered off down the adjacent back street of Gloucester Terrace and headed in the direction of Notting Hill. There, she knew of several shops where she would be able to buy replacement clothes, make-up and disguises without anyone raising an eyebrow, but until she managed to change her facial features, the trick was going to be to avoid as many cameras as possible. From what Liam had told her over the phone, it was patently clear that that pair of sleuths had links to the heavy mob and somehow persuaded them to track her down. But all she had to do now was deliver the cube to Chloe and then, even if they did manage to capture her, they'd never make the connection and find it in time. She consciously felt for the wrapped-up cube in her bag and rested her hand on it.

Keeping one eye upwards on the corners of buildings where cameras were usually mounted, she spotted Alpha Pharmacy and it looked like the kind of dispensing chemist that might not have a camera. She inwardly groaned as she pushed the glass door open and spotted the inevitable frog-eye surround of a camera behind the counter, but it was too late now, so she carried on and chose several items from the shelves before paying in cash and exiting. She estimated that the chances of anyone bothering to trawl through the chemist's CCTV were remote.

She found a quiet narrow passage between two buildings, briefly looked up and down the alley to make sure nobody was watching her, hunched over and rummaged through the bag she had been given in the chemist's, retrieved a set of gum shields and a fold-away plastic hood. The gum shields would alter part of her visage and make it more difficult to be recognised and the hood would temporarily cover her head and ears. She adjusted the pair of framed spectacles, having first bent one of the nose pads so that they were slightly skewed. She didn't need a mirror to know that her transformation was only half-complete and she still had more to do, so exited the alley and headed for any pub. The Leinster Arms was not overly large nor busy, but with an accentuated limp, swollen gums and crooked glasses, the bartender didn't bother with his usual chat-up lines as he served her a vodka and tonic and watched her sit down in the corner before turning away to attend to another customer.

Out of the corner of her eye, she let him settle down into his routine, left her V&T on the table and visited the toilets behind her. She made sure she was alone and attended to further facial make-up, this time adding a small fake birthmark across her right nostril and a convincing pair of bags under each eye. To finish off, she added a blue oval hue to her left temple, intimating that it was recovering from being hit. 'Walked into a door' was the usual excuse for such a mark. A hefty scratch across one of the lenses completed the change and, satisfied that she was now pretty safe, even when scrutinised by a digital CCTV system unless it really was close-up, she left the toilet, finished her V&T, and exited the pub without looking over at the barman.

All she needed now was a change of clothing and, avoiding the main roads just in case, she chose a couple of reasonably trendy clothes shops at random and within thirty minutes, was unrecognisable again. Confident in her disguises, and knowing that she had all she was going to need in her new suitcase, she looked at her watch and decided it was time to deliver Maurice bloody Hamilton's Christmas present. Just as well, since her wad of fifty-pound notes was fast disappearing.

Taking on the persona of a worn-out middle-aged housewife on the way to another cleaning job, she bent over and slowly limped along Porchester Road until she spotted an oncoming empty black cab which she hailed with a shaky arm. Exacting sympathy from the cabbie who loaded her case for her, she droned on in as monotonous a voice as possible about her trials and tribulations as she sat down in the back. He interrupted her.

"Where to, luv?" He was looking at her in his rear-view mirror.

"Eh?"

"Where to, luv?"

"Oh, sorry, you'll have to speak up a bit as I've lost my hearing aid." She was proud that she could still manage a slight warble to her voice

With a sigh and a drop of the shoulders in resignation of the fact that he had picked up 'one of those' the cabbie turned round and mouthed the words again. "Where are you going?"

"Oh... to drop off my niece's Christmas present."

Had he been looking forward, he would have rolled his eyes, but instead asked. "And where's that?"

"Oh..." She pretended to rummage through her bag to find a piece of paper. "Number 55 Castletown Road." She didn't look directly at him but still managed an expression that a schoolgirl might show when giving her teacher the right answer.

Other than a brief glance at her in his mirror, he didn't bother looking at her again. Had he done so he would have seen the granny-type looking up at the sights as they traversed one of the more expensive residential quarters of London, namely Kensington. Within fifteen minutes he pulled up outside No. 55.

"'Ere we are then."

"Can I ask you to drop this off for me? Saves me old back getting in and out."

He looked round and saw she was holding out a prettily wrapped Christmas present in her hand, and when she saw him wavering, she added, "It's for my favourite niece you know. Her name's Chloe."

He looked at the gift, then at No. 55 beyond the wall that divided the garden from the gaze of the passing public, and decided he couldn't do anything else but help. He repositioned his cab so that it wasn't blocking the street, turned off the engine, got out and took the offered present from the old lady. The gate to the garden of No. 55 had an intercom lock on it, and pressing the button to contacting whomever inside could take a while. These types of access were now common in the wealthier parts of London, so he wasn't put out at all when he needed to re-buzz a short while later. What he didn't know was that the old lady was using her mobile to alert the occupant that a Christmas present was being delivered, so when Chloe did answer, she didn't sound overly surprised. The lock release buzzed and the cabbie took the last few steps to the front door and handed it over to Chloe.

Erica just had time enough not to sound too hurried and used an excuse of having to dash to catch her flight. She just had time enough to wish Chloe a happy Christmas and conceal her phone before the cabbie came back into sight.

The cabbie started his engine and was about to ask where she wanted to go now, then remembered her deafness and turned round and almost shouted.

"Where to now, luv?"

"Westbourne Park... just by the Baptist Church, please."

"The one by Paddington Station?"

"Yes. That's the one... do you know it?"

He turned back to his steering wheel and went through the automatic motions of moving off while still talking; time was money. "I've been past it but never been in it." He flashed a glance at her in his rear-view mirror, but she was staring up out of the window.

Dropped off and hunching over her bag pretending to search for something inside it, out of the corner of her eye she watched the taxi rejoin the flow of traffic and disappear; she then headed off in the direction of The Royal Lancaster on foot. It was probably less than a mile and somewhere around halfway she found Sussex Gardens; a small triangular grassy area surrounded by the inevitable black painted railings. Half-hidden between a tree and an information placard there was a handy unoccupied bench which she put her suitcase on. She altered her appearance by removing the gum shields, swopping her beige raincoat for a shorter vibrant green one and changing the plastic hood for a black woollen bobble hat. She didn't think there were any cameras between her and The Lancaster, but on the off chance, she kept her glasses on after straightening them.

Back in her room, she left her suitcase where she dropped it, threw her bag onto the bed, wrenched off her clothes, leaving them strewn across the floor, and went straight to the shower. Standing under the water cascading down the nape of her neck, she felt waves of differing emotions ebb and flow. Initially she had felt dirty and had vigorously washed herself with the complimentary soap but now that that was done, just stood there occasionally blinking. Eventually she silenced the water, dried herself off and sprawled herself naked across the bed. She reached for her bag and retrieved her most precious possession and looked at it for several minutes before kissing it and placing it gently face down on her chest. Tears welled up and trickled down her cheeks as she relived the fondest of moments with her father on that beach all those years ago. Her sheer joy was countered by him being snatched away from her. Her happiness destroyed by her father's enemy. Her father's enemy was now her enemy. She could almost feel him there beside her on the bed but knew he wasn't and let out a series of despairing racking sobs. She rolled over into the foetal position and cried her eyes out. She drifted off to sleep knowing that it wasn't revenge, purely justification that

Maurice bloody Hamilton was going to die tomorrow.

***

While Justin waited for Patricia to get off the phone, he looked around The Jolly Gardener yet again to see if his sixth sense was working, but there was nobody out of place. Within an hour or less, the place would probably be full of Sunday lunch diners, but right now only a small gang of walkers and their dogs convivially congregated around the open fire. He got up and walked over to the nearest window to see if there were any suspicious cars with aerials or listening equipment on show, but nothing had changed since they had come in, so he went and sat down again.

"Good news," announced a happy Patricia. "Well, sort of. That was Mcleash and he says that as soon as he's dropped his family back at home, he'll pop round to Carl's place and ring us from there. We can both have a chat with Carl if I put it on speaker."

"Well let's hope he phones before the place fills up." He looked across at the empty table beside them.

"I've also had a reply to my text from the commander and he confirms that they've designated a certain number of cameras and will just have to wait until they get a result."

"That's not good news because she'll just change her appearance and then we'll never find her."

"No. These are the new digital cameras that pick out particular facial features such as the distance from the tip of your nose to the top of your left eyebrow."

"I know exactly what they do and I still haven't any confidence that they'll pick her out, because A they're mainly at stations, airports, Buck House, Whitehall and the like and B she's not likely to frequent those sorts of places. She'll be slinking off somewhere where we don't expect and that doesn't include Kilburn High Road. So, I ask again, if you were her, where would you go? You were going to ask your sources if they had heard anything, so have they?"

"Not much luck there. Ernie's not answering his phone 'cos it's Sunday and Jim's probably shagging one of his students in the back of his learner car. Sheila said she'd ask around but Walter the taxi driver says to give him a few hours."

"Does that mean he's going to keep a look out or ask about?"

She laughed. "No. Walter's the chap who appeared on *Mastermind* a few years ago and bloody nearly won it. He's got a photographic memory and he'll be the first to admit it, but the older he gets, the longer it takes him to remember things."

"OK then. Until Walter comes through we'll just have to make educated guesses, so let's start with a process of elimination. Countryside or city?"

"City... any stranger is more likely to stick out in the country."

"I agree. So if city, then we have to assume London. It could be Maidenhead or Reading for example, but they don't have the same transport links and in any case, there are greater crowds in London."

"Next question. North or south of the river?"

She mulled this for a moment. "I'd say north, again because of the links and on that same premise, west not east."

"OK. She's probably not rented again because of the short notice so that leaves either friends, hotels, pubs and B&Bs; or she roughs it."

"No not her. Squatting under a railway arch is definitely

not her style. If she's staying with friends then we'll never find her. As far as hotels go, they're all required to have a register but who's to say that she's not registered under another name. Only the larger ones bother to check passports etcetera and she'll probably have a false driving licence or two kicking about. Pubs are unlikely as they'll already have their rooms occupied and earning cash for their honest landlords and B&Bs fall into the same category as hotels except they don't bother to check ID. So which one do you want to start with?"

He took his eyes off his laptop and looked back at her pensively. "You're right on all counts but if I had to guess, I'd say she is either in a hotel or B&B because she won't want to rely on friends this close to the end result and my nose tells me that she won't have gone far. She'll be mingling with the crowds if and when she has to go out, which is rather unlikely at this late stage, so let's not waste any more time guessing where she is right now and instead wait until the commander or your mastermind come up with something."

"OK then, let's concentrate on models and I think we've agreed that either he or his family will be walking it through their front door because everything else goes past the dog's nose or through the X-ray scanner."

Justin raised his head in realisation. "That's why Carl was bought in on this. Think about it. It won't be your usual Airfix-type model that you have to assemble yourself because you can't hide anything that's in small pieces, so it has to be a model that's already been built. Errrrr... what's the name of that stuff with little men... you know... small soldiers etc?" He rapped his index finger on the table.

"You mean Warhammer?"

"That's it. Warhammer." No sooner had he said it than he realised the futility of pursuing that line of enquiry, and

Patricia beat him to it.

"But Carl only made his own out of wood, not the mass-produced plastic stuff you can buy in any high street."

With a wry grin in acknowledgement, he returned to his laptop and continued looking at a map of the area around Hamilton's estate and subconsciously noted that there were some stables nearby. "Dammit but there's got to be something to do with Carl and his models... how about a rocking horse... or a..."

"Trojan horse," interrupted Patricia.

"Now that's more like it..." But his voice petered off. "No it isn't because it would have to be large enough to carry enough explosive and if it's of a certain size, then it'll be delivered and go through the usual security. Anything small enough to carry into the house yourself is probably not going to be big enough to blow you up." He looked up at her. "And Aiden is the sort of chap who wouldn't want to do things by half measures. He's more likely to want to blow up the whole bloody house."

A young waitress came over and asked if they had reserved a table for lunch, and if not, could they please move to the bar area as she had to lay the table. They chose to stay where they were and have lunch. In between the appearance of the menu, cutlery, condiments, ordering and the arrival of the starters they continued to bounce ideas off each other but kept coming back to size of model and the missing link between Aiden and Gowern. Patricia's phone rang just as she was finishing off the last of her roast chicken and she kept chewing while listening finally saying thanks and goodbye.

She wiped her mouth with the cloth napkin. "That was Mcleash. According to Carl's landlady, he usually goes out walking along the riverbank of a Sunday and rarely returns until it is dark at this time of the year. Apparently, he collects driftwood and she let Mcleash know that she was none too happy about some of the smelly specimens he brings back with him."

"So he's not there, then."

"Correct. But Mcleash said that as he was on duty tonight he would find an excuse for getting out of the station to visit Carl, and then he'll phone me." She laughed and added, "Providing there weren't too many English drunks celebrating Christmas that he'd need to arrest."

"He certainly does seem to have a sense of humour and I look forward to meeting him someday."

"You're not the only one who wants to give him our thanks."

He inquisitively cocked an eye at her, so she continued. "Let's both of us go and see him when this is all over. I mean... when the pressure is off. Stay in a Highland lodge somewhere and pop in and see him on the way. Just for a long weekend perhaps."

He extended his arm so that his hand rested on hers and looked directly into her eyes. "We'll make it a whole week if it makes you happy."

They returned to her flat with one thing on their minds and spent most of the afternoon curled up with each other.

***

About a hundred miles away, Hamilton put the house phone back down on the receiver and jiggled with anticipation. "Chloe... lovely Chloe," he said under his breath as he strode off towards the front door of his mansion to meet her. Gate security had quite rightly phoned through to report that someone not on their approved list wanted to come and see him. He wondered if this might be the right opportunity to try to bed the wench and did a quick mental calculation as to when his wife and children might return from the local riding stables. Just enough time. He thought that she really ought to be compliant as he had put a generous amount of work in her direction as well as putting her name forward on a few occasions, so she owed him. After all, it was Christmas time, wasn't it? The nanny-cum-housekeeper's room in the east wing would be free as his wife had given her time off to be with her own family until the new year... or perhaps... He chuckled to himself again.

He rubbed his hands with glee before opening one side of the tall front doors just as Chloe was retrieving a bag from the back of her Audi. She was dressed in a gay blouse and Christmassy cardigan, with a knee-length skirt and he didn't miss the shapely curves of her bottom before she straightened up. He held his arms out wide as he walked across the gravel towards her. "Chloe, Chloe, Chloe. How wonderful it is to see you again and the most pleasant of surprises at this time of year." It was a genuine comment, as in his eyes, she had grown more beautiful since they had last met; even though it wasn't that long ago. He stopped just short of closing his arms around her in an embrace. "But surely... you're not my Christmas present are you?" He hugged her anyway and she awkwardly reciprocated while still holding her bag in her hand.

"Just on my way to Mum's and thought I'd drop a few presents round."

"Come on inside anyway. Here, let me take that." He motioned with his head towards her bag which was clearly containing a few presents, before ushering her into the hall where he placed it under a side table. "Follow me." He walked off in the direction of the main living room, leaving Chloe to follow in her own time.

When Chloe had visited the Hamilton's before, she had been accompanied by a secretary to a room off the hallway which was obviously Maurice's study but this one was a complete contrast and much much larger. She walked slowly across the expanse of the polished parquet floor on which were placed various rugs in suitable places. Recessed stone windows and a pair of French doors allowed natural light in from two aspects and overlooked a lawn flat enough for a full-size croquet pitch. Opposite the longer length was a picturesque inglenook fireplace surrounded by sofas, low tables and stools, plus the inevitable rug. Wood-panelled walls above which sat matching sets of ornate plates on a ledge, all lit by sympathetic lighting. She had to look closer at the ceiling to see where the painted raised patterns interlocked and met the cornice. Towards the far end stood a beautifully decorated Christmas tree, complete with fairy lights, baubles, fake mist and an angel that reached as high as the lofty ceiling. Maurice had his back to her while he attended to an enormous cocktail cabinet which was bracketed by shelves on which books and expensive-looking ornaments sat. She was just thinking that it was such a perfect room to spend Christmas in but also that it was a waste of space without people to fill it, when he turned round with a glass in each hand and stepped towards her.

"Happy Christmas," he beamed.

Her reaction was immediate and she took half a pace backwards. "Oh no, I mustn't."

"Mustn't... mustn't. This is Christmas and the season to be jolly, so take it and drink up."

"I... I really shouldn't as I'm driving and..."

"Nonsense. I won't hear any complaints and if you do get stopped, just tell them that they'll have to come through me first if they want to go after you." He thrust the delicate glass into her hand so that she had little choice but to take it. "This is one of my own specialties and I know you'll love it, so come and sit by the fire with me."

She had only ever known him as her superior and one whose authority seemed virtually absolute. Someone who was respected and feared at the same time. Someone of power, but above all, someone who had to be obeyed. In her own mind she was merely one of several lowly occasional employees who carried out his instructions, and woe betide anyone who failed. She had never considered him as the particularly approachable sort, but here he was now, befriending her, and it caught her unawares.

Hamilton recognised her state of mind and smiled, much as a wolf would do before devouring its freshly caught snack. He immediately sidled up to her when she sat down a little too far away and patted her on the knee.

She couldn't but help notice the large rather unusual coffee table centred between the sofas and had to do a double take. The surface glass covered a delicately carved wooden surface of what looked like an inset jungle scene depicting the usual kinds of animals found in that part of the world, as well as what appeared to be dwarf-like characters spit-roasting their dinner. What was just as extraordinary were the corner legs. Of slightly different hue were four monkeys in similar poses happily supporting the top, but it was the detail of the carving that really caught her attention. While she had come across carved tables before, this one was in a different class; it was exquisite. She put her glass down on one of the silver coasters next to a small marble statue of Atlas holding up the world on his shoulders, and tried to take in details of the carved jungle scene.

"Magnificent, isn't it?" commented Hamilton.

She barely had time to take it all in. "Wonderful. Where did it come from?"

"Oh that's a very long story, but I had it shipped back from Ethiopia when I was in the army. If you look closely you can see that the animals are all performing to the same sort of pattern." He allowed her a few seconds. "You get a better view if you stand up just here." He gave her a gentle nudge and as she did so, he positioned his hands each side of her hips and rotated her slightly so that his cheek was against her thigh as she bent directly over it.

She wasn't sure where to start as it was longer than her body, but she spotted a prominent lion chasing another beside the long necks of intertwined giraffes. A mountainous ridge separated the next scene of a pair of mating rhinos and the snakes below them were entangled with each other; and then she moved onto the gorilla, arm-beating his chest and showing off to his mate and probably the gazelles that were leaping over them as well. The beautiful carvings paired up the various other species and when she did twig what the link was, she involuntarily blushed. The elephant had the longest penis of all and as she reappraised each pair of animals, she realised that their sexual organs had been exaggerated. The two pigmy-like characters in the centre of the table, one at each end of a goat-like animal, were obviously enjoying themselves to full extent rather than preparing it for supper. There was even a threesome of chimpanzees.

She didn't know quite what to say. She wasn't a prude, but this was almost too much and she tried to think of it as just a table. It may have been her stiffening or slight change of position, but Hamilton detected it.

"It's a replica of a fertility table and made from the same tree... Oh, you should see the real thing... It's ten times the size and the locals really do use it for procreation."

"From Ethiopia?" She really could think of nothing else to say.

"Specifically from the southern climes, and yes, I've actually seen it working." He used his strong hands to turn her around and sit her down on the table so that she was now looking directly into his eyes. He placed a hand on each of her knees. "The story goes that because this particular wood sets its roots into the land and its seeds thrive only in the surrounding ground, their properties are such that it's supposed to increase the female orgasm ten-fold and thus produce strong offspring. Hence the need for the male of the species to have bigger organs." He moved her knees slowly apart. "The size of a man's organ is one of those mysteries of life and you'll never know how big it is until you see it for yourself." He had her almost mesmerised with his dulcet tones, but in truth she was as immobile as the rabbit that had been caught in the car's headlights.

He stood up so that his crotch was directly in front of her face, unbuckled his trousers and let them drop, revealing his bulging underpants. Initially her quandary had been how to react, but now an instinct urged her to find out if what he said was true, so she hooked her fingers each side of his pants and slowly pulled them down. Not that she was much of an expert but it seemed to her that he did indeed have a large member which now grew even bigger inches from her eyes. In fact it was now the biggest one she had ever seen and her basic primeval nature cried out for her to grab it with both hands to feel and knead it until...

Looking more closely at it, she saw spots just behind the head and then there was a slightly unsavoury smell that went with it; all in all it provoked a repellent reaction in her and as she slowly recoiled her head, she felt his strong hands on the back of hers, pushing it forwards. She knew she was supposed to open her mouth and suck until he shot his load, and she started to panic at the prospect of having to do so. She steadied herself by splaying her arms onto the table and the tip of her right fingers came across the small marble statue. Instantaneously, she grasped it round the shaft and hefted it in the direction of his nether regions; it contacted directly with his testicles. She didn't have time to react as he head-butted her in a literal knee-jerk reaction; he ended up with his back to the fire on the oriental rug with both hands clutching at his recently recovered scrotum, while she sat dazed on the table holding her hand to her forehead.

Unsurprisingly, it was she who recovered first and once she ascertained that there was no bleeding from her forehead by inspecting her hand closely, anger started to rise. She looked down at the groaning body with all the disdain she could muster. "You bastard. I bet you really get your kicks by belittling us women. Talking of kicks, here's another." She swung her foot at his midriff and we rewarded with a slight 'oooof'. "I wonder what your wife would say.... no, don't tell me. I bet you've even done it to her. You poxy shithead." Another swing of the foot and this time an 'aaaarrrgh' as it connected with one of his ribs. "Don't bother calling me again 'cos you know the answer. Happy fucking Christmas and I hope it's ruptured you."

She turned and stormed out.

***

They were both thinking about bedtime when Patricia's phone rang; they both knew it would be Mcleash. She donned her overcoat, slipped into her Ugg boots, grabbed her car keys and went outside where she could speak to him without the risk of being overheard. The car radio was playing that same old Wizzard tune and would confound any listening device nicely. She noted that it was getting on for midnight.

"I hear you're partying down there while I'm busy running around for you up here in the land of reindeer. There's enough bloody snow for a whole fleet of Santa's sleighs, and I might add, you're bloody lucky I managed to get one of traffic division's four-by-fours to drive me around tonight, so let's get on with it. I'm in Mr Jenkinson's flat so I'll hand you over to him now..."

"Hello..."

She breathed a sigh of relief when she recognised Carl's voice and for some unknown reason decided to change tack with him at the very last second. Rather than go down the official route of 'good evening sir, etc. etc.', she took the other option of familiarity.

Gleefully she said, "Happy Christmas Carl and thank that nice man standing next to you for me when you get the chance."

"Why would I do that?"

"Because I owe him a big hug and if I asked you to do that, he'd probably complain." She half-winced at her forwardness. "I believe it's called 'a Glasgow kiss' up there."

"Aye, you're right, so I'll just tell him instead then."

She thought she detected a glimmer of laughter in his voice and continued with the easy attitude. "I'll give you a big hug as well if you can tell me a couple of things about Alistair, such as why he was so pally with you."

"Oooh I wouldn't call us that pally, just occasional drinking buddies in The Cobblers and once in a while down the Comrades Club."

"The man who tried to run you over was called Aiden but do you know if he and Alistair knew each other?"

"Not a clue."

"And you never set eyes on him before that night?"

"No."

She'd already guessed the answers but had to be doubly sure. Now for the big one. "You see, I think Aiden wanted a model from Alistair, and he would have asked you but I can't think what kind of model he would have wanted. Any ideas?"

"Model for Alistair? No... he didn't want a model, only that cube."

"Cube?" A light flashed on in her head. "Rubik's cube?"

Aye... that's the one. Wanted it made out of metal so I made an aluminium one for him. Said it was for a friend of his."

She could hardly believe what she had just heard. Wow. It was that simple.

"Hello...?"

"Errr Carl. I owe you a great big hug as well." She was stunned. "Can you give the phone back please. And happy Christmas."

"Did you get what you wanted?" Mcleash's voice was deadpan.

"Oh yes and I'll tell you all about it one day and make sure you get credit."

"Right now I could do with an extra pair of socks."

She charged back through the front door and motioned for Justin to join her in the car. The music had moved onto to Slade's version of 'Merry Christmas'.

"It's a Rubik's cube. God how could I have been so blind?" She went on to explain what Carl had just told her.

"Hang on a mo and just let's think about that for a moment. What good would a metal Rubik's cube be over a plastic one?"

They sat in the dark each trying to figure out the rhetorical question and she waited until Noddy Holder had finished bellowing out of the radio. "Bollocks. He's done it to us again, hasn't he? God it's like trying to run into a headwind with the snow up to your waist."

Justin waited a moment. "Bollocks to this too. I'm getting cold. Let's get back inside."

A minute later she turned up the telly again. "Why can't it be simple? You and I are intelligent people yet we failed to spot that it was the Rubik's cube and now that we know that it is, we're no further forward."

"But are we sure that it's the Rubik's cube?"

"Oh God, don't start that again. It has to be the cube. It's the only thing that links them all together."

"I know I know. I was just testing. Well there's one good thing about it being aluminium." He looked at her waiting for the obvious answer and groaned when she gave it.

"It doesn't float."

"OK... but I was thinking about another aspect." He prompted her, but then recognised her tiredness. "Like it'll show up better on an X-ray scanner."

"Of course. Sorry. It's been a long day and I'm starting not to think straight."

"You know we're going to have to tell Commander Gibbons and that it'll probably involve MI6?"

She nodded.

"And we're also going to have to give them our suspicions

as to why we think it's a bomb instead of just a toy."

Patricia summoned here dwindling supply of logic and agreed. "I'll contact Gibbons first thing in the morning because it's too late now."

He took a couple of paces over to her and cradled her in his arms. "It's Christmas Day now so merry Christmas." He followed it with a healthy kiss.

Chapter 17

Santa venit
(Christmas Day)

Even though they had been up a couple of hours, Patricia deemed that seven o'clock on Christmas morning wasn't too early to disturb Commander Gibbons. They had spent the early hours trawling through evidence and scouring the internet trying to discover why on earth Aiden would commission a metal cube and had drawn a complete blank. The only person alive who might know was Erica. She forlornly hypothesised that Carl might be able to shed some light as he had made it, but had to dismiss that idea; and anyway, he was uncontactable.

"Gibbons," he answered.

She had it on speaker so that Justin could hear. "DI Eyethorne here, sir." Knowing that he didn't like to be kept waiting or listen to irrelevant hearsay, she got straight to the point and explained, ending up with her conclusion. "The only way we're going to know for certain is to see for ourselves."

"Go on." Gibbons obviously wanted to know how she proposed to go about this.

"We need to visit the Hamilton household, question them about a Rubik's cube and if necessary carry out a search."

The initial silence at the other end of the phone emphasised the seriousness of her suggestion. "No proof?"

"Absolutely none at all."

"What if you're wrong?"

"Then Hamilton and his family live."

Another slight silence. "You realise that if I do sanction this, particularly because it involves Hamilton as one of Her Majesty's ministers, that MI5, MI6 the Royal Protection Service and the Bomb Disposal Squad will all have to be involved, not to mention the local police force and quite probably the local hospital will need to be put on alert. If that all happens then the press will get hold of it so we would have to tell the prime minister in advance. So my question to you is, 'how sure are you?'. Because if you are wrong, not only will quite a few of us, including you, be out of a job this time tomorrow, but the PM's standing will go down a notch or two as well. You know what a struggle he's recently been having with public funding of the security services of late, and an instance such as this would go down like a lead balloon. In fact, I would go as far as saying that it might even open the door for Hamilton to make a leadership challenge."

Patricia looked at Justin for reassurance before replying. "Sir... we're damn sure," she said with what she thought was conviction. "There's only two ways of proving it and one of those is by being too late." She waited for this to sink in and then added. "But there is another way without involving all those people you just mentioned."

"Go on, I'm listening."

She drew a breath before outlining the rather vague plan she and Justin had discussed a quarter of an hour ago.

Gibbons didn't prevaricate. "Right. I'll come back to you within the hour. I need to make a couple of calls."

As she signed off, she wondered if he had a family and, if so, was this a normal Christmas for them.

***

"According to the weatherman, the odds on it being a white Christmas are very remote, but you wouldn't think so by looking outside, would you?" Hamilton's wife commented as she drew back the curtains in their voluminous bedroom overlooking the croquet lawn and tennis court. "That ground frost has probably killed off the broad beans unless Elkins has covered them up, and you can hardly see the white hoops from here."

Caroline was almost the epitome of a loyal upper-crust wife. As the adage goes, she was one of those 'who is useless in a crisis but invaluable at the Hunt Ball'. She was also oblivious to Hamilton's infidelity; well, almost, as she purposefully blanked-out any such gossip. Her Presbyterian upbringing would never allow her to countenance an adulterous husband and if Maurice was being unfaithful, then it was in London and not on their own doorstep. It was this ethos which she used to justify it to herself. She knew which side her bread was buttered and didn't want to upset the apple cart, so continued to enjoy the life that went with a government minister. She thoroughly enjoyed bringing up her two teenage boys and revelled in introducing her nearly adult daughter to the right people. Their first and much older son had left home ages ago.

"Come on, get the kids to tidy up the billiards room before brother Cyril and his family get here. You know they always like to arrive early, so I've got to put the turkey on soon as well.

She watched him make his way towards their en-suite bathroom. "Why are you hobbling?"

Waking with a headache from yesterday afternoon's events, Hamilton swore at all women in general and muttered inder his breath as he closed the bathroom door. His testes were swollen for the second time in a short period of time, when most men managed to get through their entire life with perhaps one such episode, and he cursed the fairer sex once again. He groaned at the thought of having to entertain his n-laws and their two energetic sons, but brightened up at the prospect of being able to hide away in his office after Christmas unch, round the fireside naturally. He realised he was being a little unfair on Cyril as he was a good conversationalist, but he had a worrying tendency to elicit some favour or other without one realising it.

Reaching for his razor, he managed to lightly rub his crotch against the corner of the basin, gently backed off and froze until the ache receded. It wasn't as severe a pain as when the Eyethorne bitch had tricked him, but nonetheless, he realised that today he would have to tread carefully when t came to anything remotely energetic. As he shaved, he cheered himself up by conjecturing what presents he would be receiving and then remembered that he'd left that bag from Chloe in the hallway. Much as he now hated another bitch, he admitted that at least she had had spirit, so he'd open her present anyway. He mulled on how he could turn yesterday's incident to his advantage, because he knew her parents, along with several of her contemporaries. He could quite easily turn the whole thing round to make it look like it was she who had been trying to curry his favour by using her sexuality. He paused mid-stroke of the razor as another idea sprang to mind. Yes... that would be the best way of going about it. He'd ring her parents after Christmas lunch from his office to congratulate them on bringing up such a fine daughter who knew how to use her womanly charms to further her career. That would start the ball rolling, and then he could embellish with fabricated details if they pressed him.

Gently but cheerily, he walked down the wide staircase and saw that the bag he had put down yesterday had unsurprisingly been moved. He suspected his wife's efficiency as he entered the kitchen to find her and his daughter Georgina in the process of stuffing the massive turkey. His step faltered as he admired the shapely figure of his daughter. He'd no thought of it much before as she was nearly always away at Cheltenham Ladies' College and he rarely saw her, but now her current pose got him thinking; after all, there was nothing wrong with appreciating that one's daughter had grown up. Flour and handprints on her undersized t-shirt accentuated her unrestrained breasts, and as she bent over one end of the turkey with a handful of chestnut stuffing, he tried not to imagine what the rest of her looked like; and failed.

"I suppose I'd better stay out of your way." He managed to negotiate his way past Boxer, their pet boxer dog who was still greeting him, then sidling off to one side, he opened the fridge door to see if there was any of that excellent *foie gras* pâté left that he could put on his toast for breakfast.

He received an old-fashioned look from Caroline but his daughter, who was in a more playful mood, turned round stood up and cheerfully announced. "Happy Christmas Daddy. Here. You ought to see what this tastes like?" Both hands were covered in a grainy stuffing mixture and as she took a couple of paces towards him, held an index finger out for him to sample. He forced himself not to recoil at the unusual flavour that he wasn't quite expecting.

"You can really taste the chestnuts, can't you?"

He spotted a half-full bowl of it on the countertop behind her. "And home-made, I see."

"They do teach us a thing or two at college you know

ust wait till you come to the cranberry and redcurrant sauce
ater."

Tray in hand, he disappeared to one of the smaller drawing
ooms, retrieved a suitable glass and a half-bottle of Malmsey
rom the shelf, sat down in one of the chesterfields, opened
esterday's *Times* newspaper, and tucked into his sumptuous
breakfast.

Nine o'clock came and went without any word from Gibbons
and they were thoroughly fed up with discussing the various
scenarios, but at least they had ironed out a plan if Gibbons
gave them the go-ahead. It being a lovely crisp morning, they
donned jackets, gloves and other outdoor gear, and went for a
stroll towards the river. It was only ten minutes away but they
ended-up at a small creek which was popular with the locals,
where they threw breadcrumbs for the swans and ducks.

"I envy them," commented Patricia.

"Swans or ducks?"

"Both."

"Why?"

"Because they've nothing else to worry about other than
who's going to throw the next piece of bread."

"I'd say that's pretty important, otherwise they'd die of
hunger."

"You miss my point. That's just about all they've got
to worry about... well at this time of the year anyway. One
simple thing, not multiple things like us humans."

"But isn't that what makes us human?"

She looked more closely at him. "Now you're arguing for
the sake of it."

"Well, look at it from the duck's point of view. It comes
here because it knows us humans are going to be here to feed

it. It's as simple as that." He waved his arm around. "This creek is no different to the others around, so it's become conditioned to come to this one; an automatic response to us humans." He could see her thinking. "Pavlov's dog's an example of responses... and here's another... if I dig you in the ribs, you'll move away." He went to do so and she did indeed move away. "You see, you're not that much different to that duck."

"I'm not, am I? Well let's see how you react to this." She threw a small lump of bread at his forehead and missed because he ducked. While she was tearing off another piece he managed to crumble some over her head and so it went on. Even so, she managed to hoodwink him into thinking that she had some more and she chased him round the muddy grass. He threw a small ball of dough which just happened to go into her mouth just as she opened it; she stopped and half-choked.

"That was... duck of the level."

He froze then doubled up laughing.

"What's so bloody funny?"

Once he calmed down a bit he responded, "You said 'duck of the level'." Even he started to choke but with laughter.

"Oh no I didn't." But the minute she denied it, she knew she had meant to say 'luck of the devil'.

He rested him arm on a lowish branch while they both enjoyed the moment but it was while they were walking back that her phone rang.

Unmistakably it was Gibbons. "You really know how and when to stir up a hornets' nest don't you."

Before he could continue she interrupted. "Is that mean as a compliment, sir?"

"No it bloody isn't, now shut up and listen."

Justin watched her pace back and forth for only a couple

410

minutes; she abruptly hung up. "We're on... Gibbons and another chap are coming too."

"That's it?"

"I'll tell you more on the way, but we're to wait for them in the village car park just round the corner from Hamilton's."

He put his phone to his ear. "I suppose I'd better disappoint Mum for Christmas lunch then and tell her we're indisposed."

***

As she lay in the comfortable bed and listened to the London traffic outside, Erica stroked Liam's coarse hair gently enough so as not to wake him. They'd made love sometime during the night and she knew she'd have to wake him for his daily shift soon, but for now she was quite content to doze and mull over the day ahead.

She'd already planned to enjoy a lazy day mainly in the room, and quite probably her last in the hotel. Liam had already told her that one of the cleaners had asked him about her room and it wouldn't be long before news reached the ears of those above him. It was pretty pointless going out anywhere on Christmas Day so she would use the hotel's gym and enjoy the best food that The Royal Lancaster could provide.

There was one thing that she didn't want to miss and that was the six o'clock news. Nothing short of a miracle could prevent the announcement of the death of Maurice bloody Hamilton.

***

Christmas Day at the Hamilton's was traditionally like most other English families. With the invention of the video cassette recorder some decades ago and its subsequent replacement of digital boxes, the Queen's speech on TV at three o'clock was no longer a focal point. What was far more important was to keep the kids amused, and the virtual ceremony of opening presents took place either well before or directly after lunch. In recent years in the Hamilton household, this was well before lunch, around noon.

There was ample seating spaced perfectly away from the heat of the fireplace, and off to one side a myriad of gifts heaped around the base of sparkly tree. Last to sit down was Caroline and as she did so, Georgina, her two younger brothers as well as Cyril's lads delved into the gaily coloured pile of presents and started distributing them. Caroline made a 'thank you' list on a pad of paper.

"To Harry from… Uncle Douglas."

"To Aunty Caroline… from Father Christmas."

"To Mum… that one's from me."

"To Maurice… it doesn't say who from… oh yes it does but I can't read it. Here you go."

"To Mr Nice Guy… from Mrs Nice Guy. Here you go Dad, that'll be from Mum." Cyril took it.

The presents started piling up around each individual when the front-door bell rang. Boxer made everyone jump with one of his short but loud barks and Caroline dispatched one of her sons to go and answer it.

"To me… from Mum. Oh, thank you Mum. If it's what I think it is, thanks again." Georgina was expecting a new riding hat.

"To my darling Maurice… all my love… hang on… there's more… Erica."

"Who the hell is Erica?" perked up Caroline midway through the previous message.

The son returned and announced that there were people from the police here for his father.

"On Christmas bloody Day?" retorted Hamilton. He had removed the wrapping paper as well as the transparent bubble and was ready to give the cube the first of a few twists, but instead placed it on the table in front of him. He rose and went into the hall followed by the ever-inquisitive Boxer. He didn't bother closing the door fully behind him as the sight of both Justin and Patricia almost overwhelmed him. So enraged was he that he almost didn't see Commander Gibbons and another gentleman he had never seen before standing just in front of the pair.

"What the bloody hell do you want?" This was aimed collectively at the group but mainly at the younger couple.

"You won't know me... you won't even have heard of me... but you can call me Mister." He paused momentarily. "Indirectly, it is me whom you need to thank for keeping you alive, but I don't want your thanks, just your immediate cooperation because we think you have a bomb in your house."

"Poppycock. Why the hell should I believe you? This is my house, my..."

Gibbons butted in. "We've met before and you know my reputation, so listen to my colleague here."

Mister took two rapid paces forward so that he was within huffing distance of Hamilton's face. "Listen you jumped-up pleb. Just because you've been selected to be in the Cabinet doesn't absolve you from being murdered, and I've not come all this way on today of all days just to listen to you whine. Being under direct command of Her Majesty gives me more power than you'll ever have, so don't tempt me. Both Commander Gibbons and I have listened carefully to what those two have had to say and we're convinced that there's a real threat to your lives in the form of a bomb."

Initially Hamilton was taken aback, but he was well used to these sorts of encounters and recovered quickly. He stood his ground and prepared to lambast Eyethorne and Crawford. Raising an accusing finger, he said, "They've put you up to this, haven't they? I'll bet they've given you some cock-and bull story about blackmail, drugs, and oh yes... let's add in a bomb threat, and just to make it more believable, we'll tell everyone it's going to go off on Christmas Day just when the whole family is gathered round the fireplace. The one day of the year when one is supposed to forgive one's enemies, these two smug bastards try to get their own back by showing up with some crap story just to make me fucking angry. Now get the fuck out of my house... all of you."

Nobody moved. Four out of five people in the hall had similar thoughts, while the fifth simmered with blind hatred... but then he saw the grim look on all their faces and came off the boil. "OK then, suppose you're right. I presume you want us all to evacuate while you try to find it." Scepticism echoed in his voice as he eyed the couple behind.

"Not at all," Mister continued. "We know what it is, size, shape etc. etc., but what we don't know is exactly where it is or how it got into your house. Very worrying when the security system fails." He motioned to Patricia and Justin behind him. "These two have done all the hard work but it seems that their hardest task would be to convince you, hence the commander's and my own presence."

Hamilton was indignant that the young pair should get any credit whatsoever. "They've been nothing but interfering busy bodies and bloody nuisances, and when this is all over, I want their heads on a plate. Let's be clear about that, shall we?"

"Even if we do find your bomb?" questioned Patricia.

"You bloody stay away from me." Hamilton paused but wanted to add 'even if she did find a bomb', but couldn't.

"Simple question, minister." Mister put formality back on the agenda. "Have you been given a Rubik's cube lately?"

He was about to automatically answer 'No', when he stopped, looked Mister directly in the eyes, and remembered the present he had unwrapped a few minutes ago.

Mister saw him wavering and guessed the answer. "Would you mind going and getting it for us please?"

Hamilton frowned before turning back round.

"Errrrrr, gently of course. We don't want it going off, do we?"

In almost any other circumstances, the remaining three of them would have been horrified, but such an atmosphere of calm exuded from Mister's presence that they instantly accepted that what he had just asked was right. Any of them would normally have called in the bomb squad to dispose of the item.

Mister turned to them with a hint of a slight smile on his face. "Well, it seems that the first part of the equation is right so now let's see if the second part is." He saw the look on their faces. "Oh I see you're all worried it may go off... well I really wouldn't have any concerns there, because it's obviously not movement sensitive, otherwise it would have gone off by now."

They didn't have long to wait in the hallway as Hamilton returned, gently holding his Christmas present, and this time he shut the door behind him. Gibbons, Crawford and Eyethorne stared at the cube as though it had descended from outer space.

Mister looked as though it was an everyday occurrence

and turned to Justin who was furthest away. "Would you mind opening the front door for us?" He then motioned to Hamilton using an outstretched arm. "After you, then."

With a quick flick of the eyes towards Mister, Hamilton took three soft paces and exited the front door holding the cube as gently as possible; the rest of them followed in silence. He continued walking across the gravel towards the grassed area, knowing that if it was a bomb, the best place it could go off would be in an open space. From his time in Northern Ireland, he'd seen how bomb squad officers attended to their unenvious tasks by treading as though walking on eggs, and did likewise. Ignoring everything else, after a few more paces he stopped, bent down and placed the cube on the lawn as flat as possible, stood up and started to step backwards.

Nobody could have predicted what happened next. With horror, their eyes followed Boxer as he leapt into action. After all, it was the same colour as one of his balls and needed retrieving. It was a game. Almost in unison they shouted "NO!" but to Boxer's ears, it must have sounded like an encouragement, because he clamped his jaws around the cube and started back towards the group.

Farcically, they all ran in different directions and it must have confused Boxer because he stopped on the edge of the gravel drive, looked at the disappearing party and shook his head for all it was worth, slobber arcing away from him.

Mister had sensibly taken a couple of steps back and slammed the front door shut. Gibbons headed off round one side of the building hoping to find a hedge or brick wall or anything to hide behind; in fact anywhere where the dog wouldn't see him. Patricia and Justin, with gravel spitting from their shoes, took the opposite direction to Gibbons and split up either side of the line of cars and headed towards a tone outhouse attached to the side of the main building.

Hamilton was the slowest off the mark and initially went to go indoors, but had to change his mind as he saw Mister slamming the front door. He ended up going roughly in the same direction as Gibbons with the idea of hiding in plain sight behind the mesh of the tennis court. He desperately tried to remember where the gateway was, how it opened, closed, latched... He found it and once inside, turned to see what the wretched bloody dog was doing. He whipped round trying to remember if there was another way in, spotted it and went over to ensure that it was firmly shut. Breathing a sigh of relief which manifested itself in the chilly atmosphere, he turned his attention to what Boxer was up to and was horrified to see him standing just a few feet away looking directly at him, tube in mouth. They may have been separated by what would undoubtedly be a flimsy fence which would do nothing to stop any sort of explosion, but it certainly didn't do anything to calm Hamilton's nerves. Boxer's docked tail was waggling back and forth and with his front legs slightly splayed, indicated that he wanted to play. Hamilton involuntarily jumped a little when Boxer adjusted the cube, only to catch it again... and again. This time a coloured tile flew out of his mouth, and that was enough for Hamilton. He ran to the other exit and went to escape from the imprisonment of the cage, when he spotted Boxer running round to meet him there.

"Aaaaaargggghhhh!" Hamilton stopped just short of the gate realising he was trapped; but then an idea came to him. Suppose he could trap Boxer in the cage and not the other way round? He weighed up the logistics of opening one gate, sprinting across to the other, closing it before Boxer got through, then running round the outside to close the other gate before the damn dog got there. Or even take a shortcut if

the dog looked like it was going to 'play ball' and do what h
wanted. He groaned at this last prospect since Boxer seldon
did anything he was told; especially first time.

"Aaaaaarggghhhh!" He cried out again as he realised tha
not only was the dog much faster than he, but also that ther
was a chance that with all the running around required, tha
the bomb might go off.

"Help... help!" His next idea was to get someone els
to distract the dog long enough to set the plan in motion
"Help!"

If anybody was out there, they weren't being very helpful
He looked over to where the living room windows were a
an oblique angle and saw the faces of his family and in-law
staring out at him. He supposed Mister had warned them no
to go outside. He waved his arms at them, but they didn't eve
wave back so he gave them a silent curse. He looked roun
seeking inspiration and his heart leapt for joy as he spotte
a mildew-covered tennis ball jammed against the bottom o
the wire netting. Starting towards it, he was aware of Boxe
shadowing his movements, so speeded up only to realis
that the ball was the wrong side of the mesh. The Boxer wa
homing in on him so he backed off to the centre of the cour
to give himself more thinking time.

Now he had it.

He took the dozen or so paces to the side furthest fror
Boxer and the ball, and was glad to see that the dog went a
the way round. At the last second, he reversed his directio
and went back to the gate nearest the ball to try and retriev
it before the dog got there. Not a chance. Why couldn't sh
have got a little dog that wasn't so bloody fast? A pomer..
whatever they were.

"Aaaaaarggghhhh!" This time anger crept into his tone

Trapped by a bloody dog and not just any dog, but their dog.

"Ahhhhh haaaa!" He went to the far side of the court with Boxer following him on the outside and again reversed his direction at the last moment. He ran as fast as he could towards the ball and was glad to see that his straight line was quicker than the dog's route. He went to kick the tennis ball far enough away, hoping that Boxer would drop the cube and chase it instead. His initial satisfaction of connecting with the ball and watching it travel all of ten feet soon turned to dismay. Not only did he get his shoe stuck in the diagonal mesh and his right foot come out of it, but it had unbalanced him so that he fell over against the dividing netting.

Twisting round horizontally, he turned to see what his four-legged friend was doing and was elated to see that his ruse had worked. Boxer had dropped the cube and was even now picking up the off-yellow tennis ball. As far as Hamilton was concerned, the dog could retrieve the ball as long as he liked, and sure enough, Boxer now bought the ball back to him. Out of the corner of his eye, he thought he saw someone else approaching from the house but his first thought was 'bugger them' for not coming to his aid earlier. He'd managed it by himself, just like he always did.

"Good boy." Hamilton would have patted his head had the mesh not separated them. They were only a few feet away from the cube and as Hamilton looked at it, so did the dog.

Boxer changed his mind, dropped the ball and picked up the cube. As he did so, it somehow twisted on its own axis and with an audible 'pop' released a barely visible cloud of mist.

The cube was never designed to release its deadly cargo into open air where the slightest breeze would dispel it, but even so, its effect was finite to poor Boxer who immediately collapsed and died.

Hamilton wasn't to know that it was only the faintest whiff of wind that took the majority of the cyanide in another direction before dissipating straight up into the atmosphere. Nor was he to know that had he been downwind of Boxer and just a little closer, then he too would have met the same fate. For a moment he lay there, ignorant of what had just happened, and looked over towards the house to see that Mister had nearly reached him with others not far behind.

"Took your bloody time getting here, didn't you?"

Mister ignored him and instead made a direct line for Boxer, stopped short by a few paces, and sniffed. "Smell it?"

Hamilton was now on his feet and putting his shoe back on. "Smell what?" he sniffed when he finally stood upright.

"Almonds."

"Almonds?" he sniffed again.

Mister backtracked a couple of paces, held his arm out to stop Gibbons and the others getting closer. "Classic telltale aroma of cyanide. I wouldn't get any closer if I were you." He focused on the broken cube next to Boxer's mouth and immediately understood what had been going on. "There'll be a residue in and on the dog," he stated to nobody in particular, then turned and shouted, "GET BACK INSIDE!" directed at those who would come to cuddle the family pet.

Hamilton had left the dubious security of the tennis court and joined the otherwise silent group staring at Boxer and the cube. "Cyanide, eh? They couldn't even get me with that."

It took all of three seconds before comments from the others were flying.

"You poxy fucking ignoramus…"

"… pig-headed big shit…"

"… lucky to be alive…"

They kept coming, but it was Gibbons who summed it all up. "Shame it wasn't you instead of the dog." He spun round and stormed off.

Chapter 18

The new year

Erica huffed, threw the TV remote down onto the bed and stomped off to have a shower. She cursed herself for no realising that the news she was waiting for might not b released until tomorrow morning. The death of a governmen minister was hardly the type of news the populous wante to hear about on Christmas Day and her suspicious min wondered if the authorities had forced the media to dela while they concocted some spurious story as to his sudde demise.

She changed her mind and ran a bath instead. She no knew that bathing in a roll-top bath was no different to an other bath; except that it was a little longer and that sh could reach the taps easier. She closed her eyes, let the salt she'd added permeate and allowed her mind to wander abou tomorrow. Liam had already given her a pass-key and told he the room number she was going to raid tomorrow mornin while the couple were at breakfast. According to him, th lady was about the right size and had all the documents Eric would need to make a ferry or airline booking to return to Eire She'd visit the cemetery where her father was buried and te him that his murder had been avenged; that he could now res in peace. She'd remind him that she had fulfilled the promis she'd made all those years ago and that she hadn't let g nd that Maurice bloody Hamilton was now dead. Her only egret was that she hadn't been there to see the bastard suffer.)nly then would she find Eamon and thank him personally.

***

"We're going to be a grandparents. Mandy and me," Eric nnounced to his twin brother as soon as their drinks appeared n the bar counter. "So the first one's on me. Cheers!"

"That's the best news I've heard all week… well second est because Melanie's just been promoted to head of her epartment. That's more than thirty people. Imagine that… hat's platoon size." Ernie tucked into his shandy.

The twins tended to meet at The Wheatsheaf pub on a nonthly basis and had done so for as long as the governor ould remember; and he'd been there nearly twenty years. He lidn't know exactly how far away they lived but knew it was)cal as they usually arrived on foot from different directions /ithin seconds of each other.

"So when's it due and is it a boy or girl? No, let me guess. 'ou don't want to know its sex until it arrives and it'll be a… … Leo…"

Eric made his brother wait a few seconds as they looked ach other directly in the eyes. He also tried not to give nything away by smiling, but it was no good. They could till read each other's thoughts. "Right on both counts. Due he eighteenth of August."

They both laughed and smiled at the happy strangeness. Here, has Melanie been to that new hairdressers in Fore treet yet?"

"Don't think so, why?"

"Tell her not to bother 'cos apparently it's crap. The

new owner's a real dragon and they've already branded it 'A Hamilton'.

"She must be related to the new fish and chip guy, 'cos hi fish stink and his brother-in-law's ice cream van smells like it' running on his old chip fat oil. He's called Hamilton as well.. They're all called Hamilton."

"Eh… I even caught the local newspaper chap referring t that traffic warden bloke the other day as 'A Hamilton'. He' only parked up for a few seconds in Upper Road and the g appeared out of nowhere. I was there outside the newsagent waiting for Mandy. You should have heard the language Heeeee heeee."

"It's catching on more and more isn't it? 'A Hamilton' ha now turned into a derogatory expression round here."

"Well, bugger Maurice bloody Hamilton. At least h name's of some use round here."

***

"You go first."

"No," Justin said tersely.

"Why not?"

"I'd like to say something smart like 'age before beauty or 'ladies first' but then neither of those applies to you, doe it?" There was an edge to his voice, but she missed it.

She hit him with one of the sofa cushions. "OK then." Sh sat bolt upright and lowered her voice in imitation. "It's com to my attention…"

"Oh no you don't," interrupted Justin. He knew she' been summoned to the Metropolitan Police Commissioner office, and also knew of the reputation he had for dronin on. The media almost vilified him in despair of his verbos ddresses at press conferences that were very good at saying lmost nothing of any relevance. Since he was the highest anked policeman in the land, his words were duly reported.

"Just give me the facts, not the commissioner's whole erse and chapter 'cos we'll be here all night and I'm bloody tarving."

"Spoil sport." She smirked. "OK then, I'm being romoted to detective chief inspector with my own team nder Special Branch's umbrella, specifically Commander iibbons, with a brief to prevent acts of terrorism to members f the government."

She waited for Justin to compliment her, and she got a little ross when none came. "Well come on then... congratulate ie."

"Did you accept?"

"You're a canny bastard aren't you? You're quite right, I idn't. But I've got to let him know on Monday and I see no eason why I shouldn't take the job." She frowned, wondering vhy he was being so reticent. "Aaaaaahhh, I see. Your turn hen... what happened?"

"It seems that either Hamilton or I have to go, and as he's he one who's been voted to represent his constituents, it's ie." He looked at Patricia with as deadpan a face as possible, ut inside, it hurt. "Mr Postles has little time for diplomacy vhen it is not needed and I was out of his office in less than hree minutes."

A bit of an awkward silence thickened the atmosphere etween them, then he continued. "There was no 'thank you' r a 'job well done', just an acknowledgement that my record vould reflect my few years of sterling service and that I ought o be able to pick up a job outside of the House quite easily."

He gritted his teeth. "I was even escorted out of the

building."

Patricia could see that the ignominy of the last part ha affected him in some way, so she walked gently over to hir and gave him a great big cuddle; then a lingering kiss. "We then…" She rubbed her nose against his. "We'll have to se about setting up that detective agency we talked about, won we?"

***

Group therapy works best when those who are included in : tend to have similar aspirations. In this case, there must hav been well over two hundred people in the pub with the sam idea as the volume of the countdown crescendoed to 'ONE'.

"HAPPY NEW YEAR!"

Despite most people in the pub jigging up and dow around them, Justin and Patricia stood among them huggin each other and passionately kissing. Nobody cared, minde or objected because that was what one was allowed to do i public on the cusp of a new year. A new era was beginning fo them and the auguries couldn't have been better.

Across the Irish Sea behind St Stephen's Chapel, Eamo watched Erica's car pull up; he got in. He suspected she wa going to ask him about the cube and he waited for her questior but when it didn't come, he volunteered, "There was no wa it could have failed. I made sure of that."

She was looking straight ahead through the windscree at the overcast view of a lake in the middle distance. "Hov sure?"

"A hundred per cent. Even if it had lain there undisturbe for another five years, the moment anyone twisted it, it woul

ave gone off. And anyone within three feet of it would have
ied instantly." He let her think that over for a moment. "Are
ou sure it's been used? You know... taken out of its packet
nd twisted?"

"No I'm not fucking sure, but if you saw a Rubik's cube
ist lying there, sooner or later someone would come along,
ick it up and twist it. Especially a child, so what do you
nink? Either it's still in its Christmas wrapping which I find
ard to believe, or someone's found out what it does and made
 safe, and if they have then they must also have worked out
/hat it was."

She compressed her lips in reflection. Now that she had
onfirmation directly from Eamon, she would concentrate
er efforts on finding out how anyone else knew. She had her
uspicions that it was to do with that pair of sleuths, but before
he moved onto them, she had to eliminate any possibility
nat anyone on the Emerald Isle had been the source. "I just
eed to hear it from your own lips, so say after me... 'I didn't
ell anyone else'."

She turned to look at him in the hope of catching him out
 he lied.

"I didn't tell anyone else," he said as he returned her stare.

She waited a moment before resuming her look at the
cenery. "Well help me on this one, Eamon. We all know
iden was really careful, so that makes three of us who knew.
ou, me and him... Who else knew? Who was the money?
Vho bankrolled Aiden?"

When he didn't answer straight away, she suddenly
noved her right arm and grabbed him by his balls. "Who else,
amon?" she shouted in his ear as he winced and writhed and
et out an unintelligible gasp. "Do you want me to squeeze
arder?" She did exactly that but only for a moment, then

relaxed enough for him to talk.

"I... I don't know his name but Aiden did... and Aide
trusted him... aaaaaaaaagggghhh!" This as she squeezed
little harder. "I really don't know his name... you know wha
these people are like." She relented more. "If I knew his name
I'd be dead by now."

She released him but kept her hand there, knowing that h
spoke the truth. "So nobody else then?"

When he didn't answer straight away, she clenched he
hand just a little; more of a threat than the agony he had jus
endured.

"There were the two contact chaps..."

By the time Eamon had finished describing them, sh
knew exactly what she was going to do. Then, if necessary
she'd go back to London.

***

London on New Year's Eve was throbbing with revellers as i
seemed that half the population was out celebrating aroun
Trafalgar Square. Across the river in his apartment behin
the London Eye, Hamilton reluctantly let go of the bust
secretary from the Portuguese embassy who had become hi
latest conquest. She had been bent almost double over the en
of his bed while he had pumped away and despite her crie
for him to stop, he had carried on. Now, straightening up an
smoothing her dress down her thighs, she glared at him.

The smug grin on his face said it all to her. She smilec
walked closer to him, and then kneed him in the groin.

As he doubled-over in agony for the third time that yea
she shouted, "When I say stop, that means stop."